THE GIRL
IN THE
RED DRESS

Elaine Chong

Lenora

There are raised voices outside my room. I can hear someone saying, "What do you mean, she's just eaten some ice cream?" I think it's my son, Richard. He sounds unusually agitated, fearful even, as though eating ice cream is a seriously risky business.

Another man's voice replies in a calm, authoritative tone, "I know your mother only came back from surgery earlier this afternoon but she's awake now. She's quite comfortable, and she asked for ice cream. As luck would have it, we've been able to oblige her, and at this point we're happy to let her eat whatever she wants."

Their voices slowly fade as they move away from the doorway. I strain to listen, but the remainder of the conversation is masked by the sound of a hospital trolley as it rattles and rolls along the hospital corridor like an old-fashioned locomotive.

Ice cream. It's soothingly cold and smooth, and ambrosia on the tongue when you've recently had a breathing tube inserted into your throat and the inside of your mouth tastes and feels like a dried-out dishcloth.

Aggie loved ice cream. How could I ever forget that?

I've been trying really hard not to think about my old friend, but the sweet, creamy taste of vanilla suddenly transports me to another place; reminds me of that fateful day, a day quite like no other day, when the sky was forget-me-not blue: a soft sweep of pale colour that stretched overhead, faded into the far horizon and disappeared into the sea.

The beach was sprinkled with people like Aggie and me: people with time to sit and stare at the water; watch the breakers burst onto the shore and let the sun warm their skin.

Aggie had bought me a large, vanilla ice cream cone. She tucked a paper serviette into the front of my blouse saying, "In case you dribble."

"I know I'm getting old, but I'm not gaga."

"Not you, silly, the ice cream," she said, and – as if to illustrate my stupidity – she slowly licked a trickle of pink ice cream from the end of her cone.

"I wanted chocolate," I protested.

"He hasn't got chocolate today."

"Well, why didn't you get me strawberry?"

"You didn't ask for strawberry."

"I didn't ask for vanilla either."

Aggie ignored me and looked out across the beach with vacant eyes to the distant sea. We were waiting for the tide to come in so that we could paddle our feet in the water like we used to do when we were children. Every year the church choir organised a coach trip to the seaside; they were the only holidays I had till I got married. Aggie's mum and dad used to take her to visit an aunt in Skegness, but she always said she much preferred the coach trip to Clacton.

We'd brought a picnic with us that day and bought an ice cream from the man on the pier. Aggie usually walked away from his van with pink cheeks and a sparkle in her pretty, blue eyes because she thought there was a frisson of something sexual between them – she thought he winked at her when she gave him the correct change. He was a nice-looking man with a flirtatious manner, but he really had a lazy eye.

The man who hired out the deckchairs was much less friendly and charged two pounds fifty for an afternoon. The deckchairs were those wooden contraptions that collapsed when you pulled a lever. It felt a bit like sitting on a clothes horse only less comfortable, but I always refused to sit on the damp sand like Aggie.

When Aggie's gaze returned to her ice cream, she broke off the end of her cone and scooped up ice cream so that she had two cones. "Look," she said. "Big cone, little cone."

"That joke wasn't funny the first time you told it."

"At least I have a sense of humour."

I laughed. "You'll need one when you stand up and look like you've peed your pants. Why don't you just get a deckchair like every other sensible person on the beach?"

"It's more fun sitting on the sand," she said.

We finished our ice creams in companionable silence then Aggie insisted on walking out to watch the waves come in. "You'll have to pull me out of this thing first," I told her, and I shifted myself forward in the chair.

She took hold of my hands and tugged hard. She huffed and puffed and heaved me into a standing position. "I think you're putting on weight."

"Too many ice creams, I expect," I said.

We slowly made our way across the beach. The sand was hard beneath my feet and I wished I'd worn my sandals. As we drew closer to the pounding surf, the sand had been sculpted into ridges transforming the soft, yellow grains into a strange, alien landscape.

The wind blew in short, sharp gusts and tugged at our clothes. Aggie's skirt was lifted up around her waist, and she screamed.

I laughed so much I almost tripped over my own feet. "You'll have to hold it down!" The cold, grey sea was rushing in; foam-tipped waves crashing onto the shore. Suddenly I wanted to run. "Come on, Aggie-bag, race you to the water!" I shouted at her.

Within a few, short strides she had overtaken me, her long skirt flying out behind her like an unruly kite.

We met the incoming tide with whoops and cheers; reached down and trailed our fingers in the cold, briny sea. Soon we were wet and breathless, and I could feel the pull of the current beneath my feet. I reached for Aggie's arm and hooked it round mine. "I think I could eat another ice cream after that," I said.

"With sprinkles and a chocolate flake!" Aggie shouted at the wind then she turned to me. "Are you happy now, Lenora?"

"What do you mean, 'now'?"

"Now that George has gone."

"He didn't leave me, Aggie," I said. "He's dead."

3

"I know, but are you happy now? I so much want you to be happier than you were before…" She hesitated. "Before it happened."

I considered this for a moment, but for just a moment because there was really nothing to consider. I said, "I can't remember the last time I felt as happy as I do today."

"You're free now, aren't you?" she insisted.

"Free?"

Aggie stopped walking and, as her arm slipped through mine, I felt it tremble. She was visibly trembling all over. Her long grey hair, which was more usually contained within a tight French pleat on the back of her head, now blew hither and thither, but she didn't seem to care. She was crying.

I reached out to her, but she stepped away from me. "What's wrong?" I asked.

"It was me," she said. "I did it."

"I don't know what you're talking about."

"George. I killed him."

Her voice had shrunk to a whisper, but the words resounded loud and clear inside my head. Of course, I knew that someone had killed him. Someone had driven a car at speed down a narrow country lane and catapulted him into the gutter. But all I could think to say to her was, "You haven't got a car now, Aggie."

"I've still got Daddy's old Volvo in the garage," she said. "I had it serviced."

"I don't believe you!" I cried.

She sank to her knees on the hard, wet sand; lifted the hem of her skirt; buried her face in its cold, damp folds, and sobbed.

Julia

Orchard Road, 8pm, and the humidity is over eighty per cent. The temperature is a pleasantly warm twenty-eight degrees, in fact the same temperature that it was when I left the house at 8am this morning, but it's just a day like any other day in Singapore.

Colin has asked me to meet him at the LingLang Club as usual. I can't bear the place anymore – all that dreadful, colonial bowing and scraping when somebody orders a gin and tonic. Colin loves it. That's why he leaves the office promptly at five every day, calls the driver to pick him up from the front entrance of the building, and is deposited on the Club's steps.

The low, bungalow style building is a throwback to a previous era, much like the smiling, white-jacketed man of mature years, who ushers him into its dim interior. The dark leather sofas and soft, yellow lighting from strategically placed table lamps is reminiscent of a London, gentleman's private club, and so is the atmosphere in my opinion.

Of course, young Singaporeans have no time for deference towards white expats, especially the ones who want to live like it's 1925 and the sun is still shining on the great British Empire. The world is a very different place now, but the LingLang Club lives on.

I insist on walking there when I leave the gallery, but I go through the same charade every day with Colin's driver, Haziq. I lock the day's takings in the safe, reset the burglar alarm then hand over to my assistant, Aysha, who does the evening shift. Shopping is an all-day activity in this part of the world, and if you want your business to make money then it has to be open all day, every day.

Haziq waits for me in the same parking space. He winds down the window and the car's air-conditioning unit immediately cranks up a gear. "I drive Ma'am to club?" he asks. I always shake my head and wave him away, but he calls after me, "Walking is not good, not safe."

"Walking is completely safe," I shout back at him.

The window will slowly close and Haziq be enveloped once again in dry, engine-cooled air. The car is a moving, refrigeration unit.

This evening, I actually feel the need to walk to the LingLang Club after the unexpected phone call I received from my brother, Richard. It interrupted my very brief lunch break and preyed on my mind for the rest of the afternoon. I could probably use the space and time to think through our conversation, but I don't want to think about it, I want a distraction, and a stroll along Orchard Road in the heart of the city at eight o'clock is the perfect way to banish unwelcome thoughts.

The thing that strikes me every time I walk here is the vibrancy and colour of the place. It's a complete contrast to where I was born and where I lived until I married Colin. I loathe England. It's full of dull people living out their dull lives under grey skies, especially in the winter months when every living thing is either dead, or in a state of hibernation.

Singapore, on the other hand, is perpetually bathed in warm, fragrant air. The warmth is self-explanatory, but the fragrance is something I feel is unique to this city state. Of course, New York boasts of its large expanse of woods and green open spaces in its city centre, and London has its more modest parks and gardens, but none of this compares to the scent and colour of frangipani-lined streets and bougainvillea-covered road bridges here in Singapore. In fact, almost every building is elegantly camouflaged from view behind dark green, towering trees and purple morning glory entwined in tall, bamboo screens.

Yes, it takes an army of people to keep the streets swept and clean all year round, but it's a salve to the unemployment statistics.

Colin has already decided he wants to go home when he retires. Home is a small town on the Suffolk coast. I try not to think about it, but the conversation with my brother reminded me that it's a problem I'm going to have to resolve, because I'm not leaving Singapore. His opening words sent a prescient chill down my spine.

"You have to come back here, Julia. Mum's had a fall. She's in hospital."

"Don't be ridiculous, Richard," I exclaimed. "I have a business to run."

"It's a shop," he said. "And I'm quite certain you have someone who can take over while you're away."

His casual use of the word 'shop' stung me into replying, "I have absolutely no intention of handing over the running of the gallery to one of my assistants just because our mother has fallen over and broken a bone. I suppose she has broken something?"

"She's fractured her hip."

"Well, can't she have a new one? Isn't that what they do these days? Something wears out or breaks and you replace it?"

"It isn't quite that simple," he said.

"What do you expect me to do?" I demanded. "If she can't look after herself then she'll have to pay someone to do it. I suppose she could always sell the house and go into a care home," I added, although this was an option, I knew I would never seriously consider, because I was banking on inheriting my full half-share of Hillcrest House, our family home.

There was a long, pregnant pause and I assumed that Richard was considering the options, which I'd suggested to him. I heard him take a deep breath then he said in a low but firm voice, "She'll refuse to go into a care home, and she can't sell the house even she wanted to."

Richard and I had become strangers over the years, but I recognised at once that he was speaking the truth. I understood that our mother would fight tooth and nail before she gave up her independence, but I didn't understand why she couldn't sell the house and said so.

"Like I said, it's complicated," he replied. "I just need you to come back here for a bit so we can sort things out."

Frustration rippled through me. "How complicated can it be? Honestly Richard, you can't expect me to fly ten-thousand miles because you can't be bothered to explain to me over the phone why she won't sell the family home. I'm surprised she hasn't downsized already. The place is far too big for one person."

There was another long pause and this time I knew he was doing what he'd always done: trying to break some bad news in way that wouldn't upset me or anger me, so I said, "Please, just tell me what's going on."

"I wanted to do this face to face, but if you insist…"

"I insist," I said.

His voice held a note of genuine regret when he spoke. "Mum can't sell the house because it doesn't belong to her. And if you're thinking that Dad left it to you and me, well, you're going to be disappointed." He quickly went on, "The fact is, only he owned the house and he left it to somebody else. Mum can live there until she … until she dies, but that's it."

All I could think to say was, "I don't understand?"

"Mum didn't want you to know. She said it would only upset you if you found out."

"Somebody else," I repeated. I looked out of the window for inspiration; gazed up at the puffs of low cumulus cloud hovering in the sky overhead and tried to form a rational thought that would make sense of those words. There was somebody else?

"Her name's Miriam," Richard said quietly. "Apparently, she's our sister."

The rest of the conversation now eludes me because the only thing I could focus on was that I wasn't going to get my inheritance. This is the worst of worse news and now I need to walk, cool my temper and put my shattered dreams in a place where I don't have to think about them.

As usual Orchard Road is humming, and most evenings I'm happily in tune with the sounds of the city as I stroll along, but not tonight. Tonight, I'm irritated by the noise and the sea of pedestrians. They wash along the pavement with their faces fixed on the glowing screens of their mobile phones. Of course, it's like this every night: a giant game of dodgeball.

I hate to be one of those middle-aged people, who complain about the youth of today, but it's a hazardous affair trying to avoid them and impossible to be anything other than cross when they collide with you. Whenever I remark upon it to Colin, he rolls his eyes and says, "That's what the bloody car is for."

When I left the gallery, I thought the walk to the LingLang Club would clear my head, but Richard's startling piece of news refuses to dislodge itself. Like an evil splinter, it pricks and stings and refuses to be ignored, in spite of my best efforts.

In the end, I veer away from the overflowing pavement and head to a favourite coffee bar. I sit down and order a skinny latte. I tell myself I will give this thorny little problem my full attention for the time it takes to drink it.

So, I have a sister – well, a half-sister – who has a claim to my late father's property. This is not good news. When I last asked a local estate agent to give me a ballpark figure as to its value, he told me I could expect something in excess of two-million pounds. At the time I thought, this is really very good news, because the house is going to be my *get out of jail free* card.

I don't use foul language, but I can think of only one response to the news that I have a half-sister, who's going to get my inheritance and, in the privacy of my head, I shout out the words as loudly as I can, but it doesn't assuage my feelings of anger and frustration.

Am I surprised that Daddy played away? No, of course I'm not. But to breed a bastard? Well, that's just careless and not Daddy's style at all.

The waitress brings my order and, as I sip my coffee, I consider this new line of thought, but it takes me down a road I'm now unwilling to venture for Daddy was never careless, never imprudent, and that means it was deliberate. He wanted her, this other daughter.

The road has brought me full circle and I'm back to where I started: my father left our family home to someone called Miriam and I'm now facing disaster.

Well, I won't have it! Even if it means I have to leave Singapore for a while and tend to my mother and her fractured hip.

I suddenly find myself glaring up angrily into the face of the startled waitress. I hastily rearrange my features into the semblance of a smile and ask for the bill.

At the LingLang Club Colin is already on his third scotch and soda when I arrive. The empty glasses are still lined up in front of him. I know this is a deliberate statement: a message to me that I should have got there sooner, because in ordinary circumstances the barman would have whipped them away when they were done.

His fair-skinned complexion is mottled with pink and brown. The brown blotches are ugly sunspots: a permanent legacy of thirty years living under a tropical sun. The pink ones are temporary. Any other person might attribute them to an overindulgence of hard spirits, but I know better – Colin can hold his liquor, but not his pique.

"You're late," he growls at me over the rim of the glass. "We were supposed to be meeting the Stevens for pre-dinner drinks."

"I'm really sorry, Colin," I lie.

"No, you're not."

"Okay, I'm not, but I couldn't help it. I got held up."

"If you knew you were going to be late, why didn't you ask Haziq to drive you straight here?"

"You know I like to walk," I say. "And I needed..."

"Don't give me that bullshit!" he shoots back at me before I have a chance to explain. "What the hell is the matter with you, Julia? You know how important this is. I don't ask much of you. I let you swan around that bloody gallery, pretending you're businesswoman of the year, and all I ask in return is that you turn up on time when I need you."

On any other occasion, this accusation would have provoked me into an argument, but I have more important problems to grapple with, so I waste no time in trying to defend myself. "I have to fly to London."

"What?"

I slide onto the bar stool next to him and signal the waiter to bring me a drink. "I have to fly to London," I say again. "Richard called. That's why I'm late."

"Your brother Richard?"

"Do we know another one?"

"Don't try to be smart with me, Julia. I'm not in the mood."

I wonder if I should explain about the house, but caution prevails so I simply tell him, "Apparently, Mummy's fallen over and fractured her hip."

"What's that got to do with us?"

10

"Richard has demanded that I come back and help out until she's back on her feet again."

"I don't believe you."

"You don't believe me?"

"You don't give a toss about your mother. Never have, never will."

I can't deny this, but years of making up excuses *not* to meet Colin at the LingLang Club has taught me to think on my feet. "I'm not doing it for Mummy," I say and sound suitably indignant. "I'm doing it for Richard. He says they'll want to discharge her as soon as she's well enough to leave, but they'll insist that she can't be left alone until they're satisfied that she can do things for herself."

"Like what?"

"I don't know!" Colin's eyes immediately shrink to narrow, suspicion-filled slits so I quickly rein in my irritation and try to embellish my response with a few well-chosen 'facts'. "Things like making a cup tea or using the bathroom, maybe even just getting out of bed."

"I thought she's got some woman helping her out?"

"She has a cleaner who comes in once a week, if that's what you mean." He continues to regard me with angry mistrust and my irritation gets the better of me. "Look, Colin, it's not like here. They don't have maids to fetch and carry for you or cook your meals and clear up your mess. You know how it is – it's a different world over there."

He knocks back the remainder of his whiskey and soda and asks the barman for a refill. The pink blotches are fading as his anger begins to dissipate. "Why can't Richard help out? Why does he have to drag you into it?"

"He will," I say, and I try to inject a note of reassurance into my voice. "But at the moment he's in the middle of an important project."

"If you're lying to me Julia..." He leaves it hanging there.

I pretend dismay. "How could you say something like that? I know I sometimes make excuses not to meet your business chums..." Colin's head swings round and his mouth is already forming words of accusation so I quickly I hold up my hands. "Okay, I admit it. I find most of these dinners and lunches and pre-dinner drinks

11

unendurably tedious, but never, never once have I wanted to fly back to London to avoid them."

I never want to go back, full stop, but that's an argument we can leave for another time.

He throws me another baleful glare, but this time I see a flicker of something that looks like fear pass behind his pale, blue eyes because he can't wait to go back; can't wait for a quiet retirement in his cosy, little seaside town with his adoring wife on hand to mix his whiskey and soda as the sun goes down.

I reach across the space between us and stroke his face with my finger. "It won't be for long – a couple of weeks at the most."

Actually, it's going to take as long as it requires for me to win back my inheritance, but he doesn't need to know this.

"When exactly will you leave?" he asks.

"Well, Mummy's still in hospital so I won't book my flight until I know I have to go. In any case, I have things to attend to at the gallery. I can't just leave at a moment's notice."

"You've left me before," he says sourly.

I slide from the bar stool and lace my fingers through his. "Let's go home. It's been a long day for both of us."

At once he protests. "I'm hungry. I haven't eaten yet."

I give his fingers a brief reassuring squeeze. "I'll call Siti and tell her to make something. How about cheese on toast? You like that."

"Welsh rarebit? That sounds good."

Colin swings himself off the stool, but stumbles when his feet hit the floor. A passing waiter hurries over: he's young, impossibly slender, and doesn't look as though he has the strength to prop up a drunken sot of an overweight *Mat Salleh,* but he slips his hand into the crook of Colin's arm, helps him to regain his balance and offers to walk him to the car. Colin declines with a shake of the head and the waiter backs off, but I see the look on the waiter's face as he disappears into the lamp-lit vestibule: it's a mixture of sympathy and contempt.

Richard

I watch my mother from the doorway while she sleeps. She looks smaller and infinitely more fragile than the last time I saw her, but I don't see her very often so perhaps this deterioration in her health has happened more recently. I make a mental note to ask Maggie. She sees my mother every week when she cleans so if it's something specific, it might be something that she's noticed.

I step back out into the corridor. The business of attending to the sick and elderly patients began before the sun was up. I don't doubt for a single moment that everyone working on the ward is a dedicated professional, but there's a definite feeling of conveyor belt medicine here. There are tasks to be performed, boxes to be ticked, forms to be filled... It doesn't look like nursing and sometimes it doesn't feel like nursing, but I've entrusted my mother to these people's care; I have no choice.

A voice at my shoulder interrupts these gloomy meditations. "Mr Oakley? Visiting hours are from ten-thirty. I'm afraid you're going to have to wait outside the ward."

It's the same nurse who tried to reassure me yesterday evening that my mother is expected to make a full recovery. He's a good-looking guy, reminds me of a young Denzel Washington – hair close-cropped, regular almost feminine features and kind dark eyes. I suddenly realise I'm staring back at him in a way that's wholly inappropriate, but he probably gets that all the time.

I look away, glance into the room where my mother is still sleeping. "I have to go to work now," I say. "I've brought a few things in for her – slippers, toothbrush, toothpaste..." I hand him the plastic bag I'm carrying. "I'll come back this evening, but I won't be able to stay for long. Perhaps you could forewarn her?"

"That's fine."

I have to admit I admire the guy. He doesn't step away from me, doesn't recoil in disgust, which has happened to me before, so I go on. "I've called my sister. We're going to try to make arrangements as soon as we can for my mother to be cared for at home."

He smiles. "There's no rush. She'll be moved from here to another bed in couple of days, and then the physiotherapists will take over. We need to get her up and moving before she can be discharged."

"So soon?"

"The sooner the better really."

My mother begins to stir, and I need to leave. As soon as the nurse makes to move away from the doorway, I quickly turn in the opposite direction and head for the exit. I have to press a buzzer on the wall for the door to be opened for me from the desk in the centre of the ward – it's a security measure, so it's more than a minute before I can make my escape.

The hospital walls in the outside corridor have been painted a pale shade of green. Some therapist probably advised them that it's a calming colour; something that will soothe anxieties, but I find it completely debilitating and my feet begin to drag even though I'm trying to hurry. There are windows at regular intervals along its tunnel-like length, but even with the early morning sunlight streaming in there's still an overwhelming sense of melancholy about the place, which follows me out into the car park.

As soon as I climb inside my car and look at my phone, I'm reminded of the conversation I forced myself to have with my sister, Julia, yesterday morning, and the further conversations I'll need to have with her about my mother's house and her financial situation. Of course, it *isn't* my mother's house and that's the crux of the problem.

When my father died, I have to confess I didn't even think to ask my mother about the will he'd left in the hands of our family solicitor. The circumstances of his untimely death had left us reeling, and all I could think about at the time was that the person who'd killed him was still at large. I simply couldn't grasp how a man could be mown down by a speeding car, left for dead at the side of the road, and nobody saw or heard anything.

We complain about unnecessary surveillance, we talk about erosion of civil liberties, we hate to think of nameless, faceless government agents spying on us while we go about our daily lives, but it was a simple *lack* of video camera evidence, which left my father's case unsolved. In fact, the car has never been found, the driver never brought to justice.

Julia and Colin came back for the funeral, but their stay could have been counted in hours – they flew in the day before and flew straight back out the day after. I don't remember either one of them asking about the will, but I'm sure they assumed the same thing that I did: my mother had been left my father's estate in its entirety.

It was some months after the funeral I found out about a half-sister called Miriam.

Before I pull out of the car park, I suddenly think to check for my briefcase under the coat lying across the back seat. I slide my hand beneath it and feel for the slim leather casing, but it's not there. I climb out of the car, quickly open the rear passenger door in the hope that the case has fallen onto the floor and under the seat, but it hasn't. I'm sure I remember draping the coat over the briefcase – an attempt to conceal it from light-fingered passers-by – but perhaps that was yesterday.

I close my eyes, try to reconstruct this morning's events in my head, and realise that the briefcase is still sitting on the kitchen table at my mother's house where I left it when I answered the phone in the hallway. I'll have to go back to retrieve it, and hope that the client, who'll be waiting for me later in my London office, understands that I'm not hopelessly ill-prepared but merely overburdened by a competing list of priorities.

The traffic is now in full rush-hour mode and I soon find myself in a queue of cars moving along achingly slowly at single digit speed. I realise that I might have to reschedule the meeting with the client, which would be inconvenient for both of us, but perhaps preferable to keeping the appointment and arriving late and unprepared.

As I follow the tail lights of the car in front of me, resigned now to driving back to my mother's house in Shenfield, my thoughts are free to roam, but they return to Julia and the angry exchange of words, which ensued when I told her about the contents of our father's will.

"You mean he left us nothing?"

"I told you: he left everything – except the house – to Mum. She gets a proportion of his work pension, and there were other investments, but it doesn't amount to very much and it won't be enough to keep her in a private nursing home."

"Do you know how much that house is worth?"

"I haven't checked but I guess it's a significant sum."

"Two-million pounds, Richard. Probably more. And by the time Mummy dies, definitely more. I don't believe it. How could he do this to us?"

"Did you listen to a single word I said?" I asked her.

"Of course, I did. Mummy can continue to live in the house. Well, whoopee do! That's just great for her."

"It isn't great, Julia. If she can't live there independently after this fall, then she's going to need some kind of help on a permanent basis. That will have to be funded, and she could only just about afford to live there as it was."

"Why are you telling me this?" she demanded, forever the petulant teenager.

"Because it's going to be a problem: our problem." I heard the sudden intake of breath as my words hit home. "I don't care about the house," I went on, "but I know Mum will. She won't want to move, and I can't see any other solution."

I waited for her to respond, though I guessed she was still thinking about the inheritance, which had suddenly slipped through her fingers, and I was right.

"Who the hell is this Miriam person?"

"I don't know anything about her beyond her name and the fact that she's our sister – well, half-sister."

"You should have told me, Richard," she said in a low voice.

"There's nothing we can do about it now."

"Why not? Wills can be contested."

"I think it's too late." Once again there was a sharp intake of breath as she took in this unwelcome piece of information. "About

Mum," I started to say, but she hurriedly told me she'd call me then hung up the phone.

On reflection, I realise it was a huge mistake to not attend the reading of the will, but I hadn't bothered because I hadn't spoken to my father for several years beyond a few brief exchanges at Christmas and my mother's birthday each year. We'd become what people sometimes call *estranged,* although in truth I'd always been something of a stranger to my father, unlike Julia. Although the bizarre circumstances of his death sent shock waves through the entire family, I don't believe a single one of them truly mourned him, except her. She knew him as a loving and devoted parent and refused to hear a single bad word said against him.

As the days turned into weeks with still no one apprehended, I left my mother to deal with the police and other authorities involved. I phoned her as often as I could – though probably not often enough – and I assumed that she was keeping me informed, keeping me in the loop. In truth, she was continuing to conceal from me that she and my father had been living separate lives under the same roof for a long time; that she had absolutely no idea where my father went when he left the house or how or with whom he spent his time.

The very first inkling that their marriage had effectively ended some while before was when she told me about the contents of the will.

"He can't do that," I said.

"Apparently he can, and he has."

"But why? Why would he do that to you? It's your home. This is madness, Mum! Why would he leave the house to somebody else?"

"Well, he was very clear in every detail. He's left everything to me, except the house, but I can continue to live here for the rest of my life."

"There must be some mistake."

"It isn't a mistake. I'm just sorry that he's treated you and Julia in such a shabby way. I know things weren't good between the two of you, but frankly I'm more shocked he'd do this to Julia. The only reason I'm telling you any of this is because there may be nothing left for you ... at the end."

"I really don't care about that, Mum," I said, and I meant it. "I just want to know who this person is. Have you told the police? It could be important."

She breathed an impatient sigh. "The police did door-to-door interviews in the road where he was found. Several people recognised him from the photograph I gave them. They know all about her and her mother. This Miriam is just a child, Richard."

I was still unconvinced. "Are you absolutely certain that she's his daughter?"

"Yes! She's been living with her mother in a house right there where...where it happened. Your father was a regular visitor by all accounts, but I suppose he would be."

It was strange, hearing my mother speak about him in that way – almost as though he were little more than a family friend. Of course, now I know their marriage had long dissolved into mutual indifference with my father in possession of the upper hand because my mother was financially dependent on him. Still, at the time it was hard to take on-board the fact that he had another family, and it must have been an even greater shock for her – the ultimate betrayal.

"You don't think she could have been responsible for his death – this other woman?" I asked her. "The police have interviewed her, surely?"

I heard my mother draw a long, shuddering sigh. "I think what happened to your father was just a terrible accident. This other woman ... she'd taken the little girl to visit her grandparents, so they weren't even in the country. According to my police liaison officer, she claims she knows nothing about the will, and they won't be coming back here."

"But that doesn't change anything," I insisted. "The girl's still going to inherit our family home at some point in the future."

"Well, so be it," my mother replied in a tremulous voice. "Perhaps some good may come out of this ... this horrible, horrible mess."

I argued with her over and over again, but she was adamant that all she wanted to do was move on; she still had a lovely home and money in the bank; she would be fine, I would be fine, and Julia didn't need to know about any of it – quite yet.

I knew she was wrong. I knew from painful, personal experience that even closely guarded secrets eventually reveal themselves, but as the weeks gave way to months and months to years, I pushed it all to the back of my mind and got on with *my* life.

I continue to mull over my problems until I finally pull onto the driveway of the house after a wearying and frustrating battle with the early morning traffic on the busy A12 road. I still the engine, glance out of the side window and see that the curtains have been drawn, which means that, being a Monday morning, Maggie has already arrived.

As I climb out of the car, I suddenly notice that the driveway is sown with weeds. They push through the pale, yellow stones at close, regular intervals, leaving the expanse of gravel looking more like a building site than the golden, yellow beach my mother once told me it was supposed to represent. I don't know why I didn't notice it before, and the creeping wildness of the place strikes me with such force that I fall back onto the seat. When did it get like this? I think to myself.

I cast my eyes over the exterior of the house and there's less evidence here of deliberate neglect. The windows are shiny clean, thanks to Maggie's sterling efforts, but a long streak of mould draws my eye to where the guttering has been leaking, and the front door could certainly use a new coat of paint. The place definitely looks its age though overall Hillcrest is a fine example of 1930s architecture with its red clay tile roof, herringbone brickwork and diamond leaded pane windows. For my father, it represented the pinnacle of his success, which I suppose goes some way to explain its importance to him.

I'm still running my eyes over the flaking, wooden window frames when the front door opens unexpectedly. Maggie walks out onto the front step, smiles and then beckons me inside. I follow her into the house, which in contrast to the garden is neat and clean. I explain about the briefcase.

"Oh, I saw that," she says. "I put it on the desk in your dad's study."

The fact that my father died nearly fifteen years ago seems to have had little impact on either the order or the running of the house

– though perhaps the garden tells a different story. I push my head around the door and feel a familiar nervousness, a tremor in my hand as it grips the handle. I hear my father's voice – *For God's sake, Richard. You're hanging onto that bloody doorknob like a baby with a dummy. Just get in here!*

Everything in the study is exactly as he left it, more or less. I don't understand why my mother hasn't cleared it out, but perhaps she senses the same atmosphere of ownership that I do: this was my father's private space and no one – including my mother – was allowed to enter it without his permission. When he went away, he locked the door.

I hurriedly retrieve my briefcase and carry it into the kitchen where Maggie is already preparing to leave.

"I've had a quick dust and vacuum in the rooms downstairs," she says. "As soon as I know when Mrs Oakley's coming home, I'll put fresh sheets on the bed. Is that okay?"

"That's fine," I tell her. "I'm expecting Julia to come back here at some point, so could you get her old room ready? I had a quick look in there last night and it was freezing. We might need to get someone in to check the heating."

Something changes in Maggie's warm, welcoming smile – just a fraction, just a brief stiffening of her full, pink lips and something that looks like apprehension in her bright blue eyes. She recovers quickly. "I can do that, of course, I can. But maybe she might like to have the guest room? It's a double bed, that's all."

"No en suite, though."

"The bathroom's next door."

"Is there a problem? I mean, with the room," I ask her. "If it's too much work, you only have to say."

"No, no, it's not that..." She leaves the sentence unfinished, collects her handbag from the kitchen counter and walks out into the hallway.

I follow her and tentatively put my hand on her arm. She's been working for my mother for more years than I can remember, and I don't want to upset her. "I really appreciate you looking after Mum the way you have been, Maggie. I can get someone in to give you a hand if it's too much." She hesitates, turns her head ever so slightly away from me, and I can see that her attention has moved to the

20

staircase in the middle of the hallway. I follow her gaze, but I don't know what I'm looking for. She suddenly straightens her shoulders and moves with speed to the front door. "Maggie?"

She pauses, glances back over her shoulder. "Maybe you should ask your Mum about that room, you know, when she's feeling better."

"Julia's bedroom?"

"It's just a thought," she says, and she grabs her jacket from the rack and leaves, pulling the door firmly shut behind her.

Lenora

Even behind closed lids my eyes communicate to my fogged brain that I'm not in my bedroom – too much harsh, white, artificial light, and the curtains in my bedroom are rose pink; they lend the room a gentle, early morning glow.

But I remember now – at least, I remember going to sleep in a hospital bed, though I can't quite remember why.

There's an area of flesh around my left hip, which throbs painfully. I try to slide my hand under the cover, but I quickly discover that I'm attached to something mechanical through a needle in the back of my hand. Within seconds, the monitor next to my bed beeps a critical alert and strong hands lift my arm back onto the top of the sheet.

Someone says, "Are you awake, Lenora? Do want some breakfast?"

I want to wake up, but I can feel sleep stealing back into my brain and it's hard to resist.

"Lenora, I've got some porridge here for you and some nice apple puree. Are you going to wake up and eat something, love?"

Aggie's voice is in my head, urging me to keep my eyes closed, but why?

And then it comes to me: the apple-guessing game. I would keep my eyes tightly shut and Aggie would push a piece of apple into my mouth. When I bit into it, the juice ran down my chin. The taste was sweet and aromatic, and I was always certain that I recognised the flavour.

That day in the farm shop, that was the first time I caught a glimpse of something dark and destructive in her…

"Cox's Orange Pippin," I said.
"Wrong!"

22

"Laxton Fortune?"

"Wrong again!"

I was always reluctant to admit defeat, but I said, "Okay, I give up,"

"Cornish Gilliflower."

I opened my eyes and saw Aggie grinning back at me. The apple guessing game was supposed to be fun, but sometimes it didn't feel like fun.

We'd both become ladies of leisure – the kind of people who have time to visit small, independent retailers in out of the way places. They call themselves 'farm shops', which would have made my mother smile. She sold eggs and fruit and vegetables from our farm, whatever was in season, but she had just a chair, a faded beach umbrella and a battered table on the side of the road. This shop offered customers the opportunity to 'taste before you buy' and Aggie had taken to sampling the produce like a professional wine taster.

"Now, it's my turn," she said, and she closed her eyes.

Playing 'Guess the Apple' was a bit like playing scrabble with Aggie: she always won. Growing up an only child, her parents had kept her entertained on wet afternoons with endless board games, so she was really good at that sort of thing. I'd grown up with three older brothers who beat me at everything, so I was a really sore loser and Aggie's apple game had quickly lost its appeal.

I remember that one time well. The fruit was heaped in baskets around us shiny and bright: beautiful, autumnal shades of red and orange and pink. It was really hard to choose.

"Hurry up!" Aggie said. "If I stand here much longer with my eyes closed, I'm going to get dizzy and fall over."

I glanced at the labels then reached for a piece of fruit. It was called Pearmaine... and then something I couldn't read properly without my glasses, but the name sounded familiar. It was an odd shape for an apple, but I used the knife on the wooden block to cut off a small slice and I popped it into Aggie's open mouth.

She chewed it thoughtfully. "I think this must be a new variety," she said.

Hope swelled in my chest. "Are you giving up?"

"Not yet," she said. "Give me another slice."

I cut another, larger piece of apple and pushed it into her mouth. She opened her eyes. "This isn't an apple."

"Yes, it is. It's one of these," I said, and I handed her the label.

"'Pears – Maine, US Imported,'" she read out loud then she carefully selected one of the pieces of fruit from the basket and held it up in front of my face. "Does this look like an apple?"

I screwed up my eyes and peered at the fruit. "It could be. It's very dark in here and I'm not wearing my reading glasses."

"This is not shaped like an apple," she said. "This is pear-shaped."

I was so tempted to tell her that, if nothing else, it was an accurate description of her apple guessing game, but I bit my tongue instead and said, "It was a genuine mistake."

She smiled suddenly and looked smug "It's fine. And I win."

"How did you win? It's an apple-guessing game."

"I guessed it wasn't an apple and it wasn't."

I was set to battle it out with her, but a man in a white coat suddenly loomed in the doorway. His mouth was set in a thin line. "Are you going to buy something?" he asked in a loud voice.

Even in the subdued light of the old barn I could see Aggie's face change from pink-cheeked triumph to pale-faced shock and then to red-faced anger. I quickly reached for her hand and gave it a reassuring squeeze then I turned to the man. "It says 'Try before you buy'."

"Well, now you've tried," he said hotly, "so make sure you buy something."

I looped Aggie's arm through mine, prised the pear from her hand and dropped it into a brown paper bag. "We'll take this one."

I remembered, when I was a child, if there was a glut of apples and pears, we used to sell them to the greengrocer in the high street. We had an orchard at the bottom of the garden and when it was time to pick the fruit, everyone was expected to help. There was no such thing as mechanisation back then, just hard labour. When the soft fruit was ready to be picked, my mother worked through the night bottling and jarring everything – blackberries, raspberries and plump, yellow gooseberries. They were all grown under nets, so the birds didn't get to eat them before we did. I always made jam in a large cauldron the way my mother taught me. It tasted better than anything you could buy in a shop, but I was still interested to see what they had.

Unsurprisingly Aggie wanted to leave at once, but I wanted to take a look around, even with the eyes of the man in the white coat boring into the back of my head. "Let's take a look at the 'fine preserves'," I said to her, and I pulled her with me to the far side of the shop.

"Do we have to?"

"Yes, we do."

The man in the white coat continued to watch us from behind the baskets of apples and pears as though we were a couple of teenage tearaways, intent on stealing something when his back was turned.

I rummaged through my bag to find my reading glasses so that I could read the labels properly.

"You have a cupboard full of homemade jam at home," Aggie said. "Why would you want to buy any of this?"

"I don't. I'm shopping for ideas."

All the preserves appeared to have been made by elderly ladies with old-fashioned names like me and Aggie, though perhaps not quite like us judging by the computer-generated labels on the front of the jars. My jam got a circle of wax paper and a lid, and I found out what was in it when I ate it. There were some interesting combinations of flavours though: pear with vanilla, rhubarb with ginger and a wide variety of fruits combined with alcohol.

I ignored the piece of paper pinned to the shelf, which warned that breakages had to be paid for, and began to lift down one jar at a time and study the list of ingredients. Suddenly I felt a hand on my shoulder. I spun round and found myself looking up at the man in the white coat.

"Can't you read you the sign?" he said. He peered down at me, stony-faced and unsmiling.

I think he was trying to appear intimidating, but I could have told him that he was wasting his time. "Do you mean the one that says, 'Try before you buy'?" I asked. "Because I was thinking of trying, but I can't get the lids off." I offered him the jar I was holding because I was certain that this attempt at humour would help to lighten the mood, but I'd misjudged him.

Without saying another word, he took the jar from me and carefully placed it back on the shelf. I saw his hand snake towards me again, reaching for my elbow, his intention no doubt to escort me to the till, but Aggie stepped between us. She slapped his hand away.

He was visibly shocked. "I think you should leave," he said.

"I think you should keep your hands to yourself," Aggie hissed back at him. She grabbed the brown paper bag from my hand and removed the single pear. I had no idea what she intended to do with it, but her face was suffused with rage. She passed the empty bag back to me.

It was one of those moments when you know in your gut that something bad is going to happen, but there isn't anything you can do to prevent it.

Aggie held up the pear with one hand. With the other hand she very slowly squeezed it till it broke apart between her bony fingers then she shook the pieces from her hand onto the floor.

A different man might have seen some humour in the situation – I think. But this man had suddenly staked his reputation on upholding the warning signs he'd posted around the shop. "You're still going to have to pay for that," he said.

I took out my purse. "I'll pay for it. Aggie, go and wait for me in the car." I pushed the keys into her hand now slick with pear juice. She mumbled something incoherent and quickly walked away towards the exit. "I'm sorry about that," I said. "I don't know what came over her."

He pointed to the till at the far end of the shop. "You can pay there." He began to move away then stopped, glanced back at me, and I could see that he was utterly confounded by what had just happened but then so was I. At last he said, "Don't come back. Please."

When I got outside, I could see Aggie sitting in the passenger seat with her eyes closed. "What on earth happened in there?" I yelled at her when I got into the car. "This was supposed to fun, Aggie. Remember? Guess the apple? We can never, ever come back here. They've probably got the whole thing on CCTV."

She opened her eyes. "He was a bully," she said simply in response. "I hate bullies."

26

Julia

I wake early, extricate myself from the tangle of sheets and slide onto the cool, tiled floor of the bedroom, taking special care not to wake Colin.

Last night Haziq drove us back to our apartment in River Valley Road and the mood in the chilled interior of the car was one of pleasant companionship. We held hands and spoke of our plans to redecorate the dining room – something I've been simply itching to do for months but I've been held back from hiring a designer while Colin negotiates an extension of our lease.

Siti was waiting for us at the door and had already prepared the cheese on toast. As a consequence, the bread was soggy and the cheese greasy. I took one look at it and told her to take it away. Colin grabbed the plate from her hands and told me not to be an ungrateful bitch. This has become our life: a word, a look, a shake of the head, and the uneasy truce between us is broken.

Colin immediately retreated to his study with the cheese on toast and told Siti to bring him a beer. I went straight to bed knowing that in the morning we would both act as though nothing had happened, but every little skirmish tear at the threads of our relationship. It's like an old patchwork quilt, which has been lovingly sewn together, but over the years is slowly breaking apart stitch by stitch, seam by seam.

It's still dark outside, but I know that Siti will already be at work in the kitchen making coffee and preparing breakfast for Colin. She's a good girl, I like her, but she won't stay. They like company, these young girls, and it won't be long before our elegant and generously proportioned apartment begins to feel like a prison. Here there are no lively children to mind, no elderly relatives to nurse, no family dinners to cook and serve. I feel sorry for her, but when she leaves, I'll just replace her with somebody else.

I quickly get dressed in freshly laundered gym wear. It's a short walk to my ladies-only workout studio and it's part of my early morning ritual. I deliberately avoided nasty, sweaty exercise when I first came out here, but back then I was one of those women who could eat and drink as she pleased without having to think about counting calories. The menopause has put paid to those advantages. These days I have to grind it out like all the other fifty-somethings if I want to stay a version of my younger self.

The place is already buzzing with activity when I arrive. Music seeps out into the surrounding darkness. When I glance inside the brightly lit interior, I can see that every piece of equipment is being energetically pushed or pumped or pulled by an array of lycra-clad women. A large proportion of them are successful, young professionals, who approach their working lives with zeal and commitment and see keeping fit as a necessary part of the package. I envy them their smooth skinned, well-toned bodies, and their financial independence. Of course, I have my gallery, but the income I make from selling glassware wouldn't pay all the household bills and I couldn't lead the kind of carefree existence I now enjoy.

I hurry inside because outside the acrid smell of woodsmoke permeates the air. Microparticles of ash are falling from the sky, blown to the island from neighbouring Indonesia where fires are burning day and night to clear the land.

Air pollution is a growing problem here in Singapore – something the colourful and expansive guidebooks fail to mention. It isn't unusual to see people wearing masks to cover their nose and mouth – it helps, but it's impossible to completely protect oneself from breathing in the toxic air on days like this. I love Singapore, but you only have to scratch the surface metaphorically speaking and you soon discover that it isn't always quite the tropical paradise our government promotes to the rest of the world.

I quickly find an empty locker in the changing room and leave my purse and phone locked inside it. As soon as one of the treadmills lined up in front of the window has been vacated, I reset it to a brisk walking speed at a ten per cent incline and jump on. I have a routine and I like to stick to it. My on-going goal is to maintain my weight at around 120 pounds. I know I look good for my age, but it is – quite literally – an uphill struggle.

By the time I've completed a circuit of the equipment and gone through the motions of the obligatory cool-down, I'm ready to leave. If I'm not showered, changed and sitting in the car by eight, Colin will leave without me so it's always a race against the clock.

I grab my stuff from the locker and am racing out of the exit when a breathless voice suddenly calls out to me, "Wait up, Julia!" Moments later I feel a hand on my shoulder. Nancy Sullivan drags me to a standstill in front of the building. "We have to talk, honey," she says hoarsely then she's overtaken by the need to cough. She fumbles in her bag for her inhaler, pushes the plastic nozzle between her lips and takes a deep breath. Nancy, my only true friend in the whole of Singapore, has asthma. She can barely breathe. "Fuck this!" she gasps. "I swear to God the air pollution gets worse every year."

"It won't last much longer," I try to reassure her. "Go inside and get a drink of water."

"I'll be fine in a moment," she says. She stands just inside the doorway, lays a trembling hand on the centre of her chest and makes a conscious effort to breathe slowly and evenly.

"Okay?" I ask her.

"Okay," she says.

"I can't talk now, Nancy. Call me later."

"You need to hear this, Julia."

The urgency in her tone is real, which suggests that what she has to tell me isn't merely a piece of salacious gossip. But I really haven't time to linger in the doorway, so I ask her to meet me later at the gallery. "We can have lunch."

"You don't do lunch," she says, and again her voice betrays a genuine concern.

I begin to move away from her. "I will. I promise."

"Promise?" she calls out to me.

One glance at my wristwatch is enough to encourage me to break into a run, so I answer with a wave of my hand.

Siti is serving Colin breakfast when I get back to the apartment. He glances up from his newspaper, tells me to hurry and that he won't wait for me. He says the same thing every day. One day he really will leave without me.

I shower quickly and change into my work uniform – a simple, black, linen shift dress. I always wear pearls with it – pretty earrings and a double string of plump, luminous stones. I like to look coolly elegant, which isn't easy in this climate in spite of the air-conditioning. I also like the glassware I sell to be the star attraction in the gallery. All the goods are displayed on clear, Perspex shelves with subtle backlighting so that the beautiful colours are shown off to perfection with no distractions, and that includes me.

I opened Glück Glass nearly twenty-five years ago. I was bored because I didn't work, and I was often lonely – expats tend to socialise amongst themselves and all the other wives had children, so I was never included when they met up during the day. But then I met Nancy at The Americanas Club – a much nicer and much less formal version of The LingLang. It was the usual thing: dinner, drinks and talk about the rapidly advancing Tiger Economies of the Far East. We struck up conversation at the bar while our husbands were working the room.

Nancy and her husband, Bill, had only recently arrived in Singapore. I don't know why, but we hit it off immediately. She asked me how I occupied myself and when I told her she said, "Jeez! You need to get a life. Why don't you start your own business? Isn't that what this place is all about?" She questioned me at length about what I liked doing and when I said buying nice things, she told me, "So, buy nice things and sell them to other people, who like nice things."

I made a list of all the nice things I liked to buy and top of that list was glassware.

Colin wasn't keen to fund my fledgling enterprise – I think he was still hoping to hear the sound of tiny feet pattering on the marble tiles of our lovely apartment – but I convinced him to advance me a modest a start-up capital, and promised him that if the business didn't turn a profit by the end of the second year I'd give it up. The rest, as they say, is history.

As soon as I'm ready, I join Colin in the dining room. Siti places a bowl of fresh fruit and yoghurt in front of me and asks if I would like tea or coffee. "Green tea with a slice of lemon, but don't make it too hot," I tell her.

Colin folds his newspaper and slowly gets to his feet. Unusually, the bad feeling from the previous evening seems to be lingering – the tension between us is palpable. "Are you serious about going home?" he asks in a disgruntled tone. "If you are, I want to know exactly when you're leaving and when you're coming back."

"Singapore is home, Colin."

"You know what I mean."

"I'll be arranging my flight as soon as I hear from Richard, but I can't give you a detailed itinerary at this point because there isn't one. When I know what I'm doing, you'll be the first to find out." I offer him a smile. "Priority notification."

"I think we both know that's not true," he says sourly.

I'm saved from responding to this last rancorous remark by the appearance of Haziq at the dining room door. He says, "Traffic really very bad this morning, Mr Crane Sir. I think we should be leaving *pronto.*"

Haziq's estimation of the early morning traffic is infuriatingly precise and I'm all but pushed from the moving car at Dhoby Ghaut Station at the eastern end of Orchard Road. I walk to the shopping mall at Orchard Oval and take the lift up to the sixth floor. I'm feeling flushed and fretful because I'm twenty minutes late and I can see Connie sitting on her heels in front of the gallery with her nose pressed to her phone.

"Get up!" I bark at her. "Why haven't you opened up yet?"

"Sorry, sorry, I left my keys at home," she says, scrambling to her feet.

I point at the phone. "Switch that thing off and put it away. I don't want to see it one more time today. Understand?" She quickly slides it into the back pocket of her trousers, so I reach behind her and pull it out again. "You put this in the bottom drawer of my desk, and you leave it there." The expression of contrition on her young face is immediately replaced with fear and confusion – the idea of being separated from her phone is almost unthinkable. But I can think it and, more importantly, I can insist that it happens. She takes the phone back from me with shaking hands.

I use my own keys to unlock the steel shutters which protect the windows and entrance of the gallery then let myself in. Connie

31

follows me inside and rushes into the office to switch off the alarm. "I'm putting my phone away now," she calls back to me, and she makes a point of closing the drawer in the desk as loudly as she can.

I take a quick look around, check that Aysha has dusted the shelves and vacuumed the carpeted floor, and finally cast a critical eye over the new display in the window – it's a carefully staged collection of vintage Swedish Art Glass. Although every single piece is more than fifty years old, the bright colours and bold shapes lend them a strong, contemporary feel. I prefer my glassware to be delicate and romantic, but I still appreciate the workmanship and artistry that created these.

At my request, Connie spends the morning checking the contents of boxes which arrived late yesterday afternoon while I serve customers and answer enquiries over the phone. When it gets to midday, I take pity on her and allow her to take back the phone for her lunch break. She looks suitably grateful and dashes off, promising to return promptly at one o'clock.

No sooner has Connie left than Nancy arrives, pale-faced, breathless. I usher her into the office space at the rear of the gallery and insist that she sit at my desk and drink a glass of water. "For goodness sake use your inhaler. You have got it with you?"

She nods. Once again, she goes through the ritual of breathing a metered dose of medication into her lungs via the little, plastic pistol she keeps in her handbag. "If this smog doesn't lift, I'm leaving," she gasps. "I'm thinking a couple of weeks on Hua Hin beach."

I give her an affectionate pat on the shoulder. "We all love a break from the pace on a beach in Thailand, but you'd get bored after 48 hours." (Nancy gives private tuition to stressed-out Singaporean school children – it's her life. Our education system is one of the best in the world, but it's also famously been described as a 'pressure cooker'. Teenage suicide rates have increased year-on-year – another worrying statistic that's given little publicity.)

When I explain to her that I can't go to lunch till Connie gets back, she leaves then comes back with coffee and a warm croissant. "I can't eat this," I tell her.

"Don't be ridiculous," she snaps, and she places the paper-wrapped croissant in front of me.

Reluctantly I pick it up. The folded triangle of feather-light pastry suddenly feels heavy in my hand. "What you came here to tell me ... is it bad news?"

"It's not good news, honey," she says. "We had dinner at the Club last night. Jian was there with his wife." Nancy reaches across the desk and grasps my hand. "She's pregnant."

I know this can't be true. Jian – my Wenjian – is married to his wife in name only. I wrench my hand away from hers. "They're not *together*. It was an arranged marriage." When Nancy gazes back at me, her eyes bright with tears, I insist it's not true. "It couldn't possibly be his baby," I tell her.

"They were very much together, Julia," she says.

"I don't believe you!" I cry, but I do believe her because Nancy would never lie to me.

The world, my precious, secret world, has stopped spinning on its axis. I close my eyes and feel it topple and fall.

Richard

I slip into the dining room overlooking the gravel drive and watch Maggie walk away. I expect her to glance back over her shoulder – I don't know why – but she doesn't even hesitate. One moment she's crunching yellow stones beneath her feet and the next she's disappeared from view behind the tall, unclipped privet hedge that marks the boundary with the road.

Something vaguely sinister has just happened, but I'm not quite sure what it is.

In spite of what Maggie has said, I make a note to call someone to check out the radiator in Julia's old bedroom. I'm certain she'll want to sleep in her own bed even though it hasn't been her bed for a very long time. Then I make a second note to buy Maggie something nice to thank her. I realise I have no idea what she'd like – Flowers? Chocolates? The fact that I know so very little about her, even after all these years, strikes me with some force. Her loyalty has never been fully rewarded and certainly insufficiently appreciated, except perhaps by my mother.

I decide to make myself a cup of coffee before I start work, but I've only just seated myself at the table to begin when the telephone suddenly shrills.

"Ciao, Ricardo!" Silvio's light, melodious voice sings loudly in my ear. "Dove sei? Where are you, mi amore?" He shouts in an effort to raise his voice above the noise in the restaurant kitchen behind him.

"I'm still here at my mother's house."

"Perché?"

"Why am I still here? That's a good question."

"I call your office and they say you don't work today. I don't understand. You told me this project is priority. *Molto importante*, you said."

"I'm working here this morning. I'll explain what's happening when..." Our conversation is interrupted by a series of loud crashes and bangs, followed by an angry tirade of abuse punctuated with four-letter expletives. It sounds like someone in the kitchen is breaking plates. "Why don't I call you later?"

"Call me later!" he yells, and then the line goes dead.

I feel the smile in my heart before it reaches my face. It's a sense of belonging; a consciousness of kinship. Every single person who works in their restaurant is a member or at the very least a close friend of the Mazzi family. Blood ties – they matter. Not that Silvio's ever-extending family welcomed me in the beginning, but that was more about Silvio than me. The Mazzis are a proud Lombardy family, and Mamma Mazzi had ambitions for her youngest son. Needless to say, they didn't include me, a pale, poker-faced, gay Englishman. But now everything is good. *L'amore conquista tutto,* Mamma always tells me. Love conquers everything. The Mazzi family has become *my* family.

I met Silvio about three years after my marriage broke up. I use this well-worn phrase, but it wasn't really like that; it wasn't a sudden, tearing apart; it wasn't a dramatic rending asunder of a once loving relationship. In fact, Sarah told me she'd long suspected that I only proposed to her in the first place because my father liked and admired her, and back then what my father liked was important to me. I hope that wasn't true because Sarah was and still is a good friend. I wish I could have loved her better, but then I wouldn't have married her.

After the divorce was finalised, everything changed. I could finally be the person that I wanted to be, the person who met and fell in love with Silvio. My mother was sympathetic if at first uncomprehending. My father showed me the door. In fact, we'd sat at this very table while I tried to explain, but he didn't want to listen, didn't want to know. He ordered me to leave, so I left.

I decide to send Silvio a brief text then I settle down to work.

It's completely quiet in the house except for the ticking of the large, longcase clock in the hallway. I'm engrossed in a complicated spreadsheet when I become aware of another noise above my head. It's very faint but quite distinct: a soft, shuffling sound. I stop working and listen. The noise is so faint, so soft, that I wonder if it's nothing more than the sound of the floor-length curtains in Julia's bedroom being swept back and forth across the parquet floor by a breeze. But that would require an open window, I think to myself, and then I recall that Julia has a small balcony in her room so we're actually talking open doors. I can't imagine for a single moment that Maggie would leave the house vulnerable to burglars, but the shuffling sound is unmistakable, so I feel obliged to investigate.

I make my way upstairs, irritated by the intrusion into my precious time.

I find the curtains in Julia's bedroom snugly closed. When I check, I can see at once that the doors have been securely locked with a key from the inside and bolts fasten both doors to the floor. Seized with curiosity, I draw back the curtains and at once the room is flooded with light. I don't know what I expected to see, but it wasn't this. Every surface is covered with a thick layer of dust; a grey coating of microparticles so compact that I could clearly write my name in it. Even the floor bears the imprint of my shoes. I'm utterly bewildered by this discovery because I know that Maggie has kept everywhere else in the house clean and dust-free.

It's still very cold in the room so I check the valve on the radiator and am not surprised to find it turned off. I try to turn it back on. It's too stiff to move more than a fraction without the proper tools, but I can now hear water seeping into the system. This, at least, explains the chill air inside the room.

There's something else here though that feels unfamiliar. It's a smell. It isn't exactly unpleasant – an old-fashioned, floral perfume, perhaps – but there's a staleness about it, a hint of decay, and I find myself wrinkling my nose in distaste.

Maggie has some explaining to do.

When I return to the kitchen, once again the only audible sound is the tick-tock of the hallway clock, but the experience of finding Julia's room in such a state of neglect has rattled me. I can think of no logical reason why Maggie would leave it like this, but as she's already suggested I check with my mother before the room is made ready for Julia's stay, I can only hope that *she* is well enough to offer up an explanation.

I manage to get another couple of hours work under my belt then decide to call it a day. The project I'm managing is an architectural albatross. It's going to be a boutique hotel, but for now it's a building site because our client is a lady (I use the word loosely) with too much money and too much time on her hands so the brief we've been given changes, like the weather.

I remember that my stomach has been reminding me for nearly an hour that breakfast was just a slice of toast, and I still need to drive back to the hospital to question the doctors over the prognosis for my mother. It's hard to make plans for her when I have no timeframe to work with and minimal understanding of either the immediate or short-term requirements. (I don't want to think about the long-term requirements.)

I soon discover that Maggie has cleared most of the food out of the fridge, so I decide to take the short walk to the high street and buy lunch. When the girl behind the counter in the cafe asks if I want to eat it there or take it with me, I realise I'm in no particular hurry to return to the house.

When I left my childhood home for the last time with my father's angry, hateful words ringing in my ears, it was with a mixture of heartbreak and relief. Those oddly conflicting emotions have followed me down the years. Hillcrest House was my home and I *did* have a happy childhood there, but it also represented everything I disliked about my father: stiff-necked convention, lack of imagination and bourgeois pretension. Even after his death I've continued to feel like an undesirable guest in spite of my mother's warm and heartfelt welcome and I can't throw it off, so it's an easy decision to sit in the window of the café and watch the world go by.

Just as I'm about to finish my lunch and leave, a man wearing a worn, brown suede jacket suddenly stops and peers at me through the glass. The face is familiar, but I can't remember the name. He smiles and points to the empty chair next to me. I still can't remember his name, but I feel obliged to be hospitable, so I motion to him to join me.

"Richard. How are you?" he asks solicitously as he takes a seat then carefully places his hand over mine. "How's your mother? I feel awful about the whole thing, you know. It's a good job Maggie turned up when she did because I didn't have a key to get back in." He sees my look of blank incomprehension but rattles on regardless. "The door slammed shut behind me. Of course, I'd gone and left my bag with my phone in it on the floor of the porch. It was terrible, absolutely awful ... I could see her lying there at the foot of the stairs."

"I'm sorry, I'm not sure..." I begin.

He colours up and withdraws his hand. "How stupid of me. It's just that I've known your mother for many years, and she talks about you and your sister all the time. I feel like I know you, but of course you don't really know me." He proffers his hand in a more formal gesture of friendship. "Reverend Edward Feering at your service. Sometimes known as Father Ted?" He leans in and gives me a conspiratorial wink. "Wrong denomination, but it's the thought that counts."

Now I remember. I grasp his hand firmly in mine and tell him that I should have recognised him. He brushes this aside. "I had no idea you were there when it happened," I say.

He makes a guilty face and lifts his shoulders in an apologetic shrug. "Well, I wasn't. That was the problem. I'd offered to give your mother a lift to the church hall. I only popped into the house to use the facilities, if you know what I mean. She said she was going upstairs to change her jacket, so I went straight back out. Two seconds later the front door literally slammed shut behind me."

"So, you didn't see her fall?"

"No. I waited for her in the car for about twenty minutes."

"Twenty minutes?"

The note of incredulity in my voice registers with him and once again his face colours up. "I know. I feel dreadful. But I've been doing this job for a long time, Richard, and I've learned that ladies of a certain age expect to be treated with respect and – dare I say it – deference. You don't rush them." When he realises that I'm not going to bawl him out for his ineptitude he quickly goes on. "Thank God – yes really, I do thank Him from the bottom of my heart – Maggie turned up with a key."

"Well, I'm just glad someone was there to help her," I say.

"Always a pleasure, Richard." He clears his throat – I feel a little awkwardly. "Will she be in hospital for long? I usually visit, but it's quite a long way to drive, so if she's coming home soon then I'll wait till she's back. Much nicer to be in your own in bed, I always think."

"I really have no idea," I say. I don't know why I suddenly feel compelled to confide in him – he's virtually a stranger after all – but I find myself telling him about the problem with the house, although I refrain from mentioning my half-sister. He listens very attentively and doesn't interrupt. "I don't know what we're going to do if she can't manage by herself anymore."

He nods his head sagely. "It's a big problem for lots of families, but your mother could move into the bungalow, couldn't she? In fact, I'd be inclined to recommend that she do it in any case. No stairs then, eh?"

"What bungalow?"

"The one that used to belong to your mother's friend, Agnes. Agnes Bagshot?"

"You mean Aggie?"

"Yes, of course."

"What bungalow?" I say again.

"I thought you knew..." There's a moment of pained embarrassment, and then he hurriedly gets to his feet. "It's probably best if you speak to your mother about it." He claps me on the shoulder. "It was great meeting you again, Richard. And tell your mother I'll pop round to see her as soon as she's home." Before I have a chance to question him further, he raises his hand in a farewell gesture to the girl behind the counter then dashes off.

My mind is full of questions as I walk back to the house. I feel complete and utter mystification at my mother choosing to *not* inform me that she inherited Aggie's bungalow. I try to recall when Aggie died, but I can't remember if it was ten months or two years ago. This changes everything, and these thoughts continue to preoccupy me while I close up the house and retrace my journey to the hospital.

When I get to the ward, my mother is sitting up in bed. She still looks frail and the painkilling medication has dulled her eyes, but she smiles as soon as she recognises me.

"They said you came this morning," she says. I lean over the bed, place a kiss on her cheek. She reaches up and touches my face. "I thought I was dreaming when I saw you standing in the doorway but you're real." She sighs and clutches at my hand. "It's the drugs they give you, it makes you see things."

"It's really me."

"Yes, I know. But sometimes I can't be sure."

"How are you feeling if that isn't a stupid question?"

She shrugs. "Tired. A bit sore, I suppose. They give me painkillers if it gets too uncomfortable."

"They told me this morning they're going to move you to another bed."

She nods. "I have to start the rehabilitation programme with the physiotherapist. She was here earlier. A lovely little girl, lovely warm smile, but she hasn't a clue." She points at the chair I'm sitting in. "She wanted me to get out of bed and sit there. Do I look like I want to get out of bed and sit in a chair?"

"Well, they have to get you moving, Mum. They said they won't keep you in here longer than necessary so as soon as you're able, they'll be showing you to how to use a frame to get about."

She responds with an irritated sigh. "I've fallen down the stairs and fractured my hip; I haven't just stubbed my toe on the end of the bed, you know."

"Yes, I do know, but it isn't fractured any more, is it? Now you have a nice, new hip," I reply brightly in an effort to jolly her along.

"You sound like your sister," she retorts. "She was always a fountain of sympathy in a moment of crisis."

"Ah, sarcasm. Now I know you're feeling better," I tease her. She manages a wan smile in response.

I pick up on the fact that she knows she fell down the stairs, but when I ask her how it happened, she looks away; says she doesn't remember. I know I'm going to have to question her about the bungalow, but something tells me that now isn't the right moment so instead I just describe how I met Father Ted in the cafe.

She rolls her eyes. "He's a right twerp. *Father Ted* – I ask you."

"It was lucky he was there when you fell down the stairs – lucky that Maggie was there as well."

She says stiffly, "Well, as I said, I don't remember much about it, but I do know if he hadn't called and insisted on giving me a lift then I wouldn't have gone upstairs to change my jacket."

I can't begin to understand the logic of this argument and change the subject. I tell her instead about Silvio's nephew's new baby. She lies back against the mound of pillows and listens with obvious enjoyment to my story, but she soon tires so I kiss her goodbye and tell her I'll speak with the doctor in the morning. "They won't keep you in here long, Mum. But I need to have some kind of timeframe so I can organise things for you. And for Julia as well."

She startles at the mention of my sister's name. "What are you talking about?"

"I've asked Julia to come back for a couple of weeks to help out."

"That won't be necessary. I can manage on my own."

"That will be necessary," I insist. "*I* can't do it while I'm in the middle of this hotel project, and you're going to need *someone* to stay with you until you're able to do things without any help."

The broader question of whether she can *continue* to live completely independently at Hillcrest shall remain unspoken, as shall the mystery surrounding Julia's bedroom and Aggie's bungalow, because I see that my visit has exhausted her. She yawns and closes her eyes. I hear her murmur, "Julia won't come home, not for me."

"Yes, she will," I say firmly, and for my mother's benefit I sound confident even though I'm not. But I think to myself, now that Julia knows her inheritance has been passed to somebody else, it could be the incentive she needs to come back. We have some difficult decisions to make and I won't do it without her.

Lenora

"Are you alright there, Lenora? Do you need some pain relief?"

I want to answer her, this nice nurse, who gently holds my hand, but my tongue has turned to cardboard inside my mouth while I was sleeping and it won't move, won't let me form words. It sits rigidly behind my teeth, papery dry, so I squeeze her fingers in reply.

"Do you want a drink of water? Will that help?"

I nod my head, communication now limited to parts of the body less conveniently associated with conversation. Moments later, a cotton wool lollipop saturated with water is pushed between my dry lips. I draw the cool liquid into my mouth, and my tongue is loosened from the roof of my mouth.

"Is that better?"

"Much better."

"You were calling out there, Lenora. Are you in pain, my love, because I can give you something for that?"

I am in pain. It radiates down my leg from the new hip.

"We need to reposition you," she tells me, when I explain where it hurts. "I think you've tried to turn onto your side while you were asleep. What we're aiming for Lenora is 'neutral alignment' – that's hospital jargon. It means sleeping on your back and sitting up straight." She checks my notes. "How much pain are you in – on a scale of one to ten?"

I think about it. "Six-point-five."

"Six-point-five. That's very precise. I think we'll be needing something with a bit more kick than a couple of paracetamol, so give me a minute and I'll get you something to make it go away." She scuttles off.

The pain is really quite bad so when the nurse returns, breathless and smiling, and offers me some tablets, I'm suitably grateful for her haste. She stands over me and watches, while I swallow them down with a cup of water. Then she says, "I've checked your notes, Lenora. Apparently, you refused to get out of bed this morning for our lovely physiotherapist, Lucy. What was that all about?"

I feel myself bristle. I'm not fond of the way that elderly people are infantilized when they're in hospital, but I like this woman: she's innately kind and caring, so I keep my irritation in check. "I'm not ready to walk yet. I've only just had this operation, you know."

"I do know that, Lenora, because I've just read your notes," she replies. "But if you want to leave this hospital sooner rather than later then you need to get moving. I'm warning you in the nicest way possible that if you stay in that bed, it will only slow your recovery. Don't you want to go home?"

I want to answer her with a reassuring 'Yes, of course, I do', but it's a question with which I've been wrestling from the moment that I woke from the anaesthetic and remembered starting the descent of the stairs; remembered the sudden pressure in the small of my back; remembered how I tumbled and fell, striking my head painfully against the sturdy, wooden pedestal at the foot of the stairs. Do I want to go home? No, I'm not sure that I really do.

Julia

It's six o'clock in the evening. I'm tired and feeling more than a little irritable. In fact, my nerves are as taut as a proverbial piano wire.

Aysha has just arrived and Connie is itching to leave, but this might be the last opportunity I have, before I fly to London, to impress upon them both the importance of good timekeeping, security and attentive customer service. "I need to know I can trust you," I tell them.

Connie keeps glancing down at her phone. She thinks I can't see it (and I can't) but I know that it's wedged between her knees. Any moment now I'm going to hand her a very large box then make her stand up, just to hear the satisfying sound of the phone fall and hopefully break into a thousand pieces on the hard, concreted floor of my office.

Aysha is also pretending to listen, but she's already explained to me that her mind is on her young son, who's being looked after by her mother-in-law this evening. Aysha hates her mother-in-law with a burning passion, but her own mother is unwell today and can't babysit. The boy is four years old and 'very naughty' – Aysha's own words. Aysha's mother-in-law uses an ancient but tried and tested method when dealing with naughty children – it's called *the hard slap*. I'm definitely with the mother-in-law on this one, but Aysha is sitting and fretting and not listening because she doesn't believe in 'that terrible *corporeal* punishment'.

I want to shoot myself in the head, but only after I've shot Jian first.

In those first minutes after Nancy exploded the bombshell that was the news that Jian's wife is pregnant, I seriously wanted my life to end, because Tan Wenjian *is* my life. I looked into her sorrowful, dark brown eyes and saw that it was true. I jumped to my feet, ran into the gallery and collapsed onto the floor. I wanted to rip my clothes from my body; tear every single highlighted hair from my head; drown myself in the million, gut-wrenching tears I cried into the carpet in front of the gallery window where everyone could see me and know that I'd been wronged.

As soon as Nancy realised that I was in the throes of a nuclear-scale meltdown, she pulled down the shutters and closed up the shop. When Connie came back from her lunch break, she stopped her in the doorway and told her to go home. Connie didn't argue, but then she could hear me wailing like a banshee, so I suppose she was relieved not to have to share my pain. Without asking, Nancy gathered me into her arms and held me close.

"He isn't worth it, Julia."

"Yes, he is! You don't understand, he's all I have," I sobbed.

"But he isn't really yours. He's a married man from a prominent and very wealthy Singapore family and he isn't going to leave his Chinese wife for you."

"You don't know him! He promised me we can be together."

"How can that ever happen? Seriously Julia, the Tan family are old Singapore. You know what they're like. They even arranged his marriage – brought him back a bride from China, for crying out loud."

Of course, I knew all this already, but I was still clinging desperately to the illusion of a happy ever after with the man I adored, so I said, "He doesn't love her, he loves me. You don't know what it's like for him, having to lead a double life."

At that point she pushed me away, stood up and, with a shake of her head, left me sprawled on the floor of the gallery. I knew she was frustrated with me, but I thought she was going to come back with a cup of tea and her sympathy for my horrible predicament restored. I waited and waited, but she didn't come back, so I hauled myself to my feet and went to look for her. She was sitting at my desk and had made tea, but it didn't look like she was going to offer me any kind words judging by the expression on her face.

"Are you all cried out?" she asked

I slumped into the chair opposite her. "Why are you being so mean? Why did you even tell me if you don't care how I feel?"

"Now you're just being a jerk," she said.

I reached across the desk for her hand. "Don't judge me, Nancy, please. You and Bill, you have something special, but my relationship with Colin has died a slow and painful death over many years and I can't go on pretending that we're going to walk off into the sunset together. Especially if it's on the east coast of England," I added with a tearful, conciliatory smile.

She gave my fingers a brief squeeze in acknowledgement. "I know you're unhappy with Colin, but trust me, there are no beautiful sunsets where you're heading if it's with Jian. He won't leave his wife for you: his parents would never allow it." It wasn't what I wanted to hear, and I tried to withdraw my hand, but she clung to it. "Listen to me, Julia! You've lived in Singapore long enough to know and understand that filial piety is the guiding principle of every family relationship here: respect for and obedience to your elders. The Tan family have Confucian values running through their veins. They're not going to let an ang moh break up their son's marriage."

Ang Moh. I'd heard that term a thousand times before. Jian once tried to convince me that it was almost a term of affection for expats in Singapore, but I already knew that *ang moh gui* meant something like 'red-haired devil' and was used exclusively for white foreigners.

I discovered, soon after we began our relationship, that his extended family – his grandfather, his parents, and his wife – all lived together on the north side of the island in one of Singapore's increasingly rare heritage properties: a spacious, colonial, black and white, two-storey bungalow. But Jian kept his own, private apartment in a prestigious condominium complex near the city centre, which is where we would meet. What I hadn't known at that point (although I should have guessed) was that his family also owned a penthouse apartment in one of the *most* exclusive condominiums in the very heart of the city.

One evening Jian arranged to meet me there in the lobby. Just as we were walking out, his parents surprised both of us by walking in. Jian looked embarrassed, but quickly introduced me as a business associate. I could see that his mother wasn't fooled for a single second. She told him – in front of me – that he should conduct his 'so-called business meetings' elsewhere, and she didn't want to see his 'ang moh ji nü' anywhere near their family home ever again.

As we walked away, I asked him what she'd meant. He said, "She thinks I'm paying you for your time."

I was stunned. "Is that what she actually said? She called me a prostitute?"

He answered, quite casually, "Don't worry about it. She didn't mean it. She's just not keen on foreigners." And whenever I questioned him about his family after that, he always reassured me that things would change, and I wanted to believe him.

Occasionally, I even asked him about his wife, but he always dismissed my questions with an extravagant wave of the hand, once telling me, "The marriage was arranged by our parents in the old way. Lì Húa understands how it is. She has her life, and I have mine."

Eight years down the line we're still meeting in secret and it's probably stupidly naïve for a woman in her fifties to go on believing that her young lover will keep faith with her, but I simply can't imagine my life without him, so when Nancy finally left, telling me that I should go straight home and sort myself out before I even *thought* about calling Jian, I grudgingly agreed that it was the most sensible thing to do. Thirty minutes later, after repairing my make-up and hair, I'd changed my mind and decided instead to go straight to Jian's apartment and confront him.

When I let myself in, I could hear him singing loudly in the shower. I recognised the song at once: it was an old Cantonese pop ballad from the 1990s. It brought tears to my eyes because it was a time when Jian was still dancing the night away in smoke-filled discos, but I was accompanying Colin to formal, black tie dinner events at the LingLang Club.

I checked my reflection in the bedroom mirror. I was fifty-four years old, and the face looking back at me clearly showed the strain of living two lives, both of them played out on a knife-edge, never knowing when fate would intervene and I would be exposed for what I really was: a mistress and an adulterous wife.

The singing stopped and Jian sauntered into the room. At forty-six years old, his body was still lean and strong. He wears his hair significantly longer than most of his contemporaries and he'd slicked it back from his forehead; it was as black as a raven's wing and shiny clean from the shower. Droplets of water trickled down his chest. I wanted to reach out and check their path as they moved over his smooth, tanned skin. He looked surprised to see me.

"Julia? What are you doing here?" He took a step towards me, stopped and then gaped at my face. "Have you been crying? What's happened?"

I stepped away from him. "That's what I came here to ask you."

"Nothing's happened to me," he replied.

"Really? Are you sure you haven't got any news to share with me?"

The expression of caring concern on his face began to dissolve. It started in his eyes and ended in the set of his mouth. "Who told you?"

"Does it matter?" I shrieked back at him. "What the hell is going on?"

"I can explain," he said. "Let me get dressed first."

"No!"

"Go and sit down out there," he insisted, and he pointed through the bedroom doorway to the open-plan sitting room.

I wanted to throw myself at him and beat my fists on his chest, but knowing his disdain for histrionics I left him, tight-lipped and tearful, and threw myself onto the sofa instead. What was there to explain? I thought angrily. He was having sex with his wife and not just with me. I felt ... betrayed.

When he came out of the bedroom, his hair was still dripping, but he'd pulled on a pair of shorts and a T-shirt. He immediately went to the drinks cabinet and poured out two large glasses of brandy. He carried them carefully to the sofa where I had curled myself into a foetal position around a huge cushion. I saw him hesitate, and I knew at once that he didn't want to sit next to me. He put the glasses on the coffee table then seated himself in the armchair opposite me. He pushed the glass towards me. "Drink this."

I scowled at him over the top of the cushion. "I don't need to be sedated. I just need you to tell me it isn't true."

He sipped at the brandy slowly, almost leisurely, and I could see him measuring his thoughts – how to tell her so that she doesn't make this even more difficult for me than it is already, he was thinking. Eventually he said, "I was going to tell you, in fact as soon as I saw Bill and Nancy walk into the restaurant, I realised they might see us together. But Lì Húa is my wife, Julia. We do occasionally socialize with friends."

I couldn't decide if he was being deliberately evasive, or if, perhaps, Nancy had been mistaken and I was making a complete fool of myself. This other woman in his life was his wife and he was required to go through the motions of playing her dutiful husband in public places where they might be seen by family, or more importantly by friends of the Tan family – in a society where 'face' or appearance is everything, I understood that Jian had obligations to fulfil.

I found myself watching him steadily over the edge of the now slightly soggy cushion cover and I remembered the phrase that Nancy had used: filial piety. It described perfectly the sum total of Jian's relationship with his parents: with the extended Tan clan, it was family first. I took a deep breath and plunged in. "I've always understood that you have to honour and respect your parents' wishes, Jian, but I didn't understand exactly how far that extended until now. So ... when were you going to tell me that Lì Húa is expecting your baby?"

He slowly placed the glass on the table in front of him and the two glasses sat side by side dividing us, one still half full of brandy and the other now nearly drained.

It's strange how small details can distract you in moments of drama and despair – I suddenly recognised the glasses as the whiskey tumblers I'd given him as a gift to celebrate our first Christmas together. Jian had spotted them in the window of the gallery one day and ventured inside to ask their price and provenance – that was how we met. I remembered how I'd explained that they were Victorian Wrythen glassware, over a century old. He'd considered them to be as special and beautiful as I had so the irony of the present situation wasn't lost on me: they were the very things, which had brought us together, but now they sat between us like an unbreakable barrier.

I threw the cushion onto the floor and sat myself up so that I was facing him squarely across the coffee table. I felt strangely calm. I said, *"I feel like everything you've ever told me about her, about your marriage, it was all a lie."*

He shook his head. *"It wasn't a lie, but perhaps it wasn't the complete truth either."* He leaned forward and spread his hands out on the table in front of him as if to say, 'Now I will be open with you. Now I will give you the truth you've asked for'. He looked me straight in the eye. *"I hoped you'd understand, Julia. You know, Lì Húa has been ... forgiving. She knows how I feel about you; she knew before she accepted the proposal of marriage that you were a part of my life and that I wasn't going to give you up. But ... this is what my family expects of me, and I couldn't put it off any longer."*

"Well, obviously I appreciate your wife's patient forbearance," I said with mock sincerity. *"But to have a baby with you? Seriously?"*

"Why wouldn't she?" he asked.

"Why wouldn't she?" I repeated after him. *"Why would she? That's what I can't understand, Jian, because you're going to be with me! We had plans. Remember? No more creeping around, no more hiding out in this apartment. You said we could be together."*

"We still can. Nothing has to change."

We locked eyes across the table, and I could see that he was completely serious. *"You really think that nothing's going to change?"* I asked him.

He responded by shifting back in his seat and crossing his arms in front of his chest. He said quietly, *"I never told you I would leave my wife, Julia. I honestly thought you understood that wasn't possible. We can still be together, but I'm not going to divorce Lì Húa. I love you, I really do, but this is a line that can never be crossed. I would bring shame on my family: they would never forgive me."*

I stood up and, for a moment, the room shifted in and out of focus, but I willed myself to stand straight and not give in to the torrent of emotion, which threatened to overwhelm me once again. *"I can't believe I'm saying this,"* I said quietly, *"but I think we're done."*

Jian jumped to his feet. *"Don't say that. Don't leave like this, Julia. Think about what we have together."*

It was all I could think about in that moment, which is why I knew I had to leave. *"I have to fly to London in a few days' time to be with my mother, and I will think about it. I just don't know if I can go on*

50

living like this," I said, and I opened up my arms to indicate the space we were standing in. "I know I can't stay with Colin, but if I lived here with you, what would I be?"

He didn't say anything. He didn't have an answer.

I dragged myself to the door and I didn't look back.

Richard

Silvio blows me a kiss. The shock of long, dark, unruly hair is swept across his smiling face by a sudden gust of wind. It's peppered with grey now, but he retains the same, boyish good looks, which attracted me to him across a crowded bar many years ago. He pulls an elastic hairband from his pocket and draws the hair back into an untidy ponytail.

When he gets to work, his mother will loudly demand that he get a haircut and, after a bit of lively banter, he'll respond by drawing her into his arms and planting a kiss on the top of her head. It's become a kind of ritual: Silvio's diminutive mamma admonishing him with a wagging finger and Silvio pretending to be first offended then crestfallen and apologetic, even though they both know that the hair will remain uncut until it touches his shoulders.

This is what I love most about the Mazzi family: the parry and riposte of angry exchanges, which always end with a loving embrace – so different from my own family relationships.

He makes a dash across the street to where his car is parked on the other side. Before he climbs into the car, he points at me then points at his phone. "Do it now, Ricardo!" he shouts. *"Non aspettare fino a domani!"*

"I won't wait until tomorrow, I promise," I shout back.

The last time I saw my mother was three days ago, and every day I've told myself I must phone the hospital for an update, but every day an email or a text message or a phone call has interrupted this train of thought and I've got side-tracked into doing something else.

Silvio is appalled at my inertia, but I've reassured myself with the thought that at least she's in a safe environment being cared for by people who know what they're doing. Silvio thinks this isn't enough, hence the demand to put it off no longer.

After several frustrating attempts, I get through to the ward and am then asked to wait for the nurse responsible for my mother's care today. Minutes later, a woman with a warm, friendly voice asks me to confirm who I am then she tells me that her name is Kelly and that she's just spoken to my mother. She says, "You really need to speak to her doctor, Mr Oakley."

"Is she okay?"

"Well, she's developed a UTI, so we're giving her antibiotics. That's a urinary tract…"

"I know what a UTI is," I interrupt her. "How did that happen?"

"Oh, it's not uncommon for elderly patients to get problems with their waterworks when they're in hospital. They don't drink enough, that's the usual reason."

"Isn't that something you should be monitoring?" I say. "Getting an infection – that doesn't sound good to me. I thought she was being moved to another bed for rehabilitation?"

Nurse Kelly's cheery tone holds a hint of strained impatience when she replies. "That's what will happen, yes, but Mrs Oakley isn't ready to be moved on yet. We'll be keeping her where she is on Sparrow Ward for a couple of days while she's receiving medication. If you have any further questions, then you need to speak to her doctor."

I realise that I don't know who her doctor is, but I don't want to sound like the uncaring son who not only can't be bothered to visit but hasn't even taken note of the person in whose care he's left her, so I ask if I can speak to my mother directly.

"It might be better if you come in, Mr Oakley," she says. "Your mother's not quite herself this morning, she's a bit confused."

"Confused?"

"It's not uncommon in these situations."

"What situation?"

"Speak to the doctor, Mr Oakley. I'll tell your mother you called. Okay?"

I'm not okay, but Nurse Kelly has already rung off, so I'm left to ruminate. What does that even mean, 'confused'? I've read that infections in elderly people can cause them to become disorientated, sometimes agitated, aggressive even, but is that what she was saying? Or was she referring to some other as yet undisclosed 'situation'?

I clearly have no choice but to go back to the hospital as soon as I can and speak to someone who can answer my questions clearly and authoritatively because the decision over whether my mother can continue to live on her own is going to become even more complicated if there are other health issues to consider.

I leave a message on Silvio's voicemail telling him that I won't be home till later this evening then plan the rest of my day around returning to the hospital even though work is piling up with each passing minute.

Hotel Albatross – as everyone associated with the project now refers to it – is still waiting to transform into *Hotel Phoenix* and rise from the ashes of each set of architect's drawings, which are consigned to the rubbish bin as our client changes her mind for the umpteenth time. The foundations of the building were completed nearly two weeks ago, but the whole project has been put on hold while we negotiate the changes, which she demands on what feels like a daily basis. I know that the whole morning will have to be spent making phone calls to placate one contractor or supplier after another, and the costs are mounting daily, but just as I'm about to make the first of those many phone calls, my own phone rings. It's Julia.

"I thought I'd better check with you what's happening before I book my flight," she says. She sounds breathless, anxious even.

"Well, Mum's still in hospital," I tell her. "She's got a UTI and possibly some other complication – I spoke to a nurse on the ward, but they won't ever tell you very much, so I have to go in and speak to her doctor."

"What kind of complication?"

"I don't know!"

"I thought it was routine, hip replacement surgery?"

"I don't think it's anything to do with the surgery."

There's a small, pregnant pause, and I assume that Julia is rethinking her decision to fly home, but she says, "I'm going to try to get on a flight in the morning."

"So soon?"

"You told me you need me there."

"I do, but probably not quite yet. I know you're busy with the gallery and I don't want to inconvenience you more than is necessary." Even to my own ears, this sounds dangerously like sarcasm, but she doesn't respond in the way that I'm anticipating.

"It's fine. I've got everything organised now. Colin isn't very happy about me leaving with an open-ended ticket. Although I don't know why," she adds, almost as an aside. "It's not like I'm planning to stay."

I'm completely taken aback, and I hurry to tell her how much I appreciate her giving up her time and how happy our mother will be to see her.

"Well, let's hope this *complication* isn't something serious," she says, "because I'm not leaving Singapore to look after her, Richard."

"I'm not expecting you to," I quickly reassure her.

She tells me she'll email me her itinerary then adds that she intends to stay in a hotel until our mother has been discharged from hospital. "But you can stay in the house," I say. "I've already asked Maggie to get your old room ready for you."

"I'd rather stay in London. Colin and I booked a room at the Marriott last time we were there. It's a good central location and I can get on the tube at Marble Arch."

"Well, if you're sure?"

"I'm not staying at the house until I absolutely have to, thank you very much. This whole business of Daddy leaving it to someone, who claims to be his daughter, is ridiculous. You may be happy to just hand over *our* rightful inheritance, but I'm not!" she says tartly, sounding much more like her old self.

"I'm not handing anything over," I tell her. "It's a done deal, Julia; it's what he wanted. Our only concern now is whether or not Mum can continue to live there on her own."

A little voice in my head is telling me that this might be an appropriate moment to talk about Aggie's bungalow, but I decide I need to speak to our mother first. I just hope and pray that when I see her later, she isn't too confused to explain why she hasn't mentioned it to me before this.

Julia is adamant that she'll contest our father's will, and I can't be bothered to argue with her over the phone – we have days, perhaps even weeks, ahead of us, when this issue can be discussed face to face, at length and in detail, if that's what she wants.

I wind up the conversation as fast as I can and promise that I'll contact her if the conversation with the doctor raises any significant problems.

The rest of the day passes uneventfully and, with all the phone calls made and details of changes to plans noted down carefully in writing, I clear the desk, which Silvio and I share in our study, then throw a change of clothes into a bag – just in case I have to return to Hillcrest.

When I get to the hospital, there's a long queue of cars in front of me. This is the first time I've had to compete for a parking space and somehow it underlines the stress and strain of visiting a friend or a family member at an hour that's hardly convenient for anyone in paid employment. Of course, I understand that the hospital has its own busy schedule, but adequate parking would make life infinitely easier, I think to myself, as my own irritation mounts in parallel with the minutes ticking past on the dashboard clock.

Half an hour later, I've managed to squeeze my car into a space between a monster-sized truck and an SUV. I can hear Mamma Mazzi's voice in my head bemoaning this country's current trend to drive off-road vehicles on overcrowded city streets. *"Why you need cars like this?"* she demands angrily every time a four-wheel drive mounts the pavement in front of the restaurant. *"In Italy, we have right size cars. This ... this ... è pazzo!"*

She's right, it's madness, but I'm here now, and I hope that soon I'll get some answers to my questions.

Outside, in front of the hospital foyer, there's a group of people taking hasty, last minute drags at cigarettes, and just inside anxious faces are searching signs and noticeboards for information. As patients and visitors pass in and out in a steady stream, the doors open then close with slow, almost rhythmic precision.

I suddenly notice that there are shops inside selling magazines and all kinds of confectionery, vacuum-packed sandwiches and six kinds of coffee. Even the café has music playing in the background. It reminds me of a busy airport terminal. I suppose this is what you call progress, although I feel that money might be better spent on other things.

I pass through another set of swing doors into the long, green corridor and at once feel my feet begin to drag. I can't be sure that it's the effect of the trance-inducing paintwork, but the sign to Sparrow Ward looks further and further away.

Nurse Kelly buzzes me through the security doors. She wears a badge with her name on it and a welcoming smile. "You're just the person I wanted to see," I tell her. "I'm Lenora Oakley's son – I spoke to you this morning."

"So, you did," she says. The smile wavers.

"You told me I need to speak to my mother's doctor, but I'm not entirely sure who that is now?"

"I think it's Mr Singh, but I'll need to check the board," she says, and she bustles back to the reception desk. I follow close on her heels. Behind the desk is a whiteboard showing a list of patients and the doctor in attendance. My mother's doctor is someone called Raji Singh.

"So, where's Doctor Singh?" I ask her.

"Mister Singh," she corrects me. "He's the surgeon, who operated on Mrs Oakley, but he's not here now."

"Well, where is he?"

"Probably in theatre," she says. "He was here this morning when he did his ward round."

"When I spoke to you, you didn't tell me he was here. You just said he was the person I needed to speak to."

"He is. I'm sorry, Mr Oakley, I'm not being deliberately obstructive. I did tell Mr Singh you want to speak to him, but you have to be here when *he's* here if you want to do that. I'm afraid that's just how the system works. It's by no means perfect, but hospital protocol prioritises patient confidentiality. That means only the attending doctor – surgeon or physician – can answer questions."

I suspect that this is a conversation she has to have on a regular basis, and she sounds genuinely apologetic, so I'm forced to bite my tongue, even though I want to shout my frustration into her now not so smiling face. However, I'm not going to let her off the hook quite that easily. "What's this 'situation' you were referring to?"

"Well, your mother has a UTI," she says in a confident voice and she resumes the friendly, smiley, nice nurse face.

"I know that," I say, "but this morning you seemed to be suggesting there was another problem." The nice nurse face freezes, probably because she's desperately trying to remember what she told me that she possibly shouldn't have told me due to hospital protocol. "If there's something else, I really ought to know about it now."

"Why don't you go and talk to your mother," she says. "It might be easier for me to explain, when you've seen her and spoken to her." And before I have a chance to question her further, she briskly walks off.

My mother is sitting up in bed in exactly the same position that I left her three days ago only today her hair is dishevelled, and her eyes are unnaturally bright. I sit on the edge of the bed and lean in to kiss her cheek. For a few uncomfortable seconds she stiffens awkwardly under my touch, but then I feel her fingers gently moving through my hair. "Richard, my son," she whispers.

I move to sit in the chair next to the bed, but I take her hand. I notice at once that it's unnaturally warm and the skin is flaking. "Are you drinking enough?" I ask her.

"I've got water in that … that thing there, haven't I?" she says and points at a plastic jug sitting on the table at the end of the bed. "I think I've had a cup of tea today as well… I had one when I had breakfast … I think I had tea …" Her voice trails away. She suddenly turns and looks directly at me. "It is Richard," she says, and she smiles. "Robin was here this morning. I don't know why he came. He just stood in the doorway there watching me. Didn't say a word. I thought it was you for a moment but then I remembered you've got that hotel project you're working on." Her attention suddenly switches to something in the corner of the room behind me. It's hard to read the expression on her face, but she isn't smiling anymore, in fact she looks scared.

The change in her has shocked me profoundly. I glance back over my shoulder, but there's nothing there, only the window which looks out over a concreted patch of ground with raised brick flower beds, now empty of flowers.

I reach across the bed and stroke the hair away from her face. I say, "I think you must have just seen someone who looks like Robin." (My cousin, Robin, moved to Australia about five years ago.) "It was probably one of the doctors," I go on, painfully aware that her eyes are still fixed on something I can't see. "I expect he was just checking on you."

She turns back to me and she seems to have forgotten whatever she thought she could see in the corner of the room because she smiles again. "It was definitely Robin," she says. "He was wearing that horrible navy blazer with the brass buttons. The one he wore to your father's funeral. That's how I knew it wasn't you."

Even though I've read the literature, I still can't quite accept that an infection can cause this kind of confusion, because Robin did indeed wear the blazer to my father's funeral, but the idea that he'd fly back here to visit my mother in hospital is unlikely in the extreme.

"Robin lives in Melbourne now, Mum," I say. "It must have been somebody else."

"Melbourne," she repeats after me. "That's in Australia, isn't it?"

"It is."

She withdraws her hand from mine, reaches into the drawer in the locker next to the bed and pulls out two small rectangles of paper. They look like tickets of some kind. "I found these in the pocket of my dressing-gown." She leans forward and places them carefully on the bed next to her. "I think they might be important. I want you to take them and put them somewhere safe. Somewhere where *she* can't find them."

"Who are you talking about, Mum?" I ask her gently even though I find myself unnerved by this sudden change of tack.

She puts her finger to her lips, beckons to me to move closer, whispers, "Agnes Bagshaw."

"You mean Aggie?"

She nods.

I don't know whether to laugh or cry, but one glance at the fear-filled expression on my mother's face forces me to take control of my emotions. I pick up the tickets – now I can see that they're from her local leisure centre. "These are just entrance tickets for the swimming pool, Mum. Didn't you used to go swimming with Aggie? I don't think they're important, but I'll keep hold of them for you." I slip them into the inside pocket of my jacket.

59

"I did used to go swimming with her, didn't I?" she says. She looks thoughtful. "Perhaps I'm getting them muddled up with something else."

Nurse Kelly appears in the doorway of the room. "Everything okay here?"

"Can I have a quick word with you before I leave?" I say. The tremor in my voice immediately betrays the anxiety and emotion I'm feeling and which I've been trying hard to conceal. My mother doesn't appear to notice, but Nurse Kelly gives me a knowing look and invites me to join her for a cup of tea.

"I'm going on my break soon, Lenora," she says.

"I can't stay very long, Mum," I say. "I'll try to come again tomorrow. Maybe in the evening." When she opens up her arms to me, I move to fold her in what I hope is a reassuring embrace. She's fragile, bird-like, and I'm frightened for her. How can Julia and I even begin to think of leaving her to live by herself in that dreadful house with all its sadness and secrets now exposed?

She whispers in my ear, "Sometimes I think I see her – just a glimpse of her red dress. Sometimes I smell her perfume. Can it really be her, Richard? What does she want from me?"

Lenora

The mind plays tricks. All those senses upon which we rely to confirm what we know – what we think we know – well, they're unreliable. I've learned that over the last two years and now I feel it ever more intently and it frightens me because Robin *was* here this morning. I saw him quite clearly, standing in the doorway, but Richard said that Robin is in Australia, and even with this befuddled, old brain, I can work out that he can't be here and there at the same time.

The same is true of memory. There are things, which I think I remember, but now I'm not certain if they were real or if I just dreamed them. I remember that I used to go swimming with Aggie, but we used to do lots of things together. What I don't remember is if the tickets I gave to Richard to keep safe are important because of what they are, or because I found them, and they reminded of something I didn't want to forget.

I close my eyes and try to concentrate because I know that I kept the tickets for a reason. I think about the swimming pool at the leisure centre and then I remember what Aggie told me the day she learned to swim.

"You're going to learn to do what?"

"Learn to swim. It's on my retirement list," she said. "All the things I didn't have time to do when I was working. Do you want to come with me?"

I hesitated before I answered because Aggie was annoyingly more than proficient at most things, but I was intrigued to find out more. "What else can't you do?"

She gave me an odd look. "I'm concentrating on swimming for the time being."

I'd learned to swim in that time-honoured fashion of the youngest child in the family: I was pushed in at the deep end. As a consequence, I could manage an undignified doggy-paddle, but I wasn't sure that I wanted to learn to swim properly with Aggie. Competition ran through her veins.

In the end I said, "I might just come and watch." She looked disappointed, so I offered to drive us both there the following day.

I decided to join her in the pool, but I wasn't convinced that learning to swim with her would improve either my confidence or my competence in the water, so I left her to it when the instructor, a jolly, middle-aged woman wearing a T-shirt and a pair of baggy shorts, urged her to get into the water before she got cold and then handed her a bright blue swimming float.

I made my way over to the far side of the pool and tentatively dipped my toe in the water. The sign over the reception desk said the temperature was 32° but it felt like the North Sea to me. I tried to appear graceful as I slowly climbed down the ladder, but I miscounted the rungs and suddenly found myself plunging helplessly into the water. Arms flailing wildly, legs kicking uselessly, I scrambled for the side, coughing and gasping for air. When I finally found my feet, I discovered that I was only standing in four feet of water. Feeling like a complete idiot, I looked back over my shoulder and saw that Aggie and her instructor were watching me from the other side of the pool.

I spent the next half an hour dog paddling breathlessly up and down like a frightened five-year-old that had just learned to let go of the side.

My eldest brother, Jonnie, had tried to improve my technique one summer when I was about ten years old. I think he was probably the one who threw me in the pool in the first place, so I didn't really trust him to hold me up in the water when he insisted that I had to learn in the deep end.

We didn't have floats in those days, but I did have an old, rubber, swimming ring. My father had patched it up numerous times with a bicycle repair kit, so it looked unreliable but was actually very effective at holding you up in the water. The problem with it was its size. It was quite small, but I managed to force it over my head and shoulders.

Jonnie towed me up to the deep end of the pool, holding my hands in his. He was a really strong swimmer and had clearly forgotten what it was like to be a novice swimmer stuck inside in a swimming ring. He gave me a few brief instructions and an equally brief demonstration then let go of my hands. I kicked my legs, leaned forward over the edge of the ring to attempt a front crawl and immediately turned turtle. One moment I was looking helplessly at Jonnie and the next moment I was looking up at the sky.

Of course, Jonnie couldn't stop laughing, and so did everyone else in the pool around us. Eventually he agreed to tow me back to the shallow end, and my humiliation was complete when I climbed out of the pool but couldn't get out of the swimming ring. My mother had to cut it off me with a pair of scissors when we got home.

"Waste of a good rubber ring," my father said when he saw what she'd done. And I spent the rest of the summer playing in the babies' pool and never did learn to swim like a real swimmer.

By the end of her lesson, Aggie had already learned to let go of her blue float and the instructor was showing her how to keep her fingers pressed tightly together while she propelled herself through the water with slow, controlled strokes. I was amazed and envious that she'd picked it up so quickly.

When we were back in the changing room, we chose cubicles next to one another. I called to Aggie through chattering teeth over the high divide, "How was your lesson then?" I was hoping and praying that she'd hated every second of it.

"Mary says I'm making good progress," she said, sounding pleased with herself. "She says I have an aptitude for swimming – something about some people being naturally more buoyant than others. Anyway, I've booked in for another lesson next week. Why don't you join us?"

"It's too cold," I said.

"Mary says you don't get cold if you swim properly. She says you can stay warm in the water if you relax into the rhythm of the strokes and let the water hold you where you're supposed to be."

I was used to Aggie's sly digs – I usually managed to accept them with good humour – but I was so cold and miserable that I told her, "I know where I'm supposed to be and it isn't getting changed out of a swimsuit in a room the size of a telephone box."

"Why don't you use the family cubicle?" she said. "Then you'd have more space."

"If you're trying to say I'm overweight, I already know that, but I hardly think I need space for a whole family to get changed in."

"It was just a suggestion!" she said hotly and gave me the silent treatment until we were changed into back into our clothes.

In the café she continued to talk about her lesson with enthusiasm. While I sipped my tea, she showed me how I should move my head from side to side with each stroke.

"I do know how to swim," I told her.

"Not really."

"I suppose Mary told you that," I said. "I'll have you know I was swimming at the Lido when you were still paddling your feet in a plastic inflatable."

"Did you have lessons with a professional instructor?" When I didn't reply she went on, "You're never too old to learn to do something new, or to learn to do something properly, you thought you knew how to do already."

"Well, I'm not having lessons with you."

"Why not? It's cheaper for a group lesson."

"I might need a family-sized cubicle to get changed in, but me plus you doesn't make a group."

She carefully placed her cup on its saucer. "It's important to learn how to swim," she said.

I'd been enjoying our verbal jousting – it's what we did, what we'd always done – but her tone of voice and solemn expression indicated that the fun had ended. I said, "I can swim well enough, Aggie."

Her eyes narrowed and she began to stare at a point in the café just inches above my head. It was slightly unnerving because she only had to drop her gaze fractionally and she'd be staring directly into my eyes. She said quietly, "Did you know you can drown in a bathtub? Just a little bit of water; just enough to cover the mouth and the nose."

"That's why I take showers," I quipped, in an effort to lighten the mood. "It's much safer."

"My mother died in the bath," she said, still staring off into the distance.

"Your mother had a heart attack, Aggie."

"Yes, in the bath."

Well, that was news to me. "Why would you say that? You called me when you found her. I came straight round so I know she was in bed."

"She was in bed when you got there, but that doesn't mean she didn't die in the bath," she said and she slowly lowered her head, still managing to avoid eye contact with me. "I wanted to tell you what I'd done, but you were so kind and caring. I decided to let you think I'd just found her there."

"If this is some kind of a joke, Aggie ... well, it's not funny and it certainly isn't going to convince me to have swimming lessons with you." I waited for her to say something, but she just sat there looking at the empty teacup.

We sat like that for several minutes, and eventually she spoke. "She looked so ... so undignified lying there without her clothes on and her hair sticking up like a wet toilet brush. It was horrible."

"Are you telling me you got your mother out of the bath and carried her into the bedroom?"

She nodded, and suddenly she felt able to look me in the eye. "It felt like the right thing to do."

We used to go swimming quite regularly after that, but I could never get that conversation out of my mind because I was quite a nervous swimmer and the idea that you could drown in six inches of water was frankly terrifying.

Now I can't remember if Aggie said that her mother had drowned in the bath, or if she'd had a heart attack in the bath. In fact, I can't remember if I just dreamed up the whole conversation. This is the problem.

I wanted to tell Richard that I'm seeing things and hearing things, which, if I think about it, don't make sense, but I'm certain that somewhere in the midst of this madness is an uncomfortable and unfathomable truth about life and death.

Julia

As soon as I've finished my lecture about timekeeping and maintaining standards of customer service, Connie flees, phone clasped to her breast. For the last three days she's been forced to watch me return artfully arranged baskets of flowers to the florist on the ground floor. It's humiliating having to pretend they're for somebody else, but the sight of them makes me want to weep. A particularly beautiful display appeared soon after lunch today. She grabbed them from my hands and chased after the delivery boy. When she came back, she said, "I told him, 'Enough already!'" I tried to thank her, but the words dried in my mouth.

I tell Aysha to go home as well. The welfare of her young son clearly weighs so heavily on her mind that she can barely string two sentences together when she serves customers. While it's impossible for me to truly empathise with her, the pain she's suffering is etched on her face, and I know exactly how that feels, but I warn her that she has to get her act together before I leave tomorrow.

Jian has tried to call me several times a day and left messages on my phone. He wants to see me before I leave for London, but I don't think I can bear to see him. I've spent every evening since I last saw him in my own apartment. Colin has spent every evening at the LingLang Club. He's a wily old bird and knows that something is going on. He's questioned me repeatedly over the breakfast table: 'What's the matter with you this morning?' 'Why the long face?' 'Why are you really going to London?' 'When are you coming back?' 'Have you booked your ticket yet?' It goes on and on.

I *have* now booked my ticket, and I've booked a room at the Marriott. I'll have to tell Colin when I get home. He'll complain about the cost and the inconvenience of me leaving at short notice, but now I find myself counting down the hours, so he can say what he likes.

Nancy called in to the gallery at lunchtime. When I told her what I'd done – gone directly to Jian's apartment and confronted him – she asked me if he'd ended our relationship.

"I ended it," I said.

She looked surprised. "You ended it?"

"Well, I told him we were done, but he wants me to reconsider; think it over while I'm away."

Nancy's dark brown eyes mirror her emotions: she was disappointed. "Oh," she said.

"I thought you'd be glad. You told me it was never going to work out. You said there'd be no beautiful sunsets for us."

She immediately removed her gaze from my face, pulled open her bag and reached inside for her inhaler. I'd never known her to sidestep a question before, but this was clearly an attempt to avoid responding, because she wasn't straining to breathe. Puzzled, I watched her go through the usual motions of taking into her lungs the metered dose of medication, and then I realised why she didn't want to reply: she'd hoped that Jian would do what she thought I couldn't or wouldn't do. Well, I had, so I didn't understand her dismay.

"Talk to me Nancy," I said.

"I don't know what to say to you, Julia. Actually ... I do know, but I just don't want to say it because I don't want to lose your friendship."

"If it's something that needs to be said ... well, if you can't say it, then who can?"

"Okay... I wanted, I hoped that Jian would put an end to this ... I'm not going to call it a relationship, I'm going to call it what it really is: an affair." When she saw me open my mouth to interrupt, she put up her hand to stop me. "Let me finish. Clearly, I don't know Jian as well as you do, but I do know that men who have a wife and take a mistress – because make no mistake, that's what you are..."

"It isn't like that!" I protested. "He was already with me before he married Lì Húa."

"He was never truly with you, Julia. You've only ever been an ... an appendage. Can't you see that?"

Her words were cruel, hurtful, and I was stung into replying, "Are you jealous of me? Is that what it is?"

Her eyes widened in surprise. "Jealous? Are you kidding? I feel sorry for you and I'm scared for you, and that's the truth. You're infatuated with a married man and you can't see that you're just a postscript in his life. You say you've ended it with him, but you're just angry and when you stop being angry, you'll go back. Sooner or later that husband you despise? He's going to stop looking the other way. Where will you be at the end of all this, Julia? What will you have? I wanted Jian to end the affair: I wanted him to do the decent thing and let you go. Because if not now, then when?"

I forgot my anger with Jian and told her, "It doesn't have to end. It's my choice. Jian told me we could still be together. He still wants me."

This time Nancy offered me an unflinching stare. "I know he still wants you. But why do you still want him?"

She didn't wait for me to reply; she was already walking away when she wished me a safe journey and asked to be remembered to my mother.

What will I have? It was a fair question, and I'm now pained to admit that Jian couldn't have made it clearer: I won't really have him – at least not in the way that I want. We could continue as before and I would be first in his affections, but only ever runner-up in his life. As for Colin, he knows better than anyone that the love we once shared has faded, and only the bare, frail fabric of a legal marriage unites us. If he knew, knew for certain and for sure that I'd been unfaithful? Once upon a time he may have forgiven me, but not anymore.

I take a last look around the gallery. I'm closing early tonight. In Orchard Road, the heavy fall of rain late in the afternoon cleared the air of ash, but the smell of smoke still lingers. It will pass, but for now it's a reminder that our island is forever subject to winds of change – both political and ecological. Colin says that behind the gleaming, glass towers, beyond the faces of unbridled capitalism, little worms of doubt and discontent are wriggling their way to the surface; that's why he plans to leave. But I intend to stay, whichever way the wind blows.

I've already called Haziq and told him to drive over here. He sounded surprised, asked me if I'm feeling okay. My first thought was to scold him for his insolence, but then I remembered that Haziq doesn't do sarcasm: he's a kind, thoughtful individual, who serves his employers with deference and loyalty. Colin and I could probably both learn a lot from him.

I wait for him in the foyer of the building where it's cool and I can check my emails on my phone. Out of the corner of my eye, I see the lady who runs the florist walking towards me. She's holding a small bouquet of orchids simply enclosed in white tissue paper. I turn my head away, pretend to be absorbed in reading the screen, but she taps me on the shoulder and tries to hand me the flowers.

"Mrs Crane. Your friend want you to take this," she says in a dull voice. Irritated, I begin to walk away, but she grabs hold of my arm. "You take flowers."

I shake her hand from my arm. "I thought I'd made it clear that there's been a mistake. No more flowers!"

She glares back at me. "You take flowers!" she shrills and thrusts them at the middle of my chest so that I'm forced to accept them.

I immediately look for a waste bin to dispose of them but Haziq appears from nowhere and offers to carry them to the car. Before I have a chance to protest, he's whisked them away, and only then do I spot the small, white card attached to the paper in which they've been wrapped.

Panic-stricken, I race after him. If the message on the card is filled with the kind of declarations of love and grief, which all the other cards have contained then I'm in serious trouble.

I catch up with him at the car and wrest the flowers from his hands saying, "I need those." I rip the little card from the paper and stuff it into my bag.

He looks back at me with only concern. "So sorry, ma'am. Flowers are very beautiful."

My breath catches in my throat and tears sting my eyes as the reality of this dreadful deceit hits home. Everything – the love, the lies, the pain and the hypocrisy are written in Jian's own hand. The words would surely condemn me as the careless, faithless creature that I've become in the intervening years. I realise I can't bear that Haziq should find me out.

He says nothing more, opens the rear door of the car, and I dive inside.

We drive in silence to the apartment in River Valley Road. The flowers sit on the seat beside me, fragrantly lovely, painted not in bold, tropical shades of purple and magenta, but white orchids with delicate, pale pink centres – the ones I love the best.

I steal a look at the card hidden in my handbag and recognise the handwriting at once – it isn't Jian's neat, cursive script, but Nancy's untidy scrawl. She's written, '*I hope this journey back to England will be a voyage of discovery for you; that you will return here to Singapore with your clouded vision cleared. The orchids are to remind you that this is your home and, whatever the future may hold, I will always be your friend.*'

I'm disappointed: I admit it, though it shames me. I'd convinced myself that this perfectly formed bouquet of orchids was Jian's way of telling me that he will never stop loving me; that he will wait for me. Well, I was right about the meaning, but wrong about the messenger.

I trace my finger over the words, close my eyes and thank God that I've been given this timeout, though I can't help smiling at the notion that going back to Essex is the celestial equivalent of being made to sit on the naughty step. But I do need time to think about my future and I probably should reflect on my past behaviour. Whether my vision will clear in respect of Jian I can't say, but I don't want to live this life, this lie, any longer.

Siti is waiting for me; she stands in the doorway, smiles her welcome home and takes the flowers from me, cradling them in the crook of her arm.

I tell her, "Put them in that pink vase – the one Mrs Sullivan gave me for my birthday last year."

"Pink vase with...?" She frowns in concentration, draws a wavy line in the air as she searches for a word to describe what she knows but has insufficient vocabulary to name accurately.

I offer her a sympathetic smile. "The one with the fluted edge, yes, that one."

"Fluted edge," she repeats after me then hurries back to the kitchen.

Colin is still in his shirt and tie, has apparently forsaken the comforting embrace of the LingLang Club and is watching the evening news on the television instead. I call out to him that I'm taking a shower and changing out of my dress before we have supper. He doesn't respond, but I know he's heard me because he immediately turns up the volume. It's another unspoken message. Once again, he's been waiting for me to come home and I'm late and he hasn't eaten, and he'd much rather be sitting with his buddies drinking whiskey in the Tavern Bar.

When I've washed and changed into a T-shirt and shorts – standard casual wear in Singapore regardless of age, gender or occupation – I find Colin already seated at the table in the dining room but now he's reading a newspaper. Siti has placed the flowers in the centre of the table, which is guaranteed to elicit an awkward question and answer session and as soon as I've seated myself, it begins.

"What's this then?" Colin asks me without looking up from the newspaper.

"What's what?"

He slowly folds the newspaper and places it on the floor. "When do you ever buy flowers?"

"I haven't bought flowers. They were bought for me."

A little flicker of something unpleasant passes over his face, the pale grey eyes darken and the mouth puckers into a disapproving pout. From the pocket of his shirt, he suddenly produces the white card I left in my handbag. "What about this?"

For a few seconds I'm rendered speechless. He's actually searched through my handbag. The anger at this invasion of my privacy explodes inside my head, but somehow, I manage to contain it. I say, "It looks suspiciously like a white card. You know ... the kind of card that people send with flowers."

"There's no name on it."

"Well spotted, Colin, although the message does suggest they're from a friend."

"Which friend?"

I don't have many friends in Singapore – I could count them on the fingers of one hand. Colin isn't unaware of my friend-light status so he could probably work it out for himself if he really tried, but this isn't about who sent it: it's about the content of the message. It suggests that there's something troubling me, which I haven't shared with him – which, of course, I haven't. I couldn't. This is a lie of omission.

"How do you know they were intended for me?" I say.

"Why else would you have them? Why were you hiding the card?"

"I wasn't hiding it."

"You removed it from the paper the flowers were wrapped in."

Once again, I'm lost for words. I can't imagine for a single second that Haziq has called Colin and told him what I did, which can only mean that Colin himself has inspected the tissue paper and discovered the telltale staple, which leads me to wonder what else he's discovered.

My confidence in my ability to mislead and misdirect my husband begins to falter. If I ever had a cunning plan, now would be a good time to put it into action. I haven't got a plan, never had a plan, but if this is just a fishing expedition then I have no intention of allowing myself to be caught without a fight.

I place the flat of my hands on the table and lean towards him. "You can stop playing Sherlock Holmes because I have absolutely nothing to hide. And if I ever find out that you've been rummaging through my personal things again, I'll make you pay for it in ways you can't even begin to imagine."

He looks surprised. "Don't be ridiculous, Julia!"

"I'm being ridiculous?" I cry. "The flowers were given to me by Nancy. You remember Nancy, don't you?"

"Of course, I remember her," he says.

I watch him, see that his nerve is failing, but I'm getting into my stride. I push myself up into a standing position and lean even further over the table so that I'm staring him down. I speak in a deliberately lowered tone. "My good friend, Nancy, has been trying to convince me to reconcile with my mother. Before it's too late," I add for emphasis.

"Your mother?"

"Apparently there's a complication. Richard wasn't able to go into details, but it sounds serious."

Colin looks crestfallen, maybe even apologetic. "I didn't realise..."

Oh, I'm good at this. And suddenly I know that I'm not going to tell him that our marriage is over. I'm not going to risk being thrown out on the street until I know I have somewhere else to go. Nancy is right: I have to think about my future here in Singapore, because we can't go on living like this.

I call out to Siti to serve dinner straight away, and when we've eaten, I immediately leave the table and begin to pack my suitcase.

Richard

Nurse Kelly is waiting for me at the reception desk when I leave my mother. She leads me into a small room containing a low table, a sofa and two hard chairs. Once glance at the posters on the walls confirms that this is the place where bad news is broken.

She tells me to make myself comfortable while she fetches the tea. Though quite how comfortable a person can make himself is unclear, when he's surrounded by posters of smiling-faced people offering sympathy and support in times of loss and despair. I'm worried about my mother, worried about her mental state, but I didn't think she was dying.

The reference my mother made to someone in a red dress rings a bell, but I can't remember for whom the bell rings. Not Sarah – my ex-wife is one of those pale-skinned women who only ever wear muted shades of skin and bone. And certainly not Julia – in fact I can only ever remember seeing Julia in black, but maybe that was just at the funeral. Either way, it was unsettling to hear that ghostly apparitions are more regular visitors to my mother's bedside than I am.

I'm racking my brains trying to work out this conundrum when Nurse Kelly backs into the room with a loaded tray. She's brought tea and two large slices of what looks like somebody's birthday cake – lots of brightly coloured icing and holes where the candles have been removed for safekeeping.

She puts the tray on the table then places a piece of cake in front of me. "Nurse Whitney's twenty-fifth," she informs me. "She's following some mad diet so we're helping her out."

For the next five minutes we make small talk and eat cake, but I'm impatient to find out what this 'situation' is with my mother. "You seemed to suggest, when I spoke to you earlier, that the UTI isn't the only problem with my mother," I begin.

Nurse Kelly nods. "Obviously it isn't possible to be completely certain, but there's a chance that the trauma she's recently suffered has triggered something."

"Triggered something?"

"Well, it isn't uncommon for trauma to bring on dementia in someone your mother's age." She must have registered the look of shock and horror on my face because she quickly goes on, "I'm not saying that she definitely has dementia, I'm just saying it can happen."

All the worries and concerns, which I have about my mother living independently, have suddenly multiplied by ten. The truth is that I actually have no idea if this is the case – if the trauma of the fall has somehow brought on a sudden deterioration of her mental capacities – because I've been too busy with my own life to do little more than speak to her over the phone since... I have to think back... since Christmas, and it's now October.

This is the reality: it's more than possible that it *isn't* a sudden deterioration at all. I only have to think about the weed-infested driveway and Julia's bedroom obscured by a layer of dust to know that something has changed in recent months.

A buzzer sounds outside the room and Nurse Kelly hastily excuses herself. I don't know if this was an unexpected opportunity for her to leave me on my own to contemplate this piece of information, but she doesn't return, so I decide to leave.

As soon as I reach the car park, I know that I've already made up my mind to drive back to Hillcrest. I need to take another look at the house in daylight and satisfy myself that nothing else has changed, even though I have absolutely no idea what I'm looking for.

When I call Silvio and explain the situation, he immediately agrees I should check the whole place out. "This is your mother's home, Ricardo. How do you say...? The home is the heart. If she's unhappy, *o non si sente bene* ... you will see. When my cousin, Lorenza, had the black mood, she stopped cleaning. *Tutto.* I see you tomorrow. E Ricardo. *Non preoccuparti, mi amore.*"

I'm trying not to worry, but the prospect of dealing with the consequences of my mother's fractured hip is already problem enough. The thought that she's developed dementia fills me with not only a profound sense of sadness, but also a sense of dread.

I stop in the high street on the way back and order a takeaway pizza. If Silvio knew he'd be furious with me – only Mamma Mazzi's home-baked is allowed to pass our lips – but I don't want to drive away from my mother's house in the morning with the smell of curry or chicken chow mein lingering in the recently cleaned kitchen.

The first thing that strikes me when I walk into the house is that it's cold. The second thing is that the door to my father's study is open. I don't know if I'm being paranoid, but now I see that all of the doors are open – every room downstairs. I try to remember how I left them, and I think they were closed – it's an old habit, something our father insisted on.

"It's one of the most effective ways to prevent a fire from spreading. It's a simple precaution and one that even you, Richard, should be able to remember."

Even me.

Well, the only explanation is that Maggie came back, I think to myself.

Fortunately, the house soon warms up to a comfortable temperature after I've turned on the central heating, and although the pizza isn't up to Silvio's exacting standards, it still tastes good.

The following morning, I'm woken early by the sound of someone entering the house. The front door slams shut, and footsteps echo eerily on the tiled floor of the hallway. The only other person who has a key is Maggie so at first, I'm not unduly alarmed. It's when I hear the doors being closed that I sit up and take notice. I quickly get dressed and go downstairs.

Maggie must realise I'm here because my car is parked on the drive, but there's something furtive about the way she quickly moves into the kitchen ahead of me.

"Would you like me to make you some coffee, Mr Oakley?" she calls over her shoulder.

"That would be great," I say.

"I just thought I'd check..." She hesitates a fraction too long for this to sound anything other than contrived. "Well, make sure everything's okay."

"I wasn't expecting you to be here today, Maggie."

"No, I don't usually work on a Saturday, but I was walking past, and I know the house is empty so... I just thought I'd look in, that's all."

She manages to completely avoid eye contact with me throughout this exchange, busying herself with filling the kettle and putting instant coffee into a mug. I don't know if she just feels uncomfortable in my presence because she doesn't know me very well, but my gut instinct tells me that what brought her here wasn't a spontaneous decision while she happened to be passing by. The surreptitious door closing puzzles me, so I decide to ask her.

This time there's no concealing her agitation. She blushes and her hands fly to her face. "Your dad was very strict about keeping doors closed," she gushes. "I know a fire can spread quickly if they're left open. I wasn't sure if you'd remember to check. I'm not trying to interfere or anything."

I feel like the grand inquisitor and immediately apologise.

"No, no, it's fine," she insists. "It's not my home, but with Mrs Oakley in hospital..."

"You really mustn't worry," I say. "I'll probably be coming and going quite a lot now, and the responsibility for keeping the doors closed is mine, not yours."

We stand awkwardly looking at one another. Maggie is twisting the ring on her wedding finger round and round. I notice that it isn't a wedding ring but a very expensive-looking diamond solitaire, which surprises me for some reason. Of course, I don't really know anything about the woman other than that she cleans the house once a week, and Silvio would undoubtedly chide me for thinking such thoughts, but it doesn't change the fact that the ring looks out of place on hands which have clearly spent more time scrubbing floors than having a manicure.

I suddenly remember to ask her about the state of Julia's bedroom. Apparently, this is something that she's more than willing to discuss because the look of pained embarrassment vanishes.

"I wondered when you were going to ask about that," she says.

"Well, it does seem a bit odd. Every other room in the house has been cleaned from top to bottom, but you can write your name in the dust in that room."

"I know," she says. "But it isn't my fault." She pulls out a chair and sits down, so I follow her lead. She hesitates, looks to the corner of the room as though trying to gather her thoughts then begins to speak. "Did you know your mum's friend, Agnes, lived here for a while?"

I didn't know because my mother didn't mention it, but this is just par for the course in the life of the Oakley family.

"When she was too ill to look after herself," Maggie goes on, "she moved in here. Your mum nursed her. They were very close, almost like sisters, I always thought. Ovarian cancer, that's what she had. Mrs Oakley told me Agnes hated going to see the doctor and by the time she went it was very advanced. They wanted to do an operation on her, but she wouldn't have it." Maggie suddenly smiles. "I always thought she was a bit..." She falters for a moment, searching for the right words, "...a bit prim and proper, but that was just the way she was brought up, your mum said. At the end, the Macmillan nurses were coming in every day because she needed a lot of painkillers. She was very brave, but I think your mum had had enough by that point, to be honest with you. It was very hard on her."

"My mother never told me," I say. But then my mother is very good at keeping secrets, I think to myself.

"The thing is," Maggie goes on, "she had your sister's room when she was here – because of the en suite."

"She didn't...?"

Maggie nods. "Your mum was with her when she died. Just slipped away in her sleep, but Mrs Oakley seemed to take it very badly."

Now I remember, not that Agnes died in Julia's bedroom, but that two years ago my mother was treated for depression. She told me she was feeling 'a bit under the weather', that she was sometimes lonely, and Agnes's death had underlined for her the fact that her own life was running its final course. At the time, I was involved in a large project in Manchester, so we only spoke over the phone. I can't recall the exact words I said to her, but I probably told her she was going to live to a ripe old age and that I would visit as soon as the project was completed. Did I visit her? I've no idea, and the realisation fills me with shame and remorse.

"I still don't quite understand why the room hasn't been cleaned," I say.

"It *was* cleaned regularly up until the beginning of this year."

"So, what happened to change it?"

"Mrs Oakley told me she wanted the room kept locked and that I wasn't to go in there anymore."

"Did she say why?"

"I didn't ask."

This strikes me as odd, but as Maggie is technically an employee, I assume she didn't think it was her place to question the decision. But then it occurs to me that the room wasn't locked when I was here three days previously so I say, "Mum must have unlocked it before she had the fall." Maggie stiffens. I can see her trying hard to keep a neutral expression as she meets my gaze, but her eyes betray her: it isn't quite fear, perhaps just a nervous apprehension. "Do you know something about my mother that I don't know?" I ask her.

She quickly gets to her feet and moves to leave. "I'm only here to clean once a week, Mr Oakley," she says and attempts a smile, which only reaches the corners of her mouth. "Your mum doesn't confide in me. I'm not her friend. I do what she asks me to do, and that's it." She pauses in the doorway. "I'll clean your sister's room on Monday, if that's okay?"

She doesn't wait for me to reply. She hurries out of the house, banging the front door behind her.

Lenora

When I woke this morning, the first thing I saw was Aggie standing at the end of the bed. As soon as she noticed that I was awake, she said, "How are you feeling this morning, Lenora?"

I asked her why she was here.

She said, "I'm just checking how you are."

She wasn't wearing the red dress, which confused me a bit, so I asked her why she wasn't wearing it.

She said, "My dress? Oh, I am wearing it. Look." And she opened up her coat and I could see that she *was* wearing a dress underneath the coat. I closed my eyes for just a moment and when I opened them, she'd gone.

Breakfast this morning was porridge. I wanted toast, and they said I could have toast, but I think they forgot. The food they serve here is very bland, almost tasteless. They tell me I need to eat every time they see the tray untouched, but I have no appetite, so they just take it away. They leave a sheet of paper with the next day's menu and I'm supposed to put a tick in a box next to the thing I want to eat, but I can't read it without my glasses and my glasses are in the bottom drawer of the cupboard next to the bed. I can't reach the drawer without getting out of bed, and I can't get out of bed without help.

I must have drifted off to sleep again because when I woke up, Aggie was back in the room. She was looking out of the window and she'd taken off her coat. I tried to call out to her, ask her what she wanted from me. My lips formed the words clearly, but my voice had been silenced.

That scares me; it makes me think of George. He was always telling me to be quiet; to keep my opinions to myself; not to disturb him or bother him. "Keep your voice down, woman!" he used to say if I shouted back at him, or "It doesn't matter what *you* think!" if I argued with him.

In the end, I felt like I'd ceased to exist.

Julia

Colin had clearly assumed that I would be taking the night flight to London. I might even have suggested that was the case – I can't remember – for when I rise earlier than usual and join him for breakfast, his expression is one of surprise.

"What time's your flight?" he asks.

"Twelve-thirty-five."

"Twelve *noon*?"

"Yes."

"You didn't tell me you were leaving so soon."

"Does it matter?"

He scowls into his cornflakes, and when Siti tries to top up his teacup, he pushes away her hand saying crossly, "I'll tell you when I want more tea." The amber liquid is spilled onto the white tablecloth leaving an ugly mark, which she'll have to remove by first soaking then using a stain remover and finally washing by hand, because the fabric is delicate and she knows I don't want it tossed and turned in the machine.

She doesn't say anything, doesn't look scared or offended, but I recognise the look in her dark eyes because I've seen it a thousand times before: it's something these young girls do to camouflage their emotions. Her face freezes then she turns her head away and shuffles quietly back into the kitchen.

"Did you have to do that?" I ask him.

"Do what?"

"Be so rude to Siti." I offer him a look of stern rebuke – it's the same one I use with Connie and has reduced her to tears on more than one occasion. Colin is made of sterner stuff and continues to scowl, so I say, "I know you're cross with me, but you don't have to take it out on the maid. It's going to be just the two of you here and I don't want to come home and find out the poor girl has run amok with a meat cleaver."

Colin huffs and puffs. "That isn't actually very funny, Julia."

It is funny because Siti is less than five feet tall and has the physique of a prepubescent teenager, whereas Colin is six foot three and built like a sumo wrestler. But I chose my words with care: the word 'amok' is of Malay origin and describes someone in a homicidal frenzy.

When we first came out here, it was spoken of in hushed tones at the LingLang Club by families who'd once owned rubber plantations on the peninsula – *"Whatever you do, don't upset the natives!"* I'm certain it was nothing more than a kind of urban myth, but Colin has never forgotten the tales whispered by the old colonials into his young ears of workers carrying out frenzied attacks on their employers while they slept in their beds.

Siti struggles to cut up a chicken with a heavy knife so I can't see her chasing Colin round the bedroom, but it amuses me to see the look of discomfort on his face when he seriously considers the possibility of being murdered in his own home by a maid wielding a meat cleaver.

I finish eating my yoghurt and fruit and move to leave, but Colin stretches across the table and grabs my hand. "When are you coming back?" he asks.

"I told you, I don't know exactly."

"I still don't understand why you have to go. You've never bothered about your mother before this. What's really going on?"

I pull my hand from his grasp. "For God's sake Colin! What do you think is going on?"

He gives me an odd look. He isn't usually reticent in expressing his opinions, but I can see him wrestling with something. Suddenly his face becomes suffused with anger. "I know you've been seeing someone, Julia," he blurts out.

"Who told you that?" I shoot back and try to inject a note of indignation into my voice, but even to my own ears, it sounds unconvincing.

"Are you telling me it's not true?"

I close my eyes and in the privacy of my own head I think, so this is it. It's strange, this feeling. Am I standing on the edge of an abyss or is it the first taste of freedom? I don't know what it is! For a few seconds, I'm lost to the sensation of space around me. I know I'm standing in the dining room of our apartment, but what I'm sensing is elemental. It's my future.

I don't want to cry, but my eyes brim with tears. I want to tell Colin the truth, but I don't know if I'm ready to face the consequences.

He rescues me from my indecision by leaping to his feet and pulling me into his arms. "I'm sorry," he says over and over again.

I bury my face in his chest and we stand wrapped in each other's arms until the tears have subsided.

"I have to get ready to leave now," I say.

"You are coming back, aren't you?" he asks and his voice trembles.

I nod. "Yes, I'm coming back."

Back to Singapore, I think to myself, but not necessarily back to you.

Haziq drives me to the airport. He insists that Mr Crane told him to accompany me to the check-in desk, but I insist he leaves me and my suitcases outside the airport terminal. He tries to argue with me in the politest of possible ways, but I stand firm. I'm terrified that Jian might suddenly appear, and though I know that Haziq is the soul of discretion, his loyalties would be tested if he thought I'd arranged to leave the country with another man.

I've arrived with time to spare so I make my way to the SilverKris lounge with my business class ticket tucked securely in my purse. I need a drink and some peace and quiet before boarding the plane. I'm not a happy traveller, and I've yet to be convinced that it broadens the mind, especially if Colin is a typical example of the frequent flyer.

I order a large glass of white wine, make myself comfortable in one of the oversized armchairs, and open up my phone to check for messages.

My other phone has been secreted inside the lining of my suitcase. Probably an unnecessary precaution, but I wasn't going to chance leaving it at home for Colin to find, and I didn't quite trust him not to search my bag while I was in the shower this morning.

There are several messages: one from Aysha, which assures me that Glück Glass has been left in safe hands and that she'll report any problems to me immediately. Nothing from Connie. She's probably sitting at my desk with one eye on the entrance to the gallery and the other on the screen of her phone. The other messages are business related, but as I won't be doing any business until I get back, I make a mental note to call the clients personally once I'm on European time.

The glass of wine arrives and, when I look up to tip the waiter, my gaze alights on a familiar figure sitting at the bar. Jian raises his own glass to me in a toast. He slides down from the tall stool and makes his way towards me.

"May I join you?" he asks and sits down next to me without waiting for a reply.

"How did you know I'd be here?" I ask.

"I didn't know for sure. I only knew your flight details."

"Who told you? I know it wasn't Nancy, and the girls in the gallery wouldn't dare."

"Well, you're a creature of habit, Julia. My persuasive charm may have lost its hold on you, but it's still working on others. I understand you've purchased an open ticket. Is that significant?"

"You called my travel agent?"

"She was very helpful."

"She'll be unemployed when I get back here."

He attempts a smile. "When are you coming back?"

"I've just had this conversation with my husband," I say.

I don't often mention Colin, but when I do Jian's eyes glaze over. It's an emotional response to a subject that makes him feel uncomfortable, even though he knows I only share my husband's bed in its most literal sense of the word. Hypocrisy at its very worst, I always think to myself, and now more than ever since I've discovered that Jian's wife, Lì Húa, is having his baby.

Today, he's strikingly well groomed. I don't recognise the new suit but, as always, it's been tailored to fit his slim yet well-muscled frame perfectly. When Colin finds out that Jian is the person I've been seeing – and I now accept that he will find out (either I'll tell him to his face when I get back here, or the person who ratted me out will fill in the details) – I know it will cut him to the quick. For some reason this makes me feel sad beyond words.

Jian calls over the waiter and asks for his glass to be refilled. "What about you, Julia?"

"No ... thank you," I say, and I deliberately turn my attention to the electronic board on the far side of the lounge, which shows the gate numbers and boarding times.

When his glass has been refilled, Jian reaches for my hand, but I ignore it and fold my arms around my cabin bag on my lap.

"I suppose you're still angry with me," he says. "Perhaps I didn't explain myself well enough ... my family situation ... how things are ... it's just that..."

"On the contrary," I interrupt him. "I think you explained it more than sufficiently well. You're *never ever* going to leave your wife to marry me."

He heaves an extravagant sigh. "I can't, Julia!"

I want to cry, scream; do something, anything, to voice my emotions, but I don't. I remain stony-faced and speak in a monotone. "I don't know why I ever thought you would. I mean ... if that was your intention then you'd have done it already."

"I love you and I want to be with you. Isn't that enough?"

"Well, that's the million-dollar question, isn't it?" I say. "At this point, there's only one thing I know for certain: I've finally made the decision to leave my husband because it would be cruel to go on pretending that I love him and want to spend the rest of my life with him. I'm coming back to Singapore, but I have no idea if the deal you're offering me – because that's what it amounts to, a deal – I have no idea if I want to take you up on your offer. It's a bit crap, frankly."

His cheeks redden and his tone is defensive when he speaks. "You make it sound like some kind of business transaction. You don't know what I'm offering you."

A strangled laugh escapes my lips. "I know what you're *not* offering me and that's all I can think about at this moment."

I stand up and sling the cabin bag over my shoulder. As I move to walk away, Jian catches hold of my arm. "Don't leave like this, please Julia," he implores me, but I know I can't do this here and now so I pull away from his grasp and make for the exit as quickly as I can.

Richard

When I woke this morning, my plan was to take a quick look over my mother's house to see if anything else was obviously out of place, but this is the second conversation I've had with Maggie in recent days which has left me feeling that something is being concealed from me. If my mother's behaviour has been erratic or irrational, then Maggie is surely the person who would know best and she's not telling and that irks me.

I decide to stick with the original plan and slowly make my way from room to room. As far as I can tell, nothing is out of place; in fact, everything looks exactly as it's always looked for as long as I can remember. My mother has never been a collector of *stuff* and, as a consequence, every piece of glass and china decorating the windowsills and the furniture is familiar to me because it's always been there. In fact, the long sideboard in the dining room still holds a silver tray with a crystal decanter and two whiskey glasses and I know those belonged to my father.

Upstairs, I venture first into my mother's bedroom. It's neat and tidy, although the bed has been stripped of its linen and the pillows piled in the middle of the mattress on top of the folded duvet.

I realise that I wouldn't know if anything had changed in this room because we were never allowed in here as children, Julia and I; it was one of the few rules my father instigated and my mother endorsed.

As I cast my eyes around the room, searching for something, anything that might hint at my mother's altered state of mind, I suddenly realise there are photographs missing. The last time I came into this room was shortly after my father died and I *do* remember there were framed photographs on the wall. Now there are blank spaces, the paintwork where they used to hang a slightly darker shade of green. They were family portraits, four of them, all of them taken while we were on holiday. I remember I remarked to my mother that we looked happy, and she said we were happy and that struck me as pleasingly reassuring.

It's enough to send me scuttling back downstairs to see if other photographs have been removed, and they have.

My graduation photograph in my father's study has gone (although my father possibly threw that one out when he threw me out), also a photograph of Julia and Colin when they were married at St Peter's church (that had pride of place on my father's desk), an assortment of photographs of me and Julia when we were children, and professional portraits taken of my father when he was a young man. They're all gone and only a telltale rectangle of a darker shade of paint to show where they used to hang.

The only photograph still hanging on the wall is next to the casement clock in the hallway – it's of my mother. I study it carefully because it's the only photograph that *hasn't* been removed. She stares solemnly into the lens of the camera. There's no denying that she was a really good-looking girl, but something in her expression suggests an air of resignation. Perhaps she didn't want to be captured on camera, I think to myself. Or was this just the prelude to a married life harnessed to a man, who didn't love her enough to be faithful to her? I guess I'll never know, and I'm faced with yet more questions. Why is this particular photograph still here? Why were the others removed, and where are they now?

I want to ask Maggie, but I can't because I don't know where Maggie lives, and I haven't got a phone number for her.

Frustration burns through me like blue touch paper put to the match, but then it occurs to me that Edward Feering might know. Of course, I haven't got a phone number for him either, but that's an easier problem to solve. A quick search on the internet gives me what I need.

"Hallo Richard," he says when the call connects to the vicarage and I've introduced myself. "How's your mother? Is she home already? I have to say I wasn't expecting her back for at least a week."

I quickly explain the situation with my mother but before I can tell him why I've really called, he hurries on in the same, annoyingly upbeat tone of voice. "I'm sorry to hear that. Of course, it happens quite a lot, I mean, I see it a lot, doing what I do. Very distressing for the family as well, I always think. Thank God – and I do thank Him – there's a much greater understanding of the condition nowadays and it doesn't have to be all bad; lots of people go on having a very happy life for a long time." He hesitates for a moment but not long enough for me to stem the flow. "Of course, it's a bit grim at the end. I can't pretend I haven't been a witness to some harrowing scenes. I always think it's even worse when they're in their own homes and they don't know where they are and don't recognise their loved ones anymore." He barely pauses to take a breath. "I sometimes think it's a blessing when the end comes. A blessing for everyone really," he adds as a kind of final flourish.

"I'm not actually calling about my mother," I'm at last able to interject.

"Oh, right ho," he says cheerily. "How can I help you then?"

"Do you have a phone number for Maggie? My mother's..." I don't know what to call her. 'Cleaner' sounds a bit inadequate because I'm certain she does a lot more for my mother than simply keep the house clean.

"I'm afraid I don't," Edward Feering says, and he sounds genuinely sorry.

"You don't know if she lives round here somewhere?" I say, remembering she told me this morning that she was passing by.

"I think that's very unlikely. I mean … it's quite an affluent area."

The thought that Maggie couldn't afford to live where my mother lives simply hadn't occurred to me, and now I feel very, very stupid.

"Is it important?" he asks. "Some of my other ladies have domestic help and I could check with them."

Is it important? I don't know, but it looks like I'm going to have to wait till next Monday to find out.

While I have Edward Feering on the phone, I decide that I'm going to question him about Aggie's bungalow. Once again, he suggests I should speak to my mother about it, but when I remind him that she isn't exactly in the best frame of mind to answer questions about ownership of property and that, given the situation, Julia and I might need to make plans for her future with some urgency, he relents.

"I'm really not happy about this, Richard," he says. "Your mother didn't like talking about it and I feel like I'm breaking her trust."

"Well, my mother might not be in a position to make decisions about where she lives when she's discharged from hospital, so my sister and I need to know what options are open to us. If she really does own this bungalow, then it could be the answer to our problems."

"Oh, she does own it. There's no doubt about that."

"Aggie left it to her in her will, you said?"

"Yes. She was quite meticulous about the whole thing. She didn't want your mother to have the bother of sorting everything out afterwards. As soon as she found out – you know, that she hadn't got long – your mother insisted she move out of the bungalow and move in with her, so she arranged to clear the place. All the good furniture and anything else of real value went to auction and then Marcie – that's my wife – Marcie and I helped her to box everything up and we took it to a local charity shop. When she left, she had two suitcases with her. Everything else had either been sold or given away."

"So, the place is empty?"

"There were a few bits of furniture left but that's all."

"But it's empty? I mean, nobody else is living in it? My mother hasn't rented it out?"

"Look, Richard," he says. "I really can't tell you anymore." And this time I know from the tone of his voice that he won't be persuaded.

I thank him for his help and promise to keep him informed of any developments.

I really need to get to work, but the question over the bungalow is like an itch begging to be scratched. I know I'm going to have to drive over to where Aggie used to live and see for myself because I can't believe that my mother would simply leave the place empty.

I was wrong.

Tyne Lodge is almost hidden behind an enormous privet hedge and the double-gated entrance has been padlocked shut. I leave my car on the road and am easily able to vault over the gate, which confirms my fears that anybody could have broken into the place and I might be facing a band of hostile squatters. I'm brought up short by the sight of a neatly mown lawn and weed free borders. This isn't what I expected.

I'm peering through the front window, straining to see the inside of the house, when a voice calls over the neighbouring fence, "Oi! You there!" I quickly turn around and find I'm being challenged by a tough-looking man of pensionable years holding a shovel like a sawn-off shotgun. "Bloody estate agents!" he shouts at me. "It's not for sale mate, so you can scarper."

I'm wearing a decent suit and an Italian silk tie, which Mamma Mazzi bought me for Christmas, so I'm slightly offended at being taken for the kind of rogue operator that trespasses on private property. Though I suppose it's an understandable case of mistaken identity given the circumstances. Nevertheless, I stay where I am, because the shovel-wielding neighbour is glaring at me across the fence and he looks like the kind of man who strikes first and asks questions later. I've a few questions of my own to ask so I shout back to him, "I don't know who you are, but this is my mother's property."

"Yeah, right mate!" he yells. "You think I was born yesterday? You're like a pack of thieving magpies. I've told you – it's not for sale."

I decide to risk walking within striking distance so that I don't have to shout, and cautiously approach the fence, although I know before I even consider the consequences that I'm not going to offer my hand to him. "I'm Richard Oakley – Lenora Oakley's son."

"How do I know you're who you say you are? You could be anybody. Mrs Oakley never said nothing about having a son," he says belligerently.

I take my wallet out of the inside pocket of my jacket, flip it open and show him my driving licence. "Is that enough to convince you?"

He leans the shovel against the fence, folds his arms in front of his barrel chest. He peers at me like I'm some strange species of animal that crept into the garden and he doesn't quite know what to make of it. He says, "I haven't seen you round here before. Has something happened to her?"

"She's in hospital. She had a fall and fractured her hip."

He grimaces. "Nasty. My missus done the same thing last year. Tripped over one of the grandkids' bikes in the garden. I told the little beggars to put them away in the shed, but they never take no notice. Do what they like these days, kids do."

I nod my head in agreement – it's seems like the sensible thing to do because I'm guessing that this could be the person who's kept the garden from turning into the jungle of overgrown shrubbery I was expecting to find. In case I've jumped to the wrong conclusion, I ask him directly then thank him profusely when he confirms that he's been looking after the garden and generally keeping an eye on the place to make sure no one breaks in.

"No trouble," he says, and his face finally cracks a smile He suddenly points at the hedge. "She didn't want me cutting that thing back though; said she 'prefers the privacy'. It's a bit of a bloody eyesore, in my opinion."

I have to agree with him but suggest that my mother probably had her reasons for allowing the hedge to grow almost as tall as the bungalow itself.

"Well, the house is empty, isn't it," he says. "Don't want no squatters moving in."

"Have you got a key?" I suddenly think to ask.

"For the house and the padlock on the gate there? Yes. Not for the garage though."

I can't see a garage and must look confused. He indicates with his head the far end of the back garden, and now I can see a low concrete building partially covered by ivy.

"There's a lane that runs along the back of the houses," he explains. "It's supposed to be an access road but it's full of potholes now. Nobody uses it."

I'm not really interested in the garage, but I am interested in the state of the house. "What's it like inside?"

He shrugs. "It's been empty for two years so bound to be mice. Windows are all locked though." He gives me a sharp look. "You're not thinking of selling the place?"

"It's not mine to sell," I say.

His eyes narrow and his mouth hardens into a thin line. "Your mother told me she'd give me first refusal for my boy if she ever sold it. I wouldn't like to think she'd go back on her word, not after everything I've done for her."

91

Sensing that hostilities might have been resumed, I back away from the fence. "I just wanted to take a quick look at the place. And like I said, it's not mine to sell."

He picks up the shovel, muttering under his breath, and walks straight back into his own house, slamming the front door shut behind him.

Maybe that's why my mother has chosen not to live in the bungalow, I think to myself, but why not sell it? That's what I still don't understand.

Lenora

I think I must have drifted in and out of sleep all morning. Aggie seemed to come and go from the room with surprising regularity – like one of those little figurines in a cuckoo clock popping in and out when the hour strikes. Though I'm no longer certain what's real and what's imagination, my own good sense tells me that I must have been dreaming about her some of the time.

I don't understand what she wants from me.

Lunch was chicken soup. I managed to eat some of it, and the nurse who they call Kelly told me I was a good girl when she took the tray away. If she noticed the angry glare, which I gave her in response to this condescending observation, she did a good job of hiding it.

The physiotherapy midget with the fake smile came in after lunch.

"Are we going to get you out of that bed today, Lenora?" she asked me.

"No," I said. "Not unless you've got a hoist and a glass of wine to celebrate the occasion."

The stupid girl laughed. "We don't serve alcohol, but you can have a cup of tea."

"In that case," I said, "I think I'll just stay in bed."

She shook her head. "*We* have to get you moving. *We* can't let you stay in bed."

I told her, "I'll think about it. Perhaps when you come back without your *imaginary friend*?" Of course, she hadn't a clue what I was talking about because they all speak to you like you're a wilful child when you won't cooperate.

She then had the temerity to wag her finger at me and say, "I'm not taking 'no' for an answer when I come back on Monday." She actually looked like she meant it, so I expect she'll be bringing reinforcements.

Lying back on the pillows, I suddenly notice a strand of cobweb hanging from the ceiling; a single, silvery thread the cleaners have missed, probably because they spend most of their time mopping the floor and don't think to look up.

Most of my married life was spent making sure the house was clean and tidy for George. It was a thankless task, and when we moved to Hillcrest House, I insisted we employ someone to help. He wasn't keen on the idea, thought I should be able to manage it all on my own, but it was one of the few occasions when he gave in without a fight.

I don't think about him very often now but whenever I do think about him it's with a sense of sadness, although this generosity of spirit is something that's only come about since he died. Before he died, when we lived our own, very separate lives, I felt nothing but contempt for him.

Of course, I didn't always feel like that. Once upon a time I think I was in love with him, but it was such a brief flowering of passion, and ended disappointingly abruptly after our wedding.

I didn't want to marry him, and George didn't really want to marry me, but my father insisted. He wasn't a gentleman in the social sense of the word, my old dad – he was a tenant farmer with a large family to feed – but he did possess the moral certitude of a man who understood that reputation is important. He wasn't about to allow his only daughter to squander hers when the 'situation' in which she suddenly found herself could be so easily rectified.

George's parents were less enthusiastic about the union: their ambitions for their only son hadn't included a shotgun wedding to a farmer's daughter. But ... the banns were called, and the wedding went ahead, and four months later our son, Richard, was born.

I remember lying in a hospital bed not unlike the one in which I'm now confined, looking down into the pinched little face of this mewling baby and praying with all my heart that I would grow to love him, because at that point I didn't love him. I was twenty years old and had recklessly abandoned the principles my parents had spent their lives instilling into me because a handsome man with a modicum of charm had taken a bit of a shine to me. I felt like my life had ended, and in a way it had.

George didn't love him either – he made that clear from the moment Richard was dragged out of me by a pair of surgical forceps. It was very bloody, very brutal. They wrapped him up in a muslin cloth and offered him to George, but he took one brief, disinterested glance at the screaming bundle and shook his head. No, he didn't want to hold his son.

In the days that followed his birth, I did grow to love my baby, and eventually, when he could walk and talk, I think George developed a fondness of sorts for him, but in the beginning it was impossible to look at him and not be reminded that we were bound together till death parted us because this little scrap of humanity had inadvertently come into our lives.

If there had once been a few, brief months of blossoming romance then they came to naught, and the truth is that the marriage blessed by God was blighted from the start.

The strange thing is that when death did finally part us, only then was I able to look back and see that George had suffered too.

Julia

As the plane descends into Heathrow airport, I look out of the window. The London skyline is painted in its usual depressing palette of grey. Why on earth does Colin think that I would want to come back here to live?

I send Richard a text message telling him I've landed safely and intend to go straight to my hotel. Fortunately, my British passport allows me to speed through Passport Control – 'speed' being a relative term. But at least I don't have to wait in an excessively long queue like my fellow Singaporean travellers, who are forced to stand in line like beggars in a soup kitchen, which is ironic considering that most of them would rather sell their souls than live under British leaden skies.

As soon as I've collected my suitcase, I make my way outside. Last time we were here, Colin insisted on taking the tube and we arrived at the Marriott Marble Arch sweating and breathless. I'm going to take a taxi, which is what every sensible woman does when she wants to make a dignified entrance.

The taxi driver isn't English, but he does know where to find the Marriott Hotel in George Street and he doesn't want to engage me in pointless conversation, so I can sit back and relax.

At the hotel, I'm checked in with effortless efficiency, and then a porter carries my suitcases up to the room. It's late and I'm tired so I unpack, take a shower and go straight to bed.

I wake the following morning having slept only fitfully in a strange bed and am immediately aware that my body clock is frantically trying to adjust to the tail end of British summer time. The roads outside are quiet, which surprises me, but then I remember that it's Sunday.

Richard has left a voicemail on my phone.

"Hi Julia. Look ... if you haven't got anything else planned, Silvio and I wondered if you'd like to have lunch with us at the restaurant? You can get on the Central Line tube at Marble Arch and get out at Chancery Lane. It's about a five-minute walk from the station. If you fancy it, just turn up. Around two? Yeah, that should be fine. I thought we could visit Mum later, but obviously only if you're not too jet-lagged. Actually, text me. Okay, Ciao!"

Do I have anything else planned? Well, no, but do I want to have lunch with the entire Mazzi family buzzing round me? Probably not, but I might just have to show willing if I'm going to convince Richard to help me contest our father's will. At least Silvio should be good company.

Colin once asked me if I'd known that my brother was gay when we were growing up and I could honestly tell him that I had absolutely no idea. This isn't because I was especially unobservant or insensitive: it's because Richard did everything that he possibly could to fit in with my father's ideas about what a man should be, and that included marrying someone of the opposite sex.

I liked Sarah, his ex-wife, well enough, although I'd only met her a handful of times before we moved to Singapore. I think she was good for Richard, helped him to escape my father's heavy-handed influence. Of course, once that happened and he was finally free to be his own person – well, the person he wanted to be, perhaps was always destined to be – that was someone who liked men. That must have been hard for Sarah, but she took it really well, apparently. I have to say I would have been much less understanding and much more inclined to take a pair of scissors to his wardrobe and a key to the paintwork on his car.

My father, not unexpectedly, took it very badly. I don't think he ever forgave Richard.

Colin, on the other hand, was surprisingly understanding when Richard finally tiptoed out of the closet. For a man whose views on most other subjects verges on blind bigotry, he was actually incredibly supportive and told Richard not to look back, disregard everything my father said about "nonces" and "queers", and get on with his life.

When Richard met and fell in love with Silvio Mazzi, I was probably even a little bit jealous. Silvio is one of those men, who attract attention wherever they go. Tall, dark, handsome and with the kind of good dress sense that only a stylish, metropolitan Italian can own, he is the opposite of my brother in every way you could possibly imagine. I'm not sure his family welcomed Richard in the beginning. I think Silvio's mother (the matriarch of the family) was still hoping that her beautiful son would find himself a beautiful wife and make beautiful babies, but my brother is now an integral part of the Mazzi clan and much happier for it.

I decide to text him back, accepting the invitation to lunch, but declining the offer to visit our mother. I just can't face it – not yet.

Even though the temperature outside is still in double figures, it feels like the inside of a refrigerator to me. I only managed a cup of coffee for breakfast – the after-effects of a long-haul flight and food served every time you blinked – but by one o'clock I'm hungry and looking forward to lunch, so I decide to leave early.

There's more traffic on the road than was suggested by the sounds penetrating the hotel window, but I forget that every building here has double-glazing. At least the grey sky that greeted me yesterday has now been replaced with a cheerful shade of blue. It's not quite a cloudless sky, but I can feel the sun on my face.

I've spent the greater part of my life *not* living in this country and Singapore is now my forever home, but it's impossible to forget and not appreciate (albeit grudgingly) the fresh feel of an English autumn day. The air is cooler than is comfortable for someone used to living in a tropical climate, but it's pleasant after being cooped up first in an aeroplane for more than fourteen hours and then in a hotel room. As a consequence, the walk to Marble Arch tube station is really quite enjoyable.

The Mazzi family restaurant – 'Bocca Felice' – was first opened in 1898 by Silvio's great-great-grandfather, and then closed down in 1941 by his grandfather, Antonio, after Italy weighed in on the side of Hitler. The whole family removed themselves from London and went home for the duration of the war. But Papa Mazzi, Silvio's father, always wanted to re-open the restaurant and at the first opportunity moved his wife and now grown-up family back to Clerkenwell Road.

How do I know all of this? It's because it's been repeated to me by Silvio's mother every time I've visited the restaurant; I can count those times on the fingers of one hand and I'm sure I wasn't listening to the story with particular attention, but somehow the facts and figures have stuck in my head.

When I arrive at the restaurant, it's obvious from the first glance through the large, well-polished window that business is brisk. As soon as I set foot inside, Silvio peels away from a lively group of customers and envelops me in a huge hug. People don't do this in Singapore, neither friends nor family (an invasion of personal space such as this is usually met with wide-eyed alarm and rigor mortis like stiffening of the limbs), but I attempt to respond with an appreciative smile.

"Silvio! It's lovely to see you again."

"Benvenuto a casa, mia bellissima, Julia!"

"English please, Silvio."

"Of course, my darling girl. Welcome home." He slips an arm around my shoulders and draws me to the rear of the restaurant. "Come, come. We have a little table waiting for us. You want a drink? What do you want to drink? You want wine, yes?" He rushes off to the bar and leaves me standing by myself.

The restaurant is full of people speaking Italian loudly and punctuated with laughter. It's a Sunday afternoon and the Roman Catholic Church of St Peter (known locally as the Italian church) is just around the corner so I'm guessing that Midday Mass is over, sins have been confessed, and now it's time to drink and be merry.

Richard appears at my shoulder. "Julia! You're early." He knows better than to attempt the big welcome home hug thing and instead kisses me chastely on both cheeks. "You're looking well," he says. "Good journey?"

"Well, I'm one those people who never turn right when they get on a plane," I say, "so yes, it was a tolerable journey."

He looks puzzled. "Never turn right? Oh, I see. Business class."

"It's very noisy," I say. "Are we really going to eat here in the restaurant?"

"No, No. We're going to eat upstairs in the flat."

He leads me though a doorway just inside the entrance to the kitchen, which is a cacophony of people shouting angrily at one another in Italian; stainless steel pots and pans being flung around with abandon; huge, white porcelain plates clattering together as they are carried in and carried out, and enormous extractor fans whirring round like the blades of a helicopter before take-off. The noise is deafening.

Richard takes my hand. "Come this way," he mouths at me. He closes the door behind us, and immediately the noise is halved, and we can hear each other speak. "It's a fire door," he explains. "I don't know how they work like that; it's no wonder Silvio thinks he's going deaf."

"Is he going deaf?"

Richard laughs. "I think it's called selective hearing."

At the top of the stairs, we go through what looks like yet another heavy fire door, but I have a sneaking suspicion that the reason for it is simply to block out the noise from the restaurant, because inside the flat everything is calm and quiet.

"You don't live here now, surely?" I ask him.

"No, no. But Silvio and Eduardo sometimes stay over when they're on a late shift. Did I tell you they opened another restaurant in Canary Wharf? That makes three now. Toni's managing it. Marina's finally taken over the restaurant in Muswell Hill because Luca and Antonia are both at high school."

I shake my head – Richard probably mentioned it to me, but I have to confess I have little interest in the Mazzis' empire building.

"Who does Mamma live with?" I suddenly think to ask.

Richard looks surprised. "She still lives here, of course."

"She's not here now?"

"She's gone home for a few weeks. Her sister Vittoria's organised a big family reunion. Apparently, they're taking over a hotel. Four generations under one roof."

"Sounds like my idea of heaven."

"Liar," Richard says, and we both laugh.

He guides me through to the kitchen where a small, round table has already been prepared for lunch with a red and white-checked tablecloth, three glasses and three sets of cutlery. Other than a sink unit, a gas cooker and a continental dresser, the room is surprisingly free of clutter and actually has none of the homely charm of the restaurant below us.

"How hungry are you?" Richard asks.

"Very," I say. "I only had coffee for breakfast."

We hear the fire door slam and seconds later Silvio bursts into the kitchen. "Let's eat. What do you like, Julia? Pizza? Pasta? Please don't say salad. We Mazzis, we don't like skinny women."

"You don't like women full stop," I tease him.

"I love women!" he exclaims.

"Why don't you order for us all?"

"Good idea. Then Ricardo cannot complain that he made a bad choice. I choose for everyone."

While we wait for the food to arrive, Richard brings me up to date.

"So, you really think Mum's got dementia?" I ask him.

"I'm not sure what to think," he says, then he relates a story about tickets to the swimming pool and Mum's old friend, Agnes. "She wanted me to hide them from her for some reason. I mean, the woman's been dead for nearly two years. A couple of days ago," he goes on, "she told me Robin had been in to see her. Apparently, he was wearing the same jacket he wore to Dad's funeral."

"And you're not sure if she's got dementia?" I say. "Seriously?"

He purses his lips and considers it briefly. "I'm really not sure. Silvio and I have been reading up about it and those aren't typical symptoms. You more usually get problems with memory loss and changes in personality and mood. The only thing that makes me wonder is something we saw on one website. It talked about difficulties with tasks, which need planning and organisation. She's definitely got some issues with that."

"You're going to have to explain," I tell him.

"Well, the house and the garden for a start," he says. "You know how much she loves the garden, but the back garden hasn't seen a lawnmower for about two months by the look of it, and the seaside-inspired front garden is covered in weeds."

"Perhaps she's just lost interest," I say. "Or maybe she can't manage it anymore?"

"What about the house then?"

"What about the house? She's still got ... what's her name ... Maggie, isn't it?"

101

"Yes, but that's something else that's bothering me. I swear Maggie knows what's been going on."

"Did you ask her?"

"Of course! But she said that Mum doesn't confide in her."

"I don't suppose she does," I say. "I can't imagine confiding anything to any one of the people who Colin and I employ – not even the name and number of my manicurist."

"It's not like that here," Richard says sharply.

"What's wrong with the house then?" I say. He looks away, rearranges the cutlery with one hand and scratches the back of his head with the other. Patience has never been one of my strengths, and my blood sugar levels are now running dangerously low, so it doesn't surprise me when I find myself barking at him, "For God's sake, Richard, spit it out!"

He finally finds the courage to meet my eyes. "She locked your bedroom door."

"So?"

"So, it hasn't been cleaned since ... I don't know, probably last year judging by the depth of the dust that's accumulated."

"Only my room?"

"Yes."

"That is strange."

Richard doesn't respond immediately and there's definitely something shifty in his expression. I haven't seen my brother very frequently over the last thirty-odd years that I've lived in Singapore, but I recognise that look. "What are you hiding from me?" He does the same routine with the cutlery, but this time he swivels the plate round and adjusts the position of the wine glass. "Good grief!" I explode at him. "I hope you don't cheat on Silvio, because poker-faced you ... are ... not!"

"I was hoping to avoid telling you."

"I think we're done with that, don't you Richard?" I say, sarcasm oozing from every syllable.

"Okay. According to Maggie, Mum nursed Aggie for the last few weeks of her life in *your* bedroom. And she died there, in your bed."

"Oh. I see. Well, I can understand why you didn't want to tell me that," I reply, because I'm not a squeamish sort of person, but the idea of anyone breathing their last breath between my sheets does fill me with a certain distaste.

I can still remember Aggie quite well even though she wasn't a regular visitor to the house. My father had taken against her for reasons, which were never fully explained, but I know that whenever her name came up in conversation with my mother, an odd look passed over his face; on reflection, the same look I just saw on Richard's face. Daddy had probably made a pass at her – something he was more than capable of doing after a few drinks – because she was a nice looking woman: tall, slim, pale-skinned with dark brown hair and pretty blue eyes, although the thing I remember most clearly about her was the perfume she always wore: *Je Reviens*. She once showed me the blue glass bottle it came in and sprayed some onto my wrist. It smelt like summer.

"I really didn't want to tell you," Richard goes on, "because I know what you're like and..."

"I'm not the hysterical, teenage sister you remember from your youth," I interrupt him. "I'm a grown woman, and in any case I have absolutely no intention of sleeping there when I'm already staying in a nice hotel with room service."

"But when Mum is discharged?"

"I'm still not moving in."

I know Richard is ready to argue the issue. I see the way his mouth compresses into a thin, angry line, but I'm saved by Silvio: he swings through the fire door with three plates balanced precariously on one arm and a bottle of wine tucked neatly under the other.

"Mangiamo! Let's eat," he calls out.

"Lovely," I say. "And just in time. Richard was priming himself to launch into a lecture. Something I don't need."

"Lecture?" Silvio enquires with a frown.

"About me staying with my mother at Hillcrest when she comes out of hospital?"

He rounds on Ricardo. "Of course, Julia is going to stay there. What were you thinking of?" He offers *me* an unwavering smile and says, "We eat and then you go and see your mamma. I know you can't wait."

Richard

After lunch, when Julia has excused herself to go to the bathroom, I tell Silvio, "You're positively Machiavellian. Did you see the look on her face when you told her you know she can't wait to see Mum?"

"Niccolò Machiavelli was diplomat, Ricardo."

"I thought he was an evil genius?"

"Non è vero!"

"Well, *you* are a genius. Although she's still going to take some convincing to stay over at Hillcrest now that I've told her about the bedroom."

He reaches for my hand, brings it to his mouth and slowly wraps his tongue around my index finger. "You taste of pizza." He licks his lips. "Pomodoro e basilico." He suddenly makes a face. "You need more salt."

"I blame the chef."

He looks aghast. "I'm the chef!"

"Well, you need to shape up," I tease him. "Or I'll be taking my custom elsewhere."

He leans in to kiss me, but Julia suddenly appears, and he pulls back. "Are you ready to leave?" he asks her with another winning smile.

My sister is stony-faced in response. The cheerful expression she struggled to maintain throughout the lunch has been abandoned, wiped away from her lovely mouth with the last traces of *Linguine Carbonara alla Bocca Felice*. She says, "You know, I have a terrible headache. It's probably the red wine. I think I might just go back to the hotel."

"No!" Silvio exclaims loudly. "I will drive you both to the hospital. It's no trouble."

"I'd really rather go straight back to the hotel," she says.

Silvio leaps to his feet and gathers her into his arms. "Oh, poverina, mi dispiace tanto. I'm so sorry, poor Julia. Come. I give you some nice, cold ice water to drink and you take an aspirin. You'll be fine."

I watch her hesitate; watch her rapidly sum up the possibilities of persuading Silvio that today really isn't the best day to visit her ailing mother, but I think she knows he won't be diverted by feeble excuses. She sighs loudly, and he simply kisses the top of her head and leads her back to the bathroom.

Silvio insists that everything is left on the table to be cleared away later, but just as we're leaving, he's called to a crisis in the restaurant kitchen downstairs. I take the car key from him, but he accompanies us to the car. "Give my love to your mother," he tells Julia. "She will be so happy to see you."

Julia manages a tight-lipped smile in response, but as soon as we drive away, she says, "Take me back to the hotel, Richard, I really do have a headache. You know I struggle to deal with our mother when she's compos mentis. I can't talk to her if she's lost the plot."

A surge of anger washes over me. This is typical of Julia: selfish to the end. How Colin has lived with her all these years is beyond me, but I think he's always treated her with the same paternal indulgence that my father did. Julia only had to say the words 'Please, Daddy, darling,' and the chequebook was on the desk; the car keys were laid on the table; misdemeanours dismissed with a wave of the hand. That's why she always struggled with our mother: because *she* saw through Julia; *she* recognised self-serving manipulation where our father only saw smiling entreaty.

I rein in my temper and tell her bluntly, "We're going to the hospital. We don't have to stay long, but if Mum does have dementia then the sooner you get used to it the better, because we're both going to have some difficult decisions to make if she can't live at Hillcrest on her own."

Julia turns her face away from me and looks out of the window. She says in a quiet voice, "I'm never coming back here to live, Richard. Even if Colin decides he wants to leave Singapore, I'm not leaving, and I'm not being made responsible for our mother either. I don't care what you say; I don't care what you think of me. I'm only interested in what happens to our family home."

Anger swells in my chest once again. "Let me get this straight, just so we understand one another; just so that we're on the same page. You only came back here to claim your inheritance?"

Her head swivels round, and she says defiantly, "What's wrong with that? I only want what's rightfully mine. I need that money!"

"Since when?"

Her voice is full of raw emotion when she replies. "Since I decided to divorce Colin."

So, that's it.

I suddenly realise I don't want to know the whys and the wherefores of this decision – Julia's private life can remain her own concern – but I still care enough about her to want to make her understand that she's heading down a road marked 'no entry' if she thinks she can contest our father's last will and testament.

At the first opportunity, I pull over to the side of the road and still the engine.

"Why are we stopping?"

Yet again, I find myself assuming the role of the older brother: I want to protect her – if only from her own selfish desires. "Look, Julia, I'm not interested in your problems with Colin." I take a deep, calming breath; prepare myself for the backlash. "If you've been banking on getting money from the proceeds of the sale of Hillcrest then you're going to be disappointed. You can't contest the will. It's too late. You don't have a right to anything from Dad's estate. The will might not be fair, but it's legal."

"It can't be!" she cries.

"I'm sorry, but it is."

"There has to be some way..."

"There isn't."

I realise I've been anticipating an outburst of hysterical fury from her, so I'm struck with wordless surprise when she doesn't scream her frustration into my face the way she used to do. Instead she takes a paper tissue from her bag, carefully wipes her eyes and blows her nose then leans back in the seat and closes her eyes. She says in a low voice, "I suppose I might as well tell you – even if you're not really interested – but I've been involved with someone else for about eight years. Colin doesn't know ... well, I thought he didn't, but now ... I don't know." She opens her eyes and blinks back tears. "I can't stay with him, Richard. We make each other miserable. He wants to retire in a few years, come back here and buy a cottage in the country, and I can't do it. Suffolk, for crying out loud! What am I going to do in Suffolk?"

"If you get a divorce then surely money shouldn't be an issue?"

"It will be. For me, at least. We don't own our apartment: we accept a generous living allowance from the company. Colin has money invested, but I have nothing in my name except the gallery and that won't me allow me to live in Singapore, at least not the way that I want to. I don't wish Mummy dead, obviously I don't, but I've been thinking of Hillcrest as my ... I don't know ... my eventual escape route, I suppose. I don't understand why Daddy would do this. It doesn't make sense to me."

"Which bit doesn't make sense? That he decided not to leave us anything, or that he had a second family?"

She looks thoughtful, and I can actually see in her face that she's considering which part of this conundrum pains her the most. Eventually she says, "If I'm being completely honest, it's the fact that he left us nothing. I mean ... even if he was seriously involved with someone else for years and had a child with her, he was still married to Mummy; we're still his children." She turns her face towards me and asks with complete sincerity, "What did we do to deserve this?"

As her eyes meet mine, I wonder how long it will take her to recognise that this was the wrong answer. And it does take her several minutes of increasingly awkward silence to realise that I'm not responding with resounding agreement. When it does sink in she demands, "Well, what did you expect me to say?"

"I hoped that for once in your life you might think about someone other than yourself. He had a second family, Julia. He didn't just have a bit on the side, he had a second home with another woman, who effectively lived as his wife, and they had a child together." She opens her mouth to interrupt, but I put up my hand to stop her. "Let me finish. I don't think he left Hillcrest to this other daughter, this Miriam, because he didn't care about us – not about you, anyway. I think he did it to punish Mum, and I know that sounds mad, but I think it was his way of making sure that she continued to live her life in thrall to him. So that she had nothing of her own; so that he still had all the power."

"That's ridiculous!"

"Is it? They might have lived under the same roof, but they lived separate lives. Mum never knew where he was, what he was doing or who he was with. Why didn't he just leave her? He could have paid her off and then he would have been free of her, but he chose not to."

Naturally Julia jumps to his defence but she clearly isn't thinking when she says, "She could have left *him* if she wasn't happy." No sooner have the words been uttered than the significance of them hits home and her face burns, I think with shame as well as embarrassment.

"This act of malice wasn't about you," I say quietly. "This was about our mother."

I restart the engine, wait for a pause in the flow of traffic then pull out into the road. Julia goes back to looking out of the window, and we spend the rest of the journey in ruminative silence.

I don't know why I'm surprised to find the car park full to overflowing on a Sunday afternoon when we get to the hospital. We have to queue, and then we have to wait until someone leaves, before we can park the car. The anticipated outburst of impatience from Julia doesn't manifest itself until we're walking into the hospital itself.

She says, "I don't know why I let you drag me here. It's taken us nearly an hour. I really do have a headache, you know, so don't expect me to play the kind, caring daughter for too long."

"Mum wouldn't recognise you if you did."

"She might not recognise me anyway," she says and sticks out her tongue at me.

We're buzzed into the ward and I lead Julia straight to the room where I last saw my mother, but she's not there anymore. Another even more elderly and bewildered-looking woman is lying in the bed. She starts to cry when she sees us.

Julia looks horrified and quickly backs out of the room.

"They must have moved her," I say. "Wait here and I'll check where she is."

Julia grabs my elbow. "Don't leave me on my own. I'm coming with you."

The nurse at the reception desk checks the whiteboard on the wall behind her and informs us that Mrs Oakley has been moved to bed eight in the side ward at the end of the corridor. We find her sitting up in bed and her face breaks into a delighted smile when she sees Julia.

"What a wonderful surprise," she says.

Immediately Julia replies, "You sound like you weren't expecting me."

"I wasn't."

I stoop to kiss her cheek and she reaches up and touches my face very gently. "It's so good to see you again."

Julia continues to stand at the foot of the bed. She glances over her shoulder, her gaze resting briefly on each of the other elderly women on the ward. She passes her small handbag from one hand to the other; shifts her weight from side to side; tries to form her mouth into an attractive smile every time her gaze returns to our mother's face, but the effort of trying to look like the caring daughter is hard to sustain. At last she sinks onto the end of the bed, and I breathe a sigh of relief.

"We're not going to stay very long," I say. "Julia only arrived yesterday evening and she's a bit jet-lagged."

My mother nods her head in response. Her eyes look bright, but not feverishly so. I notice that the tubes, which were attached to her hand and her abdomen, have now been removed and she definitely seems more comfortable.

"How are you?" I ask her.

She points to her hip. "I've got the mother of all bruises there where they sliced me open, but I'm feeling more like my old self." She turns to Julia, "It's so lovely to see you, dear. Although it really wasn't necessary for you to rush back here."

"Richard insisted," Julia says then her mouth snaps shut again.

This juvenile attitude irritates beyond measure, but I ignore it for my mother's sake. I say, "I just told Julia we might have to make some changes to your living arrangements. I mean ... if you're going to struggle to live on your own at Hillcrest ... well, then we might have to..."

"I've been thinking about that," she says abruptly. "I suppose you've told Julia that the house isn't mine?"

Before I have a chance to reply, Julia jumps in. "Why didn't you contest the will?"

My mother looks surprised at this sudden turn in the conversation and I'm stung into asking, "Do we really have to do this now?"

"But I want to know," Julia insists. She turns back to our mother. "When you found out what he'd done, why didn't you do something about it? You do know it's probably too late now, don't you?"

"I do know," our mother says. "But you have to realise, Julia, there were so many other things to think about at the time, not least of which was the fact that your father had been knocked down by someone, who then drove off and left him dying on the side of the road. Do you know the police investigated *me*?"

This is yet another piece of information she's kept to herself, and now I can't help wondering what other closeted skeletons are waiting to reveal themselves. I realise I want to ask her about the bungalow, but one look at Julia's face confirms that now isn't going to be the best time.

Julia hasn't finished being crass and insensitive and exclaims loudly, "What did you expect? As soon as they found out that Daddy was involved with someone else, you would have been the prime suspect."

"For God's sake, Julia, keep your voice down," I scold her. "This really isn't the time or the place to conduct a post-mortem of Mum and Dad's marriage." I turn my head so that only she can read my lips and say in an undertone, "You're not exactly in a position yourself to criticise."

Julia's response is to fold her arms over her chest and clamp her mouth shut.

Mum's response is to utter a hollow-sounding laugh. "I don't think a post-mortem's going to tell you anything you don't already know." Her expression darkens suddenly. "Your father never made a secret of the fact that he had little time for me, and his behaviour towards Richard was shameful. I think that's what hurt the most, actually. But you, Julia, you never lacked for anything; you always had his love and his affection, and you certainly had more than your fair share of his money while you were growing up." She hesitates and I see a look of pained disappointment in her eyes. "Is this the real reason you've come back? Because you think you're entitled to an inheritance?"

"I am entitled!" Julia snaps.

A look of sad resignation passes over my mother's face. "Well, clearly your father thought differently."

I know I have to end this torturous exchange quickly. I tell Julia, "I think it's time to leave." I lean across the bed and draw my mother into a gentle embrace. She's lost weight, I think to myself. I can feel the bones beneath her withered skin: fragile, brittle as ancient brickwork. I picture them crumbling to dust, and the thought of it fills my heart with sadness. I kiss her cheek. "We can talk about the house another time. I just wanted to bring Julia to say hallo."

Julia stretches out her hand across the starched bed linen, which separates her from our mother, and briefly touches her fingers to the age-spotted skin. Immediately she withdraws her hand, as though this physical contact with infirmity is somehow contagious. Her lack of humanity sickens me.

She says, "I'll come back when you're feeling better, Mummy." For a brief moment, she looks like she might apologise for her behaviour. "I didn't mean to upset you, but..."

"That's enough now," I tell her, and insist that we leave.

We slowly make our way back to the car, Julia wisely keeping her ungracious thoughts to herself until we find ourselves in a queue to get out of the crowded car park. She looks up at me and says, "Are you sure she has dementia? She didn't sound to me like someone whose memory's fading. I know she looks as frail as a bird, but that brain is still firing on all cylinders."

Lenora

The morning after Julia's surprise visit, I'm woken by the tea trolley. It's now a familiar, jarring concerto of crockery and cutlery reverberating on a metal tray as it's wheeled from bed to bed.

At home, I wake up to Radio 4. The newsreaders have mildly annoying voices but at least they can be switched off; the sound of the tea trolley and its driver – today a lady called Brenda with a Birmingham accent – can be heard long before they've arrived at bed eight and can't be dismissed in quite the same way.

Brenda checks the board behind my bed for instructions and prohibitions before she asks, "Cup of tea, Lenora?"

I push myself up into a sitting position then together we pull the table from the bottom of the bed and station it so that I can reach it without straining my stitches.

Brenda carefully places the cup and saucer in front of me. "Enjoy," she says.

"I will enjoy it. I won't get this kind of service at home."

I know she's in a hurry, but she stops for a moment, smiles. "Haven't you got a nice husband to wait on you when you get back then?"

I want to say that I had a husband, but he wasn't very nice, and I don't think he ever, even once, brought me tea in bed. Instead I explain that I live on my own – although I'm no longer quite certain if that's true.

"Well, make the most of it then," she says. "See you later."

The tea tastes surprisingly good and it perks me up, so that when I'm reminded that it's Monday morning and the physiotherapist will be round later to get me out of bed, I don't immediately plead an excuse to stay where I am.

The problem is that I don't want to go home.

The first time I became aware that Aggie had come back, I was in bed. The alarm clock had sounded and someone on Radio Four was announcing the weather forecast for the weekend, but my attention was focused on the unmistakeable smell of a sweet, floral fragrance. I say 'come back' but now I don't know if she ever actually left. The irony of it, however, wasn't lost on me: it was Aggie's perfume I could smell. *Je Reviens* – 'I will return'.

Of course, I did that thing that every up-to-date person does these days: I googled it. I soon discovered that smelling something, which isn't there – otherwise known as a phantom smell – is potentially a sign of something seriously wrong with the brain. The more I read about olfactory hallucinations, the more worried I became, because it was associated with all sorts of unpleasant conditions like epilepsy and Alzheimer's disease.

In the end I asked Maggie if she could smell it. When she said she thought she might have noticed it on a few occasions, I was momentarily relieved – it meant I wasn't on course for a temporal lobe seizure. But that then begged the question: where was the smell coming from?

The answer presented itself one evening when I went to bed. The small, blue glass bottle of perfume was sitting on my dressing-table, and then I nearly did have a seizure because it definitely hadn't been there when I'd got dressed in the morning.

I thought I'd cleared Julia's bedroom of everything, which had belonged to Aggie. I thought I'd boxed it up and given it away. Of course, I checked the room and it *was* empty apart from a few bits and pieces Julia had left behind, though the absence or otherwise of Aggie's belongings still didn't explain how the bottle came to be sitting on my dressing-table.

When I showed it to Maggie she said, "Well, that explains everything, doesn't it?"

"Does it?"

"It explains what you've been smelling."

"I rather think you've missed the point," I told her. "I know what I've been smelling is Aggie's perfume. What I don't understand is where the bottle came from." At first, she looked back at me with blank incomprehension, and then the colour drained from her face. "Now do you see what I mean?" I said.

She nodded then she took the bottle from me and threw it in the bin.

Three weeks later it was back on the dressing-table.

I didn't immediately jump to the conclusion that Aggie had somehow come back. I understood that I'd become forgetful over recent years and so the first time I found the bottle of perfume on my dressing-table, I realised that if I'd found it in the house then I could have put it there myself in a moment of distraction. It was when it reappeared that I began to doubt what I thought to be true. Of course, I knew that Aggie had died – I'd been with her when the last gasping breath left her body, and I watched as it was taken away.

I suppose the point I'm trying to make is that I saw the corporeal manifestation of Aggie being loaded into the back of a vehicle and I think I can rely on the fact that this earthly body was put into a coffin and cremated – I watched the curtains close around it at her funeral. But what happened to *her* afterwards? That was the question, which began to bother me.

I've been a churchgoer all my life even though my relationship with God and his only son has fluctuated between faithful devotion and disappointed scepticism. What I have never *seriously* doubted, however, is that there's a place for all of us in the afterlife, so I just assumed that Aggie had left this world for the next one, never to return.

The appearance of the blue glass bottle marked *Je Reviens* consequently made a gaping hole in my long-held belief system. Was it possible that Aggie had somehow come back or indeed had never really left? I wrestled with these thoughts and confided some of them to Maggie.

She told me she'd recently read an article about something called 'unresolved grief'. She said the symptoms sometimes included disbelief in the death of a loved one, an inability to accept the death, and overwhelming feelings of emotional pain and sorrow. Well, I knew it wasn't that. I'd spent a lot of time with Aggie while she was dying; became her true confidante; the recipient of her final confessions. When she died, I knew things about my friend, which should have gone with her to her grave. I was actually unreservedly relieved when Aggie finally passed away.

Julia

Last night I dreamed of Jian. He was standing on the balcony of his apartment, so he didn't hear me when I entered. It was almost dark outside; that time of the day when the warmth of the sun has heated every leaf, every flower, and the fragrance is suddenly released into the air. I could still hear the busy hum of the traffic on Orchard Road, but Jian radiated peace and contentment.

I wanted to draw my finger down the length of his spine; feel his naked flesh shiver under my touch. As I slowly walked towards him across the cool, marble-tiled floor, I saw that he was holding something in his arms. A surge of joyous recognition ran through me. I knew what it was. He'd bought me a puppy, a French bulldog, and it wasn't even my birthday. As I approached the balcony, he turned. His face shone with happiness...

Needless to say, it wasn't a puppy he cradled lovingly in his arms: it was a baby. His baby.

The shock drove me from restful slumber into gasping, wide-eyed, wakefulness, like someone who has filled their lungs with air, dived to the bottom of the ocean and is propelled back to the surface. Whoosh.

I scrambled out of bed and ran to the bathroom. I could taste the vomit before it spewed between my clenched lips into the toilet bowl.

This nightmare scenario of Jian sharing a beautiful moment with the offspring of his loins was only partly responsible for the violent eruption of the contents of my stomach: the main reason was drinking too much red wine the evening before.

Richard had driven me back to Bocca Felice after visiting our mother in hospital and then Silvio insisted that I spend the rest of the evening with them in the empty flat upstairs because he didn't want me to be left on my own in a 'horrible hotel room'. I was desperate to be left on my own in a hotel room, but he can be very persuasive, and I couldn't be bothered to argue.

"Drink. Be happy, Julia," he told me.

"I want to be happy," I said. "But finding happiness, lasting happiness, is a bit like searching for the Holy Grail. You've read that it exists, and you want to believe you can find it, but every time you think you're getting close, you're disappointed."

Silvio pushed a ridiculously large glass of wine into my hand and said, "Roma non fu fatta in un giorno."

"What?"

Richard took the bottle from him and poured himself a somewhat smaller measure of wine. "He said Rome wasn't built in a day."

"True, or not true?" Silvio demanded of me.

"Well, of course it's true, but how is that relevant to my situation?"

"It's not," Richard said.

"It is," Silvio insisted. "You must keep trying to be happy. You're not happy with Colin? What's wrong with you? You have a good man."

"She doesn't love him anymore."

"Oh ... I see now." He cocked his head to one side and peered at me with mistrustful eyes. "You fell in love with someone else. Yes?"

"She's been having an affair."

"Mamma mia! Julia! What were you thinking? This is not good. Who is he?"

Richard dragged out a chair from under the table and sank into it. "Yeah, who is he, Julia?"

"You're both so mean!" I cried. "You don't understand what it's been like for me."

I spent the rest of the evening trying to explain and then justify my behaviour. I think Silvio was only pretending to be appalled, but Richard looked genuinely dismayed.

At the end of the evening, they put me in a taxi and sent me back to my hotel, but not before Richard had extracted a promise from me to go and take a look at my old family home.

"Just take a look over the place," he said. "See if you can find any more evidence."

"Evidence of what?"

"Anything else, which might indicate that Mum's not looking after the place or looking after herself properly."

"Why didn't you do it when you were there?"

"I don't know what I'm looking for."

"Don't know what you're looking for? Oh right, and I am supposed to know because I'm a woman. Is that it? Are you stupid? I don't know anything about ... domestic stuff. I have a maid at home."

"Well, you have to have a better idea than I do, if she's not looking after herself," Richard replied, slurring his words slightly.

"Why exactly do I need to do this?" I asked. "What purpose does it serve?"

"We have to know if she's going to be safe, Julia."

"And if she's not? What then?" I retorted.

He put his finger to the side of his nose and tapped it.

"Is that supposed to mean you know something I don't know?"

He then had the temerity to laugh. "There may be a way out. That's all I'm saying." And he refused to say any more.

With yesterday evening's overindulgence voided, I feel quite a lot better, although the picture of Jian with his baby lingers unhappily in my mind. That is how it will be, I keep thinking to myself. It doesn't matter how much he tries to reassure me that nothing will change, I know that everything will change, and the dream only proves it.

I decide to order room service then I shower and dress.

It's another short walk to the tube station, but this morning it's a much less pleasant experience compared to yesterday's trip to Bocca Felice because the streets are busy, and the sun isn't shining. I've waited until rush hour has passed so that I don't have to (quite literally) rub shoulders with the hoi polloi, but the trains are still crowded and claustrophobic, and the habit of walking and looking at the screen of a phone has become an international phenomenon. How some people don't fall over the edge of the platform and in front of a train is beyond me.

I checked the route to Shenfield station before I left the hotel, though I ought to know it well enough. I commuted from there into Liverpool Street station for several years, specifically until I married

Colin, but only until then because my father had this outdated idea that married women shouldn't work. As he was the one who was *giving me away* – another completely outdated notion – Colin had no choice but to accept his terms if he wanted to have me. We moved to Singapore two years later, and I suppose I could have found gainful employment in another office after that, but Colin never asked, and I never offered.

Liverpool Street station has been transformed since I last boarded a train there, but it's still a dark, grimy, cavern compared to the shiny, glass and steel, shopping mall-like Dhoby Ghaut station where I occasionally hop on the MRT if I'm meeting Nancy. If cleanliness really were next to godliness, then the Singapore Mass Rapid Transport system would be a holy shrine.

I search out a seat, which doesn't look like someone has recently rested his filthy shoes on it, then check my phone for messages. Singapore is seven hours ahead of London so Colin will be leaving the office for the LingLang Club at about this time – I'm surprised he hasn't tried to contact me already. In fact, nobody has tried to contact me.

It's strange finding out that everyone I know in Singapore can get on with their lives without reference to me. I never seriously thought that I was indispensable; I didn't actually imagine that I was instantly forgettable, but it is a sobering discovery that nobody needs or wants to speak to me.

I did think – and probably hoped – that Jian might message or mail me, but there's nothing on either of my phones to indicate that he's even *tried* to get in touch, so I turn my attention to the landscape outside the window of the train.

I've forgotten what it's like to live in a vast, urban environment like London and frankly I'm horrified at what I see. Of course, Singapore is a *tropical* island but it's actually just as much a concrete jungle as any other city on the planet. There, however, the resemblance ends. In Singapore, emphasis is placed on creating an eye-pleasing backdrop. Trees and flowering plants are used to soften the hard lines of steel bridges and towering, hi tech office blocks as well as utilitarian housing developments and futuristic shopping malls. It would be true to say that there's an element of theatre about the place – things aren't always quite as lovely as they seem at first glance – but I know I could never live anywhere else and I certainly couldn't come back to this. London may have the edge as far as culture and history is concerned, but a city is judged by its streets and its architecture, and everything I can see is litter-strewn and grimy.

Thankfully, with each passing mile, the dismal buildings gradually give way to green fields – a much more pleasant vista to gaze upon – and then I remember that my father made this journey every working day of his life. It can't have been very enjoyable, but I don't remember him ever complaining, though he probably had his nose in a newspaper for much of the time.

It's difficult to reconcile my memories of him with the picture that Richard has painted. My mother was right: he rarely denied me anything. I was the apple of his eye and it was a wonderful place to be. I felt loved by him; appreciated for my wit and my intelligence.

When he took my arm and walked me down the aisle, he whispered to me, "You'll always be Daddy's girl, Julia." He placed my hand in Colin's and withdrew to my mother's side in the pew at the front of the church, but I could feel his eyes on me, and I knew they were filled with tears. This is what I can't understand: why would you turn your back on someone you love? Why would you deny them what's rightfully theirs? I don't care what Richard says: I have to find out why Daddy did this. Before I return to Singapore, I have to know.

When the train stops at Shenfield, I'm quick to disembark. A brief glance up and down the high street when I emerge from the station soon establishes that it hasn't really changed and is the same, unremarkable, small town that I left more than thirty years ago.

A taxi takes me on the short journey to Hillcrest House. The driver attempts to make polite conversation and I confide that I'm returning to a home I haven't lived in for a long time. He asks me if I've missed 'the old place' and I tell him, truthfully, that I haven't missed it for a single second.

As soon as I get out of the car, I see what Richard tried to explain to me about the state of the garden: it looks quite neglected. The trees, which grow along the side of the house, are shedding their leaves and clearly no one is sweeping them up. I don't know very much about trees, but I do know that leaves on the ground rot if you don't remove them. Over the winter, these leaves are going to decay and form a layer of black slime, which isn't going to improve the saleability of the property, so *someone* is going to have to do something about it.

Last night I remembered to ask Richard to give me a key, but when I search my bag for it, I find I've left it back the hotel. Thankfully I'm saved from being locked out of my own house by the appearance at the front door of a woman whom I take to be Maggie.

"You must be Julia," she says, and backs into the hallway.

At first glance, she seems to be a person of pensionable years, but I think the green, flowered housecoat she's wearing over her clothes has influenced my estimation of her age. On closer inspection I can see she's probably not very much older than me. She reminds me of Agnes Bagshot. She has the same shy smile, same dark brown hair and bright, blue eyes. When she was a girl, she must have been what my father often referred to as a 'true beauty'. Richard and I both inherited our mother's blonde hair and hazel eyes.

As soon as I step inside the house, I'm filled with a feeling of homesickness. I miss Singapore. I don't want to be here, and I remember why I was happy to leave.

Richard

After Julia left us yesterday evening, Silvio made strong, black coffee. He said we needed to talk. Having just listened to my sister's story of unhappiness and betrayal, I sobered up pretty quickly, but it was my mother that he wanted to discuss.

"You must settle this problem *velocemente*, Ricardo," he told me. "Julia is not a bad person, but I know women like this. All she thinks about is me, me, me. As soon as she is absolutely certain that the house Hillcrest can never belong to her, she will leave, go back to Singapore." He sighed. "Probably she will go back to her poor husband and still see her lover."

"I know you're right – about everything," I told him. "But doing something in a hurry isn't possible. I'm as certain as I can be that the house doesn't belong to my mother, so selling it to fund her care isn't going to happen. We're going to have to consider other options."

"You have options?"

"Maybe." I hadn't told Silvio or anyone else about the bungalow because I wanted to discuss it with my mother first – I still couldn't understand why it was standing empty and unused when it could be lived in or generating an income for her. I had, however, considered something else. "I've been thinking about the possibility of letting Hillcrest, but I don't know if that's allowed under the terms of the will," I said.

Silvio responded with a surprised and happy smile. "*Fantastico!* You don't sell it, but you get the money for her."

I nodded agreement. "She could rent a flat in supported living accommodation. It's probably not quite what she wants after living in a four-bedroomed detached house for the last forty years, but she might not have a choice, if she can't look after herself anymore."

Silvio's happy smile instantly dissolved. "I think maybe it's too much to ask of her."

I knew he was right – that it was a lot to ask of her – but I couldn't see any other alternative.

When he leaves me at Bocca Felice the following morning, he reminds me that I need to contact my mother's solicitor. That's going to necessitate a drive back to the house we share in East Finchley because our bedroom in the flat over the restaurant only holds the basic essentials – some casual, weekend clothes and a few toiletries – and I'm going to need access to my computer.

I quickly throw on my clothes from yesterday evening because I want to get on the road, but I'm forced to take a more leisurely drive because of the traffic.

Back at home, as soon as I've showered and changed, I first phone the hospital to check on my mother's progress. I'm told she's with the physiotherapist and I can call later for an update after the doctor has made his rounds: all being well, she'll be discharged by the end of the week.

"The end of the week?" I know I sound surprised, and not in a good way.

"That's right, Mr Oakley. The physiotherapist is going to get her walking to the toilet with a frame. I understand her bathroom at home is on the first floor?"

"Uh, yes, I suppose it is. Is that a problem?" I say, and I try to suppress the note of hope in my voice.

"Well, it just means he has to get her walking safely up and down stairs."

"Oh, I see. I suppose that could take a while then?"

"Not usually. If she can manage to walk comfortably with the frame today and tomorrow, then they'll be tackling the stairs the next day. You'd be surprised how well people manage after an operation like this."

I don't want to be surprised. I need my mother to remain in the care of people, who know how to look after her, so I decide to mention my worries about her mental state.

The nurse responds immediately with, "Just let me read through her notes. I wasn't aware there was a problem?"

"I think there might be," I say. "One of your colleagues spoke to me about the possibility of her having dementia."

"I'll have to call you back about that, Mr Oakley." I tell her that's fine, but then she adds, almost as an afterthought, "Your wife didn't mention this when I spoke to her this morning."

"My wife?"

"Mrs Oakley."

"There must be some mistake," I say.

"Let me check the board," she says at once. "I know Oakley isn't a common name, but we might have two patients with that name." And it takes her no more than a few minutes to get back to me and confirm that there's only one patient called Oakley currently on the ward. "She's phoned almost every day to check on your mother, Mr Oakley. I spoke to her myself this morning. She said her name was Sarah Oakley. I told your mother that she's been asking after her and she seemed to recognise the name."

There are several things wrong with this scenario. The most obvious is that I'm no longer married to Sarah – we've been divorced for almost twenty years. The second thing is that Sarah is working in New York so this morning in Essex would have been the middle of the night where my ex-wife now lives with her new husband and teenage daughter. More worrying, however, is that Sarah *never* called herself Oakley: she always used her maiden name – Hollingsworth – in both her private and professional life. Whoever has been calling the hospital isn't the person I was once married to.

I can't decide if I should explain this to the nurse. I'm not sure she'd believe me and then *I* might be labelled the person with the mental health issues. Instead, I tell her it must be Sarah, who *used to be* my wife. She seems to accept this explanation readily enough, but I'm intrigued to know who's been masquerading as the current Mrs Oakley, and why.

The phone call to the solicitor takes less time. He's out of the office and won't be back till tomorrow according to his secretary, but she assures me that he'll be able to see me promptly as he has few appointments timetabled for this week. I realise that Julia will want to attend any meeting I arrange, so I leave a message for him that we want to discuss the provisions of our father's will, in particular the arrangements for our mother and the property he owned, and she still lives in.

With too many unanswered questions buzzing around inside my head, I leave the house and head for the office, but before I leave, I email Sarah in New York. It's a short message asking after her and her family, and then enquiring if she's heard about my mother's fall, and has she phoned the hospital. God knows what she'll make of it, but she's a stickler for answering emails promptly so with luck I'll have an answer before the end of the day.

Lenora

You know you're being treated like a child when you're offered cake as a reward.

The physiotherapy midget's partner in crime – a young man calling himself Frankie – arrived at my bedside this morning with a large slice of Battenberg on a paper plate. It looked disgusting: bright pink and yellow sponge cake covered in something that was supposed to be marzipan. It positively reeked of almond essence, but I had grave doubts whether anything growing on a tree had contributed to its manufacture.

"What's that?" I asked him.

"It's cake," he said.

"Are you sure?"

He looked at the piece of Battenberg then looked back at me. "I thought you might like to have this with your elevenses, Lenora. You know ... a nice cup of tea and something sweet ... but obviously only after you've had a go with the walking frame." He made a half-hearted attempt at a friendly smile and placed the cake on the table in front of me.

I was immediately seized with the urge to pick up the cake with my fingers and throw it across the room, but realised at once that that kind of behaviour – albeit very satisfying – would only confirm their opinion that I needed to be dealt with like a naughty child, so I put the temper tantrum on hold. I said, "If you want me to use the walking frame, you only have to ask."

The faked friendly smile disappeared. "I think we already tried that, Lenora, but you weren't very cooperative."

"You seriously thought cake was the answer?" I asked him. The mouth didn't move, but I saw a glint of appreciative humour in his eyes. "I'll get out of bed," I said, "but only after you've removed this corruption."

He went away with the cake and came back with the walking frame.

The truth is that I love cake and have always enjoyed baking. It was one of the few things I could do really well, and Aggie couldn't.

I can't stop thinking about Aggie, and the Battenberg cake has reminded me of something that happened a few years after George died. I was at home, working in the garden. The phone rang. It was Aggie.

"Could you come over and help me make a cake?" she said. "I've been invited to a Bake and Buy sale next door and I've got to bring something homemade."

I looked down at my hands and, even though it was only May, there was already a thin line of compost under my fingernails. "I'm not really dressed for it," I said.

"You weren't actually invited," she replied, not sounding in any way apologetic. "I have to make a cake and I just need you to tell me what to do. I really don't think I can do this on my own, Lenora."

We both knew that she was probably right.

As an only child, Aggie had grown up the centre of attention of her rather elderly parents – at least they looked old to me, but my parents were barely in their twenties when they married and my brother, Jonathan, was supposedly a honeymoon baby. Money was tight for everyone in those days of post-war austerity, but she seemed to get pretty much everything she asked for, and she didn't have to do chores to earn pocket money like me and my brothers.

I think Mr Bagshot worked in a bank, but I know Mrs Bagshot stayed at home. He loved to be in the garden and spent most of his free time in the potting shed or working on his car in the garage at the bottom of the garden, but she loved to cook. The kitchen was her kingdom and there she reigned supreme.

Where my brothers and I were dragged inside to help out with everything, including the cooking, Aggie was forbidden from entering the kitchen, and ate all her meals with a napkin on her lap in the dining room. As a consequence, she grew up with impeccable table manners, but didn't learn how to boil an egg or even toast a piece of bread until she was an adult. Even when Mrs Bagshot was old and infirm and very short-sighted, she would still insist on overseeing every meal that Aggie prepared for them.

Of course, Aggie never married so after they died, she lived on her own in the house, but the spirit of Mrs Bagshot continued to hover over the hob and fill Aggie with fear and dread whenever she tried to prepare food. If it hadn't been for the invention of the microwave and the ready meal, she would surely have faded away from malnutrition.

When I arrived at the Bagshot bungalow, Aggie was waiting for me on the doorstep.

"I think I've got everything you need," she said.

"You asked me to come here and tell you what to do," I said. "I didn't realise you expected active participation."

"But you're so much better at this than me," she pleaded, and she ushered me through the hallway into the kitchen.

She'd already placed all the ingredients on the kitchen table in readiness so I told her, "Just watch what I do so you can do it yourself next time. It's not exactly difficult."

"Yes, it is," she shot back at me. "My mother was meticulous about preparing food and she said that making a really good Victoria Sandwich was an art in itself."

"Well, I've always used a bit of artistic licence when it comes to baking cakes," I said. "As long as you weigh things carefully, you can pretty much just throw everything in together."

"That's not what my mother told me," Aggie replied. "You also need to use the correct utensils."

I remember I stopped beating the butter into the caster sugar and offered Aggie my cross face. "For someone who doesn't know a lemon zester and from a potato peeler, you aren't exactly in a position to offer advice on anything connected with cooking."

"I'm only trying to be helpful."

"Don't," I said. "Just watch and learn."

I talked her through each stage, explaining why you beat in the eggs but fold in the flour, and it soon became clear that she was really only interested in the science of the process; she didn't give two hoots whether we made a coffee cream gateau or a lemon drizzle cake.

"But you must have a zester," I exclaimed in surprise after we'd agreed that lemon drizzle was nicer than coffee cream.

"Possibly," she said. "But if it looks anything like a potato peeler then I probably threw it out when Mother died."

"Why would you do that?"

She sighed and looked back at me as though I were an exasperating child. "When Mother died, I went through the whole house and threw out everything that we had two of: it seemed such a waste of space to keep a lot of unnecessary equipment that I was never going to use."

"But now we want to use it," I pointed out with some irritation.

She rolled her eyes at me. "Can't we just use a potato peeler? Surely it has the same essential function?"

In the end, we opted for a simple chocolate butter cream cake and when it was done, Aggie happily added the finishing touch with a light dusting of icing sugar sieved through a lacy paper doily she found in a box in the pantry.

I examined the doily with interest. "I didn't think they made these anymore."

"I'm sure they must," Aggie replied. "That's how you serve cake."

"Not in my house," I said.

"Well, perhaps not these days," Aggie admitted, "but Mother always set a nice table for tea."

"We only had cake on Sundays," I said. "And then we had to take it outside, so we didn't drop crumbs on the carpet. In fact, I spent most of my childhood eating in the garden."

Aggie looked horrified. "Not breakfast, surely?"

"Especially breakfast," I said. "I must have been about five when Jonnie showed me how to toast bread and spread a bit of jam and butter on it. Being the eldest, he took it upon himself to teach the rest of us everything we needed to know so we didn't starve."

"What about your mother?" Aggie asked. "What was she doing?"

"Working, I expect," I said. "Farming was a very different business in those days, and everyone had to muck in. We never went hungry though."

Aggie looked sad. *"I feel bad now – about you not having cake for tea."*

I laughed, lifted up my blouse and demonstrated the expanding, elastic waistband on my trousers. *"As you can tell, I've made up for it every day since."*

Something in Aggie's face changed. It was an expression that was hard to interpret but looked rather like an unwelcome memory had suddenly resurfaced. *"Do you remember the little blonde girl who used to work with me?"*

"Very short hair and lots of black eyeliner?"

"Yes. Melanie Mitchell. She told me she and her friends used to bake fairy cakes with marijuana in them. Because they didn't smoke," she added by way of explanation.

"My brother Angus tried that once with disastrous consequences..." I started to say.

Aggie ignored my interruption. *"When she told me that,"* she went on,*" it made me realise you could put anything in a cake."*

"Anything?"

"Anything. And nobody would know because the person who ate the cake would have eaten the evidence."

"Isn't that why they have autopsies?" I pointed out.

"Only if the person died under suspicious circumstances," she said, and then she laughed a little awkwardly and looked away.

I remember I was struck by the incongruity of this conversation; I sensed that something of importance had unwittingly been confided to me. It was only much, much later that I learned the truth.

129

Julia

Hillcrest House. Once upon a time this was my home, and by the look of it I think it hasn't changed since my wedding day when I left it for the final time as Miss Julia Oakley.

Daddy and I were driven to the church in a white Rolls-Royce hired specially for the occasion. I remember I felt like a princess in my voluminous, white dress – Princess Diana had a lot to answer for when it came to wedding dresses in the 1980s. Mine was a veritable explosion of white lace and taffeta and I looked like one of those dollies they used to dress to cover the immodesty of an unused toilet roll. It makes me shudder when I think of it now.

Mothers are supposed to cry when their daughters get married, but my mother looked relieved.

Daddy, on the other hand, was tearful throughout the whole ceremony, and when we had our father and daughter waltz at the reception after the wedding, he whispered to me that I was the most beautiful girl in the world and that he would love me forever.

Sometimes I used to think that my mother was jealous of me. There were days when her sadness was etched clearly in her face.

Sometimes I think that my marriage to Colin is history repeating itself, but I didn't marry Colin for money – although if I'm being brutally honest, it did play a part in my decision to accept his proposal: I wanted to have a nice life. I did love Colin in the beginning though, and he completely adored me.

Maybe that was how it was for my parents in the beginning, but when I was a teenager, I never heard them say a kind word to each other and my mother used her acerbic wit to mock my father – but almost always behind his back. In fact, the only time she told him to his face was when she was emboldened by alcohol.

The really strange thing is that I don't remember us being an unhappy, dysfunctional family: we were actually quite conventional, going on holiday together and celebrating birthdays and Christmas just like everybody else.

The real reason I was so keen to leave home was that I was bored with my nice, safe, conventional existence: marrying Colin and moving to Singapore had seemed like a huge adventure.

If I'd only realised…

I tell Maggie straight away that I'm going to have a look round. I explain that I haven't been home for a number of years. She nods and smiles and offers to make me a cup of tea. I don't know what I'm looking for, but Richard seemed to think there would be clues, which would confirm that our mother's mental health is rapidly deteriorating. I'm not wholly convinced this is true after our visit to the hospital yesterday, but I'm prepared to do as he's asked, and see what I can see.

The very first thing I notice is that my wedding photograph on Daddy's desk is missing. I cast my eyes around the room and it's evident that other photographs have been removed from the walls.

Upstairs, it's the same. There are no family photographs anywhere to be found so I make my way back downstairs and head to the kitchen and Maggie. I'm used to dealing with hired help, so I have no inhibitions in demanding to know what's happened to them.

Maggie looks embarrassed. "I think your mum took them down."

"Why?"

"She didn't say."

"Where are they now?"

She shrugs. "I really couldn't tell you."

"Did she destroy them?"

"I don't know!"

"Do you know for a fact that *she* took them down?"

Maggie looks shocked at this bold line of questioning. She says, "I didn't see her take them down and she didn't talk to me about it. She doesn't tell me everything she does."

I don't like the tone of her voice and if she were in my employment, I'd tell her so, but this isn't Singapore and I have to tread more carefully. "Well, I'm going to take another look round the house and see if I can find them."

She then tells me that the tea is ready and asks me if I'm going to sleep in my own bedroom or the spare bedroom because she still needs to get the house ready for when my mother is discharged from hospital. As I have absolutely no intention of moving out of the hotel, I suggest she leaves both rooms exactly as they are until we know where my mother's going.

Once again, her face immediately reflects her feelings and her hand flies to her chest. "She's not coming back here?" she gasps.

I now feel obliged to tell her, "Nothing's been decided yet. We have to see if she can still manage by herself."

"But where will she go?"

"I don't know!"

"What about the house?"

"What *about* the house?"

"I mean ... if she's not living here ... what will happen to it ... it can't stay empty ... not a big house like this..." The words tumble out of her mouth.

"If I have anything to do with it, it will be sold," I tell her abruptly. I want to end the conversation quickly: I'm not used to being subjected to examination by the domestic help and I know I'm going to say something unpleasant if I don't walk away.

As I leave the kitchen, I hear her say, "You know the house doesn't belong to Mrs Oakley?"

"What?"

"She's only allowed to *live* here," she says in a low voice.

I can do quite a good impression of someone who looks like they mean trouble, so I don't hesitate to walk back into the kitchen and square up to her. "What did you say?"

I'm expecting her to back down, but she doesn't. Her bright blue eyes are chips of ice. "Your mum told me she doesn't own the house." (Now I'm genuinely angry: my mother has chosen to confide her secret to the cleaner, but not to me, her only daughter.) Without breaking eye contact she goes on, "When you know what's happening, perhaps you can let me know? Otherwise I'll be back here next week at the usual time." And then she sweeps out of the kitchen, grabs her coat from where it's hanging in the hallway, and slams the front door behind her as she leaves.

I am speechless. The impudence of the woman, I think to myself. I wonder if Richard has seen this side of her. Though now that's she's gone, I actually feel more at ease; feel like I can take a proper look at the place without her hovering and monitoring what I'm doing.

I decide to start with the garden at the rear of the house. The key to the back door always used to be kept in the kitchen drawer and it's still there when I search for it. I use it to let myself outside. What greets me isn't exactly a surprise having already seen the unkempt state of the front garden, but I feel a pang of real sadness. The garden was our mother's pride and joy: it was where she spent much of her time when the weather allowed. It gave her a reason to remove herself from the house when she and Daddy had fallen out, which was quite a frequent event in the years before I left.

It's evident that the grass hasn't been cut for some while, and the borders don't look like they used to do when my mother spent her summer in the garden, so I'm guessing that what's growing between the larger plants are simply weeds. The only thing that hasn't obviously changed is the tall wooden fence. It's still covered in pretty flowering plants and, though horticulture really isn't my thing, I still remember their names: honeysuckle, clematis and passionflower.

The reason I remember them so well is because I infuriated my mother by treading on the garden and pushing the plants out of the way and sometimes breaking them when I climbed through a gap in the fence by way of a broken fence panel. It hung from a single nail and made it possible for me to swing it to one side then make my escape with no one the wiser. I might even have facilitated the other nail's removal myself; I can't remember. I don't know if Daddy ever knew about the gap in the fence, but I used it as a means to get in and out of the house without him seeing me, and I realise now that my mother must have been a co-conspirator because, although she complained about the plants, she never commented on the fence panel.

When I investigate further, I discover that the wooden panel is still hanging from a single nail and, though it's difficult to be completely certain, it looks like someone has been getting in and out of the garden through the gap in the fence.

I add this to the list of the things I'm making in my head, which suggest that my mother is indeed losing her marbles.

I take a last glance around the garden and go back into the house, remembering to lock the back door and leave the key in the drawer.

On an impulse I decide to check out my old bedroom first. Nothing in it has changed, not even the cream coloured floor length curtains or the pale yellow-painted walls.

I remember it was a bright, sunny room, and I simply adored the little balcony, which my father had built for me. It overlooked my mother's pretty, well-tended garden. I used to pretend I was living in romantic Italy with the sounds of a piazza drifting into my room where I lay on my bed waiting for my lover to scale the wall of the house and rescue me. By the time I turned sixteen, I'd got fed up with waiting to be rescued and used to climb down the drainpipe to make my own getaway.

The room looks like it's recently been dusted and vacuumed so Maggie really has been attending to business as usual while my mother's away, although there's a lingering smell of Aggie's perfume. I don't know when Aggie died but I do know that it wasn't recently so I can't understand why the fresh, floral fragrance of *Je Reviens* is still evident.

The wardrobe is empty of clothes although there are still coat hangers swinging from the metal rail. I take a cursory look inside the chest of drawers standing next to it. It's also empty although the drawers are still lined with a decorative paper.

At the back of the top drawer, something draws my attention. At first glance it appears to be a piece of white cardboard tucked under the drawer liner, but when I pull it out, I can see that it's a photograph in a decorated mount. It immediately piques my interest because all the other formal family photographs have disappeared from the walls of the house, but when I take it over to the window to get a better look, I can see at once that it isn't a photograph of one of us: it's a photograph of Aggie.

I remember Aggie as a rather buttoned-up, monochrome individual and this was reflected in the clothes she chose and the way she wore her hair. The person in the photograph is neither of these things. In the photograph her hair has been styled and falls in soft waves around her face, and someone has carefully applied make-up to her pale complexion. But most surprising is the dress that she's wearing: it's red. No, not just red. It's an eye-catching shade of scarlet; a brilliant burst of flaming colour. This is Aggie as I've never, ever seen her before.

On closer examination, it's obvious that the photograph was taken shortly before she died because I can recognise that this woman is in her seventies – there are some things that even a really good foundation and flattering blusher can't conceal and I consider myself to be a bit of an expert in this area. I study the photograph more carefully and decide that a youthful transformation isn't what Aggie was trying to achieve.

I put the photograph back into the drawer for safekeeping.

I decide to do a circuit of the house after that, checking each room thoroughly even though I don't know what I'm expected to find. I have absolutely no idea how dementia affects people other than mental confusion and there's clearly no confusion in the way the house is being kept. It looks exactly as it did when I last visited.

After another half an hour of pointless wandering from room to room, I'm ready to give up. Whatever it is Richard thinks is here which points to the fact that our mother is checking out early in the mental health department – well, I just can't see it. Then I remember that I haven't found the missing photographs. They have to be here somewhere, I think to myself, unless our mother has consigned them to the rubbish bin.

The only place I haven't searched is the garage, and that's where I find them, wrapped in brown paper and shoved into a box. I use the word 'shoved' advisedly because I have professional expertise when it comes to packaging fragile objects and I can see that neither time nor care was taken to pack them in such a way that the glass wouldn't break, and the frames wouldn't warp. This was done in a hurry.

One by one I take out each photograph and lay it on the floor. The pictures tell the story of the life of the Oakley family, but they give me no pleasure because it was all a lie. Maybe that's why Mummy took them down, I suddenly think to myself.

In the bottom of the box is a pile of smaller frames and when I lift them out to check that the glass is still intact, I nearly drop them back into the box. They're pictures of our family on holiday. We're all there – me, Richard, Mummy and Daddy – and we're at the beach, walking through a field of flowers, eating ice creams in a café ... It looks like we're having a jolly time except that every face in every picture has been obscured, blacked out.

I don't know quite how to react to this. With shock and horror? Yes. Probably even anger and hurt. But my overwhelming emotion is blank incomprehension. Why would she do this?

I don't waste any more time. I quickly rewrap the photographs in the brown paper and put them back in the box. I need to leave here and get back to the comfort and sanity of my pretentious and overpriced hotel room. Richard can do his own sleuthing from now on, I think to myself.

Richard

Sarah Hollingsworth
Re: Your Mother
To: *Richard Oakley*

Dear Richard
It was a pleasant surprise to hear from you. I hope, you're well. I'm sorry to hear that your mother has been hospitalized - I didn't know. Please do keep in touch and let me know when she's been discharged so I can arrange for some flowers to be sent to her at home. I remember how much she loved her garden.

With kind regards
Sarah

Sarah's email pings into my laptop just as I'm preparing to leave the office. I read it through several times, but the content is clear and to the point: she doesn't know that my mother is in hospital.

I sit back down at my desk and anxiously try to work out what this means, although the meaning is obvious: someone has been calling the hospital pretending to be Sarah.

I know that the hospital has a very strict policy about disclosing information over the phone so the only thing this person would have been told is that my mother is recovering from the operation, but probably little else. Whoever it is knows *something* about our family, but not enough to realise that Sarah is now living in America. Even my mother's circle of friends and members of her own family have to know that much, so I can't understand why any one of them would masquerade as my ex-wife.

I'm still sitting at my desk and mulling over the email when Julia calls.

"I've just got back to the hotel," she says a little breathlessly.

"You sound like you ran," I tease her.

"It's called power-walking. I haven't had a chance to get to the gym since I arrived, and these days I do whatever I can to stay in shape. I'm not like you; I take after our mother. With my genetic heritage, if I didn't work out, I'd have the fifty-four-year old body of an Anglo-Saxon housewife."

"But you *are* fifty-four."

"Only on my driving licence. You have no idea how depressing it can be standing next to the other women at my gym. Middle-aged Singaporeans just don't get fat."

This is an absurd assertion, so I decide not to waste time and ask her, "Did you go to the house today?"

"I did. And I met that Maggie. She was very rude."

That doesn't sound like the Maggie I thought I knew, but Julia has a tendency to bring out the worst in people when she meets them for the first time. She's just a little bit too straight-talking and it's a character trait, which has developed year-on-year since she's lived the expat life in Singapore.

"What did you discover?" I ask her. "Other than that Maggie can be rude."

"Well, all the family photographs have been taken down and put in a box in the garage. You're never going to believe this, but Mummy's actually defaced all those holiday photographs she had in the bedroom."

I already know the photographs have been removed but I'm more than a little concerned to hear that something has happened to them. "What do you mean, 'defaced'?"

"Defaced as in every face has been blacked out."

"What about the other photographs?"

"Oh, those are fine, they've just been wrapped up in brown paper."

"Why would she do that?"

"I don't know. I had a look round the back garden, and I think she's been using my old escape route."

"I have no idea what you're talking about," I say.

"The fence panel: the one I took out, so I could get in and out of the house without Daddy seeing me. You must remember?"

I do remember. Julia was quite the rebel in her teenage years, but only as long as our father didn't find out. Our mother turned a blind eye to her late-night comings and goings, but I think it was because she knew what it was like to feel a lack of control over your life: my father held the purse strings and he wielded them like the sword of justice.

"This doesn't make sense," I say.

"I know and I take back everything I said yesterday about her brain still firing on all cylinders."

"You don't *know* that she's been climbing through the fence. I mean, why would she do that? It could just be kids from the estate getting into the garden and causing trouble. Maybe that's why she's stopped going out in the garden – because she's scared."

"That doesn't explain the photographs though does it?"

I can't disagree.

"Are you going to visit her?" I say. "I thought I'd pop in for half an hour."

"This evening? Good grief, no!" Julia exclaims. "I plan to have a nice long soak in the bath, room service, and then an early night. I don't usually suffer from jet lag, but I'm exhausted. I'll speak to you tomorrow." And with those parting words, she rings off.

I recount the conversation to Silvio when I arrive home, but he shakes his head in disbelief and tells me that there has to be a sensible explanation for all this madness.

I'm just not convinced. "What *sensible* person would scribble out the faces of their children on an old holiday photograph?"

"Perhaps Julia is mistaken," he says. "Perhaps it's just ... how do you say ... discolouration. Old photographs ... they don't stay nice." He wags his finger at me. "That's why your mamma took them off the wall." He wrinkles his nose and makes a face, which leaves me in no doubt that he's about to express his dislike or disapproval of something. "It's the weather in this country. So cold and damp. We have a big cellar at Bocca Felice. Can we use it to store food? No! In Italy, we keep everything nice. It's cool, it's dry. *Perfetto*! In England, *impossibile*!"

"But the photographs aren't being stored in a cellar."

He shrugs. "Garage, cellar ... it's all cold and damp."

"Okay, but that still doesn't explain why Mum took them down in the first place."

He bestows on me a look of benevolent pity, draws me into an affectionate embrace then kisses my cheek and says in a gentle voice, "I know your mamma, Ricardo. There will be a reason for this. Old people ... when they are ill ... they get confused sometimes, and *she* had a big operation; *she* had anaesthetic. When my uncle Beppe was in hospital, just like your mamma he had ... how do you say? ... *allucinazione.*"

"Hallucinations?"

"Yes. He saw the Holy Ghost!" He throws back his head and laughs. "He is accountant. He still *cooks the books* for his brother Emilio." He points a finger at my head. "The brain is still working fine." He kisses the other cheek. "Why don't you just ask her why she did it when you see her tonight?"

So, that's what I decide to do.

At the hospital, the long, green corridor is busy, peopled with anxious-looking visitors rather than members of staff at this time of day. The expression on their faces is mirrored on my own. I don't want to ask my mother why she's storing the family photographs in the garage, but I know it has to be done if I'm going to be persuaded that she isn't suffering from dementia.

She looks up from reading a magazine when I walk onto the ward. "Richard! I wasn't expecting you. This is a lovely surprise." Her eyes are bright and there's colour in her cheeks, and when I bend over the bed to kiss her, she hugs me tightly and there's warmth and strength in her embrace.

"Wow! I can see a real improvement in you," I say.

"Well, they insisted I get out of bed this morning and use the walking frame. I hate to admit it, but I actually feel much better for it. It's nice to get a bit of independence back even if it's just to take myself to the toilet."

"I can see you feel better."

"They also insisted I sit in the chair after lunch. They're very bossy."

"They're only doing their job."

She frowns suddenly. "Whose side are you on?"

The question surprises me. "I'm always on your side, Mum. Always have been, always will be."

The frown gradually fades, but I note that it isn't replaced with a smile. She says, "They keep talking about discharging me, but I'm not ready to go home yet, Richard."

"That's okay," I try to reassure her.

"It's not okay because I don't actually have a choice in the matter and neither do you. As soon as *they* decide I'm ready to go home, I'll be loaded into the back of an ambulance and that'll be it. It's all very well the Department of Health throwing around terms like 'bed-blocking', but they seem to forget they're talking about vulnerable, elderly people often going home to an empty house with no one to look after them."

Her face is now flushed with righteous indignation, but it only underlines the impression that, while she might still be physically recovering from the surgery, in all other respects she's back to her old, combative self.

"You won't be going home with no one to look after you," I say. "That's why Julia's here."

My mother looks aghast at me. "You can't be serious?"

"Why not?"

"I know your sister better."

"But she is here, Mum," I say.

"Where is she?"

"She's staying in a hotel in London at the moment. But that's because you're still in hospital. She went to the house this morning. We're going to get everything organised so you can go home and have someone staying with you until you're back on your feet properly."

"And this 'someone' is Julia?"

"Yes." I don't know why I choose this moment to ask, but I find myself saying, "When she was at the house, she noticed you'd taken down all the family photographs. We were wondering why you did that?" My mother freezes and the colour drains from her face. "You do remember doing it then?"

"Of course, I remember."

"So…?"

141

She looks away. She doesn't look embarrassed, and I think to myself, Silvio was right: she did have a reason for doing it.

Watching her compose her thoughts before she answers, I see her gentle, hazel eyes harden and I'm suddenly aware that whatever answer she's now preparing isn't necessarily the truth – after all, she spent years concealing from everyone around her the real nature of her relationship with my father.

At last she says, "After your father died, I left everything as it was, didn't change anything in the house really." A wry smile emerges. "I even left his study exactly as he left it and I can assure you that wasn't a tribute to his memory."

"I don't imagine it was," I say.

She goes on, "It was and still is our family home." I open my mouth to interrupt her and point out the error of this statement, but she lifts her hand to stop me. "Of course, I found out after he died that he'd left the house to this Miriam girl, but that doesn't change the fact that it's *still* my *home,* and still the place where you and Julia grew up. There are lots of lovely memories in the house and that's why I didn't want to change anything."

"So what? You changed your mind?"

"After Aggie died," she says carefully, "I realised we never know what's waiting around the corner for us. I could live to be a hundred years old, but I could also be struck down suddenly by some awful illness, so I thought: I'm going to make the house mine – while it is still mine."

"I assume an explanation for the photographs is going to be forthcoming at some point."

"Good grief! You sound just like your sister," she snaps.

"So?"

"I'm going to have the house redecorated. I took down the photographs, wrapped them in brown paper and put them in a box in the garage."

"But what about everything else?"

"Well, I'd only just made a start before this fall happened." Her eyes meet mine almost defiantly. I can see her thinking, 'Challenge me if you dare.'

At that moment a bell sounds somewhere on the ward, and everyone begins to move.

"I think it must be time for you to leave," she says guilelessly, and pats my hand.

"I think it is."

"You're such a dear, coming to visit me. I know you're busy with work." She hesitates. "I really do appreciate Julia coming back here. I know she's busy with work like you. It's just that ... I know Julia better than anyone. She only agreed to help when you told her about the will, didn't she?"

"I couldn't possibly say," I tell her, and I gather her into my arms once again.

A knowing smile creases the corners of her mouth. "Give my love to Silvio. Oh yes, and can you thank Sarah for sending in the magazines for me please? I can't concentrate for long, but they do help to pass the time."

Lenora

I've always been a good liar. I think it comes from being the youngest in a large family. You don't get much attention when there are siblings who have come before you and gobbled up your parents' patience and forbearance like greedy little ducklings. By the time I came along, my mother either ignored my bad behaviour with a wearied sigh or dragged me roughly to sit on the naughty step at the bottom of the stairs with dire warnings if I moved 'so much as an inch for the next thirty minutes'. In some ways, she was ahead of her time in her child-rearing methods – most of my friends got the belt or the slipper. I hated the inactivity and the sheer boredom of it, and in the winter, it was freezing cold in the unheated hallway. As a consequence, I learned from a young age to talk myself out of the naughty step punishment, usually by giving a less than honest account of what had happened.

I hated lying to Richard though, but I couldn't tell him the truth, or at least the part of the truth which explained *why* I'd removed the family photographs from the walls of our home – I'm certain that he wouldn't have believed me anyway.

It started with the wedding photograph on George's desk in the study. I rarely went into the room, but I'd noticed that the door, which was usually kept shut, was open again and again. At first, I thought there must be something wrong with the catch and when I opened the door wide enough to take a proper look at it, I noticed that the photograph was lying face down. I assumed that Maggie had cleaned the room and forgot to put the photograph back as it should be and of course I set it straight. Two days later, I found the wedding photograph lying face down on the desk and Richard's graduation photograph on the floor. The glass in the frame was unbroken and the hook on the wall still fixed firmly into the plaster.

For the next few weeks, framed photographs of our family found their way onto the floor, turned upside down and once or twice hidden amongst rubbish in a bin. Of course, by that point I was already afraid that Aggie had come back to haunt me. When I discovered my favourite holiday photographs with the faces of the children blacked out like something in a horror movie, I made the painful decision to remove all of them to the garage for safekeeping.

I decided to talk things over with our local vicar, Edward Feering, after Sunday Service. I couldn't think what else to do. We were standing just inside the dark porch because it was raining, so I couldn't clearly see the expression on his face when I asked him if he believed in ghosts, but what followed was a torturous conversation.

"Do I believe in ghosts?"

"Yes. Do you think it's possible to be haunted?" I asked him.

He gave me one of his infuriating, little, self-conscious chuckles. "Obviously I believe in the Holy Ghost." I think I must have given him one my slightly scornful looks in return because he quickly went on, "But as for visual manifestations of the dearly departed ... well, the bible's pretty clear on the matter."

"What does it say?"

"There are various passages, but the overall view is that when people die, they go to heaven ... or hell, I suppose."

"So, what are ghosts?"

"Hard to say really ... never seen one myself ... and it depends who you talk to, at least within the church community."

This wasn't at all helpful.

"I'm a bit confused here, Reverend Feering," I told him. "Are you saying that ghosts categorically do not exist?"

He shrugged nonchalantly. "Like I said, it depends who you talk to, and I've talked to people inside and outside of the church, who are absolutely convinced they've experienced some kind of haunting activity." He threw up his hands in a gesture of baffled inconclusion. "Is it an evil spirit? Is it a memory of someone somehow captured within a landscape – you know, the old stone tapes thing?"

I didn't know.

He put his arm around my shoulder and drew me out of the porch and into the rain. "I really don't know where you're going with this,

Mrs Oakley, but if you're experiencing things that you can't explain then you're probably better off speaking to your GP. I know it's hard to hear, but maybe you're becoming a bit confused ... you know, memory playing up ... think you've put your glasses down in one room and find them somewhere else ... catch a glimpse of someone you know and then realise that it's somebody else." He gave an awkward laugh. "It happens to all of us in the end."

I wanted to hit him over the head with my umbrella.

He shuffled back into the warmth and solace of his lovely church, and I was forced to return to my haunted house with my question unanswered.

Julia

I was dragged into consciousness this morning by the sound of the phone ringing loudly on the other side of the room. In my dream state, I was in the throes of an almighty argument with Jian. We were standing in his apartment – well, he was standing. I was crouched behind the sofa because he was hurling whiskey glasses at the wall behind my head. I could hear someone ringing the doorbell and I knew (because you *can* know when you're dreaming) that Colin was on the other side of the door. The ringing went on and on and then my brain finally worked out that the sound was real and wasn't part of my dream.

I flung back the cover and staggered across the room to the phone.

"Hallo?"

"Mrs Crane?"

"This is Julia Crane," I croaked.

"I have a call for you. Hold the line and I'll put it through."

I lowered myself onto a chair and waited. It seemed to take forever but it was probably no more than a matter of seconds before a different voice repeated the question. "Yes, yes, this Julia Crane," I said irritably.

"I'm sorry, have I woken you, Julia?"

The voice was familiar, but I couldn't place it. "Okay, you're going to have to tell me who you are," I said. "I'm afraid my brain isn't yet working on Greenwich Mean Time."

"It's Jason. Jason from Castle Glass. I called your office and the girl there – I think she said her name was Connie – she told me you were in London. I tried calling your mobile, but you weren't answering."

"Jason? Where are you?"

"I'm in Norwich but I thought it would be nice to meet up. I don't think Dad and I have seen you for about four years."

Phillip Glass and his son, Jason, had been supplying me with antique glassware for nearly twenty years. Phillip had started the business many years before that. He told the same anecdote over and over again: that when he was first looking for premises, he'd chanced upon an empty building with space for a showroom and a workshop in Castle Street – a stone's throw from Norwich Castle. He said he knew it was an omen of good things to come. A Castle within a castle. I liked him a lot and we'd maintained a friendly business relationship for two decades although in recent years it was Jason who called me when they had something come in that they thought I might like.

Jason went on. "We've just had a real find at a small local auction: Victorian cranberry glass. Decorative mostly. Dozens of pieces, though. All in mint condition."

"I'm not actually here on business," I told him.

"That's fine. We could still meet up if you're free?"

I arranged to call him in a few days' time when I had a better idea what I was going to be doing. "If I have time, I'll come up to Norwich on the train. The cranberry glass is still really popular although more and more people are drinking wine these days and looking for nineteenth century cut glass. Singaporeans have money and know how to spend it."

"Well, that's good for both of us. I'll wait to hear from you," he said.

As soon as I put down the phone, I knew I was going to have to call Connie, and now that I'm showered and dressed and have a healthy breakfast inside me, I'm ready to give her a piece of my mind.

"Glück Glass. How can I help you?" Connie's voice simpers down the line.

"You can help me by not giving out personal information about my travel plans," I bark back at her. "I've just had Jason Glass call me at the hotel. Who else have you told where I'm staying?"

"Ohh … Mrs Crane … so sorry … Mr Crane said, go ahead."

"Mr Crane? My husband? He was at the gallery?"

"Yesterday. But it's okay, he just wanted to use the computer in the office."

Just use the computer. This doesn't sound good. In fact, this sounds absolutely terrible. I do a quick mental recce of the documents, which might be lying on my desk. I can't think of anything incriminating, but I have a secret internet bank account. If Colin had the password, he could look at my statements, and that wouldn't be good. I know I haven't written it down anywhere, but it wouldn't take much imagination to crack the code.

I try to sound casual when I ask Connie, "Did he say what he wanted? Was he looking for something specific?"

"He closed the door."

My heart skips a beat. Now I know I'm in trouble. Of course, I'm angry – how dare he shut himself in my private office and look at my computer – but I'm also a little bit scared, and it isn't because I think he's going to find anything I don't want him to see. It's because he *thinks* he's going to find something that will confirm what he fears – that I'm having an affair. If he's actively looking for evidence, then how long will it be before he pays someone to look for things, he can't access himself? It won't take long for the right person to discover what I've been hiding for eight years.

I know I have to tell him myself, but I want it to be on my terms. I want to choose the place and the time. I don't want him ferreting around my office for clues and confirmations, so drastic measures are going to have to be employed.

"Listen to me very carefully," I tell Connie. "I want you right now … as soon as you put down the phone … as soon as the shop is empty of customers … I want you to turn off all the lights in the gallery, pull down the shutters and put the 'Closed' sign in the window."

"You … you want me … you want me to … to lock myself in here, Mrs Crane?" she splutters.

"Don't be stupid. Of course not!" I scold her. "I want you to close the gallery to the public, but you can stay in the office. There are still orders to make up and phone calls to answer. Just make sure you keep the door locked. And don't go to the door if anyone knocks," I add as an afterthought.

"What about Aysha?" she asks in a trembling voice.

"Call Aysha and tell her she doesn't need to come in till I get back."

I can hear her breathing heavily at the other end of the line, probably remembering the day she came back from lunch and heard me howling like a lovelorn lunatic. At last she says, "You okay Mrs Crane?"

I have to close my eyes, hold my breath and count to ten before I can find a calm, quiet voice to answer her. "I'm fine, Connie. Just do what I said."

Richard

Henry Silver, my father's solicitor, is prompt in getting back to me: a message has been left on my phone to call his office at my earliest convenience. When I ring back, his secretary tells me that he's free this afternoon and would be happy to meet Julia and me whenever it suits us.

Julia is shopping in Regent Street when I call her.

"Can you get to Shenfield by three o'clock?" I ask her. "It's a short walk to Silver's office from the station."

I press the phone close to my ear to hear her reply because the background noise of traffic muffles her voice. I *think* she says 'okay', but I *know* she sounds cross, which I find extremely annoying because it was Julia who wanted this meeting. I'm happy to let this half-sister have whatever is legally if not rightfully hers.

I have to spend the remainder of the morning fielding questions from long-suffering contractors about the progress not yet being made at 'Hotel Albatross'. Yes, the building work finally began this week, but no we won't need plumbers or plasterers, electricians or painters and decorators until we actually have a pile of bricks that resembles a hotel. Everyone is unhappy except the client although she's now dithering over colour schemes and flooring materials. It's at times like this that I wish I were a pizza chef and not an architectural project manager.

Thankfully I manage to get away from the office in good time to drive to Shenfield and meet Julia: she's travelled by train out of Liverpool Street station, so we don't actually meet up until she walks through the barrier. She has an anxious look about her, but she greets me in her usual perfunctory way. "I hope it isn't far," she says waspishly. "I don't mind walking, but I only bought these boots this morning and they're a tad too tight. Couldn't you just drive us?"

"My car's parked behind the station already and it's literally five minutes from here, Julia," I tell her.

"Oh, alright then," she says. She quickly moves the conversation onto Henry Silver. "He must be at least as old Daddy would have been if he hadn't … you know … In Singapore, most solicitors specialise. How can we be sure he knows what he's talking about?"

"For goodness sake, Julia! You haven't even met him and already you're questioning his competence.

"Have you?" she lobs back at me.

"No, but I'm going to assume that Dad appointed him as his solicitor because he trusted him."

In fact, I'm as certain as I possibly can be that our father wouldn't have appointed anyone to represent his interests either ante or post mortem unless he was completely convinced that he'd do the job with the same attention to detail that my father would have given it, and my father gave his last will and testament the most careful consideration before he signed it. The old bastard, I think to myself angrily, but I keep this thought to myself – Julia doesn't need to be antagonised.

We find the offices of Silver, Reid and Bateman in a brightly lit, modern building. The reception area is spacious and uncluttered, tastefully decorated with contemporary furniture and a large, modernist-style canvas on each white painted wall. Henry Silver and his colleagues appear to be doing well for themselves and are not the stuffy, old-fashioned figures Julia probably imagined.

The receptionist is a young woman and takes her job very seriously. She writes down our names on a notepad, asks us when we made the appointment and double-checks the schedule on her computer screen, all with an unsmiling expression, before she finally rings through to Henry Silver's secretary. I can see Julia becoming irritated by the unnecessary officiousness of the situation, so I tell her to sit down and rest her aching feet. She clearly doesn't appreciate the reference to her new boots and tosses me a withering glance over her shoulder as she takes a seat, but she doesn't argue.

We're kept waiting no more than five minutes before Henry Silver strides into reception with his hand already outstretched to greet us. "Mr Oakley … Mrs Crane … It's a pleasure to meet you. Come through to my office."

Henry Silver clearly wasn't one of my father's contemporaries when he was appointed as the family solicitor because he doesn't look a day over fifty. He looks fit and tanned in the way of all people who enjoy outdoor sports, so I'm guessing they met at the country club where our father was a long-standing member.

"Please sit down. Can I get you tea, coffee?" he offers in a friendly fashion.

I decline, but Julia says she would like tea with lemon.

"How exactly can I help you?" he asks.

Julia jumps straight to the point. "It's about our father's will."

"Yes … I understand you have some questions regarding the house. I have to tell you straight away," he quickly continues, "your father was very specific about the provisions of the will. Of course, he had no idea his own life would be cut short in the dreadful way that it was, but he very much wanted your mother to be able to live out *her* life in the family home, regardless of anything else."

"Are you referring to the fact that he left the property to this daughter, Miriam?" I ask.

"Well, yes." He hesitates. "I take it you don't know her?"

"We had no idea she even existed!" Julia bursts out indignantly.

"*You* didn't know," I correct her. "Mum obviously found out when the will was read."

Julia rounds on me. "That's what I don't understand. Why didn't she contest it?"

I note that Henry Silver is watching this exchange with sympathetic interest and it makes me warm to him. I say to Julia, "It doesn't matter now, does it. It's too late. We have to just accept it."

Julia swings her attention back to Henry Silver. "Is too late?"

All this while he's been sitting in his chair looking relaxed and unruffled, but he quietly picks up a pen and begins to tap it on the desk. It's the only visible sign of agitation, but I think he's suddenly realised that my sister isn't going to 'just accept it'. He says in a deliberately neutral-sounding voice, "Under the Inheritance Act of 1975, you have six months from the date of the grant of probate to contest the will and, under certain circumstances, a further four months…"

"But I didn't know!" Julia shrills at him. "I would have contested the will if I'd known about it."

"I do understand, Mrs Crane, but the time restriction is strict."

"There must be a way," Julia insists angrily.

"The only way you can contest the will is if it's invalid and I really don't think…"

Julia abruptly leans forward in her chair and fixes Henry Silver with an unwavering glare. "It has to be invalid. He must have been pressured by this girl's mother to cut us out."

I place a cautioning hand on Julia's arm. "You can't possibly know that," I say, but she isn't listening to me.

She says to Henry Silver, "If the will's invalid, then we can contest it, yes?"

"You could."

"On what basis would it be invalid?"

"Well, if wasn't executed properly, but I can assure you that it was."

"What else would invalidate it?" Julia demands to know.

He begins to list the reasons. "If your father lacked the mental capacity to make a will, which in my opinion he did not. (Though I suppose you could check with his doctor at the time.) If he lacked knowledge of the content of the will – obviously he didn't because he discussed it with me in great detail. If the will was fraudulent or forged – again, it wasn't, and I know that because I sat here with him in this office, drafted it together with him, was present when it was witnessed, and it's been kept here ever since. The only way you could contest the will, in my opinion, is if you thought he was under undue influence and I don't know how you'd prove that now."

"Undue influence from the girl's mother. That's it!" Julia cries jubilantly. Her face is flushed with the promise of succeeding in getting her hands on her inheritance, where only a moment ago it looked as though all was still lost.

I don't want to pour cold water on this happy possibility, but it seems to me that someone needs to state the obvious. "This is madness, Julia. We don't know where the woman is, and in any case the daughter's an adult now. She must be … what … twenty-five years old? You can contest the will, but she can also fight to keep what's hers."

"Your brother's right, Mrs Crane. You could spend an awful lot of money pursuing this and still end up with nothing."

Julia's eyes flash defiance. "I already have nothing."

Henry Silver flicks through the file in front of him. When he looks up, I can see his reluctance to share the information he's just confirmed is in his possession, but I suppose he feels he has to pass it on. He says, "I have an address for her mother in a place called Urk. Her name's Lena Bartok, in case you didn't know. Obviously, she might not be living there anymore, but we could try to trace her if she's not."

"Urk." Julia repeats after him.

"It's in The Netherlands. That's where she was when your father's accident..." He stops and looks at me. "I do understand why you feel aggrieved, but this is what your father wanted." He writes down two addresses on a piece of paper and hands it to Julia. "That's where they were living, Miriam and her mother, when they lived here with your father and that's the address her mother gave me to contact her after your father died."

Julia takes the paper from him, puts it into her purse and immediately rises to her feet. "I'm sure I'll be speaking to you again soon, Mr Silver," she says briskly but a tremor in her voice betrays her true emotions. She swiftly moves towards the door. "Are you coming, Richard?"

"I'll see you outside," I say.

Henry Silver looks relieved when Julia leaves the room. "I wish I could be more helpful," he says in a low voice, "but your father was quite insistent."

"He didn't mention us at all?" I ask.

"He did – briefly. I didn't want to say in front of your sister." He takes a deep breath and grimaces. "He said that you and your sister had already had the best of him and didn't need his money, and that your mother would only have what she deserved."

I swallow down my anger. "That sounds about right." I get to my feet and then remember why *I* wanted to speak to him. "There's one other thing. There's a possibility that my mother won't be able to stay on in the house – she has some problems with her health. I just wondered, if she'd be allowed to rent it out? It was all very well leaving her a house to live in for the rest of her natural life," I say bitterly, "but he didn't leave her the means to do it. If she has to move somewhere else, then we have to find a way to fund it."

155

It's obvious from the pained expression on his face that he knows the answer. He says, "Your father set up a trust, and your mother was made a life-tenant. If she doesn't want to live in the house, she can rent it out, but my concern is that your sister seems intent on contesting the will. She might even succeed in getting it overturned, however, if she did succeed, Miriam would still be a beneficiary. Nothing's going to change that, in my opinion. My advice would be to do nothing with the house until the situation with the will has been resolved one way or the other."

I nod my assent. I know Julia and she won't accept what's happened until she's explored every avenue to change it.

As I make to leave, he says, "Have you thought about talking to Miriam face to face? I don't know if it would help the situation, but it might be worth it. Especially if Mrs Crane succeeds in her challenge," he adds. "It would help everyone if you were at least on speaking terms."

"I wouldn't know what to say to her," I tell him.

"Well, think about it," he says. "She *is* your sister."

Lenora

Frankie the physiotherapist has returned today to plague me with polite requests to get out of bed and practise walking with the frame he left behind yesterday.

"I have a challenge for you, Lenora," he says as he adjusts the position of my hands on the top of the frame. "I want you to walk to the end of the ward and back again."

"What happens if I fall over?"

"You're not going to fall over. Firstly, you have this fabulous walking frame to hold on to, and secondly, my job is to make sure that you don't fall."

"What happens if I feel dizzy?"

"Do you feel dizzy?"

"Not yet."

"Well, if you feel dizzy at any point between here and the end of the ward, tell me and I'll fetch a chair for you."

We slowly perambulate the length of the corridor and back again. Frankie tells me I'm doing really well – he even manages to say it without sounding patronising.

I feel feeble and weak and I don't like it. Even when George was being particularly difficult and I knew I had to tread a fine line between standing up for myself and not antagonising him, I never felt completely powerless, but the situation at home and now this physical infirmity has left me with an overwhelming sense of being vulnerable and unprotected and it scares me. How can I go back there and feel safe?

Frankie shows me again how to move from the chair to the frame and he makes me repeat the movement while he watches. He says, "As long as you don't feel dizzy, you can practise walking with the frame; go up and down the corridor like we've just done this morning. Nice and slow and keep your head up – look where you're going."

"Where else would I be looking?"

"You'd be surprised how easy it is to get distracted when it's busy on the ward. One more day and then we can tackle the stairs."

"Super," I say, and roll my eyes.

He laughs. "That's the spirit, Lenora. We'll soon have you on your way out of here."

That isn't what I wanted to hear, but I have to accept that it's the inevitable conclusion of my stay in hospital.

I doze in the chair for a little while and try not to think about returning to Hillcrest, then the cleaner appears. I point out the cobweb to her and she thanks me, but she doesn't look especially grateful for my contribution to her list of things that need to be dusted and wiped down. She mumbles something about having to get a ladder and goes away again. I haven't seen a single speck of dust since I've been here so I can only conclude that her lack of enthusiasm isn't reflected in her workmanship.

Maggie is an excellent cleaner. I remember the day quite clearly when I told her, I didn't want her to clean Julia's bedroom anymore. The expression on her face was a mixture of confusion and disappointment. I thought she'd be glad to have one less room to keep clear of dust, but she took some persuading that I was serious.

"It's no trouble, Mrs Oakley. It takes five minutes to put the vacuum cleaner round and I only dust every few weeks because the room is not used anymore."

"That's why you don't need to clean it," I said.

"What about the other bedrooms that aren't used anymore?"

"I do use them," I told her. "I like Richard's room to be kept nice in case he stays over and I use the box room to store things."

"But it seems such a shame," she said. She very gently put her hand over mine. "It isn't because of your friend, Agnes, is it?"

I snatched my hand away. Having Aggie's name mentioned was the last thing I needed.

Her hand flew to her chest in an unguarded expression of both surprise and heartfelt apology. "I'm so sorry, Mrs Oakley. I didn't mean to upset you."

"It's fine, Maggie. Honestly."

"Why don't I just give the room a quick clean after I've done the other rooms upstairs," she persisted.

"No!" When I saw the care and concern in her pretty, blue eyes – ironically so much like Aggie's – I was certain she must be thinking, that I was finally overcome by grief and loss.

Nothing could have been further from the truth, but I couldn't explain, for how could I have told her, 'You can't clean the room, because Aggie left a message for me written in the dust on the mirror.'

Je Reviens! I couldn't believe my eyes but there it was, plainly written across the mirror in large letters. I remember I ran into the en suite bathroom and grabbed a face towel. My hands were shaking when I went back into the bedroom, I could actually see my face reflected in the spaces where the dust had been wiped away and it was as white as the proverbial sheet. I stretched out my arm and swiped at its surface. Microparticles of dust were released into the air along with the letters spelling out my nightmare.

I kept the mirror free of dust for weeks and weeks then one day I walked into the room with the duster in my hand and some unseen hand had written those two death-defying words across the mirror in bright, red lipstick. Aggie's lipstick. It was the lipstick we'd chosen together; the lipstick, which perfectly matched Aggie's red dress.

Something inside me broke.

I turned around and walked straight back out. The very next day a locksmith came and while he was fixing the door, I cleaned the mirror. He put the key into my hand and I never went back in there again.

Julia

Richard and I walk back to the station in silence. I know he's cross with me, but I'm not going to simply walk away without at least trying to do something about the will. He leaves me sitting on a bench while he fetches the car. I offered to walk to the car park, but he reminded me that my boots are too tight, and my feet hurt, which I'd forgotten in the throes of my angry indignation at Henry Silver and his 'this is what your father wanted' speech.

Richard has always been the consummate caring big brother. He's a man, who expresses his love and devotion, not in grand gestures, but in small acts of kindness. I realise much too late that I should have looked for a husband like my brother and not like my father – though perhaps not exactly like my brother in view of his *volte face* over his sexuality.

As soon as I get into the car he says, "I'm going to show you something."

"What is it?"

"I'll explain when we get there."

"Explain to me now."

"No."

"Why are you going all mysterious on me?"

"Because I need to think about what I'm going to say to you when you find out what it is. I don't want you blowing up, and I especially don't want you to interrogate Mum when you see her."

"So, it's not something nice then?"

"I didn't say that."

"So it is. Is it something for me? Something I'm going to like?"

"Those kinds of tactics might have worked in the past, Julia," he says, staring doggedly at the road ahead, "but I'm immune to them now."

"What tactics?" I exclaim and pretend to sound like I've been unjustly admonished, but I know exactly what he's talking about – though persistence in the face of refusal has always worked well for me before this.

"Just wait and see," he says and refuses to be drawn into further conversation.

We leave Shenfield behind us and are soon snaking our way along narrow, country lanes. I haven't driven around the area since before I married Colin so I quickly lose track of where we might be heading, but it isn't too long before Richard pulls up in front of a very high hedge. I can't see the property it conceals but the road looks familiar.

"Recognise it?" Richard asks.

"Not really."

He inches the car forward so that it sits in front of the padlocked gates. "This is Tyne Lodge."

Now I remember. "It's Aggie's bungalow. Why are we here?"

Richard gazes out of the window and says in a quiet voice, "It belongs to Mum."

Well, that's a surprise. "Since when?" Richard's head whips round and he stares into my eyes with a look of wide-eyed incredulity. This response to my question bears a theatricality of gesture that confounds me until I suddenly realise what I've said. "Oh, yes of course, she died, didn't she?"

"About two years ago."

As this latest piece of new information sinks in, I feel anger inside me begin to build. When I open my mouth to express my indignation at being excluded yet again from our mother's circle of trust, the anger quickly becomes outrage. "This is too much!" I shout at him. "What else are you hiding from me?"

Richard remains calm as always. "I only recently found out myself and, before you ask, I don't know why she didn't tell us about it."

"I can't believe this! You make me fly back here because she can't afford to pay someone to look after her and all the while she's sitting on a goldmine."

"It's hardly a goldmine, Julia," he protests.

"It's as good as money in the bank!"

Richard continues to stay calm in the face of my fury, which infuriates me even further. I throw open the door of the car and scramble out as quickly as I can because I want to hit him with my handbag. I march over to the padlocked gates and realise at once that I'm going to have to climb over them if I want to get into the garden. I can feel Richard's eyes on me. I'm wearing a new and very expensive pair of designer trousers, and I hesitate for a moment. I know he's expecting me to fall at this first hurdle, so I force myself to forget about the cost and I clamber over.

The first thing I notice is that this garden is neat and tidy; the grass mowed short and the narrow borders filled prettily with late-flowering shrubs. It instantly halts me in my tracks. I think to myself, what on earth is going on here? Why does Aggie's bungalow get the good garden treatment and not Hillcrest?

I hear first one car door and then the other slam shut. Richard has decided to follow me. He does a kind of scissor stride, hops over the gate and comes to stand next to me. He puts a consoling arm around my shoulder and gives me a brief hug.

"Circle of trust," he says. "I like that one."

My anger melts away and I feel myself smile. "I think it's from a film – 'Meet the Fuckers'."

"I think it was 'Fockers'," he corrects me.

"Really?"

"Definitely." He gives my shoulders another affectionate squeeze. "I can't get my head round it either. I mean … I understand why she doesn't want to live here."

"It looks nice enough to me," I say. "Who's taking care of the garden?"

"Ahhh…that would be the neighbours. And that might also be the problem with it – although in fairness, I only met the husband."

"They can't be that bad."

"Well, *he* was. Threatened me with a shovel. And he insisted that Mum had offered him first refusal if she decided to sell."

"Why hasn't she sold it if she doesn't want to live here?"

"That's the million-dollar question. Why indeed."

He breaks away from me and begins to circle the house, inspecting the window frames and checking over the roof tiles with an expert eye. "It all looks in pretty good condition still," he says. "I'm sure she could get a good price for it. Let's go around the back. There's a garage at the bottom of the garden. Do you remember if Aggie had a car?"

"I can't remember if she had a car of her own, but I know she could drive," I say. "When I was here four years ago and we all met up at my hotel, I remember Mum telling us that she'd twisted her ankle walking into the station. You asked her why she didn't get a taxi and she said Aggie had given her a lift to the station, but she'd tripped over the kerb getting out of the car. She made a big fuss about it. I think it was because I wouldn't visit her at home. She seemed to forget that I was here on business. I had to go up to Norwich by train the next day to see my supplier, Castle Glass, and she said Shenfield was en route and why couldn't I stay over at Hillcrest for a change."

Richard listens patiently to this lengthy explanation, but as soon as I finish speaking, he moves away from me. He says, "I'm going to take a look."

I trundle after him across the wet grass. The pale tan leather of my new boots darkens ominously as water soaks into them. I don't think they were made for country walks.

I catch up with him at the bottom of the garden. He's inspecting the padlock on the garage door. "Logic dictates there has to be something of value in here, otherwise why keep it locked?"

I push my face close to the small window next to the door and try to see inside. "I'm sure there's something quite large in there, but it's covered up with a tarpaulin."

"Could it be a car?" Richard asks.

"It could be, but then it could be anything – a stuffed elephant, a small biplane..."

Richard nods and smiles at my attempt at humour. "The funny thing is, the neighbour said he's got a key to the house and a key for the padlock on the front gates, but he doesn't have a key for this. He indicates the padlock holding the garage doors together. "She has to be storing something in here, doesn't she?"

"The mystery deepens," I tell him.

"Shall we just ask her?" he says.

"Does she know that you know about the bungalow?"

He shakes his head. "I've been waiting for the right moment to broach the subject. I don't want to upset her unnecessarily. She obviously doesn't want us to know about it, but I can't think why."

"Well, you'd better be the one to ask her. If I do it, apparently she'll feel like she's being interrogated."

He offers me a rueful smile. "You know what I mean."

"Well, I won't be worrying whether or not I upset her," I say. "She should have told us, Richard, then we wouldn't have spent the last two weeks fretting about her finances."

"We'll ask her tonight."

"*You* can ask her tonight," I say swiftly. "I'm going back to the hotel. I have plans for this evening."

Richard insists on driving back to the station via Hillcrest. He says he wants to check the place over again.

"Why bother?" I ask. "I didn't notice anything of the ordinary when I was there, and that Maggie would have said something, surely?"

"Maybe. Maybe not. Every time I've met her there, I've had the feeling that she's hiding something from me."

"That smacks of paranoia," I tease him, but he responds with an uncertain smile. "You can't be serious? What could she possibly have to hide from you?"

"Well, I think she knows a lot more than she's letting on about Mum's mental state, for a start."

"So is the jury still out on whether or not she has dementia then?"

"I think so. Silvio said there are tests they can do, so I'm going to ask the hospital before we agree a date for her to come home."

"Surely that won't be yet?" I say, remembering how weak and vulnerable she'd looked. "How's she going to look after herself properly?"

Richard snorts his displeasure, though I'm not sure if it's aimed at me because I haven't immediately voiced my thrilled anticipation at the prospect of being her carer for the next however many weeks, or whether his ire is directed at the NHS, who seem intent on getting rid of her at the earliest opportunity. Eventually he says, "As soon as she can manage to walk up and down the stairs, she'll be leaving hospital." He pauses. "And as soon as she leaves hospital, you're going to have to move back home." He glances round at me then returns his attention to the road. "I know you don't want to, Julia, but it's a question of needs must."

I know he's right, but I *don't* want to do it, so I don't reply.

At Hillcrest, the weeds are manifestly multiplying day by day. A keen gardener would probably see the multiplication of weeds as a sign that the soil is fertile and the sad, shrivelled up leaves a reminder that life is a circle. I haven't a poetic bone in my body and can only see a whole lot of work that needs to be carried by a willing pair of gardening hands – and the sooner the better. I remark on this to Richard as we walk into the house.

"Why don't I just add it to the list of things to ask Mum," he says with a sardonic twinkle in his eye.

The inside of the house presents a welcoming contrast to the garden outside: it still looks and smells clean and fresh. Maggie might be deceitful and disrespectful towards authority but she's a damn fine cleaner.

"Show me the fence panel," Richard says so we trudge outside and I show him. He prods the soft soil with the toe of his shoe. "Those look like footprints. Someone's definitely been getting into the garden through here, but I don't think it's Mum."

"Perhaps you're right then. Perhaps it's kids from the estate."

"I'll soon put a stop to that," he says manfully, and he goes back into the house and returns with a handful of nails and a hammer.

As I stand by and watch him drive the nails into place, I feel a pang of remorse and it's for two entirely different reasons. I feel sad because the loose fence panel represented a time in my life when I actually felt free to do what I wanted, and the future seemed full of bright promise. Yet I'm also stung by the thought that some horrible little oik might have driven my mother out of her beloved garden and kept her imprisoned in the house. I'm musing on these two thoughts when I realise that Richard is staring up at the house and his face has dramatically paled.

"Are you okay?"

"I thought I saw someone at your bedroom window."

"Perhaps Maggie…"

"No, no … it was a woman … a woman in a red dress."

"I found a photograph of Aggie in one of the drawers in my bedroom. She was wearing a red dress."

"That isn't funny, Julia," he says.

"I wasn't joking. Come on," I say, "I'll show you."

Richard

Julia is quick to go back inside the house. I can tell by the disgruntled expression on her face and the worried glances she keeps giving her feet that the new boots haven't held up well to wandering around gardens in the middle of a typically cold and damp British autumn.

My own shoes are now smeared with mud and I don't want to walk it over the recently cleaned kitchen floor, but that concerns me less than the thought that there might be an intruder in the house. Nevertheless, I suggest we take off our footwear before we investigate, and Julia agrees at once.

We quietly make our way upstairs. I'm listening hard for anything out of the ordinary, but Julia seems more concerned about laddering her tights.

The door to the bedroom is closed. I cautiously put my hand over the knob – my hand is actually shaking slightly as I apply pressure to turn it. Of course, the room is empty, though the curtains have been drawn back.

"No ghost then," Julia says and pokes me in the ribs. She elbows me out of the way, pulls open a drawer and takes out a photograph then hands it to me and excuses herself to go to the bathroom.

It's definitely a photograph of a woman in a red dress though I wouldn't have immediately guessed it was Aggie if Julia hadn't told me. Aggie always wore her long grey hair tied up in a bun on the back of her head and her dress sense was funereal. This woman has shoulder length brown hair and she's wearing … well, she's wearing a scarlet cocktail dress. Julia's right, it is Aggie and not a young Aggie.

When Julia comes back into the room, I hand the photograph to her. "What the hell was that all about?" I ask her, pointing at the picture.

She shrugs. "It's called a makeover."

"Yes, but why? She must be ... I don't know ... at least seventy in that photograph. Isn't she a bit old for that sort of thing?"

Julia immediately bristles at this suggestion. "So what? Age is just a number. I think she looks great and I admire her for doing it."

"Yes, but why?" I say again. "She always had grey hair and always dressed like she was in mourning, but she looks a different person altogether in this photograph."

"Maybe that's the point," Julia says with an enigmatic smile.

"Well, I don't understand."

"Well, I liked her." She props the photograph up against a small glass vase on top of the dressing-table. "She always wore the same perfume, which I thought was very chic, and she was always polite and well-mannered, even when Daddy was being obnoxious. She was a good friend."

"I bet you're still not going to sleep in here though, are you?"

"God, no!" As we move to leave, she asks, "So what do you think you saw at the window then?"

"Probably just a trick of the light," I say, but I'm remembering the day I worked in the kitchen and heard soft, shuffling sounds from this room upstairs. I don't usually allow my imagination to rule my head, but there's something here I find disquieting and I hustle Julia out of the room, telling her that I need to get going if I'm going to avoid the traffic.

I drive Julia to the station, and she promises me that she *will* stay at Hillcrest as soon as our mother has been discharged from hospital, but "not a moment before".

The traffic isn't as bad as I'd anticipated so I decide to go straight to the hospital because Silvio is working this evening. A valued customer has booked the whole restaurant for a family party, so he feels obliged to be on hand. These kinds of occasions can often run on late into the night so I'm not expecting him to come home till tomorrow morning.

My mother isn't in her bed when I arrive on the ward or sitting in the chair next to the bed, but I sit down as the sign on the toilet indicates that it's engaged. However, when the door opens, it isn't my mother shuffling behind a walking frame, but another very elderly woman in a hospital gown.

"Uhhh … do you know where my mother is?" I ask her.

The woman peers at me short-sightedly. She says, "Is that you, Arthur? Why are you sitting over there?"

I get to my feet and introduce myself properly.

"Oh, you're Lenora's Richard, are you? Well, she's probably gone walkabout. She's a dab hand with that frame now. I'm still struggling."

"But where can she have gone?"

"Wherever she likes, dear. We're not prisoners, you know." She shakes her head at me. Clearly, I'm an imbecile.

I start back down the corridor that leads to the exit doors and spot my mother coming out of a side room accompanied by Nurse Kelly. I hear her say, "There's your son come to visit you, Lenora."

My mother smiles and waves. She's walking well if a little unsteadily, even though she's holding onto the metal frame with both hands. We meet in the middle of the corridor and she reaches up and brushes my cheek with her parched lips. "Richard, how lovely to see you! I really didn't expect you to come in this evening."

"I thought I'd surprise you," I say. "You look like you're making good progress with the walking frame. I'm impressed."

"I'm still a bit wobbly on my feet, but the new hip is bearing up well. The physio chap says he's going to have me walking up and down the stairs on Thursday, but I think I need a bit more practice walking on the flat first."

I accompany her back to her bed and watch with bated breath as she carefully transfers from standing with the frame to sitting on the edge of the mattress.

"This is the tricky bit," she says, but she manages to get into bed and shuffles her bottom till she's sitting upright against the pillows though the effort of lifting herself into position leaves her breathing heavily. "Phew! I can't believe how unfit I've become. Goodness knows how I'm going to get up and down the stairs when I get home."

"They won't let you home until they're satisfied you can do it safely," I tell her. "In any case Julia's going to stay with you."

My mother looks surprised. "Is she still here?" She gazes up at me with an expression of wide-eyed astonishment as though the idea that Julia might have agreed to help out is so implausible as to be totally unbelievable. Either that or she's already forgotten that this is the *reason* Julia flew over in the first place.

The seed of unease about my mother's mental state has sprouted and is now growing leaves. I realise I'm going to have to insist they do this test that Silvio told me about. We have to know.

I sit down on the edge of the bed and take my mother's hand. "Of course, Julia is still here. As soon as the hospital says you can leave, she's going to move out of the hotel where she's staying now and move back home."

"Won't Colin mind?"

"Why would Colin mind?"

"I just thought…"

"She's not moving back here permanently, Mum."

"Oh, I see…"

I have to ask her about Aggie's bungalow and I know I have to ask sooner rather than later because if I don't do it soon then Julia will, but this confusion is disconcerting and I wonder if it's fair to question her about something that she clearly doesn't want to share with us.

I take a deep breath and dive in. "I need to ask you something, Mum," I say gently. "It's about Aggie's bungalow." She immediately looks away and tries to withdraw her hand from mine, but I hold on. "Your vicar friend, Edward Feering, let it slip I'm afraid."

"He isn't my friend, he's an idiot. He should know better than to break a confidence," she snaps, and she tears her hand away from mine.

"Why didn't you tell me that Aggie had left you the bungalow?"

This time when she gazes up at me, her eyes bore angrily into mine. "It's none of your business. If I'd wanted you to know, I would have told you."

"But this is important, Mum. If you need help to stay living by yourself at Hillcrest, then somehow that has to be funded. Dad didn't leave you much, I know, and I'm just trying to be practical. That bungalow is sitting empty when it could be sold or even rented out to generate some extra income for you. If it came to it, you could even move in yourself."

"Move into that bungalow? Never in a million years!" she exclaims angrily.

"Why not?"

"Because."

Once again, she turns her head away from me, and I can tell by the jut of her chin that she's still smarting with indignation, but I'm going to have to press the point home. "You might not have a choice."

"I'm never moving into that bungalow!"

"Then sell it or rent it out."

"No!"

"Please, Mum," I plead with her.

Her hands pluck at the bedcovers. "You don't understand."

"Then explain it to me."

"I can't because I'd just sound like a foolish old woman."

I reach for her hands once again. "You have to tell me."

She still won't look at me, but she says, "Aggie made me promise that I wouldn't sell it. She never had children of her own and she wanted *her* inheritance passed on to you and Julia because she knew what your father had done. I know I could live there, but I don't want to live in *her* family home – both of her parents died in that bungalow and Aggie would have died there as well if I hadn't insisted that she move in with me. It's got death written all over it."

"Okay," I say. "I understand why *you* don't want to live there, but somebody else could."

"I'll think about it," she says and her voice wavers. "But I'm not making any promises."

Unwilling to distress her further, I decide to leave it at that. When she's back in her own home, I think to myself, we can talk about it again. I spend the next half-hour doing what I know she likes best: telling her about the exploits of Silvio's extended family.

When it's time for me to leave, she suddenly gets tearful. "I'm not ready to go home yet, Richard, and they keep pressuring me. I know I can't stay here forever, but when something like this happens, it undermines your confidence. I've lived alone since your father died and I've been happy on my own for the most part, but I realise now that anything could happen to me and no one would know."

She's right. Julia and I have to rethink this, but first I have to find out what I'm dealing with, so when I see Nurse Kelly sitting at the reception desk on my way out, I decide to ask her about the test Silvio mentioned.

"I think you're talking about an MMSE," she says, suddenly looking serious. "That's a Mini Mental State Examination. It's the most commonly used test for dementia."

"Well, can you get it done?"

"The only thing I can do is make a note of your concerns, Mr Oakley. Obviously, your mother's clinician will decide if he thinks it's necessary. Nothing's been written in her notes so far, but I could have a word with him tomorrow if you'd like me to?"

I have a feeling Nurse Kelly is backtracking, so I tell her that our mother isn't going anywhere until we've had some kind of reassurance, that she's both physically and mentally well enough to look after herself.

"Well, mild symptoms can be quite difficult to diagnose," she says. "You might be better off speaking to her GP after she's been discharged and asking for a referral to a dementia specialist. Your mother was admitted as a surgical patient and as soon as she's ready to leave from a surgical point of view, you're going to have to arrange for her to go home."

"It sounds to me like you're washing your hands of the problem," I say.

"We don't know if there is a problem, Mr Oakley."

"That's not what you told me before."

Her face reddens and she gets to her feet. "I'll make a note of what you've told me and pass it on to the appropriate medical specialist, but that's as much as I can do."

"Just make sure you do," I say, and I quickly leave before I'm tempted to say any more.

Lenora

I watch Richard walk away, and this time I'm overcome with guilt and remorse, but it had to be done – the bending of the truth. I don't doubt for a single second that he's thinking to himself, 'As soon as we get her home, we'll persuade her to change her mind.' But they won't.

The bungalow became a bone of contention between Aggie and me from the moment that she moved out of it and moved into Hillcrest, and we continued to argue about it right up to the day that she died.

"I don't want you to leave it to me," I told her.

"But I don't have anyone else to leave it to, Lenora."

"You must have cousins, or aunts and uncles," I insisted.

"Why would I want to leave it to them?"

"Uhhh ... because they're family. Your family."

It was late one afternoon, and Julia's bedroom was very warm, so I'd opened up the doors, which led onto the balcony. A breeze disturbed the curtains and the gentle undulation of the light fabric seemed to have an almost hypnotic effect on Aggie, who was stretched out on the bed for the afternoon rest prescribed by the doctor. As she watched the movement of the curtains, her eyelids began to flutter and within a short time she'd fallen asleep.

I was sitting comfortably in an armchair on the far side of the room. Edward Feering and his wife had volunteered to haul it upstairs from the sitting room for me so that Aggie and I could talk while she was resting. I was grateful to them because otherwise I would have been perched on the hard, dressing-table stool.

It was heart-breaking to see how the flesh had fallen away from her bones; how the dark hollows under her beautiful blue eyes had deepened; how her hair had thinned and coarsened – it was like the

172

finest, steel wire, and when I supported her head over the sink to wash it, I had visions of it cutting into my skin, which was macabre but probably indicative of my underlying suspicions about her.

When we're young, we tend to think of death like a thief in the night creeping into the room while we're sleeping and stealing away our life, but it's rarely like that. Most usually it's like it was for Aggie: a drawn out, painful cutting of the threads, which bind us to this earthly existence. I saw Death slowly snip, snip, snip, and knew that Aggie's life would soon be hanging by a single thread. It was only a matter of time.

Julia's room looks out onto the back garden and I was glad for Aggie to be able to spend her final days watching the birds fly to and fro and smell the scent of things growing and ripening in the earth below. Though perhaps the sights and sounds of life moving ever onwards like a wheel in perpetual motion only served to underline that she was also part of that process of growth and decay.

I watched Aggie's chest rise and fall, but it no longer moved with metronome precision. Aggie's breathing was ragged, and every now and then she would appear to stop breathing altogether. It was like a practice run for death and I was the sole spectator.

Soon I too fell asleep.

When I woke, I saw that Aggie was now watching me.

She told me, "I've thought about what you said, but I still want Richard and Julia to inherit the bungalow."

I rubbed the sleep from my eyes, stretched and yawned; it took me some minutes to realise what she was talking about. "I don't know why," I said.

"I'd have thought it was obvious," she replied.

Her eyes met mine and I saw that she wanted me to understand, and I did understand, but the property was a gift that came with the price tag still attached. "I've haven't forgotten what you did," I said. "I remember that day on the beach when you told me what you'd done, and I still can't take it in."

"Did it really require an explanation?"

"I think so."

"And yet you wouldn't let me explain. I remember how you ran from me. I can still see you striding up the beach; you were so angry.

I thought you were going to leave without me. I was so relieved when I saw you sitting behind the wheel of the car. You said..."

"I know what I said."

"You wouldn't let me explain."

"You did it for me, I know that," I said softly.

"Can I explain now?"

"Well, I suppose it's now or never, isn't it?"

It was probably a cruel thing to say to a dying woman, but she nodded and began to speak.

"I don't know how I hadn't seen him with that woman and their child there before – they were living just a few streets away. I knew what he was like, Lenora. He'd made passes at me when he was drunk, and Daddy said he'd always had a reputation." Up till that point, she'd gazed solemnly into my eyes, but now she shifted her gaze to the window, revisiting the past in her head. "I was driving home after visiting you – I still had my black Ford Fiesta back then. I saw them in the front garden – the woman and the child. They were waving to a man getting into a car. I didn't even realise it was George they were waving to until after I'd driven past and glanced in the mirror..." She faltered; her voice shrank to a whisper. "He looked really happy; happier than I'd ever seen him before."

I felt the blood drain from my brain; knew that a different kind of unconsciousness beckoned. I leaned forward, put my head between my knees and breathed deeply. I'd told Aggie that day at the beach that I didn't want to know any more, but it hadn't stopped me speculating. I still wasn't sure if I wanted to know, but she took my silence as a sign to continue.

"After that, I often used to make time to drive or walk past, and I often saw them all together. I couldn't stop thinking about how badly he'd treated you all those years – like an unpaid skivvy. Somehow he didn't deserve to be happy."

I jerked back up to a sitting position. "He probably didn't deserve to be happy with somebody else, but he didn't deserve to die, Aggie!"

She sighed and turned to face me. "I didn't plan to kill him, Lenora. I just wanted to scare him."

"What happened?"

"I was driving Daddy's car because my Fiesta was off the road. I panicked at the last moment and my shoe slipped. When I found the

pedal again, I'd put my foot on the accelerator instead of the brake. It happened so quickly. I drove straight home afterwards, put the car back in the garage, and covered it over with an old tarpaulin."

Beads of perspiration began to ooze from my skin, but I was shivering. "It's still there, in the garage, isn't it?"

She nodded, sank her head back into the pillows and closed her eyes.

The following day, I drove over to Tyne Lodge. The neighbour saw me poking around in the garage and called over the fence. He was and still is quite an unpleasant individual, and I didn't trust him not to do a bit of poking around himself, so I told him about Aggie and explained that I was making sure that everything was secure. I'd brought a heavy padlock with me and I pulled the garage doors tightly shut then fastened it in place.

The car has remained there to this day, and I've been banking on the fact that, by the time I'm dead, it will also be dead; the bodywork rusted away and Aggie's guilty fingerprints on the steering wheel unreadable.

Now I'm going to have to review the situation.

Julia

Another day of mournful grey skies greets me when I leave the hotel. I work out that it's only Wednesday. I've already spent more time here than I really want to and I still have the prospect of leaving the Marriott with its wonderful room service and moving into Hillcrest to look after my mother. Doesn't Richard realise that I haven't ever looked after anyone in my life? In fact, I'm not sure that I really know what 'looking after' actually entails.

The meeting with Henry Silver yesterday afternoon darkened my spirits. I was absolutely certain – in spite of what Richard had already told me – that we'd be able to contest the will without too much trouble, but it seems I was wrong. Will I allow that to deter me? Absolutely not!

As soon as I got back to the hotel after Richard had dropped me at the station, I put a call through to Colin's solicitor. Although his expertise is in Singapore corporate law, I knew that he'd trained in London. Due to the time difference, it went straight to voicemail, but he called me back early the next day (Singapore time) and close to midnight here. Fortunately, I was still awake – my body clock is keeping its own, peculiar time and refuses to adjust to GMT.

"Mrs Crane, how can I help you?" he asked me.

I outlined the situation. "Is there anything I can do?"

He was blunt and to the point when he replied. "Time is money, and this could take a long time. You'd have to *prove* somehow that your father made the will under the influence of this woman. Have you spoken to his doctor? If I were you, I'd do a little bit of detective work before I engaged someone to fight this on your behalf. Find out as much as you can about her: speak to the neighbours, people she worked with. She might have said something to someone; inadvertently let something slip."

"That's not very encouraging," I told him.

"I realise that, but you need to be realistic. Unless you can show it's very likely if not indisputable that she persuaded him to make his will in favour of her daughter, then you haven't got much of a case. In view of your father's age, in all probability there was already a will in place so that would be a good place to start, in my opinion."

I thanked him politely for his advice, but inwardly I was seething, so this morning I called Henry Silver and asked what appeared to be the crucial question: Was there already a will in place? The answer was an unequivocal 'yes'.

This is why I'm travelling back to Shenfield and hiring a car for the day. Colin's solicitor recommended a private detective agency of all things and I suppose it might be useful, but at this point it seems prudent to do some of the so-called 'legwork' myself. I am my father's daughter after all, which is why I'm going to drive over to the address that Henry Silver gave me and find out as much as I can.

The house turns out to be a modest chalet bungalow, but I'm not sure what I was expecting. My father didn't own the property – at least as far as I know, but there are many nuggets of information, which have been deliberately concealed from me, so this could be one more.

When I was first told what had happened to my father, I couldn't comprehend how something like that could take place without someone witnessing it, but now I understand. The house is situated in a narrow lane and every property enjoys a degree of privacy from its neighbour that would cost its owner millions of dollars if this were Singapore. On the other side of the road, a line of closely growing trees marks the boundary of an open field. Anything could happen in this place on a dark night, and no one might see or hear it. Richard told me it was a hit-and-run *accident,* but it could just as easily have been planned, though I suppose the police would have investigated that possibility. Could my father have had enemies desperate enough to want to kill him? It seems unlikely, but I suppose it's not impossible.

As I approach the house, I realise that I haven't got a plan, but I'm good at thinking on my feet, so I walk up to the front door and ring the bell. I don't have to wait long till someone comes to the door. It's a girl, and she has a toddler with her. He clings to her skirt with one hand and holds a bottle of something, which could be milk, in his other hand. His blonde hair has been cut in what I'm guessing is the latest style – shaved short at the sides with longer floppy hair on the crown. It looks sticky, unwashed, in fact the whole child looks like it could do with a good scrub.

I put on my nicest smile. "Hi there. I'm hoping you can help me. I'm looking for someone…" but the girl is already closing the door.

She says, "Sorry, but we've only just moved in," and she grabs the child by the arm and pulls him after her. Before I have a chance to say any more, the door has been closed in my face.

Well, that was just rude, I think to myself.

From the corner of my eye, I notice a movement in the garden next door, so I quickly walk back to the road. The neighbour is an elderly woman around the same age as my mother judging by the colour and cut of her hair. I hesitate to use the word 'style' to describe it because it's the same androgynous shape that so many women of her generation choose to adopt when the menopause has faded to a distant memory and femininity seems to be a choice rather than a biological imperative – not a trend that I intend to follow.

I slip into position my brightest 'May I be of assistance to you?' smile – even though I'm the one who requires the assistance on this occasion – and walk confidently up the garden path. "Hallo there!" I call out to her. When she returns my smile, I approach with my hand already extended. It's a tactic I've perfected. It's now impossible for her to *not* take my hand without appearing appallingly rude, and most people in my experience hate to *appear* rude regardless of how they actually feel about a situation – especially the British, who still believe (erroneously as it happens) that they're famed for their good manners.

"Can I help you?" she asks and gives my hand a friendly shake.

"I hope so," I say.

I was going to spin her a line about working as an investigator for Silver, Reid and Bateman Solicitors, but I stop myself just in time. This woman probably knew my father quite well, though possibly not well enough to know that he had another family – at least not until it was mentioned in the newspaper after his death. If she'd had a fondness for him, his lovely companion and their darling daughter Miriam, then she probably didn't feel quite the same way when she found out that he was effectively a bigamist, so a straightforward introduction suddenly seems a better bet.

"My name's Julia Crane and my father was George Oakley."

Her face immediately lights up with interest. "Come in," she says. She gives me a long look. "You don't look very much like him, you know. Miriam's the spitting image of him. No doubt about who *her* father is."

I can't decide if there's some sort of innuendo hidden in this observation, but I just keep smiling and when she turns and walks into the house, I follow her.

She leads me into a sitting room at the back of the house. It's crammed with dark, replica period furniture, whose outsize proportions would be better suited to a country hotel rather than a modern bungalow, and there's lots and lots of chintz. It's everywhere – the curtains, the upholstery, even the feature wall behind the fireplace is covered with exotic flowers. The effect is overpowering, and I can actually feel my chest tighten and my lungs contract so when she offers to make a cup of tea, I accompany her into the kitchen.

"Go and make yourself comfortable on the sofa, dear," she says.

I ignore her. The kitchen is light and uncluttered and a much more welcoming space, so I pull out a chair at the dining table. "I'll sit here," I say and then I distract her by admiring the garden and asking her how long she's lived here and if she knew my father well.

"Oh, we moved here when Reggie – that's my husband – when Reggie retired. That's nearly twenty years ago." She smiles. "I'm Shirley, by the way. Shirley Pym."

"It's really kind of you to invite me in, Shirley," I say. "I hope you don't mind me ... don't mind me asking you a few questions about my father when he was living here with ... with..." I hover awkwardly over the unfinished sentence because the words are like bile in my mouth.

Shirley misinterprets and oozes sympathy, but she doesn't hesitate to supply the missing information. "It's Lena. Lena Bartok. I think she said the name was Hungarian, but I know she was born in Holland."

"In a place called Urk," I volunteer. "At least that's where her parents were living when Daddy had his accident." I tell her this as though I know the family.

Shirley nods. "That's right. That's where she was when your dad was knocked down." Her cheery expression visibly saddens. "Such a nice man. And he was a wonderful father to Miriam." She must have noticed my smile falter because she quickly adds, "Of course, we had no idea he was still living together with your mum when he wasn't here."

"What do you mean?"

"Well, we all thought they were separated. You know, legally separated. He told everyone at the club that she was a churchgoer and she wouldn't agree to a divorce. Was she Roman Catholic? I know they don't hold with divorce." She places a cup of tea in front of me and puts her hand on my shoulder. "It must have been horrible for you all when he died. Such a shock." I feel her hesitate, feel her hand tremble. "He made some mistakes, I realise that, but he *was* a lovely man, Julia, a real charmer. He didn't deserve what happened to him and it breaks my heart when I think that the person who did this terrible thing is still out there. It's a travesty, it really is."

A travesty of justice, she means, and two weeks ago I would have immediately agreed with her, but now I wonder... What other secrets was he hiding? What other lies did he tell?

"You said he told everyone at the club? Do you mean the country club where he used to play golf?"

"That's right, dear. Reggie's still a member. Goes off most mornings – he's a bit of a fair-weather golfer these days mind you, but he likes the company."

"So that's how you knew my father? Through the golf club?"

She nods emphatically. "It was my Reggie, who told him about the house next door. They had a lovely little flat over one of the shops in Shenfield high street but then when Lena found out she was in the family way, he wanted to find a place for them all to live. Somewhere quiet with a nice garden, he told Reggie."

"They had a flat in Shenfield high street," I repeat after her. She nods again and I realise that, somehow in the course of our conversation, she's forgotten who she's speaking to. I could remind her. I could tell her that my mother was neither a Roman Catholic nor a wife from whom her husband had legally separated. I could tell her that the lovely flat he shared with his mistress – because that's what Lena Bartok really was – the flat in the high street was just a stone's throw from our family home and my mother must have walked past it every time she went shopping and she never knew. He knew though. He knew and he clearly didn't care. Perhaps Richard was right about him after all, I think to myself.

Shirley likes to talk. I think she's lonely. She tells me that Lena Bartok came back for the funeral without the child, and that she couldn't afford to stay in the house next door, so she sold off most of the furniture on eBay and took what was left with her when she moved out.

"She still lives around here?" I ask, hoping against hope that Shirley Pym has a forwarding address.

"I've no idea," she says. "But she kept on working at the club for a while. Reggie said they all missed her when she left. She was a good worker, always cheerful and conscientious." A sad, wistful note creeps into her voice. "I miss her too."

She walks me to the door and tells me, "Your father was a good man, Julia. He had his faults, no doubt about that, but him and Lena were a lovely couple."

I've successfully managed to keep my anger tightly zipped up till this point but a picture of my mother frail and helpless in her hospital bed pops into my head and it acts as the catalyst for an outpouring of furious indignation.

When I finally leave, I tell her, "Lena Bartok wasn't a lovely person and, as it turns out, neither was my father. She was just another money-grubbing opportunist and he was a liar and a cheat. We've lost everything because of that woman."

Shirley Pym stands on the doorstep speechless and red-faced. It wasn't kind a thing to do – reveal to her how my father left virtually everything he owned to little Miriam, the bastard child of his mistress, and nothing to his *real* family – but it was the ugly truth.

I'm not sure I've learned anything new about him, but I have discovered where he probably met Lena Bartok. If she continued to work at the club after she moved away from here, then I should be able to find out where she went when she left. There's even a small chance that someone there still keeps in contact with her. That could be just the little bit of luck I need.

Richard

Silvio woke me with a kiss this morning then climbed into bed. He wrapped himself around me, yawned extravagantly and murmured, "*Buongiorno mi amore.*" Within seconds he was fast asleep.

Yesterday evening, the party at Bocca Felice went on into the night. He phoned me at around midnight to tell me that no one had left yet, people were still eating, and the wine was still flowing. I told him to stay at the flat, and he agreed it was the best thing to do because he didn't think he'd get to bed much before three. I'm not sure Mamma Mazzi would have approved, but fortunately she's still staying with her sister in Varenna and what she doesn't know she can't oppose.

When I was certain that I wouldn't wake him, I disentangled myself from his arms and crept into the kitchen. A cup of espresso from Silvio's very expensive coffee maker soon had the desired effect and I've been able to quickly settle down at my desk to work.

The hotel project, which has plagued my waking hours for the last few months, has suddenly gathered momentum. I think the client has herself grown tired of it all and now wants it finished, but probably not quite as much as I do. I make a string of phone calls to suppliers and contractors, impressing on everyone the need for speed and efficiency now that final decisions have been made and we have a non-negotiable deadline to complete the work.

At around eleven o'clock, Silvio stumbles out of bed, rubbing the sleep from his eyes and demanding coffee. I remember that I haven't eaten since the previous evening, so I hurry away to our favourite delicatessen to buy a selection of sweet pastries for him and a more substantial breakfast for me – a baguette filled with ham and cheese.

When I return to the flat, Silvio is lying on the sofa. There are purple rings under his eyes and his honey-coloured skin has lost some of its healthy glow. Once again, he demands coffee.

"It's a good thing your mother can't see you like this," I tell him. "If she knew that you'd kept the restaurant open late just for that guy, she'd be mad as hell. I know you value his custom, but really…"

"It was a private party," he says and shrugs. "It's okay. It's just one night."

"I know. But now you've set a precedent," I argue back at him. "What are you going to say when he wants to do it again?"

He forces a smile. "We worry about that when it happens. *Caffè Latte. Presto per favore.*"

With the coffee and pastries consumed from a prone position on the sofa, Silvio ambles away to have a leisurely shower. When he returns, he looks refreshed but there's still an underlying air of fatigue in his handsome face. He drops back onto the sofa and motions to me to join him. He knows I worry about him when the work in the restaurant is grinding him down, but I understand it isn't easy to turn away customers when the business is all about service and goodwill.

I close the file I've been leafing through and sit down next him, put my arm around his shoulder and find the smooth skin at the back of his neck with my lips. He drops his head onto my shoulder and sighs.

"We both need a holiday," I tell him. "All these problems with my mother and Julia. As soon as everything's sorted, we're going away, Silvio. Just the two of us."

"Julia must sort her own problems," he says.

"And my mother?"

"It's not a problem, Ricardo."

"But what about this MMSE? What if it shows she's got dementia? She can't live on her own if she's got dementia."

"You are … how you say? Putting the cart in front of the horse. You don't know!"

"But if she does?" I persist, and I hear the fear in my voice.

He lifts his head and with the tips of his fingers turns my face to meet his, presses his lips to mine and kisses me with such warmth and tenderness that tears spring to my eyes. He whispers, "We worry about that when it happens."

He spends the rest of the morning lying on the sofa listening to music through headphones, while I get back to work. When his brother calls from the restaurant about an urgent problem with the plumbing in the flat upstairs – apparently there's water dripping through the ceiling – he quickly gets dressed and leaves, telling me once again not to worry. This is like asking a cat not to purr. When there's a problem, which needs to be solved, I worry. It's my default setting in all uncertain situations. And now that the subject of my mother has been raised once again, I find I can no longer concentrate so I decide to drive to the hospital and find out what's happening.

As soon as I reach the reception desk on the ward, a nurse I've never met before springs to her feet and asks me if I'm Mrs Oakley's son. When I confirm that I am, she takes me into the room where I shared the multi-coloured birthday cake with Nurse Kelly. This looks like the bad news I've been anticipating.

"What's going on? Is there a problem with my mother?" I ask her straight away.

"No, not a problem really, just a few concerns," she says. She's younger than Nurse Kelly, probably not much more than a teenager, and I can see from the nervous hand-wringing that she's been given the task of telling me something I may not want to hear. "The consultant had a chat with Mrs Oakley this morning..." she begins.

"You mean this MMSE – Mini Mental State Examination," I say.

She swallows hard. "No, he just had a little chat with her about going home."

"So, she hasn't had this test?"

"No." She consults the notes on the clipboard under her arm. I open my mouth to protest but she's obviously been prepped for this confrontation and continues quickly on. "Because Mrs Oakley was admitted to the ward as a *surgical* patient," – and she emphasizes the word for my benefit – "the orthogeriatric consultant makes the final decision that she's well enough to be discharged, together with other members of staff involved in her care. Nurse Kelly did mention to him that you were a bit worried about your mother. He doesn't have any concerns and, like I said, he spoke to her this morning, but he can make a referral to the memory clinic."

"Where she'll have the test?" I attempt to confirm.

"She'll be seen by the geriatric consultant – a specialist in dementia."

"But meanwhile she has to go home?"

She nods.

The constricted muscles in my chest begin to relax. It isn't precisely what I wanted to hear, but at least she's going to have the benefit of a professional opinion, I think to myself. It then occurs to me that I've been brought into this room for a reason. They still have concerns.

"Mrs Oakley is probably going to be discharged before the weekend."

"Okay..."

"We've spoken to her about this, but she says she isn't ready to go home."

"Okay..." I say again.

The nurse looks up at me and I recognise the expression in her eyes – it's one of anxious hopefulness. It says, *please help me out here because I can't do this without you.* "We have to discharge her, Mr Oakley. We understand that your sister..." she glances at her notes. "Your sister Mrs Julia Crane, is going to be staying with her?"

"Yes, that's correct."

She offers me a small, grateful smile. "As far as we can tell she's making a good recovery. The physiotherapist has confirmed that she's now progressed to using elbow crutches, and the plan for tomorrow is to teach her how manage the stairs then discharge her on Friday."

"What exactly are the concerns that you have?" I ask her.

"Well, from a medical perspective, she *is* ready to go home, but if she refuses..." She leaves the sentence hanging in the air.

"I see," I say. "You want me to speak her?"

"If you could, please. We've tried talking to her, but it's difficult because she refuses to say specifically what's worrying her. I don't know if you can think of anything?"

Can I think of anything? Well, maybe the prospect of being forced to leave the home you've lived in for the last fifty years. Yes, I think that might just do it.

"I'll speak to her right now," I say.

185

She's sitting in the chair next to the bed and greets me with a surprised but very happy smile. "Richard, how lovely to see you. You're not working this afternoon?"

"I decided to take the afternoon off." I fetch another chair and place it so that we're facing one another. "You look well." And she does look well. The colour has returned to her cheeks and her eyes are bright with curious interest. Before she has a chance to deny the obvious improvement in her health, I tell her, "They're planning to discharge you on Friday. That's good news, isn't it?"

Her expression immediately sours: the upturned corners of her mouth change direction and the curious interest is replaced by ... I think it's anger. "Is that what they've told you?" she says. "Well, then I suppose it must true. I've told them I'm not ready to go home – I haven't even done the stairs yet but they're dead set on getting rid of me."

"They're not 'getting rid of you'. They're discharging you into the care of your own doctor because you don't need to be in hospital. I thought you'd be glad to get home. Why do you want to stay here?"

"I don't want to *stay* here," she shoots back at me.

We could bat this ball backwards and forwards for the next five minutes, so I decide to get straight to the point. "If you're worried about being able to keep living at Hillcrest, then don't be. I took Julia over to Tyne Lodge yesterday and she agrees with me that leaving the place empty is ridiculous." My mother's expression sharpens even further, but I ignore it. "I understand why you don't want to live there and that's fine, but it needs to have someone living in it or it's going to deteriorate and the value of it depreciate. You could let it out through an agent, and when I say 'you' I simply mean that this is what can be done. I'll arrange it for you. You personally won't have to do anything except put your signature on a piece of paper."

She glares back at me, but there's something else in her expression, which I can't quite put my finger on. She says, "So you've got it all worked out between the two of you then."

"We're just trying to do what's best for you."

She raises a sceptical eyebrow. "And, of course, you'd know that, you and your sister, who hasn't actually lived in this country for the last thirty years."

186

I don't want to argue this out until it's time for me to leave, but I'm not leaving until I find out what's behind the reluctance to deal with Aggie's bungalow. I pull the chair forward so that I can take her hands in mine. "Please tell me what's wrong, Mum." She shakes her head in response. "I need to know," I say. "Renting out the bungalow would generate some extra income and that would make it much easier for you to stay living at Hillcrest. It would pay for carers when you need them."

"I don't need a carer!"

"Okay, maybe not a carer, but you clearly need some help with the garden now."

"The garden?"

"Yes, the garden. Julia and I went back to the house, after we'd been to Tyne Lodge. Please be honest with me," I plead with her. "Have you had kids messing about? You know … getting into the garden through that loose fence panel?" She looks blankly back at me. "I've nailed it back in place because it was still just hanging from a nail when we found it. I thought I could see footprints in the soil. I can't think they belong to you because the garden doesn't look like it's had anything done to it for months." She begins to blink rapidly, and her breathing quickens. "What's going on, Mum?"

All the while she holds my hands with steady pressure, but I can see in her face that she's struggling to conceal her feelings. Something has happened, I know it has, but why won't she admit it?

"I think you might be right," she says at last. "That's why I haven't felt like going out there very much."

"You mean you think you've had someone trespassing on the property?"

She nods. "I think so … just a glimpse of someone every now and then. I know it sounds ridiculous because why would anyone want to get into the garden?" She gives an odd, nervous laugh. "I'm probably just seeing things. I'm getting old and going a bit gaga in my old age."

Well, we all hope and pray that isn't true, but I try to reassure her. "Don't worry, it happens to all of us sometimes. When Julia and I were in the garden yesterday, I looked up at her bedroom window and thought I saw a woman in a red dress standing there. How mad is that?"

187

This time she drags her hands from mine and clasps them in her lap.

I find myself uttering the same nervous laugh. "Julia said it must have been Aggie. We found a photograph of her in Julia's room."

A strange mixture of emotions passes over my mother's face. I want to question her further, but she reaches for the buzzer to call for the nurse and tells her that she needs some pain relief, which ends the conversation. We spend the rest of the visit talking about Silvio and the restaurant and how much he and I need a holiday. "Obviously it's going to wait until you're safely back on your feet again," I say.

Before I leave, I talk to her again about the bungalow and this time she agrees, albeit reluctantly, that letting the property would give her some useful extra income. "But maybe not the garage," she says.

"It looks like there's something pretty big stored in there."

"Oh, that's just something that Aggie left. It's not valuable in any way, and I'll get rid of it eventually." She smiles and blows me a kiss goodbye.

Lenora

I watch Richard walk away and wonder how long I can keep up the pretence. When he said he'd seen a woman in a red dress at Julia's bedroom window, I thought my heart would burst out of my chest. 'How mad is that?' he said, and it is a kind of madness, for how can it be true?

I try not to think about Aggie, but she steals into my thoughts and into my dreams.

She would have hated being in hospital like this where there's no privacy at all. At some point during your stay, your every bodily function will be either overheard or overseen by somebody else. The curtain around the bed acts like a Japanese paper screen: it's a psychological barrier rather than a physical one.

The lady in the bed opposite me died in the night. Her name was Fleur. She had dementia and used to spend much of the time calling out for someone called Libby. We all thought it was a daughter or a sister, but it turned out to be a dog.

Her husband and son came in very early this morning to collect her belongings and argued about whether or not Libby should be allowed to stay on in the flat or whether they should just put her out of her misery. I'd only just woken up when they arrived and didn't know that Libby had been Fleur's constant, canine companion so I was horrified to hear them talking about euthanizing a member of the family. I kept thinking, 'This is outrageous! Don't they realise people can hear them.' Obviously, I was still a bit groggy, it being so early, and Fleur's son was very tearful, but I didn't understand that they were discussing her dog until the husband complained about the constant barking.

Aggie sometimes talked about euthanasia – or the E-word as we later referred to it after she got her diagnosis. If she hadn't been such an obstinately private person, she would probably still be here today, and the E-word wouldn't be a part of my vocabulary.

She'd always been very slim, not a single unnecessary ounce of fat on her whole frame, but one day when we were leaving the swimming pool, I noticed that she'd put on weight around her tummy. Of course, I felt compelled to mention it.

I stabbed my finger into her rounded belly. "Finally!"
She winced. "That hurt."
"Hurt your pride maybe. You're getting fat, Aggie. At long last."
"I'm not fat, I'm bloated. There's a difference."
I looked again and saw that her abdomen was noticeably distended. "What's wrong?" I asked her.
"I'm having tests to find out," she said and immediately moved off to go into the changing rooms.
I grabbed hold of her arm and forced her to stop walking. "What sort of tests? Why didn't you tell me?"
"Just blood tests."
"What are they testing for?"
"You wouldn't know what it was even if I told you," she said sharply and pulled away from me.
I had to practically run to catch up with her as she deliberately strode away to the area where you're supposed to take a shower before you enter the pool but actually only shower when you've come out of the pool and don't want to smell of chlorine for the rest of the day. I was a bit scared of even walking fast around the edge of the pool because the tiled floor got slippery when it was wet – bizarrely, in my opinion, in view of the fact that it was a swimming *pool – so I didn't manage to catch up with her until she was washing her hair. She pretended she couldn't hear me when I asked her again what the tests were for.*
While I was washing my *hair and had my eyes closed for the fraction of time that it takes to get rid of the eye-stinging shampoo, she dived into one of the cubicles. It wasn't until we were seated in the café that I was able to raise the subject once more without her doing a disappearing act on me.*
"They're testing my CA 125 levels," she said in a matter-of-fact voice.
"And that is?"
"I believe it's a type of protein found in the blood."
"Okay," I said carefully. "Why is it significant?"

190

She slowly stirred sugar into her coffee, kept her eyes fixed on the spoon. "I don't like talking about these things, Lenora. They're personal. And it might not be significant."

I reached across the table and removed the spoon from her hand. "I'm your friend, Agnes Bagshot. Possibly your only real friend. If you can't confide in me, then who?"

"I don't need to confide in anyone," she said, sounding irritated.

"If you don't tell me, I'll just go home and look it up on the internet so you might as well just say," I told her.

I could see by the stubborn set of her jaw that she was still unwilling to disclose anything to me, so I just sat and waited. We sat without speaking for nearly five minutes. I expected her to get up from the table and walk out, but then I remembered I'd driven us here, so I reasoned that I had the advantage.

I think it cost her to tell me what was wrong. Cost her in pride and dignity, but at last she said, "The doctor suspects that I have ovarian cancer."

Well, it was a shock. Had it been anyone other than Aggie sitting opposite me, I would have instantly got to my feet and enveloped them in a huge hug, but I knew she would have recoiled from that kind of attention in those circumstances.

I gently put my hand on her arm and said, "Let's go home."

Over the following weeks and months, Aggie had tests and scans; she was examined and probed in places that no woman should have to endure, and the final diagnosis of ovarian cancer was not only confirmed, it was extended because the cancer had spread to other parts of her body. She was offered surgery and chemotherapy to give her a fighting chance of prolonging her life, but she refused it all.

We were out shopping for a new coat one day because Aggie had begun to lose so much weight and few of her clothes fitted her, when she told me about the red dress.

"That's who I always wanted to be," she said. "The girl in the red dress."

"Is she someone you knew?"

"Oh no. It's just that Mother insisted that I dress modestly and didn't draw attention to myself, but I always thought how nice it must feel to have people look at you in an admiring way. I always had this idea that *if I wore a red dress, I'd be a more interesting person: a girl with a dash of adventure in her veins. I wouldn't be plain old 'Aggie-bag'."*

I was surprised and saddened. "But you've never been plain, Aggie. You're a very attractive woman and you've certainly had plenty of admiring glances."

"Really?"

"Honestly."

"Well, it's too late now," she said and sighed.

'It's never too late," I shot back at her. "Come on, let's find you something outrageous!"

We found the dress in a small, independent store – what they used to call a boutique back in the day. It fitted Aggie perfectly, and I decided it was time – before it was really was too late – to seize the moment and go all out for it. I knew a photographic studio that would style your hair and do your make-up as well, so I booked an appointment for the following day.

Aggie wasn't keen on dying her hair so we opted for something that would wash out although there was still a tinge of colour in it when she was put in her coffin.

On the day she was as excited as a child looking forward to its first ever birthday party, and when she finally stepped into the red dress, I understood exactly what she meant: it was a total transformation.

We did the whole 'standing in front of a mirror and closing your eyes' for the big reveal. Aggie burst into tears and the make-up girl had to do a quick repair to her eyeliner. She looked beautiful, and I think she cried, because she finally saw herself as the person, which she'd always secretly longed to be.

When I thought about Aggie after she died, I always tried to recapture that moment. I would hold the image of her in my head, when she still looked well and I hadn't been forced to hear her deathbed confessions – though why she couldn't have whispered those words into Edward Feering's ears, I have no idea.

That she's chosen to appear to me as the girl in the red dress still confounds me, but every time I've seen her, whether it's been in the garden or somewhere in the house, it was the flash of the scarlet fabric that caught my eye and remains ingrained in my brain.

Julia

The sun peeps at me between the curtains where I'm still lying in my lovely hotel bed even though it's nearly eleven o'clock in the morning. After a succession of grey sky days, it really ought to have the effect of cheering me up, but nothing can cheer me up – not even nice bed linen with an eight-hundred thread count.

I ordered room service at nine o'clock – green tea and yoghurt with organic honey and fresh blueberries. I was looking forward to breakfast.

After I returned the hire car yesterday afternoon, I got straight back on the train at Shenfield and spent the rest of the day checking out showrooms in West London, which specialise in antique glassware. None them compared favourably to Glück Glass – obviously I'm not unbiased in my opinions – but it did keep my mind occupied, which was necessary after the less than successful trip I'd made to the country club to ask about Lena Bartok.

The only thing the manager had been willing to confirm was that she'd been a member of staff till approximately twelve years ago. He wasn't at liberty, he insisted, to disclose any further information: he must have repeated the words 'data protection' twenty times.

As a consequence of my frustration and my efforts to relieve that frustration, I forgot to eat dinner and then couldn't face ordering food to the room when it was time to go to bed.

Unfortunately, breakfast was brought to the room with an unwanted side order – a message left with the concierge late last night with the request that it be delivered to me in the morning. It was from Colin.

'Flight scheduled to arrive London Heathrow 15.40. Table for dinner booked 19.45.'

I couldn't believe my eyes. Twelve words. That's all it took to ruin my day, no not my day, my life.

What am I to do? Because I know why he's here. Somehow, he's found out about Jian.

I've been lying in bed since then, breakfast untouched, and checking through the emails, which I should have opened. If I'd opened them, I would have discovered that Colin returned to the gallery. Connie had written to me immediately afterwards outlining in unnecessary detail what he'd said, what she'd said, how he tried to *'force his way onto the premises'* when she told him it was closed for business. I don't think Colin could force his way out of a paper bag so perhaps it was forceful words rather than a shoulder in the doorjamb.

If I'd opened my emails, I would have read that Nancy bumped into Colin at The Americanas Club. He asked her if she knew how long I'd been cheating on him.

'Of course, I told him that it must be a mistake. I said that you sometimes entertain regular, valued customers. He said, "You mean people like the Tan family?" I told him I didn't know their names: I said that kind of information was confidential. He laughed, Julia. Not in a good way.

I really hope this trip to London has helped to clear your head and put things in perspective.

You're in my thoughts and my prayers.

Love Nancy'

Put things in perspective? They were never out of perspective. I know exactly how I feel about Colin – or rather no longer feel about Colin. I don't love him. I don't even like him much of the time. I wonder, frankly, if I ever did.

He's not really my type and looking back I think I married him because he asked me. I was flattered that someone eight years older than me wanted me to be his wife. I'd had boyfriends before I met him – actually quite a few and certainly far more than my parents ever got to know about – but it was all about having fun, having a laugh and making out.

Colin was always the perfect gentleman, so we kissed, and we touched – but never below the waistline – and the first time we had sex was on our honeymoon. It was … disappointing. I remember lying there afterwards thinking, 'Is that it?'

It got better and there was probably a period of time in our marriage when I wasn't unhappy or dissatisfied, but it wasn't long enough to sustain the kind of relationship that endures into and beyond middle age. And though I don't *not care about him at all*, for how can you *not* care about someone you've spent most of your life with, the feelings that I *do* have for him aren't going to persuade me to leave Singapore to see out my twilight years in a small, English seaside town. It simply isn't going to happen.

Have I reflected on the future of my relationship with Jian? Perhaps every now and then my thoughts have strayed in that direction, but they've been reined in pretty quickly because I can no longer bear to consider the consequences of being romantically attached to someone who is *legally* attached to someone else – especially someone else with whom they have a child.

My dearest friend Nancy was right about one thing: I'm never going to be more than adjunct; Jian's *bit on the side*. It pains me dreadfully to think it, but it's true. The real question, I suppose, is will it be enough? And I don't know the answer to that – not yet.

I realise that I'm going to have to make plans. Somehow Colin must be thrown off the scent until I'm ready to deal with the situation in its entirety.

I'm mulling over the options when I get a call from Richard.

"Where are you Julia?"

"I'm in my room at the hotel."

"Okay, well you need to get packed. I've just had a call from the hospital. Mum's being discharged. I've told them we can't do anything until tomorrow, but you need to get over to Hillcrest and get her room ready."

"Ready for what?"

"Ready for her to sleep in. Until she's independently mobile, she's going to need help with everything."

"How can it be any more ready than it is now?" I say. "It's got a bed in it, hasn't it?"

"Of course, it has! But Maggie stripped off the bed linen last week and it wasn't made up again when I last checked."

"Well, can't you call her?"

"I haven't got her number."

I don't want to leave the hotel, but I also don't want to stay here now I know that Colin will be checking in. The absurdity of the situation strikes me forcefully and I find myself laughing out loud.

"What's funny about that?" Richard demands.

I hesitate for moment, not sure if I should confide my misgivings to my brother, but then I realise that having Colin here will allow me to spend one more night at the hotel and on reflection it's probably worth it. I'm going to have to face him at some point and at least this way I can genuinely plead the excuse of leaving tomorrow to look after my mother.

I say, "I'm just surprised. You're usually much better organised than this."

"I can't do everything!" he exclaims angrily. "I have to work, Julia."

"So, do I," I say. "And yet here I am in London, when it's the last place on earth I want to be." The truth of this statement could never be more heartily felt than at this very moment.

I hear him take a deep, calming breath before he speaks again. "Please get yourself to Hillcrest before the end of tomorrow afternoon. I'm picking Mum up from the hospital around half past two. If I have time I'll go shopping first. If I run out of time, I'll order online, but you'll still need to be there, Julia. There's no point in getting food delivered if nobody's going to be at the house to take it in."

"Oh, stop fussing!" I tell him. "I've said I'll be there, haven't I?"

When he answers, I can tell that I've exhausted his usual patient forbearance. He says hotly, "I have neither the time nor the inclination to deal with you acting like a rebellious teenager. Grow up, Julia! If you can't do that, pack your bags and go home. I really don't need you here and Mum definitely doesn't need you here if you can't for once in your vacuous existence act like the responsible adult you're supposed to be." Then he hangs up on me.

That was quite a speech, I think to myself. I dare say he'll be bragging to Silvio tonight that he's told me a few home truths.

It does, however, give me pause for thought because I've always relied on him to bear the burden of care for our mother; always used the excuse that I'm too busy, too far away, too important to be able to tear myself away from the gallery.

Well, first things first, I tell myself. Tomorrow, I'll assume the mantle of responsibility for my mother, but today I have to deal with my husband.

To cheer myself up, I spend the afternoon browsing in my favourite stores. It's a pleasant enough way to while away the hours and at least it's not raining. I buy Colin a cashmere jumper – not something I would ever think to do if I were shopping in one of the malls back home – but it's a tactical purchase.

Singapore's reputation as *the* place to shop has changed over the years. When I first moved there, you could buy practically anything you wanted, and it was fifty per cent cheaper than anywhere else in the world. Everyone who travelled there had heard of Lucky Plaza and the department store C K Tang. Today, you can still buy anything you want but now it's designer goods, which people crave, and Singapore's Orchard Road doesn't disappoint.

I miss my life in Singapore so much.

When I get back to the hotel around half past five, Colin is waiting for me. They wouldn't let him into the room because his name isn't on the reservation, so I'm greeted with a scowl.

"Where the hell have you been, Julia?" he barks at me.

"Hallo to you too," I say.

"What?"

"Hallo Colin. Welcome to London." I pass him the bag with the cashmere jumper wrapped in white tissue paper.

"What's this?"

"It's a little gift. I'm guessing Siti packed your suitcase for you?" He nods, but still looks confused. "Well, the weather here is about fifteen degrees cooler than it is in Singapore so I thought you might appreciate having something to wear that keeps you warm in the evenings." I reach up and brush his cheek with my lips. "You don't have to thank me, darling."

I quickly move away from him to the reception desk and before he has a chance to further voice complaint, I explain who is and that he'll be sharing my room.

In the lift, I keep talking, I don't give him an opportunity to tell me why he's here, and by the time we reach the room, much of his unexploded anger appears to have evaporated.

"Would you like me to order you something from room service?" I ask.

"I'm not hungry."

I point to the mini-fridge in the corner of the room. "Something to drink?"

"I don't want food or alcohol, Julia. What I want is an explanation."

I give what I know is a rather hollow-sounding laugh. "I rather think you're the one, who needs to give the explanation. Why on earth are you here?"

He slumps onto the bed. "I know all about it, this affair you've been having."

I take my time to reply. I keep thinking, 'Damage limitation, Julia'. I don't do the obvious thing and fling myself onto the bed next him promising that it's all over. Instead, I walk away from him and seat myself on an upright chair in front of the window so that my face is in shadow. I'm a good liar, but I don't think even I could look him directly in the eye and not expose my true feelings.

"What is it that you think you know," I ask him.

"John Tan. You've been seeing John Tan. How could you, Julia?"

The look of surprise on my face is real because I've never heard anyone call Jian by that name before, although it isn't unusual for Singaporeans to adopt a western name, especially when they do business with the expat community. "I don't know anyone called John Tan."

"Yes, you bloody well do!"

"No, I don't!"

"Don't tell me you've never heard of Tan Techtronix?" he says.

"Of course, I have." And this is where thinking on one's feet is crucial. I assume an air of shocked incredulity. "Surely you don't mean Tan Wenjian?"

"Don't pretend, Julia!" he shouts at me.

"I'm not pretending anything. Mr Tan is one of my best customers. He collects Victorian Wrythenware. I've sold him dozens of pieces over the last eight years or so. He's been hugely supportive of my business and yes, we are in regular contact, and yes, we do meet for dinner on occasion."

"Regular contact?" Colin sneers. "I've seen your last phone bill. I'd call four or five times a week a bit more than regular contact."

So that's what he's found on my desk at the gallery, I think. But there has to be more. I wrack my brain to think what else I left there, but I can't think of anything, so I say, "I've been helping him find something special."

Colin's face is now suffused with anger. His eyes have shrunk to hate-filled slits and his top lip is turned upwards in a furious snarl. "Something special?" he roars. "You must take me for a complete and utter fool. Well, I'm not! Not so bloody foolish that I don't now see what's been going on right under my own nose."

A burst of hysterical laughter threatens to erupt, for how many years have I been seeing Jian? Eight years, and all of them while Colin has stupidly been looking in the opposite direction. I want to tell him. I want to spill my guts and never, ever again have to play this ridiculous game.

But I can't, not yet, so instead I ask him, "Have you met his wife at The Americanas Club recently? Her name's Lì Húa. They're expecting a baby." Oh, how much it hurts to say that, but I quickly go on. "He wants to find something special to give her. It's their first child … a boy … yes, a boy, I think." The words stick in my throat, the sour taste of vomit fills my mouth, tears flow unchecked down my face. I can't do this. I run to the bathroom and lock the door behind me.

Who's the fool now? I chide myself. Never was there a more obvious admission of guilt.

Colin waits half an hour before he knocks on the door. "You have to let me in, Julia. I need to take a shower and get changed."

Reluctantly I open the door and we change places. He doesn't say anything, just strips off his clothes and climbs into the cubicle. I resume my seat in front of the window.

When he comes out of the bathroom he says, "I'm going to assume that you're not coming to dinner with me."

"I'm not hungry," I say. "I don't want food or alcohol. I just want an explanation."

A smile tugs at the corners of his mouth but it doesn't reach as far as his eyes. "You want to know why I'm really here? I'll tell you. I've been offered early retirement. It isn't a great package, but fortunately I still have useful contacts and dinner this evening is an interview of sorts. All being well, I'm going to be able to carry on some consultancy work."

I can hardly bear to ask, but I have to know. "You're leaving Singapore, aren't you?"

"Yes," he says. "From April next year, I'll be working out of Felixstowe. That's Suffolk, Julia, in case you've forgotten your 'O' level geography of the British Isles." He finishes getting dressed, checks his appearance in the mirror. "It looks like I'll be coming home much sooner than I expected. I have absolutely no idea what you intend to do and at this precise moment, well, frankly my dear, I don't give a damn!" And he slams out of the room without a backward glance.

Richard

When I wake this morning and remember that it's Friday, I immediately experience a feeling of nervous anticipation for the day ahead, but not in a bad way – for a change.

I've wrung a promise from Julia that she'll move out of the Marriott hotel and as a consequence I'm able to eat breakfast, get showered and dressed and not feel an overwhelming sense of dark foreboding. To further enhance my good mood, my mother's consultant has declared himself happy to discharge her this afternoon and confirmed his opinion that she isn't showing any obvious signs of dementia.

I've already arranged with the office to take a day off work so when I set off for the supermarket en route to Hillcrest, I'm beginning to feel a cautious optimism. It's early and the car park isn't full; I find everything I want without having to ask, and in no time at all I'm wheeling a trolley with a bag of essentials back to the car.

Even the traffic on the A12 is flowing freely so when I finally pull onto the drive at Hillcrest, I'm whistling a happy tune.

I let myself into the house and immediately hear the sound of a vacuum cleaner buzzing from one of the bedrooms upstairs. I think to myself this isn't Monday but perhaps my mother has thought to phone Maggie and ask her to make up the bed.

The vacuuming continues unabated, so I put away the food I've bought and fill the kettle – I'm certain Maggie will appreciate a cup of tea before she leaves. I think, it's the least I can do under the circumstances.

When the vacuuming stops, I make my way upstairs. A woman I don't know meets me in the doorway of my mother's bedroom. She looks a bit surprised to see me, but as she's wearing a pink polo shirt with the words Hutton Home Help embroidered in large black letters on the front pocket, I don't immediately jump to the conclusion that she's someone who's broken into the house to open the safe.

"Who are you?" I ask her.

"I'm Jackie," she says and then points to the logo on the pocket of the uniform. "Hutton Home Help. Maggie sent me."

"Oh, I see." I glance into the room and notice at once that the duvet and pillows are still piled in the middle of the bed so I say in a jovial tone, "I'm not sure where the clean bed linen is either but I'm sure we can find it between the two of us."

A small frown cleaves her brow. "Maggie didn't say anything about making up the bed."

"Oh, really?" Now I'm confused. "Why are you here then?"

"She asked me to clean up the broken glass. I've done the best I can. I've wrapped up all the bits I could pick up with my hands in newspaper, but I've had to use the vacuum cleaner to pick up the rest of it. Didn't have a choice really with the long pile on this carpet, but I'm sure it'll be fine." She pushes her way past me. "I have to get off now."

Now I'm really confused. "What broken glass?"

Her expression is a mixture of embarrassment and irritation. "Look, I'm just doing what Maggie told me to do. I don't know how it happened. You'll have to ask *her*."

"What broken glass?" I say again. "You mean a window? A mirror?" She shakes her head. She quickly heads for the stairs and I follow her. "I need to know what you're talking about," I say in my sternest voice. "How did something get broken when there's nobody here and the house is locked up?"

She halts at the top of the stairs and swings round to face me. Her eyes flash defiance when she says, "I came here to do a job and now I've done it. I didn't come here to get interrogated. You've got a problem? Talk to the boss." She sprints down the stairs and is out the front door and pulling it closed behind her before I can stop her.

I slowly walk back to the bedroom, trying to digest what's just happened. There isn't a single speck of glass on the carpet as far as I can tell, and no sign of any broken glass wrapped in newspaper. The window and the mirror are both still intact so it has to be something that was sitting in the bedroom – an ornament or a vase perhaps –

although that still doesn't explain why this Jackie and not Maggie came here to clean it up, or how it got broken.

As a precaution, I walk around the house checking all the windows and all the mirrors. Nothing has been damaged, but when I enter the dining-room I know that something has changed: something is missing that's usually here. It's the crystal decanter and whiskey glasses. They're gone.

I find them – or rather what's left of them – wrapped in newspaper at the bottom of the bin in the kitchen. How the hell, I think to myself, did a bottle of whiskey and two glasses get from the dining room to the bedroom? It just doesn't make sense.

What makes even less sense is that the twenty-year-old malt whiskey must have disappeared as well because there isn't a trace of it anywhere, not even the faintest whiff. Logic dictates that whoever broke the bottle drank the whiskey first and Maggie must have known about it.

Determined to get some answers, I grab my phone and search for 'Hutton Home Help'. The website soon pops up in the browser. It doesn't say who owns or runs the business, just lists the kinds of domestic help it offers, but there's a number to call and I call it. A recorded voice asks me to leave a message and a contact number. The voice sounds a lot like Maggie. I briefly consider leaving a message but decide on reflection that this is a conversation she and I need to have face to face.

What the hell's been going on here, I think to myself angrily. Has she been using the place for parties? For secret, romantic trysts? Whatever it is, I think perhaps her services are going to have to be terminated.

Lenora

When Frankie the physio arrived early this morning for a second round of staircase gymnastics, I thought, no hoped, he'd changed his mind about me being discharged. He stood at the foot of the bed and gave me a long, penetrating look. I offered in return an unwavering stare: our eyes were locked together for several increasingly uncomfortable seconds before he asked me, "How are you feeling this morning? Ready to go home?"

"If I say 'no', will it make any difference?"

"Why don't you want to go home? Is something worrying you?"

"Worrying me?" I said. Of course, I couldn't tell him the real reason so I made up the best excuse that I could think of on the spur of the moment. "I don't want to go home because I'm not convinced that I can *walk* safely with crutches never mind negotiate the stairs on my own."

"But you were fine yesterday," he said. "You were a superstar, Lenora."

"If you're going to use that kind of language, I can tell you right now I won't be moving from this chair."

He looked puzzled. "What kind of language?"

"The kind of patronising language people use when they want small children to cooperate."

He gave me a sheepish grin. "Sorry. Force of habit."

"It's degrading."

"I know it is."

"No, you don't know! If you were sitting in this chair instead of me, would the staff talk to you like you had the functioning brain cells of a five-year-old? I don't think so!"

He heaved a sigh. "I know exactly what you're saying and I'm sorry, okay? I promise I won't do it again." He handed me the crutches. "One more time, up the stairs and down again. Just to make completely sure."

After Frankie had gone, the doctor stopped by my bed for a final consultation. He told me Richard wants him to refer me to the Memory Clinic. I told him there was nothing wrong with my memory and he said I was probably right, but it wouldn't hurt to check, especially as I can't remember how I came to fall down the stairs. Well, that shut me up.

I dream about falling down the stairs. In my dreams, I feel Aggie's breath on my cheek, smell her perfume; I feel the pressure of her hand on my shoulder. As I fall, I turn and see her clearly at the top of the stairs. She's already walking away. The dark curtain of hair swings from side to side; her hand glides over the wooden rail; the red dress slides over her thighs: it's a confident, sinuous movement. She has become the consummate 'Girl in the Red Dress'.

When I wake, I remember that it didn't happen quite like that.

What do I actually remember?

I remember walking from my bedroom to the head of the stairs. I remember becoming aware of the scent of '*Je Reviens*' – it struck me like a blow to the back of the head, left me feeling shaky and fearful. I was anxious to get out of the house. I remember setting my foot on the first step and that's when I felt it – the pressure of a firm hand in the small of my back.

Even now I'm not certain if I fell because I was shoved, or if I fell because I couldn't move my feet fast enough, because I was terrified of what I might see if I turned around.

As I fell, I caught just a glimpse of her: a woman in a red dress.

This is why I don't want to go home, because if Aggie did it once – pushes me or scares me so much that I fall down a flight of stairs – then she can do it again and I might not be so lucky next time.

I've had a lot of time to process this experience.

If I'm *not* going gaga, then Aggie's presence in my house *isn't* a product of an atrophying mind – and I'm pretty certain everything is still functioning in that department – so it has to mean that Aggie really *is* a ghost. I can live with that even if it flies in the face of everything I've believed about life and death up till this point. What I can't live with so easily is the idea that she wants me dead as well.

205

Aggie was my friend. I was her deathbed companion. Why does she want to kill me?

I can only think of one explanation. It's hardly rational, but having listened to her tell me why she felt she had to end her father's life after he had a stroke, and why she allowed her mother drown in the bath, never mind running George off the road in that old Volvo – well, there can be only one explanation: she thinks she's saving me again.

Never was there a more dysfunctional form of empathy, but I'm certain that's what it is.

In the days before she died, we spent a lot of time together reminiscing although she didn't tell me about Mr and Mrs Bagshot until the very end.

During those days, we had many intimate conversations, some of them about life and death.

"I'm not scared of dying," she said one day. "I've thought about it quite a lot and I've come to realise that it's a natural conclusion so there's not much point fighting it."

"Well, nobody lives forever, I know," I said, "but I'm not sure I agree with you about not fighting it."

Her bright blue eyes probed my face. "Is that a dig?"

We were sitting as we usually sat: Aggie propped up against a mound of pillows on the bed and me sprawled in the chair. It was early evening, that time of the day when the late summer sun is sitting like a huge, golden globe on the horizon; no hint of darkness yet but somehow you can feel it gathering in the corners of the room. A bit like death itself, just waiting for the moment to arrive when it can creep in and extinguish the light.

I smiled. "I've forgiven you for choosing to leave me like this."

Her expression was serious. "I don't want to leave you, Lenora. In fact, I'm really worried about you."

"Well, don't. Worry, that is."

"But I do," she insisted. "You'll be all by yourself."

"I've got Richard and Julia."

"Not really," she said.

It was the kind of comment from Aggie I'd grown used to. It wasn't meant to offend. It was just a statement of truth, and I couldn't deny that I no longer 'had' Julia in any sensible sense of the word – she'd been living her own life in Singapore for many years and I didn't have a place in it. Richard, on the other hand, still kept in touch. Not as often as I would have liked, but I don't think he had many happy memories of living at home, so he phoned, or we met somewhere for lunch.

However, when other people draw your attention to something, which you'd prefer not to dwell on, it hurts. In the past, I would have been stung into offering some waspish response, but Aggie was dying a slow and painful death and I wasn't going to add to her pain. It took me several minutes to think of a suitable response.

"Birds always fly the nest. That's how it's meant to be."

She grimaced. "You're having another dig at me, aren't you?"

I jumped to my feet and slid onto the bed next to her; gently took her hand in mine. "I'm not having a dig at you. You're right. Julia isn't really part of my life anymore, and Richard is usually too busy to do more than eat the occasional meal with me." I squeezed her hand. "But I've had your friendship all my life, Aggie. That's been a blessing. And you've had my friendship too. We've had each other."

A single teardrop rolled down her cheek. "When I die, you won't have me anymore. You'll be all alone. I can't tell you how sad that makes me, Lenora."

"I'll have you in my heart, Aggie," I said. "You'll always be with me."

Well, those turned out to be words of breathtaking prescience – 'You'll always be with me'. The trouble is I think Aggie now wants *me* to follow *her* into the afterlife. She thinks I'm sad and lonely and that actually I'd be better off dead.

Julia

I hear Colin before I see him. His stertorous breathing rumbles from the direction of the foot of the bed. I untangle myself from the bedclothes and crawl towards the sound. He's sleeping on his back on the floor, head supported by one of the pillows from the bed and from somewhere he's found a blanket. I didn't hear him enter the room last night, but I made use of the minibar after he left, and a cocktail of spirits is as good as any sleeping pill.

I tiptoe to the bathroom, trying hard not to wake him, but when I return to the bedroom, he's sitting on the end of the bed. I'm trusting, hoping that last night's argument will be dealt with in the usual way: by not referring to it and acting like nothing has happened, but Colin takes up where he left off last night.

"I don't know what your plans are, Julia, but I'll be staying in London for at least a week." When I open my mouth to respond, he quickly adds, "That wasn't a question. I have no interest in your plans – either immediate or long-term."

"I don't know what my long-term plans are either," I say. "My immediate plan is to check out of the hotel and move in with my mother. She's being discharged from hospital today."

He looks surprised. "So that really *is* the reason you flew back here?"

"Yes! I've told you Richard can't look after her. She's had a hip replacement and she needs someone to stay with her until she's *independently mobile*." I have no idea what those two words actually mean in practice, but it seems to make an impression on Colin because his face softens. I try to take advantage of this change of disposition by asking him if we can discuss the issue, which he raised yesterday evening. "Like sensible adults," I say, and I throw in a hopeful smile.

"Sensible adults," he repeats back to me. "I don't think you've ever been a *sensible adult*. What is there to discuss, anyway? And please don't do me the discourtesy of continuing to pretend that your relationship with John Tan is a professional one. You owe me that much."

I sit down on the bed next to him and he doesn't move away so I take his hand and hold it in my lap. I keep thinking, I can put up a convincing defence. I can talk him round even if I can't persuade him that he's completely wrong, but I need to get a grip on the situation before it spirals out of control.

"Colin," I begin in a calm voice. "I'm not going to lie to you. I have been seeing him … romantically … but it's only been for a few months. I was telling you the truth when I said that he's been a client of Glück Glass for about eight years. And that he's an avid collector – that's how I've got to know him so well. We've had dinner together, I promise you, that's all."

"Oh, Julia…" Colin stifles a sob, squeezes my hand and then withdraws it.

I throw my arms around his neck. "I'm so sorry, Colin. It shouldn't have happened, but I haven't been happy for so long. I know you've always wanted us to come back here; spend our last years together somewhere quiet on the coast when you retire but I can't bear the thought of it. I want to stay in Singapore."

I feel certain that he'll relax this seemingly implacable stance until I realise that, although he hasn't pulled away from me, his whole body has stiffened. It's like holding a corpse that's still in the grip of rigor mortis. I close my eyes and wait for the explosion but when he speaks his voice is little more than a whisper.

"I spoke to Tan's wife. I saw her at The Americanas Club the same evening I spoke to Nancy. She knew all about you. She used the word 'qiè' to describe you. My Mandarin isn't great, but it didn't matter because her English is excellent, and she translated it for me. She said it means 'concubine'. I actually apologised to her, but she just shrugged her shoulders. It was such a small gesture, but it spoke volumes. Shall I tell you what it meant, that shrug? It meant your Julia is the bit on the side that can be discarded like a dirty rag, but I'm the '*forever wife*'."

He stands up and walks to the bathroom. When he gets to the door he turns around and says, "I don't think I've ever known a greater humiliation in my entire life. Now I'm going to take a shower and then I'm having breakfast. When I get back to the room, I expect you to have packed your suitcases and checked out of the hotel."

My heart starts to beat wildly in my chest and suddenly I feel like I'm drowning. I try to suck the cool, dry air of the hotel room into my lungs, but they don't respond. I think I must be having a panic attack. Colin watches me impassively from the doorway of the bathroom. "I can't breathe," I manage to grind out between my teeth.

"You're fine," he says. "It's just the shock."

After several agonising minutes, I manage to calm myself. This isn't how it was meant to be – I was supposed to be the one calling the shots. My mind races trying to piece together this new puzzle because I don't understand why I've reacted like this. So, Colin knows about Jian. So, what? Mentally I try to reproduce Lí Huà's nonchalant shrug, but it won't work because what I feel is … fear.

It's a moment of revelation. I know I don't love Colin. I know I want to be with Jian, but the truth is that I'm actually terrified of ending my marriage.

Colin is still standing, waiting. His face is a picture of unrelieved misery. "You need to go now," he says.

"But I don't want to leave you," I protest.

"You left me a long time ago, Julia," he replies. "I just didn't realise that you'd gone."

I've been left with no choice but to do exactly what he says, and as soon as he's showered and dressed and closed the door of the room behind him, I begin to pack. I'm not sure what to do with my card key but when I return it to reception, the girl behind the counter tells me that the account has already been settled in full by my husband. She gives me an odd look, so I'm guessing that Colin has checked out of *my* room and checked into another one on his own.

I hail a taxi and ask to be taken to Liverpool Street station. It's a slow journey from one side of the city to the other and it gives me time to contemplate my situation, but can I seriously contemplate leaving Colin? Where would I go? A picture pops into my head and it isn't a pretty one. It's me sitting on my own at Jian's Elizabeth

Heights apartment, watching the clock, waiting for him to decide whether he'll go home, or whether he'll steal away for a few hours to be with me, his *mistress*. It takes two seconds to work out in which direction he'll be heading.

I try to reassure myself, tell myself nothing would fundamentally change. I'd still be working at the gallery each day, still meeting Nancy for lunch, still seeing Jian – when he isn't with his wife and new baby.

I squeeze my eyes tightly shut, but a tear escapes, and the picture is still there. Oh, God ... I really didn't think this through.

Richard

Still smarting from my surprise encounter with the indomitable Jackie from Hutton Home Help, I nearly forget that I need to pack some clean clothes for my mother to change into before I leave Hillcrest to drive to the hospital.

I go back up to her bedroom and search through the wardrobe for something suitable. The weather is noticeably cooler than it was when she was admitted two weeks ago, but it occurs to me that pulling on trousers over a recently replaced hip might be difficult, so instead I choose a soft wool dress.

I'm congratulating myself on my foresight and good sense when I hear a door slam shut. It sounds like it's somewhere downstairs and it really unnerves me because I know – because I've only just checked them – that every window is not only closed but locked so it can't have been caused by a gust of wind through an open window.

The silence after the loud slam is even more unnerving. I stand in the bedroom and listen. I can't hear a thing, but I gradually become aware of a strange tension in the atmosphere – it reminds me of the eerie sense of oppression one sometimes senses before the outbreak of a storm.

When the door slams a second time all I want to do is grab the bag I've just packed and head for the front door, but if someone has got into the house then I'm going to have to confront them.

As I cautiously retrace my steps downstairs, I notice that every door is open including the door to my father's study. Now, my mind begins to race, and a cold sweat breaks out on my face and neck. I feel every trickle of perspiration running down my back and my chest. Did I leave the doors open when I checked the windows? And how could someone get into the house when the both the front and back doors are locked?

I stand at the foot of the stairs and strain my ears to listen for anything that might reveal an intruder: a footstep, a movement, even heavy breathing. Once again, I'm greeted by the sound of silence, but my eyes are suddenly drawn through the open doorway of the kitchen to where I can see a door that's still closed. It's the door to the garage, a door rarely used but which both Julia and I have opened recently because the garage is where my mother put the family photographs.

I place the bag containing my mother's clothes on the floor and as I do, I become aware of the old casement clock ticking away. It's like the heartbeat of the house. As I move towards the kitchen, the space between each drawn-out tick and tock grows longer, as though time itself is slowing.

My limbs feel heavy: I struggle to place one foot in front of the other, but I'm determined to reach the door to the garage because somehow, I know that's where I'm supposed to go.

When I reach the door, I take a deep breath, place my hand on the handle and push. The door is heavy, but it swings open easily. Light from the kitchen rushes in but it only illuminates the area immediately in front of the door and I can sense something moving in the far, dark corner.

"Who's there?" I shout.

I feel for the light switch and press it down. It takes several agonizing seconds for the overhead fluorescent tube to flicker and then flood the garage with harsh, white light.

There's nobody there. The garage is empty except for my mother's small car and a pile of boxes.

Relief overwhelms me, but it's soon replaced by nervous curiosity. Some unconscious unravelling of the mystery of the slamming door has propelled me in the direction of the garage. The answer lies here somewhere, I think. I look about me for something, anything, that will explain it but there really is nothing here.

On an impulse, I check the up-and-over door, which opens out onto the driveway. It's old, made from solid timber in a steel frame, and I have no doubts about its security until I notice that it hasn't been pushed back into the correct position so that it locks. All you'd need to do to gain entry to the garage from the outside is pull on the handle and the up-and-over door would swing up and over into the roof space. In fact, if the internal garage door had already been left unlocked as well – which it evidently has – then anyone could get into the house. No need to break in; no need for a key.

Is this what I was meant to find? Was it this door from the garage into the kitchen, which slammed once, twice?

All I can think after I've secured both garage doors is: what the hell has Maggie been up to? Because it has to be Maggie who's responsible for all of this: the whiskey, the broken decanter and glasses, the garage door deliberately left unsecured. There can be no other explanation, but as I'm driving away, I can't help asking myself, why would she do this? It really doesn't make sense.

On Sparrow Ward at the hospital my mother's bed is empty, but I can see at once that it's waiting for a new occupant because the overhead whiteboard has been wiped clean and the bedding has that freshly laundered look about it.

The woman in the opposite bed who mistook me for Arthur calls out, "Hallo, Richard. Have you come to collect your mum?"

"Yes," I say, "but she seems to have left already."

"That's right, dear. You need to go to the departure lounge."

"Departure lounge?"

"It's on the second floor. They need the bed, you see, and Lenora told them you were coming to collect her. I told her – I said, 'You're lucky you've got someone to help you out.' My Arthur – that's *my* boy – he's abso-bloody-useless. They told him I'd be good to go this morning, but he said, he can't take time off work, so I've got to wait here till they know they can book me an ambulance. I mean, you'd think they could organise something a bit quicker than this. I've been waiting here since half past nine."

I don't quite know how to reply to this outpouring of discontent, so I just wish her well and hurry back the way I came.

I take the lift to the second floor and a sign points me to the 'Discharge Lounge' so I guess I'm heading in the right direction.

My mother greets me with an anxious expression on her face. "Did you go up to the ward?" she asks.

"I did. But Arthur's mum told me where to find you."

"Is she still there? She won't be happy."

"She's not. And Arthur's still in the doghouse."

Her mouth smiles in response but her eyes carry a look of nervous apprehension. "I'm still in my nightie and dressing-gown, but they insisted I had to come here to wait for you."

"That's okay." I show her the bag of clothes I've brought with me. "Do you want to change?"

"Maybe put my coat on," she says, and she immediately shuffles off the dressing-gown.

A nurse appears at my shoulder. "Are you here for Lenora Oakley?" When I say I am, she hands me an envelope. "You need to give the letter inside here to her GP. It just lets him know that she's been discharged from hospital and any changes to her medication. There are some information sheets and some exercises from the physiotherapist, which she needs to do at home." She looks down at my mother with what I know is intended to be a compassionate smile. "It's really important that you read the instructions carefully, Lenora. If you need help understanding anything, I'm sure your son can explain it to you."

I glance at my mother. Any anxiety she felt about leaving hospital has been replaced with angry indignation and before I can intervene, she replies in an icy tone, "I was the one who taught *him* to read. And, by the way, my GP is a *her*."

The nurse pats her distractedly on the shoulder: her attention is already on another patient.

Before my mother can launch into a full-blown rant against ageist and sexist attitudes, I pull her coat from the bag and insist that she puts it on straight away. "Let's go," I say.

While we slowly make our way to the car park, I compliment her on how well she's managing with the crutches. "I'm amazed," I tell her.

"What are you amazed at? That I can walk and talk at the same time?"

I laugh. "It's nice to have the old *you* back again. And by old, I don't mean ancient."

"You make it sound like I wasn't *me* while I was in hospital."

"Well, you weren't – at least, not for a while. To be honest, Mum, I've been quite worried about you."

"Ah…" she says.

"Ah?"

"Is that why you told the consultant you want him to refer me to this Memory Clinic? If it is, I can tell you right now there's nothing wrong with my memory."

We've reached the car, so I suggest we continue the conversation once we get on the road. It's not one I'm looking forward to, but I remember my mother once confiding in me that she always arranged to have difficult conversations while she was driving whether it was with my father or with me and Julia. She said it gave her an excuse to not have eye contact while she said what she wanted to say, and the other person was forced to sit and listen. Either that or do a James Bond-style getaway.

As soon as we've left the hospital grounds and are back on a main road I begin. "While you were in hospital, you were very confused sometimes, Mum. You said Robin came to see you, which obviously he didn't because he's living in Melbourne. And you gave me those old tickets for the swimming pool at the leisure centre: you told me you didn't want Aggie to find them. Do you remember any of that?" I glance at her face but it's unreadable. "Mum?"

"Why are you asking me if I remember when you've already decided that I've got a problem with my memory?"

"You just told me there's nothing wrong with your memory."

Another sideways glance establishes that she can see she's slipped up: the tightest of smiles puckers the corners of her mouth. She says. "I had a UTI. That sometimes causes confusion and paranoia. Apparently, it's something us *old folk* are especially prone to, but there isn't anything wrong with my memory. And before you ask – because I know you *will* ask – because the doctor has *already* mentioned it to me – yes, I do remember how I came to fall down the stairs."

"You told me you didn't remember!"

"I know."

I'm distracted for several minutes by the driver of a white van who seems intent on overtaking me even though the markings on the road clearly indicate that it's prohibited. But I'm keen to know what happened the day that she fell so as soon as he's accomplished his objective, I turn to her again. "So … what happened that you didn't want to tell me?"

216

"I still don't want to tell you. I know you're going to think that I'm going gaga."

This time I'm the one reluctant to reply, but she doesn't seem to notice my hesitation. She leans her head back against the headrest and closes her eyes. We sit in silence for perhaps ten minutes. I think she's fallen asleep, but when I look at her face to check, she's opened her eyes again.

"Do you believe in ghosts, Richard?" she asks in a strained voice. "Before you answer, let me tell you that I've asked Edward Feering the same question. I hoped he might be able to help me, but he … prevaricated; didn't want to commit himself. Apparently, the Anglican Church is happy to promote the mysterious workings of the Holy Ghost, but not yet ready to recognise the existence of *other* incorporeal beings. Actually, he had the same reaction I know you're going to have when I tell what you happened. You've hinted at it already – I know why people get referred to a memory clinic by the way and it isn't because they can't remember where they put their spectacles."

"Mum…" I begin, but she immediately cuts me off.

"Let me tell you everything. Then you can decide for yourself if I'm sliding into senility or if, God forbid, there really is something else going on."

And then she tells me.

Lenora

Poor Richard. Forced to listen to the ravings of a mad, old woman. I'm surprised he hasn't pulled over to the side of the road and asked me to climb into the back seat of the car so that he can press down the kiddie locks and keep me secured for my own protection. Instead he's listened attentively and without comment.

"When did this all begin?" he asks.

"Well, obviously after Aggie died." I don't want to sound snappish, but I know how this all sounds and I feel foolish beyond words, now that I've actually told my story out loud. "Please don't tell me it's a form of unresolved grief. I've already had that lecture from Maggie."

"Really?" He glances at me with an eager, expectant expression on his face.

"She said she read about it in a magazine – the inability to accept the death of a loved one caused by powerful feelings of pain and sorrow."

"I suppose it's possible…"

"No, it's not!"

"But…"

"I was sitting next to her when she died, Richard. I saw them take her body away and I sat in the chapel at the crematorium and watched her coffin slide into a fiery furnace. I know she's dead." His mouth opens to contradict me once again, so I shut him up quickly. "I'm not mourning. I'm not suffering from unresolved grief. The woman had terminal cancer and at the end, when she died, both of us were glad she'd gone."

He's shocked. He can't believe I said I'm glad Aggie died. Of course, I'm not exactly *glad* that she died, but under the circumstances, well, it was definitely a case of a welcome end to overwhelming suffering.

218

"She was your closest friend," he begins again. "You must have been grieving..."

"Oh, for goodness sake! Of course, I grieved for her after she died. She *was* my closest friend. But I'm not grieving for her anymore."

"Okay..." he says slowly. "So, what do you think has been happening?"

I stall for time to reply because that's the burning question, isn't it?

Before I fell down the stairs, I couldn't make up my mind. Was I imagining everything or had Aggie returned from the dead to haunt my waking – and unwaking – hours? Had she ever really left?

As Edward Feering had been less than useless, I eventually confided my fears in Maggie. It's fair to say she was a bit shocked, but she didn't dismiss it as just the wild imaginings of a batty, old woman who needs to go a memory clinic. She said she would think about it and the following week she told me she thought she had a solution. She said she didn't know if it was unresolved grief like it said in the magazine, or if perhaps Aggie *was* finding it hard to leave this world behind her, but she thought it might be useful either way if I went to the cemetery where her ashes had been placed in the columbarium. She said, she thought I should say a final goodbye to Aggie; tell her I was fine, and it was time for her to move on.

I had nothing to lose, so that's what I did. I went to the cemetery and I stood in front of the urn which housed Aggie's ashes. I told her I was happy on my own and I didn't need her to watch over me; that she could leave Hillcrest and this world safe in the knowledge that all would be well.

For perhaps a couple of weeks everything *was* well, and my home once again became a haven of peace. Then Aggie appeared behind me at the top of the stairs, gave me a nudge and I fell.

Richard is waiting patiently for a reply and I can only say to him, "I don't know what to think."

He looks thoughtful. I can tell by the way he bites his lower lip that he's considering the possibilities. At last he says, "I'm going to tell you something – well, two things actually. Don't freak out."

"I won't," I say. "I promise."

"I think something *is* going on at Hillcrest, but I don't think it's anything … supernatural."

"What's happened?"

"I told you I called in a couple of hours ago to drop off some shopping and pick up some clothes for you. Well, guess what I found? A cleaner from Hutton Home Help in your bedroom."

"Not Maggie?"

"No. Someone called Jackie. She was clearing up broken glass; she said Maggie told her to do it. After she left, I discovered that the broken glass was Dad's crystal whiskey decanter and glasses. The ones on the silver tray in the dining room."

This doesn't strike me as especially worrying because it's happened before – when Maggie was on holiday or unwell – but she always asked my permission first before she sent someone to the house with a key to let themselves in. "How on earth did Maggie know what had happened?" I ask him.

"That's what I couldn't work out," he says.

"What's the second thing?"

Richard is studying the road ahead of him, but he casts a cautious glance in my direction before he replies (he always hates to be the bearer of bad tidings). "I discovered that the door to the garage – the up-and-over door – it was unlocked. Anyone could have got into the house, and I know you won't want to hear this, but I think Maggie's responsible. I think she's been using the house to meet ... to meet men."

Meet men? I suppose I don't *really* know Maggie well enough to comment on her private life, but it seems highly unlikely to me. "Why would Maggie need to leave the garage door open when she has a key to the front door?"

"Perhaps she left it open for the person she's been meeting."

"Couldn't she just give him her key?"

"Perhaps that was too big a risk."

"Bigger than leaving the garage doors open so that he can get into the house and drink your father's whiskey?"

"I know it sounds unlikely," he says, "but didn't you say you thought you'd seen someone lurking in the back garden?"

"I *thought* I saw Aggie," I say.

"But it could have been a man."

"In a red dress?"

"Are you sure it was Aggie?"

"Am I sure it was Aggie? Are you mad?"

Richard's head swings round and he says sharply, "Am *I* mad? Are you kidding me? You're the one who thinks that it's more likely to have been your dead friend wafting around the garden in her red dress rather than consider the possibility that Maggie has a boyfriend waiting to meet her."

His brief lapse of focus on the road propels the car dangerously towards the kerb but Richard quickly corrects it. The situation has shaken up both of us and, even though I'm not thrilled at the prospect of returning to my haunted house, if I have to do it I'd rather do it in one piece so I choose not to respond with the displeasure I actually feel and instead point out in a calm voice, "Maggie only works on a Monday morning."

He's obviously still feeling rattled because he exclaims crossly, "Well, she's not going to bring him into the house when she's cleaning your carpets, is she!"

I have to say, this persistent sarcasm is quite out of character for Richard, but I'm forced to agree with him. "Probably not," I say. "But why would she need to secretly meet *anyone* in my house?"

"I don't know! But somebody was drinking whiskey in your bedroom and somehow managed to break the bottle and the two glasses. Somebody is responsible for leaving the garage doors unlocked. Was that Aggie?"

As neither one of us can be sure, we lapse into silence for the rest of the journey home, each lost in our own private thoughts.

When we arrive at Hillcrest, Julia comes out of the house to greet us. She smiles and tells me I look well. I can't say the same for her. She's usually immaculately and expensively turned out from head to toe but today she's wearing a simple cream sweater with a pair of jeans and not a scrap of make-up. If I didn't know her better, I'd think she'd been crying.

She leads us into the house saying that she's made up the beds in both my room and the guest room. I don't ask her why she isn't sleeping in her own room because I already know the answer.

I've quickly discovered that walking around on crutches is exhausting so when Richard offers to make me a cup of tea, I ask him if someone will bring it up to my room. "I think I need to rest for a while," I tell them.

They both stand at the foot of the stairs and watch my painfully slow ascent. I hear Richard say to Julia in a low voice, which he probably thinks I can't hear, "You'll need to keep an eye on her when she's going up and down the stairs."

"Why?" Julia asks. "She looks like she knows what she's doing, and I can't help her if she falls."

"I'll explain later," he says.

I manage to get to my bedroom without tumbling down the stairs, and carefully lower myself onto the bed – Frankie the physio gave me precise instructions before I left. He told me he hoped – in the nicest way possible – that he wouldn't see me again soon. I told him his feelings were reciprocated and we said goodbye with a friendly handshake.

Now that I'm back in my own bed, I have a mixture of emotions running through my head. On the one hand, I'm happy to be home surrounded by my own things and not having to listen to the vapid conversation of the medical staff with the other patients. Dementia is a cruel and careless thief of intellect and dignity and if that's the alternative explanation for what I've been experiencing then perhaps being haunted by Aggie isn't such a high price to pay. On the other hand, if my brain is still functioning normally and this *madness* is Aggie intent on helping me to join her in the afterlife then moving out of my lovely home would certainly be the wisest course of action.

I'm considering my dilemma when Julia appears in the doorway.

"I hope this is up to your usual standards," she says, placing a mug of tea on the table next to me. "And before you complain about the mug, Richard said it would be safer for you. I told him you're more than capable of balancing a cup in a saucer, especially seeing the way you went about walking up the stairs carrying your crutches," she adds. She offers me a sympathetic smile.

"Oh, you know your brother," I say. "Caution is his middle name." I deliberately catch her eye. "Not like you, eh Julia?"

A pained expression passes over her face. "Well, it's no bad thing, is it?"

I want to ask her what's happened, but this clearly isn't the right time so instead I say, "I'm going to rest upstairs here for a while so don't worry about me."

"Don't try to come downstairs by yourself," she tells me. "Shout out and one of us will …" she gives a strangled laugh. "Actually, I don't know what we'll do, but when we've worked out what it is then we'll do it."

I wave her away.

The tea tastes good although I think Richard just swished a bag around in some hot water because the mug has a telltale rim of brown scum around the edge of it. I think to myself: I'll have to tell him about my tea-for-one teapot, but no sooner has the picture of the little blue and white teapot burst into the forefront of my memory than another picture takes its place and my hand actually begins to shake. I'm reminded of the day that Aggie came into my room with a cup of tea, sat on the end of my bed and insisted on telling me what she'd done.

It was early, a Monday morning, and I was woken by the sound of someone moving around downstairs. I immediately assumed it must be Maggie even though the clock said it was only seven thirty.

I didn't want to get up. I was dog-tired. Caring for Aggie was taking a huge toll on both my physical and mental health and I wasn't sure how much longer I could go on. We'd talked about what might happen at the end, but Aggie was adamant that she wasn't going to die in a hospital bed. The medication she took made her dull and drowsy: it eased the pain and was helping her to make an exit from this life with dignity and calm, but it didn't help me.

I was on the point of forcing myself to get up when there was a tap on the door. It slowly opened into the room and Aggie shuffled in bearing a cup of tea, no saucer.

"I'm sorry, Lenora," she said, "but I've got a slight tremor in my hand this morning so I couldn't carry a cup and a saucer." I began to throw off the bedclothes, but she told me to stay where I was. "I have to take my tablets in half an hour, but I want to talk to you first."

"You didn't have to make me tea," I said, knowing that I sounded ungracious.

223

"I wanted to. I can't do much of anything anymore, but this morning I can make you tea."

I took the cup from her shaking hand and placed it on the table next to me. "For goodness sake sit down before you fall down."

She slumped onto the end of the bed, but it was clearly an effort for her to sit unsupported, so I ordered her to change places with me. Reluctantly, she agreed.

When she'd settled herself, I said, "So what is it then? What do you want to talk to me about?"

She immediately looked away.

I studied her profile. The soft light of the pink-curtained room lent her face an almost healthy glow from this position, but I knew it was an illusion because the cancer growing inside her had affected every cell in her body. She was dying from the inside out. Only her beautiful blue eyes had survived this desolation and they now seemed to shine with a bright, feverish light.

I waited.

At last she turned to me. "I have to tell you these things, Lenora, because there's no one else that I can trust. I have to tell you because I owe you the truth. Please don't think badly of me. Everything I've done, I've done for a reason."

And then she began.

I sat still and listened. I sat still and listened even when I wanted to stand up and walk out of the room. I sat still and listened even when I wanted to stand up, walk out of the room, pour myself a large glass of brandy, turn on the radio, turn the music up to full volume and forget that Aggie had ever been my friend.

When she stopped speaking, a dreadful silence filled the room.

"Please say something," she whispered.

"I don't really know what to say, Aggie. You've just told me that you gave your father an overdose and allowed your mother to drown in the bath."

"You make it sound like I murdered them. It wasn't like that."

"But your father wasn't dying, Aggie! He'd had a stroke, but he wasn't dying. You can't even justify it by calling it euthanasia. You put it in the chocolate blancmange, so that he wouldn't know, and your mother would get the blame if it came to light."

Her expression changed from anxious pleading to one of childish vexation. "It was a kind of euthanasia! You don't realise how unhappy he was. He hated having to rely on my mother for everything. And I mean everything, Lenora. I know he wanted to die!"

"What about your mother? Did she want to die?"

Aggie's tone is one of pained exasperation when she replies. "She'd already had a heart attack when I found her in the bath. I didn't do that!"

"But you left her in the bath. You didn't try to help her. That's the point."

"She was cursing me, Lenora! Calling me terrible names. Telling me that I was stupid and useless when I know I've spent my whole life trying to please her; knowing that whatever I did would never be good enough. I had to walk out of the room before I lost my temper and said things, which I knew she'd never forgive."

I could see in her face that she wasn't about to admit that what she'd done had been anything less than completely justifiable, so I pointed out to her, "You lied about what happened, Aggie. You knew that leaving her in the bath was wrong."

"I know I lied to you when you came to the house, but I told you the truth afterwards, and I told the truth to the police."

"Really? Did you tell them that you left her to drown?"

"I didn't leave her to drown. Not really."

"Did ... you ... tell ... them?"

With her face pushed into the pillow, Aggie's skin now appeared the same colour as the bed linen – chalk white. "No," she said.

I rose unsteadily to my feet; walked with slow, deliberate steps to the bedroom door but my mind was racing. I had to ask her: I had to know if she'd used the same twisted logic to remove my husband from my life. "What you did to George, it wasn't an accident with the car, was it?" She refused to answer me, but in my heart I knew.

I left her in the bed – I didn't want to hear any more. When I went back to the bedroom to get dressed some while later, she'd returned to her own room. I put my head round the door, I don't remember what I planned to say to her, but she was sleeping. She looked quite peaceful and I think she was because she'd unburdened herself to me and now the burden was mine.

Julia

As soon as Richard has reassured himself that our mother is still resting in her room, he drags me into the kitchen and closes the door. I tell him he needs to buy green tea when he goes shopping and he tells me I can take care of the shopping myself while I'm here. When I begin to argue with him, he orders me to sit down because he says he has something to tell me and I'll probably need more than a cup of green tea afterwards.

The 'something' he has to tell me is short and to the point, but not lacking in detail: family photographs mysteriously removed from the walls, messages written by an unseen hand in lipstick on the mirror, perfume bottles, glimpses of a red dress, and the final coup d'état: a shove which sends our mother tumbling down the stairs.

"Are you trying to tell me that our mother is being haunted by Agnes Bagshot?" I ask him. "Seriously?"

"No, of course I don't think that!" he exclaims. "But *she* does. I think there's a much more mundane explanation – at least for some of it."

"Go on."

He tells me about the missing whiskey and broken crystal decanter in our mother's bedroom; about garage doors left unsecured and secret trysts. He tells me he's certain that Maggie is responsible. "It's the only explanation I can think of," he says. "We already know she comes and goes as she pleases."

"Why would she use our house to meet up with men? Doesn't she have a home of her own?"

"Perhaps she's married and doesn't want her husband to know what she's up to," he says. "Maybe the boyfriend is married as well and they think if they meet here, nobody will find out. Desperate people do desperate things."

If this last remark is a nod to my own situation then the allusion isn't lost on me. "It doesn't explain everything though, does it?" I say. "Why would someone write *'Je Reviens'* on the mirror?"

"Maybe it was a message," he suggests with a weary sigh. "Doesn't it mean, 'I will return'?"

He slumps in the chair opposite me and I notice for the first time since I arrived that an air of utter exhaustion pervades every movement, every word he utters. Then I remember that he's been juggling work and hospital visits for nearly two weeks without a break, and I'm briefly seized by a feeling of remorse, because I could have done more, and I wouldn't.

On the other hand, I *have* drawn the short straw by moving in with our mother when the hinges of her good sense and reasoning are clearly hanging off, though Richard isn't much better if he's willing to believe our mother's cleaner is using Hillcrest as a secret love nest. I tell him, "Isn't the more mundane explanation that Mummy is losing the plot? She could have been unwell for a long time and we just didn't realise. Perhaps she'd been coping well but Aggie's death acted as the catalyst for her condition to deteriorate suddenly."

"It's possible we're both right," he says. "All that weird stuff Mum told me obviously happened before she went into hospital, but the house has been empty for two weeks. Maggie could have seized the opportunity to make use of it. I know someone calling herself Sarah Oakley was phoning the ward and asking about Mum. That could have been Maggie."

"You're going to have to speak to the woman," I tell him. "Have you got a telephone number or an address for this Hutton Home Help?"

"I'm going to the office when I leave here," he says.

We spend the next hour arguing about my attempts to track down Lena Bartok and have our father's last will and testament declared null and void. He thinks I should accept the situation and get on with my life. I'm almost tempted to tell him that my life has just been thrown into turmoil by the arrival of my cuckolded husband, though I'm still hoping against hope that Colin might change his mind about leaving me while my finances are still in a state of flux and uncertainty.

I think about it some more after Richard has left and I realise that I'm actually being hopelessly optimistic. Even if Colin were to accept that the affair with Jian is over, I know he isn't going to change his mind about leaving Singapore and that's the real game changer. If Colin leaves, how can I stay?

Richard

As I pull out of the drive at Hillcrest, I have the strangest sensation that I'm being watched. I know it isn't Julia because she closed the door in my face when I told her that she needs to deal with the rejection she feels at being left out of our father's will. And it isn't my mother because I checked on her before I left, and she was still sleeping.

Ever since my father kicked me out, I've never really felt welcome at the house so what I'm sensing is possibly linked to that unpleasant memory. Still, it troubles me because, for every word I've spoken *against* the notion of Aggie as a restless spirit roving our home, I can't forget the sight of the woman in the red dress at Julia's bedroom window. I know what I saw.

For everyone's peace of mind, I must confront Maggie.

It doesn't take me long to locate the office of Hutton Home Help. It's situated above a charity shop a short walk from the railway station. The entrance door has a panel of clear glass and through it I can see Maggie speaking to someone on the phone. In a pink blouse and tailored, black skirt, she looks rather different from the Maggie who cleans my mother's house on a Monday morning.

I tap on the glass then walk straight in. She doesn't look surprised to see me and she doesn't smile but she's probably been waiting for me to contact her and knows that our conversation isn't going to be a friendly one.

When she finishes the call, she invites me to sit down.

"I expect you know why I'm here," I say.

"Yes. Jackie told me you were at the house." Maggie's bright blue eyes look steadily into mine. Her gaze doesn't waver. "I would've cleaned up the mess myself if I'd been free. I didn't think Mrs Oakley would mind if I sent someone else under the circumstances. I've had to do it before."

"What exactly are the circumstances?" I ask her, expecting a flush of embarrassment to match the colour of her blouse, but her self-assurance doesn't falter for a single second. Instead she assumes an air of bewilderment.

"I don't want to seem rude, Mr Oakley, but *I'm* not responsible for that ... that incident." She emphasizes the word 'I' loudly and emphatically and I suddenly realise that the person being accused of breaking the crystal whiskey decanter is probably me. She goes on, "I knew Mrs Oakley could soon be discharged from hospital and I wanted to make sure that everything was cleaned up properly."

"You think *I* did this?"

She shrugs. "You, or your sister. It's not my place to ask questions about how it happened."

I feel myself bristle in response to this accusation. "To my knowledge there are only four people with a key to the house," I say. "One of those was in hospital with a fractured hip, and I know it wasn't me or my sister so that only leaves you."

"Me? That's ridiculous! Why would I be drinking whiskey in your mother's bedroom?" She pushes back her chair, rises quickly to her feet and walks over to the window looking out onto the busy road in front of the building. She appears to be watching the traffic with some interest, but if I were her and had been caught out, I'd be racking my brain for an alternative explanation and I'm certain she's doing the same. When she turns back to the room, she asks me, "Are you sure no one else has a key? I know Mrs Oakley's friend, Agnes, had a key. It's possible someone else does. Maybe a neighbour? My neighbour keeps a spare key to *my* house in case I get locked out."

It's an explanation of sorts, but no more believable than the one I've already offered her. "Look, Maggie," I say to her, "you have to understand why I'm concerned."

"I do understand," she says at once. "Mrs Oakley's been with Hutton Home Help for a long time. We wouldn't usually hold a key, you know, but it's what she wanted. Sometimes I've had to send someone else, but all of our employees have a Criminal Records Bureau check."

"If you keep a key then anyone working for you could get hold of it then," I argue.

She shakes her head. "The key's kept in the safe." She walks stiffly and self-consciously back to the desk, resumes her seat and addresses me directly in a clear confident voice. "I've been working for this company for more than twelve years, Mr Oakley. I started as a cleaner and now I manage it. I've got a few favourite customers – people who've been kind to me – so I still help them out if I can because I know having a stranger in your home isn't very nice. Your mother is one of those people. I'd never take advantage of her good nature."

All the while she speaks, she keeps her blue eyes trained on mine. If she's lying, then it's a mesmerizing performance, because sincerity shines through. I find I want to believe her, if only because she's been a friend of sorts to my mother for all of those twelve years and I don't like to think that my mother's trust has been misplaced. Still...

"I'm glad you've come here today," she continues. "I've wanted to speak to you about your mother for some time. I'm really worried about her."

"She told me she'd been confiding some of *her* worries in you."

She nods. "Things have been hard for her since her friend, Agnes, died. We've talked about it and I've tried to help her but..." She shrugs and shakes her head.

"She told me."

"Then you know she thinks that lots of strange things have been happening?"

"She told me about that as well. It's made her quite fearful. I don't think she really wanted to come home."

"I'm so sorry," Maggie says, and she looks genuinely sympathetic. "It can difficult … in this line of work you get to know people quite well. Sometimes you're the first person to notice something has changed, if they live on their own."

"Are you saying you've noticed something wrong with my mother?"

She looks away, places her hand over her heart. I feel like I can hear her breathing quicken but perhaps it's just a reflection of my own fears because this is what I've been waiting to hear: that my mother probably has dementia and Maggie knows because in Maggie's line of work she gets to know people quite well, who live by themselves.

She turns back to me. "Obviously this is just my … my impression. I think some of the things she believes happened… Well, she just got confused. Things like photographs get moved when I clean, and I think she forgets. I wonder… Maybe she just *wants* to see her friend then imagination does the rest?"

She stands up and I assume it's a signal that the interview is over. She says, "If you want to end the contract with Hutton Home Help then you need to let me know soon. But please don't do anything until you've made some other arrangement."

I thank her for her time and tell her I'll speak to my mother first before any decision is made. She nods and smiles but she looks relieved when I head for the door. At the last moment, I remember the garage doors.

"There's one last thing," I say. "When I was at the house this morning, I noticed that the garage doors had been left unlocked and I couldn't work out why that would happen because you have no reason to go into the garage. It's just that … well, anyone could get in and they wouldn't even need a key."

Once again, her hand flies to her chest. "I'm so sorry, Mr Oakley. I had no idea…"

At first glance, she looks genuinely shocked, but there's something else: it's the same expression I saw on her face that day after my mother's fall. It's as though she *knew* something had happened at the house – something that troubled her. I realise I still don't trust her.

Lenora

I can't, won't open my eyes. I know Aggie is in the bedroom with me. I try to calm my shattered nerves by slow, deep breathing, but now I can smell her perfume. The light, floral scent of *Je Reviens* has become her signature. It proves that she's here, but why are you here Aggie?

Behind my closed lids I *see* a shadow pass in front of the curtains: it's just a flicker of movement against the pink fabric lit by bright morning light. My heart is racing, and my mouth is drier than a piece of driftwood. When I feel her chill breath on my face, I can't contain my fear any longer.

It's an odd experience hearing your own scream: it sounds like the panic-stricken voice of a stranger. No words just noise, but there are no words to describe blood-curdling terror.

Julia bursts in. "What's happened?" She casts her eyes frantically about the room, but with my eyes now open wide, I can see that there's no one here except the two of us.

I still can't speak even though I'm hugely relieved it's just her standing beside me. I point to the glass of water on the table next to the bed.

She presses the edge of the glass to my lips, pours some of the water into my mouth but most of it trickles down my chin. "You scared the life out of me," she says.

I let the water soothe my parched mouth, but my voice still croaks when I find it. "Aggie was here. In this room."

Julia sinks onto the bed and pats my hand. "You were dreaming," she says.

"I don't think so. When I woke up, I could smell her perfume."

Julia lifts her head and sniffs. "I can smell *something* a bit like perfume, but I think it's just fabric conditioner on the bedsheets."

"I saw her!"

"You had your eyes closed when I came into the room."

"I felt her breath on my face."

Julia's eyes narrow and she regards me calmly. "How is that possible?" she asks. "She doesn't have lungs. She's dead."

"I don't know how any of it's possible," I declare despairingly. "I think she wants to kill me, Julia!"

"Why would she want to kill you?"

"I just know she wants me dead," I tell her.

I remember the look on Richard's face yesterday afternoon when I told him why I think Aggie wants to kill me. He didn't say anything, but he didn't look convinced either. Of course, I didn't tell him about the other deaths, which Aggie was responsible for – he doesn't need to know how Mr and Mrs Bagshot were removed from the picture, and I haven't yet decided if I'm going to confess what happened to George.

Obviously I'm a party to that particular crime since I didn't report Aggie to the police after she told me what happened, that day on the beach at Clacton, but the issue of the car hidden in the garage at Tyne Lodge is going to have to be addressed sooner rather than later. I don't like to think of it as the murder weapon but I'm quite certain that a judge and jury would have little sympathy with viewing it otherwise.

Julia gives my shoulder a sympathetic squeeze. "Nightmares are horrible. I've been having some pretty awful dreams myself lately." She hesitates briefly. "I've got something I need to tell you, Mummy. Will you be okay while I make some tea for us? I promise I won't leave you alone for long."

"I'm fine now," I say, but I'm not fine. I've known Aggie almost all my life and when you've been close to someone like that, you have an almost supersensory connection with them. Richard and Julia can tell me a thousand times that this is my imagination, but I *know* Aggie is here in this house.

Julia is as good as her word and soon returns to the bedroom carrying two steaming mugs of tea. "I haven't had English Breakfast tea for..." she cocks her head to one side and considers it for a moment. "...Good grief!" she exclaims. "It must be the last time I stayed here – what's that? Nearly twenty years ago."

"It was January two-thousand – our ruby wedding anniversary. You and Colin wanted to stay in a hotel in London, but everything was booked up because of the millennium celebrations."

"You're right," she says. Her face clouds suddenly. "How did he do it? How did Daddy stand in that room downstairs and welcome all our family to celebrate forty years of *happy marriage* when he knew he had that Bartok woman and her child living five minutes from our home?" A small smile parts her lips. "He wasn't exactly truthful with her either though. Apparently, he told her you wouldn't agree to give him a divorce."

"Is that what she honestly thought?"

"Well, did you ever ask him for a divorce?"

"Yes, and he always refused," I say. "He told me I was free to leave whenever I wanted, but he wasn't going to lose his house to..." I use my fingers to quote mark his actual words. "...pay for it."

"So, you chose to stay with him."

I shake my head. "I chose *not to leave* – it's an important distinction. The harsh reality is that I had no money of my own and nowhere to go. But I didn't *stay* with him. It wasn't a marriage; we just went through the motions."

Julia's smile, which had been laced with schadenfreude for Lena Bartok and her daughter Miriam, abruptly crumples, and then she does something completely unexpected: she clambers onto the bed next to me. I haven't spent time like this with my daughter for more years than I can count. When she links her arm through mine, I'm first overwhelmed with love and gratitude then I find that I already know what she wants to tell me. Perhaps I've recognised in her face the thing that she's long concealed: the pain of pretending to be happy.

"I think I understand why this business with the inheritance is so important to you," I tell her gently. I feel her stiffen so I quickly continue, "I know I could have contested the will but you see, it wasn't a huge surprise to me that I was excluded from it, and I was actually grateful I could continue to live here."

"But what about us?" she asks. "What about me and Richard? Why were we excluded?"

"Believe me, I was as shocked as you were when I discovered he'd left you nothing," I say.

"Why didn't you tell us? Then *we* – me and Richard – *we* could have contested the will."

I attempt to explain. "You have to remember the circumstances of your father's death were anything but normal, and I was in a terrible place, emotionally. It took me months to recover from the shock of it all. Henry Silver was very good to me, very understanding, but if I told you now, what he told me at the time, I don't think it would take away the hurt you're feeling. George had clearly thought everything through very carefully. It was all written down in a letter. Obviously, he didn't expect to die prematurely, he probably even hoped he'd outlive me, but the purpose of the will was to ensure that I couldn't benefit *in any way* from the sale of the house."

Julia throws her head back against the pillow and sighs loudly. "It isn't fair and I'm going to challenge it." Her voice sinks to a whisper. "I need that money."

I don't want to spoil this moment; I don't want to question her love and her loyalty, but I know I have to ask my daughter, "Is that why you really came home?"

She laughs awkwardly. "Would you believe me, if I said 'no'?"

I wrap my arm around her shoulder and hold her close. "It's okay, Julia. I understand, I really do. You have a right to be angry with me. I should have tried to fight this. Whatever you decide to do now, I'll support you."

She begins to cry. "I can't do what you did, Mummy. I might as well tell you because you're probably going to find out anyway, but I've tried to ... to have my cake and eat it." She gives a hollow laugh. "That won't surprise you, I know."

"Has Colin found out?"

She nods and then uses the edge of the sheet to wipe away her tears. "He's already making plans to leave Singapore. Someone has offered him some consultancy work. He's coming home ... home to Suffolk." In the closeness of my embrace, I feel her shudder. "I can't do it," she says. "Even if I was happily married to him, I couldn't live in some East Anglian backwater."

"Does this ... *piece of cake* ... does he have a name?"

"He has a name." She chokes back more tears. "But he's doing the Singapore sidestep."

I don't know what that means, but I can make a good guess. I tell her. "Oh my, Julia, you don't make things easy for yourself, do you? How can I help you?"

She sits up and blinks away the tears. "I still have the gallery. It's been more profitable than I've ever let on to Colin. I guess I can just about manage on the income from it, but I'm going to need somewhere to live. I'll never be able to afford to buy but I could rent a one-bedroom apartment if I could get a deposit together. Colin might help me. He's a good man." She offers me a wry smile. "He won't see me turned out on the street."

"So, you really need this money," I say.

She nods. "I'm not going to give up fighting for what's rightfully mine, but in the meantime..." She leaves the sentence unfinished, but I think I understand what she's asking of me. The difficulty is, only I know the true price that will be paid if I sell Tyne Lodge.

Julia

My mother insists that she doesn't need help to shower and dress, and I don't insist that she does. I do, however, stand outside the door of her en suite – just in case – and when she returns to the bedroom in a towelling bathrobe, I offer to find her something easy to put on. We both agree that it's too soon for trousers but argue over a dress. It's a green, shirt style in a crisp linen mix. "Why don't you wear this?" I hold it up for her to see. "You could wear it with a narrow, leather belt."

Her response is a scornful laugh. "If you did your own ironing, you'd know why that isn't a good idea."

"But it's pretty," I say.

"I think something practical would be better. In any case, I find linen itchy at the best of times. When women get to the age that I am, Julia, it's always comfort over style."

I smile and she smiles back because she thinks I agree with her, but in my head, I'm thinking that's one compromise I'll never be making.

She eventually decides on a navy flared skirt with an elastic waistband – a frankly hideous piece of clothing. She wants to wear it with a navy and white-striped pullover and is only reluctantly persuaded to choose a pink blouse.

"What's wrong with the pullover?" she says a little wistfully. "It's cashmere."

"There's a reason why they call blue and white stripes the nautical look. If you fall off a boat, they can spot you in the water a mile away. Do you really want that kind of visibility?"

"But I like it," she insists. "It's comfy."

"It leaches the colour from your face and you're still as white as a…" I nearly say the word 'ghost' but stop myself just in time. "…as a hospital sheet. You need something that reflects a healthy glow. Pink is perfect. Just put it on."

"You're very bossy," she observes with a mock frown. "I'm not used to being told what to do."

"Well, I'm *very* used to ordering people around so you're going to have to put up with it while I'm staying here," I tell her.

"I think I liked you better when you were curled up next to me crying about Colin."

"I wasn't crying about Colin. I was just feeling sorry for myself. I think we both need to pull ourselves together. You need to forget about Aggie for a start. She was given the celestial red card two years ago and there's no coming back after that kind of sending off."

"How can you be so sure?" she asks. The teasing note in her voice has disappeared.

"I could ask you the same question?" I say.

My mother's expression darkens. "I've seen her."

"Really?" I fail to keep the note of sarcasm out of my voice, but she doesn't seem to notice.

She says, "Sometimes I see her clearly even though it's dark outside. Sometimes it's just a flash of red out of the corner of my eye. Other times … it's like a faded photograph. I can only just make out her face."

I gently push her onto the bed and sit down next to her. I take her hand and hold it really tightly, and then I kiss her cheek. I haven't kissed my mother since … since I was just a girl. Her skin is soft and smells of lemon balm. It's still warm from the shower. I sense a frailty and a vulnerability that I've never experienced with her before. It frightens me. I'm frightened *for* her, because it doesn't really matter whether Aggie is real [if ghosts *can* be real] or if Aggie is a product of her decaying brain: all that matters is that my mother is now scared to live in this house on her own.

"I'm going to make us some breakfast," I say.

My mother glances at the clock. "I think you'd better make that brunch."

"Even better," I tell her. "I don't do much cooking, but I think I could manage bacon and eggs. Would that be okay?"

She offers me a tremulous smile. "That would be marvellous."

With breakfast and lunch successfully negotiated at the same time, I suggest we place an order for some more food online. I'm thinking ready meals or anything that can be heated up in the oven. My mother is intrigued by the idea of the supermarket delivering her shopping and seems to have forgotten her fears about Aggie returning from the dead.

"This is how it used to be," she says smiling broadly. "Just like the old days."

"The old days? The internet wasn't invented till about nineteen-ninety."

"Oh, I know that, Silly. I mean, getting groceries delivered to your house."

"Well, there isn't much alternative," I say.

"You could take a taxi to the supermarket. Then you could have a proper look round."

"That just isn't going to happen."

"Don't you go food shopping in Singapore? Or do you order online like Richard does?"

"I have a maid, Mummy. She does all the boring things I don't want to do. That's what she gets paid for."

My mother sniffs her disapproval then makes changes to the list I've made. "I'm not eating microwave meals every day, Julia."

"But I can't cook."

"I'll tell you what to do," she says. "That'll make a change, won't it? You being bossed about." She digs me in the ribs and laughs – a little too heartily, I feel, as the joke is at my expense.

Our delivery slot is from four till five, so we have a whole afternoon to while away. We watch a film then I insist that she does the exercises, which the physiotherapist showed her. They seem to involve various kinds of leg raises while she holds onto the back of a chair.

I'm admiring the way she manages to balance and suggesting a few changes to her technique when the doorbell rings. Thinking it's the early delivery of our food shopping, I rush to answer it. Standing on the doorstep is Colin. For a moment I'm completely bewildered, and I think I must be looking at up him as though he's a total stranger, because he looks rather cross.

"Aren't you going to invite me in?"

I recover quickly. "Yes, yes, of course. Come in." He walks straight past me into the sitting room. "Hallo, Lenora," I hear him say. "You're looking very sprightly." I don't hear her reply, but I know my mother is more than capable of holding her own, so I leave her to it while I retreat to the kitchen to make coffee.

When I return to the room, my mother continues to exchange pleasantries with Colin for about ten more minutes before she excuses herself. "Time for my afternoon rest, I think."

Ever the well-bred gentleman, Colin quickly gets to his feet and waits while she makes a slow but dignified exit. She deliberately catches my eye as she limps towards the door and her smile is warm and encouraging.

"So..." I say to him. "What brings you here? I mean ... why did you come? I thought ... well, I didn't know..." Even to my own ears, this rambling attempt to open the conversation sounds utterly pathetic.

"It's okay, Julia, I'm not checking up on you: things have gone way too far for me to waste any more of my time doing that." He sits down again, pours himself a cup of coffee.

I feel my face suddenly become uncomfortably immobile, but my heart has broken into a gallop. I never thought, not for a single moment, that our marriage would end this way: Colin detached and emotionally unresponsive; me flustered, even confused.

He continues in the same matter-of-fact tone. "I've been in Suffolk looking at properties. Found a nice bungalow in Nacton. It's about a fifteen-minute drive to the port at Felixstowe, so perfectly placed for work." He finally turns his head and looks at me, grey eyes as cold and uninviting as the bleak North Sea. "I decided to pay my respects to your mother as it wasn't too far out of my way. I'm surprised how well she looks."

This is more than I can bear. I feel tears spring to my eyes. "I'm so sorry, Colin," I blurt out. "For everything."

His response is a compression of his pale pink lips. He says, "You've never truly been sorry for anything in your whole life."

"I'm sorry for this."

"You're only sorry that you got found out."

There seems little point in denying it, but I didn't want to hurt him: that was never my intention. I blink back my tears. "I'm not going to bore you with excuses for my behaviour; I know it was wrong and I know it's over between us. But we are still married, Colin, and we need to talk about the future."

"I know where my future lies," he replies. "My working life in Singapore was always going to end like this. We aren't exiles, Julia. We're *expats* and there was always the expectation that we'd come back here. You knew that right from the start."

"But we don't have to!" I cry.

"I want to," Colin says. He looks down into his coffee cup and for the first time since he arrived at Hillcrest his voice falters. "I've had my suspicions about you for a long while. Always working late; always going out to dinner; always *unavailable.*" He looks up at me and adds, "In every conceivable way." He utters a mirthless laugh. "It was one of *my* clients who gave me the idea to check your office at the gallery. He was talking about criminal activity at the port in Singapore. He said, there's always a paper trail, you just have to know where to look." He finishes his coffee and gets to his feet. "We can come to some arrangement about the apartment, but you can't stay there indefinitely."

"I realise that," I say weakly.

"Do you want to involve a solicitor?" he asks. "If you do, you'll have to pay for it yourself."

"You know I don't have any money."

"I don't know. We stopped … communicating … a long time ago and anything you did tell me was probably a lie."

My instinctive reaction is to protest because the only thing I ever deliberately concealed from him was my relationship with Jian, but it's a fair comment under the circumstances. I take a deep breath before I respond. I don't want to antagonise him while I still need his assistance, but I'm not going to be browbeaten into simply giving up my home and my possessions because he wants rid of me.

"I think…" I say in a calm and controlled voice, "…I think it would be sensible to spend some time apart. I don't know how long my mother's going to need me here, but it'll be long enough for us to give some considered thought as to how we're going to manage this … this separation."

I accompany him to the door, but before he leaves, he says, "What really rankles is that I tried my best to give you a good life and I believe I succeeded in doing that, but it wasn't enough, was it?" His face contorts with suppressed emotion; his eyes brim with involuntary tears. "I wanted a family. I wanted children and grandchildren, but it was always about you and what *you* wanted." He cups my face in his hand, looks deep into my eyes and asks, "Have you really got what you wanted, Julia? I wonder…" And then he leaves, firmly closing the door behind him.

Richard

It's still dark outside when I wake and after thirty minutes of turning restlessly from one side to the other, I accept that I'm not going to be able to get back to sleep.

Silvio is lying on his back snoring softly. His mouth sags open, and every now and then he gives a little pig-like snuffle, but this only endears him to me more deeply. I press my lips to his temple then carefully slide out of the bed so that I shan't wake him.

I don't suffer from insomnia, but when I have a difficult decision to make, I'm inclined to sleep lightly and I'm disturbed easily – on this occasion by the sound of passing cars, even though it's a Sunday morning.

I tiptoe to the kitchen and make myself a cup of camomile tea. Silvio will demand espresso as soon as he wakes, and I don't need a double dose of caffeine when I'm already feeling anxious about the day ahead.

I don't like keeping secrets. Nothing good ever comes from concealing the truth. It's like trying to hide the bone from the dog. You just know he's going to sniff it out, chew it up and the only thing left will be a big mess, so this is my dilemma: do I tell Julia that Henry Silver has arranged for me to meet our half-sister, Miriam. I've been wrestling with the question ever since I arrived home on Friday evening.

When I left Hutton Home Help, I headed straight back to the flat. Silvio had already left for work, so I threw together some bits and pieces from the fridge for dinner then checked my emails. There were a dozen or more work-related messages which I ignored, because I saw there was something marked 'Urgent' from Silver, Reid and Bateman Solicitors.

Henry Silver had discovered a recent phone number for Miriam in a file. He said he'd taken the liberty of contacting her because he felt it would be in everyone's best interest to have a working relationship, especially if Julia was adamant about contesting the will. He'd taken the further liberty of making an appointment for me to meet her and offered the use of a private room at Silver, Reid and Bateman offices on Monday morning, when he would also be available if his services were required. He apologised profusely for this presumption but assured me that he was trying to act in the best interests of everyone concerned. Could I please confirm my availability?

I replied immediately that I would be available and that I was grateful for the opportunity to speak to her, but then I thought about Julia and how she would react if she only found out about the meeting when it was done.

I wasn't able to talk it over with Silvio until the following day and his response was an enthusiastic endorsement of both the meeting but also of letting Julia know about it.

"That's great news! Of course, you must go, Ricardo. Julia sarà molto contenta."

"Will she be happy? I wish I felt your confidence." I said. "I know if I tell her about it, she'll want to come with me."

"Why is this a problem?" he asked.

"Well, she hasn't been invited for a start, and I know my sister: she's not going to sit in a room with the person who stole her inheritance without offering an opinion on the situation. That's the last thing we need."

"This girl, she is also your sister. Perhaps she will understand."

"She might be our sister but she's still a stranger, and I think if she wanted to offer us our fair share then she would have been in touch before this."

Silvio pursed his lips and wagged his finger at me. "You don't tell Julia ... this is not good."

"I'm going to tell her – obviously – but maybe not till after I've met the girl. Henry Silver said we can arrange to rent out Hillcrest, but he doesn't think we should do anything until the situation with the will has been resolved one way or the other. After the

conversation I had with my mother yesterday afternoon, she clearly can't go on living there by herself. She's convinced that the house is being haunted by Agnes Bagshot."

Silvio was draped across the sofa with his feet in my lap after a late night working the dinner shift at Bocca Felice, but he immediately sat up and stared at me with a look of utter disbelief on his face. "Aggie?" he said. "Her friend, Aggie?"

"Yes, her best friend Aggie. And that's not the worst of it," I went on. "She thinks that Aggie is trying to kill her."

Silvio swiped away this idea with the back of his hand. "She's just confused. She hit her head, no?"

"Well, she fell down the stairs so it's highly likely she hit her head. The point is we need to get things moving if I'm going to help her, whether it's hiring a ghost-buster or a carer." My attempt at humour didn't go unnoticed – he knows how much I worry – and he immediately threw a comforting arm around my shoulder. "As far as I'm concerned," I went on, "Miriam can have the house and do what she likes with it when my mother isn't here anymore, but while Mum is here it's going to have to pay for the help she needs. I'm worried that if I bring Julia with me to the meeting, she'll just antagonise the girl and things could drag on for months, even years."

Silvio's eyes glazed over – in his family, everything is discussed openly; everyone has an opinion, which they express loudly and passionately; everyone disagrees with everyone else and, when the shouting has stopped, they kiss and make up.

"When we see her tomorrow, just don't say anything, please," I pleaded with him.

"I think you make a big mistake not telling her, Ricardo," he told me. "You going to regret this."

Am I going to regret it? Well, only time will tell, I think to myself. Tomorrow has come and the plan is to spend the afternoon with Julia and my mother – take them out for a nice lunch and afterwards try to lighten both the mood and the atmosphere at Hillcrest House.

Silvio is a master extraordinaire when it comes to generating the feel-good factor. His positive outlook on life can be infectious so that even when in the darkest of moods, you allow yourself to be swept along on a wave of optimism and good cheer.

My mother and Julia are ready to fall under the Mazzi spell when we arrive at Hillcrest. They're dressed in outdoor coats and waiting in the hallway when we pull onto the drive. Silvio jumps out of the car and races into the house, envelops them both in a huge hug, tells them they are '*le più belle signore*'. My mother rolls her eyes at being told they're 'the most beautiful ladies', but Julia smiles appreciatively.

Silvio removes one of my mother's crutches then links her arm through his. He guides her with great care to the car and helps her to sit in the back seat, adjusts the seat belt tightly across her lap and kisses her cheek. Julia follows after them carrying two handbags and appears slightly miffed at being overlooked.

I've already booked a table at a pretty riverside restaurant where we can gaze out over the water, relax and enjoy watching the little sailing boats flit and float like pale-winged butterflies. Even the weather is joining in the party atmosphere: the sun is shining; the sky is a deep shade of blue, and the breeze still holds a touch of summer warmth even though it's October.

On occasions like this, I fall in love with Silvio all over again, not because he's handsome and charming, but because he wants the people he cares about to be happy, and it isn't long before Julia is laughing. She looks carefree and untroubled. My mother also seems much more at ease although I notice that she glances at Julia from time to time with genuine concern in her eyes.

I see that Silvio has noticed it too. He invites Julia to take a stroll while we wait for the bill, and smiles encouragement at me as they make their way down to the riverbank.

As soon as they're out of earshot I ask my mother, "What's wrong with Julia?"

"Nothing's with Julia," she says. "She seems fine to me, anyway."

"Are you sure?"

She suddenly looks serious. "Has she spoken to you about ..." She hesitates, turns her head so that I can no longer read her expression.

"She told me that things with Colin aren't too good," I say.

My mother sighs. "He came to the house yesterday."

"Who? Colin? I didn't realise he was over here." She nods. She still won't look at me, but I think she doesn't want me to see how much this has upset her.

"He's been offered early retirement and he was looking at property. He said he'd found a nice bungalow in a village near Felixstowe and all being well he'll move back here in the spring."

"Oh, I see," I say.

She fishes in her handbag for a tissue and dabs at the corners of her eyes. "He didn't use the word 'divorce' when he told me about it, but he didn't mention Julia's name even once when he was outlining his plans. I found I couldn't ask him and then I felt such a coward afterwards. I mean … she is my daughter."

I don't mean to sound uncaring, but Julia made this mess herself, so I ask my mother, "Did she tell you why this has happened?"

"I know she's got involved with another man."

"She's basically done what Dad did," I say, knowing that those words will strike a chord with her albeit an unhappy one. "She didn't want to be with Colin any more but she didn't want to give up all the advantages of being married, so she kept her mouth shut and just had an affair – actually a bit more than an affair because she's been in a relationship with this man for eight years. "

My mother's head swings round, and she looks back at me with shock and surprise written large in her expression. "I had no idea!"

"That's why she's been banging on about this inheritance. She wants to divorce Colin, but she can't manage on her own financially, and they'll have to give up their apartment if he retires and comes back here. She needs money if she's going to carry on living in Singapore."

Something changes in my mother's face. She feels a kind of empathy for Julia, I know. I understand. I don't doubt for a single moment that there are similarities between their situations, but it's Colin who's been deceived.

"I'm pretty certain she won't be able to contest the will so don't encourage her to think that she can," I say.

"I still have Tyne Lodge."

"But you don't want to sell it, remember?"

"I could if I had to."

"Not to fund Julia's uptown lifestyle," I say firmly.

I know she wants to argue the point, but Julia breezes back into the restaurant with Silvio on her arm, so we all make ready to leave. My mother mouths at me, "I'll speak to you later about this."

By the time we get back to Hillcrest, it's obvious to everyone including my mother that she needs to rest. I stand at the bottom of the stairs and watch her climb with slow but now practised ease. She calls back to me, "Don't forget I want to speak to you before you leave."

Julia and Silvio are discussing Thailand as a potential holiday destination when I join them in the sitting room. She insists we go to Hua Hin beach resort – apparently, it's a favourite haunt of Bangkok's rich and famous. According to my sister it's the only place to go if you want an authentic taste of Thailand. I just want a nice beach and good food, but Silvio is completely sold on the idea when she tells him about the Monsoon Valley vineyard only twenty miles from Hua Hin town centre.

The afternoon passes quickly, and I only notice that it's beginning to get dark outside when Julia rises from her seat to close the curtains and switch on the lights.

"I think I'd better wake Mum up," I say.

"When you come down, I'll make tea," Julia replies.

As soon as I step into the hallway and close the door behind me, I'm immediately struck by the change in temperature and the lack of light. The sitting room was cool but comfortable, and the windows and patio doors opening out to the back garden made it possible to enjoy the last, golden rays of the setting sun. The hallway on the other hand is simply cold and dark.

As my hand searches for the light switch, a movement at the top of the stairs catches my eye. "Mum? Are you okay?" I call out. My question is met with a pregnant silence – no not silence, not an absence of sound, but rather an *unarticulated* cry. It sends shivers down my spine.

I can't find the light switch, but I *can* smell something. It's the slightly musty scent of stale perfume, and I recognise it. This was what I could smell in Julia's bedroom.

I'm propelled to the bottom of the stairs, not by bold curiosity but by fear for my mother, because *something* is moving on the galleried landing above me. As my eyes adjust to the dark, I can just make out the shape. I would swear on my life that it's a woman – a woman in a red dress with long dark hair.

There's a second switch on the wall next to me, yet somehow I know, if I put the light on, what I believe I can see will disappear, and I can't allow that to happen, because I have to know what it is.

Walking up the stairs feels like scaling a mountain with ankle weights attached: I have to drag each foot forwards and upwards; the effort makes me sweat. It's that and fear for what I might find.

When I reach the top, I can see at once that the door to my mother's bedroom is closed but there's a sliver of light on the floor where it doesn't quite meet the carpet. The radio is playing in the background, not music but a muffled, monotone conversation.

The door to Julia's bedroom on the other hand is wide open and I can feel the draught before I see the curtains blowing.

The woman in the red dress has vanished.

This time my hand finds the switch on the wall easily, and the room fills with light.

The balcony doors are open.

I walk on unsteady feet towards them, and I don't close them. I was led to this room for a reason, just as I was led to the garage.

I step onto the narrow ledge, place my hands on the top of the safety railings, and that's when I hear it: the sound of metal grating against brickwork. I know what it is: it's the bolts, which anchor everything into the wall; they grind and release and the whole thing shifts beneath my feet.

I quickly step back into the room. The balcony is quite literally a death trap.

Lenora

Scaffolding is being erected at the back of the house. The workmen arrived here at eight o'clock this morning. I must say Richard is a marvel getting it organised so quickly. He was straight on the phone last night after he discovered that the balcony in Julia's bedroom isn't safe to stand on, insisted that the door to the room be kept shut at all times until it's been secured.

The workmen told Julia they won't know if the balcony can be repaired until they take a proper look at it, but it seems likely it will have to be removed completely. I'd quite like a new balcony, but Richard is adamant the doors are going to be replaced by new brickwork and a window.

I wanted to speak to him about Tyne Lodge before he left, but he was visibly trembling when he told me how very dangerous the balcony had become, and he left with Silvio soon after. I think it really shook him up.

Julia brought me tea in bed this morning, which was lovely, but then she announced that she was walking to the church to put flowers on her father's grave. "I'll wait till Maggie gets here. I don't want to leave you by yourself," she said.

"I'm sure I'll be fine," I told her.

"I'm sure you will. Nevertheless, I'm not going till she gets here."

Over the last couple of days, we've settled into a routine first thing in the morning now that she's satisfied that I won't keel over in the shower or somehow fracture the other hip getting dressed. As soon as I'm ready I shout out, then she stands at the bottom of the stairs and watches my descent with eagle eyes. It's actually quite off-putting, but I don't like to tell her.

This morning she seems particularly anxious and distracted. I don't really understand this decision to visit George in his final resting place, but if it makes her happy…

When Maggie arrives, Julia explains that she's going out and won't be back for a couple of hours and doesn't want me to be left alone in the house.

"That's okay, Mrs Crane," Maggie says and promptly switches on the vacuum cleaner.

I have no idea if these two have ever met before, but you could cut the atmosphere with a knife.

"I'll see you later, Julia," I call out to her as she leaves, but she just waves back to me in reply.

Almost as soon as she closes the door behind her, Maggie switches off the vacuum cleaner and insists on accompanying me back to the kitchen where I was having a leisurely breakfast. "I feel so bad, Mrs Oakley," she says. "I was going to visit you in hospital, but I just couldn't get away from work. Did you get the magazines? Jackie dropped them off for me."

"Yes, I did," I say, "although I was a bit confused at the time. I think I told Richard they were from Sarah because the nurses told me several times that Mrs Oakley had phoned and asked after me. I don't know why I forgot that she isn't Mrs Oakley anymore."

Maggie has a face which reflects her emotions so it's immediately evident that she's unhappily surprised at hearing this piece of information. "Someone phoned the hospital?"

"Yes. It's a bit odd, isn't it?" Probably got the wards mixed up. They named them after birds, though I can't think why. I was on Sparrow Ward but there's also a Starling and a Swallow, so you can see how it might happen."

She smiles and nods, but she doesn't look convinced. She says, "Perhaps there was another Mrs Oakley on the ward."

"I have no idea. Anyway, I'm home now," I tell her. "Richard said you've been looking after the house while I've been away and making sure no one's broken in?" Maggie's hand flies to her chest – it's now a familiar gesture though I don't know why she needs to be concerned. "It's fine," I reassure her. "I'm glad to come home to a house that doesn't need dusting. I know Julia's glad not to have to do it," I add. I've often spoken to Maggie about Julia and the pampered lifestyle she leads in Singapore, but she still looks anxious.

"How long will Mrs Crane be staying with you?"

That's a question I've been asking myself ever since I learned she was here, but I'm not going to ask her, so I tell Maggie, "I really don't know. She's got a business to run so I can't imagine she'll be staying past the point that she and Richard are happy to leave me on my own."

"But should you be living here on your own now?" she asks. "I mean ... Hillcrest's a big house ... and with the stairs ... after what happened ... I just wondered ... well, you could always move ... you know ... into that bungalow ... I just thought..." The stuttering sentence seems to have exhausted her because she falls into a chair opposite me and grasps both my hands in hers. "I've been so worried about you."

I realise that she reminds me of Aggie not just the long dark hair and pretty, blue eyes, but in the way she struggles to contain her emotions and then they get the better of her. I like her, even though I don't know her as well as I should after all these years. I like her warmth and her honesty, so I don't hesitate to tell her, "Richard thinks I should give up Hillcrest and move into Tyne Lodge."

"It might be for the best," she says.

"I suppose it might," I say, and then something inside me suddenly revolts. For even though I quail at the prospect of living with Aggie's restless, murderous spirit, I really don't want to leave my home. It feels like giving in, so I shake my head. "But no. No, I'm not doing that."

I've carried a little seed of rebellion with me all my life. It never had the chance to truly flourish, but it seems I've kept it alive. I fought with George all the time and he tried to smother it, extinguish it, but I guess it never died.

I've always wondered why he only left me the house to *live* in but now I think I know the answer. He wanted to defeat me; wanted me to give it up; wanted me to surrender. He made sure that I could only ever be the keeper of the house but never the holder, the one with the power. It might be for the best to move out of Hillcrest, but I'm not going anywhere. Perhaps this is our last battle. If it is, I won't let George win.

Julia

I could feel Maggie's arctic eyes on the back of my head when I left the house. Why my mother thinks so highly of her, I can't imagine, but at least she's doing something useful by remaining with her while I go out. Fortunately, it's not far to the high street and the florist's shop. I just hope I can remember the way to St Peter's after I've bought the flowers – the last time I was there was for the funeral and we were driven directly from Hillcrest in the back of a blacked-out hearse.

I haven't thought about my father very much since he died, but last night after Richard and Silvio had left, I couldn't stop thinking about him. It was because of the balcony.

My bedroom didn't have a balcony until I asked for one. My mother had taken me to see the Franco Zeffirelli film of Romeo and Juliet. I was fourteen, and instantly fell in love with Leonard Whiting. Profoundly affected by the music and the romance and the drama, I went to my father and begged to have a balcony of my own. He held me close against his chest, kissed the top of my head and said, "You can have whatever you want, Julia. You're my girl."

I was always his girl, and that's why I don't understand what's happened, so I'm going to bring him flowers and ask him. It's silly, really, but I can't think of any other way to feel close to him again.

I find the walk to the florists a welcome break. Caring for my mother hasn't been quite the onerous task I thought it would be, but it feels good to get out of the house. I don't do much walking in Singapore during daylight hours – it's just too hot – but walking in England is a much more pleasant experience and I find that I'm enjoying the fresh air and the freedom.

I discover that the shop carries a good selection of flowers and it's hard to choose. I don't want to buy white lilies – there's something uniquely funereal about them and I don't need reminding that I'm going to visit a grave. The orchids just aren't up to scratch, but the roses look nice, so I buy a dozen yellow ones. Yellow is the colour of sunshine and happiness and I could do with a little bit of both of those things in my life at the moment.

When I arrive at St Peter's after a few false turns, the churchyard is empty of the living but there are lines and lines of graves, then I realise that I don't remember where my father was buried, so I'm forced to search for him. When I find him, I see my mother has chosen a plain, rectangular, black granite headstone engraved with gold. Even the words are plain.

> *George Arthur Raymond Oakley*
> *Died 15th January 2002 aged 67 years*
> *Rest in Peace*

Well, that didn't take much imagination, I think to myself.

I remove the roses from their cellophane wrapping and place them directly on the ground in front of the headstone. I spread them out in the shape of a fan, but they still look sad and lifeless, and now I wish I'd thought to bring a vase with me.

I'm quietly berating myself for my lack of foresight when I spot someone walking purposefully towards me on the narrow gravel path between the lines of graves. It's a man wearing baggy jeans and a rather shabby looking brown suede jacket, but they're teamed with a dog collar so at least I know he's not a vagrant. I married Colin at St Peter's, but it wasn't this scruffy individual who officiated at the service.

"Hallo there!" he calls out to me as he approaches. "Edward Feering," he says and offers me his hand to shake. "I saw you walk up the drive with those roses and I didn't recognise you so I guessed you wouldn't know the rules."

"There are rules?"

"Not rules exactly ... it was started by my predecessor."

"So, what have I done wrong?"

He throws up his hands and follows it by an awkward laugh. "Nothing wrong, nothing wrong ... it's just that we don't encourage the placing of *cut* flowers." His expression veers from mock solemnity to an embarrassed smile. "They die so quickly, you see.

Especially when they're just left on the grass." He looks pointedly at the yellow roses on my father's grave. "What we like to see is sympathetic planting and by 'sympathetic' we really mean evergreen if possible, although I personally won't say no to a hardy annual."

I haven't the faintest idea what he's talking about and I'm certain that my ignorance is written clearly on my face, but he carries on regardless.

"I'm afraid it's a matter of cleanliness. People want to leave flowers as a token of remembrance for their loved ones – which I completely understand by the way – but they don't think about what happens to those flowers when they've died. I can tell you, it isn't a pretty sight, although I actually think it's worse when they're left in a vase because we then have nasty, smelly water to get rid of." He glances down at the headstone then back at me. "George Oakley," he says.

"My father."

He does the jazz hands gesture all over again only this time it's followed by an enthusiastic cry of recognition. "Julia! How lovely to meet you at last! Is your mother out of hospital yet? I told your brother – Richard, isn't it? – I said, as soon as she's back in her own home, I'll come around."

I can't think of anything I'd like less, but my mother has always been a conscientious churchgoer, so he probably knows her quite well. I try really hard to respond with a friendly smile, but I'm definitely not issuing a visitor's pass, so I tell him, "She was discharged on Friday and I'm staying with her while she recuperates. You can call round after I've left."

He nods his agreement as though I've just suggested the perfect plan. "Don't worry about the flowers," he says. "And just tell Lenora to give me a call when she's ready to receive visitors again." He suddenly leans towards me and says in a conspiratorial tone, "I didn't know your father. He wasn't one of my flock, if you see what I mean. I wasn't here for the funeral either, but I heard what happened – you know the incident with the car? There was a lot of *loose* talk afterwards and I just wanted to say that it isn't our place to judge. Only the Lord knows what's in our hearts and in our minds. I'm sure your father was a good man."

256

He gives me a quick, sympathetic pat on the shoulder then marches back the way he came.

Was my father a good man? Once upon a time I might have agreed with him, but now I'm not so sure. And as for loose talk – well, I can well imagine what people said about him. I just find it hard to believe that my mother didn't know about his *other* family until after he died.

I'm not the kind of person who indulges in introspection but standing here at the graveside of my father I'm forced to consider the possibility that I might be quite a lot like him, because I managed to conceal the truth from Colin for eight years.

Did my mother have her suspicions? I wonder. Colin said he long suspected. What was it he told me? 'There's always a paper trail, you just have to know where to look.' He waited until I'd left the country to search my office, and he found what he was looking for: proof of my adultery.

And then it hits me – *you just have to know where to look.* That's what Colin said.

My father kept the door to his study locked so that my mother couldn't snoop, which suggests he had things he wanted to conceal from her.

I look down at the grass beneath my feet – it's my father's final resting place. "What were you hiding behind that locked door, Daddy?" I ask him. "Whatever it was … well, the door isn't locked anymore." I kneel down in front of the headstone. Tears spring to my eyes because I know I'm never coming back here again. I whisper, "I did love you, and I think you loved me best, but I can't understand why you cut me out … cut all of us out of your will. I can't decide if what you did was wrong, but I know it wasn't fair, so now I'm going to do everything in my power to put it right." I gently place a kiss on the cold, hard granite. "Goodbye Daddy. Goodbye."

Richard

When I went to bed last night, my mind was in turmoil. I tossed and turned, pushed and pulled at the quilt until Silvio sat up and ordered me to leave the bedroom.

"Nothing can be done until tomorrow, Ricardo, but if you cannot rest till then, get up and let me sleep."

All I could say to him was, "I'm really sorry. It's the balcony – I can't stop thinking about it."

"I understand," he told me. "You cannot let go of this worry, so do something else. Make tea. Listen to music."

So, I got up and I made tea, I lay on the sofa and I listened to the radio. I don't remember feeling even remotely sleepy but the next thing I knew, Silvio was waking me with a cup of coffee.

"I have to go," he said. "Good luck with your *sorellina.*"

"I'm not calling her 'little sister' yet," I said. "At this point she's Julia's legal adversary and I don't think she's going to want to be a part of our family if she's forced to share her very generous inheritance with us."

I watched Silvio weigh up my reply then wordlessly shrug his response. He lifted his fist to the side of his head with the thumb and little finger extended. "I call you later. Ciao, ciao."

As soon as he left the flat and I was on my own, my thoughts immediately returned to Julia's balcony. I'm certain it hasn't been used in years, and its safety has certainly never been checked, so it's highly likely that over time the bolts have gradually loosened – the weather alone would cause deterioration. But last night I couldn't get out of my head the idea that the bolts had been loosened deliberately.

I still keep thinking that the balcony has been tampered with. Why and by whom, I haven't the faintest idea. It smacks of paranoia, but with everything I've experienced over the last couple of weeks it's hardly surprising that my imagination has got the better of me.

I try to push all of these thoughts to one side because I need to give my full attention to the meeting this morning with Miriam. I can only hope that striking up some kind of relationship with the girl will help to smooth things over in time, if Julia persists in this quest to have the will overturned. Now she's a part of our life whether we like it or not.

Unsurprisingly for a Monday morning, the traffic is slow and heavy, and I arrive for the meeting at the offices of Silver, Reid and Bateman nearly thirty minutes late. Henry Silver is pacing up and down in front of the desk in reception. He has the look of someone who has asked to see the inside of the lion's cage and is now waiting to find out if he's going to be eaten alive or allowed to escape.

"Ah good, you're here at last," he greets me.

"Sorry ... Monday morning traffic on the A12 ... it's always dreadful."

"She's waiting for you."

"Okay. Let's get started then," I say, but he doesn't move; he takes my elbow and draws me to the far side of the room.

"I realise it's a bit late but, before I take you in and introduce you to each other, I feel compelled to tell you I'm not convinced this is a good idea after all."

"What do you mean, not a good idea?" I ask him. "You were the one who instigated this meeting."

"I know, I know, and in principle it *is* a good idea, but I hadn't met the girl before this. I remember her mother from the club. She was a delightful person, always happy to help you out, but the daughter's cut from a different cloth. When she found out you weren't here, I had a real battle on my hands persuading her to stay."

"Well, I'm here now."

"Just be warned, Mr Oakley. Something tells me that you and she have very different motives for agreeing to meet. I'm not at all optimistic for the outcome."

I follow him back to the reception desk, where he advises the receptionist that the meeting in room one is not to be disturbed under any circumstances, then he guides me through a short corridor into the main office.

From there I'm led into a large, well-lit room with windows which look out over a paved courtyard garden. There's an enormous table in the middle of it surrounded by chairs. This is clearly a conference room and not the type of intimate space, which encourages friendly conversation, but Henry Silver has already intimated that my half-sister has her own agenda.

She's standing with her back to the room staring out at something beyond the courtyard and she doesn't turn away until Henry Silver calls her name and introduces me.

"I won't hang around," he says. "I arranged this meeting for the two of you, but if or when you want me to be present, just press the buzzer on the wall next to the lights." He points to a row of switches next to the door. "Take as long as you need."

When he's left the room, she promptly takes a chair on the opposite side of the table, opens up a bag, pulls out a laptop computer and places it on the table in front of her.

"Miriam," I begin awkwardly, "this obviously isn't the nicest way for us to meet for the first time."

"You're late," she snaps.

She fixes dark, serious eyes upon me. There isn't a single trace of interest or warmth in her expression, but I find myself wanting to laugh because she looks exactly like my father and the moment is surreal. She has the same slim upright figure; holds herself with the same unnatural rigidness; she even has the same air of haughty disdain. Her hair is pulled back into a tight ponytail and the hairstyle accentuates the sharp contours of her face. She really is the image of my father in every way.

I've played this game before and my father always won because I never *completely* stopped wanting his approval, but I'm not playing today, so I smile back at her. "You look just like him. Julia and I look like our mother."

Her expression doesn't change. "What do you want? I assume you want something because you've never bothered to get in touch with me before."

"It's complicated," I say, not wishing to reveal to her quite yet that Julia only very recently learned of her existence and now wants to take her to court. "My father … our father," I quickly correct myself. "…our father was … what shall I say … economic with the truth … yes, I think that's the right expression. He didn't disclose to anyone in our family that he had another daughter, so we only found out about you after he died. If he'd told us, things might have been very different," I add.

"You still haven't explained what you want," she says.

"I want to get to know you," I say. It sounds like nonsense, even to my own ears, but we have to start the conversation somewhere.

Her mouth contorts into an unpleasant sneer. "Get to know me?"

"Well, you have that advantage over me, I suspect."

"How's that?"

"I think you probably grew up knowing you had a brother and a sister?"

"Half-brother. Half-sister," she corrects me.

I shrug my indifference. "Nevertheless, you've always known, and I expect you asked questions about us – it's only natural you'd be curious. I suppose that's why *I'd* like to know a bit about *you*."

She sits back in the chair and folds her arms in front her. "What do you want to know?"

I try another smile. "I was going to say 'everything', but we don't really have time for that today, so how about telling me what happened to you after our father died. It's a bit of a mystery, frankly."

Her eyes narrow and the hostility she feels towards me is palpable. "You want to know what happened? I'll tell you. I was left with my pious, overbearing grandparents in a fishing town called Urk. I was left there because my mother suddenly became an *unmarried* mother with nowhere to live and no money. Not the best outcome for someone in a place where the bible is the *go-to* reference book for lifestyle choices."

"I've never heard of Urk," I admit.

"Nobody outside of Urk has heard of Urk. It used to be an island and it might as well still be. It's the arse end of Europe." She unfolds her arms, pushes the laptop to one side, props her elbows on the table and rests her chin on a bridge of her slim fingers. "Shall I tell you why I hate you?" she says, and once again I'm impaled on the point of her malevolent gaze.

There isn't a sensible response to this question, so I say nothing and wait.

"I hate you and your sister because you had the life I should have had. You had tennis lessons and garden parties and holidays in exotic places, and you lived in nice, middle-class Shenfield with both your parents. I didn't. I had bible study classes and church outings and my only holidays were visits to my mother because I was forced to live in Urk with my grandparents. When I left, it took me four years to get the stink of fish out of my skin."

"Four years?" It seemed a random number.

"I spent four years in Amsterdam – the devil's playground according to Oma and Opa. I was a student at the university. That was a *real* revelation. It showed me what I'd been missing out on."

Guessing that I'm treading on sensitive ground, I ask her gently, "Where was your mother all this time?"

"Here!" she exclaims angrily. "Working two jobs and sending money back to my grandparents."

At first, I think I've misheard. "You mean your mother continued to live *here*?"

"You look surprised."

"Does she *still* live here?"

"Why shouldn't she? This is her home now. She wasn't going to stay in Urk if she didn't have to." She leans across the table and says in a low, confiding voice, "That's the problem, you see. I'm conflicted. I completely understand why she didn't want to live there. It's just that she left me behind when she went. I spent a lot of time at university reading about the consequences of abandonment. Apparently, sometimes it causes irreversible psychological damage."

I realise I'm being toyed with – it's something my father used to do. It seemed to give him a perverse pleasure watching me squirm. Of course, I'm no longer the small boy who hovered, trembling, in the doorway of his study, but it's interesting to note that both his looks and his disposition have been passed on to his daughter.

I feel an inappropriate bubble of laughter in the back of my throat, but I swallow it down. Miriam is … what? Twenty-five, twenty-six years old? Her childhood isn't a distant memory and so the hurt of being left behind is still fresh and painful. I tell her, "I'm genuinely sorry that your mother had a hard time when Dad died. And that she was forced to leave you with your grandparents. Like I said earlier, if he'd been more open and honest then things might have been different for both of you, but he wasn't so it isn't really fair to lay the blame at my family's feet."

"You didn't lose your home when he died."

"Yes, we did," I say. "One day Hillcrest House will belong to *you*."

"The house is *already* legally mine."

Well, she's right on that score, I think to myself, but it might change if Julia has her way, and I'm not certain what the legal situation would be after that when it comes to ownership of the house. As things stand, however, one thing I am clear on is that the will provided for my mother to live out the rest of her life there, so I tell Miriam, "Our father might have *bequeathed* the house to you, but you can't take possession of it while my mother's still alive. That's what he wanted."

Anger sweeps through her. "You don't know that!"

"It's written in the will."

"I don't care what's written in the will! Why should I be forced to wait? I only want what's rightfully mine, and I have every intention of making sure I get it. Trust me, you won't stop me."

Her words have the ring of childish, petulant outrage, but the expression in her eyes is one of ferocious intent. "Is that why you agreed to meet me?" I ask her. "Because you think you can have the house *now*?" Disappointment overwhelms me: clearly there aren't going to be any friendly discussions or working relationships. If Miriam imagines that she's going to oust my mother from her home, then her hopes will soon be dashed. I slowly get to my feet because the meeting is over. "You *will* have to wait," I tell her. "My mother isn't leaving Hillcrest."

The sudden smile she offers me in return would curdle milk. "I wouldn't be so sure," she says, and she presses a button on the keyboard of her laptop computer. It emits an electronic sigh. She's been recording our conversation.

Lenora

The man who put up the scaffolding is knocking on the kitchen window to get my attention, so I go out into the garden.

"It'll have to come down," he says.

"It can't be fixed?"

He shakes his head. "If you want a balcony then you'll have to get a new one, but I wouldn't recommend getting one like that." He points up at the back wall of the house, which now has a climbing frame of poles and boards and ladders erected in front of it. "If you don't want a window, you could always have a Juliet balcony. They're quite popular."

"What's that?"

"Your architect calls it a balconette. It's usually a nice metal railing or a piece of safety glass at the outside plane of the window. It's a much safer option in my opinion."

"So not a balcony at all really?"

He gives a rueful smile. "Not really."

My first thought is that Julia will be disappointed, but I have a strong feeling Richard will insist that it's replaced by a window whatever we say.

"Are you going to take it down today?" I ask.

"That's the plan," he says. "We'll come back in a couple of days and board up the doors. I know Mr Oakley wanted it done today, but I've had to fit this in around other jobs. We'll stick some red and white safety tape across the glass. You're not using the bedroom, are you?"

I assure him that the bedroom has been declared off limits.

When Julia returns, Maggie immediately leaves. The phrase 'passing strangers' comes to mind, but I suppose that's what they are.

As soon as Julia has removed her jacket, she goes directly into George's study.

I follow her. "Are you okay?" I ask her.

She's standing in the middle of the room casting eager eyes over the cupboards and shelves behind his desk. She says, "I was standing in front of Daddy's headstone…" Her head flicks round. "And by the way, was that really the best that you could do for him?"

"Are you talking about the headstone?"

"The headstone itself is … inconsequential. Name, age and *Rest in Peace*. Is that all you could think of?"

I feel my hackles rise. "I hope you haven't come back from laying flowers on your father's grave just to chastise me for my lack of imagination. What else was I supposed to say? Always in our thoughts; forever in our hearts? Loving husband and father to Richard and Julia? Oh yes, and Miriam. I think 'Rest in Peace' was a more than generous epitaph considering the mess he left behind him when he went."

"That's not a very Christian sentiment," she says peevishly.

"Well, I didn't ask God for his advice." I look around the room. "Are you searching for something in particular?"

"I'm not sure what I'm looking for. What I was about to say to you…"

"Before you interrupted yourself," I quickly interject.

She rolls her eyes at me. "Before I got *side-tracked*. I was standing in front of Daddy's headstone and I suddenly remembered something Colin said to me. He said there's always a paper-trail, you just have to know where to look."

"A paper-trail?"

"Something that will prove Lena Bartok used her influence to persuade Daddy to make his will in favour of her daughter. A letter maybe?"

"You think you're going to find something in here? Richard's already looked though the files – they're mostly bank statements and insurance papers, that kind of thing."

"I don't know," she says again. "This is where he kept everything isn't it? Locked up in his study?"

"I wouldn't think he kept anything relating to…" I hesitate. I haven't had to talk about Lena Bartok and her daughter, Miriam, for a very long time – not since George died – although I remember a reporter from the local newspaper turned up on my doorstep not long after it happened and asked me if I knew my husband had a second family. I told him he was mistaken, that she was just a friend. We both knew I was lying. Now, I'm not sure how I should refer to them.

Julia slips a consoling arm around my shoulder. "It's just an idea," she says.

"He did keep the door locked when he wasn't here. He kept the key with the car key, so it was always with him whenever he went out."

"What was he hiding in here, do you think?"

"Let's find out, shall we?" I say.

We set to work going through each file on the shelf behind his desk, systematically scrutinizing each page. I discover that he kept the invoices and receipts for all the major purchases in the house – furniture, electrical equipment, painting and decorating. I'm also reminded that over the years he became a member of lots of different clubs and societies because there's paperwork relating to each and every one of them. His whole life is here in this room – except the life he shared with Lena Bartok.

I've been standing for too long and my hip is beginning to throb painfully, so I tell Julia I'm going to make a cup of tea and sort something out for lunch.

The first thing I notice when I return to the room is the temperature. It's noticeably colder. "Have you opened a window?" I ask her. "It's freezing in here."

She looks up from where she's sitting at George's desk. She's found an envelope in the bottom drawer. "Never mind about that," she says. "Look at this." She holds up a receipt. "It's from the jewellers. Did he buy you a diamond ring in 1992? He bought someone a diamond ring." She quickly scans the page. "Hang on second … he asked to have a name inscribed on the inside of it."

The pain in my hip is a finger of fire and I know I need to sit down, but I don't sit down because I want to see what she can see. I look over her shoulder. "What does it say? Did he buy it for *her*?"

"Mag…da…le…na," she reads out loud, emphasizing each syllable. "That has to be her, doesn't it?"

I'm peering at the receipt when I notice, from the corner of my eye, a shadow pass fleetingly in front of the window. I look up. There's a sudden charge in the atmosphere and my first thought is that a storm must be brewing with dark clouds scudding across the sky.

All at once the curtains billow as though a gust of wind has rushed into the room. A picture hanging on the wall facing the desk falls to the floor. The frame breaks apart and the glass shatters, shooting tiny shards in every direction.

"What the hell was that?" Julia exclaims.

"I asked you if the window was open," I say. "Don't worry, it's just an old photograph of Lake Windermere." I limp across the room to close the window, trying hard not to step on the frame or grind glass into the carpet.

"When did you go to Lake Windermere?"

"I've never been, but your father..." I begin to say, but I see that Julia is staring at the broken frame on the floor with a startled look on her face.

She gets to her feet and walks towards me. The mood in the room has changed suddenly: it's charged with suspense and the feeling is electric; it feels like Julia is moving in slow motion. She bends down and picks up the frame with careful hands. The sticky tape holding the backing cover in place has torn away revealing a second photograph. Julia slides it out from behind Lake Windermere. It's a studio portrait of a woman in a white, strapless evening gown. Her long, dark hair has been twisted into a single ringlet and it sits prettily on one bare shoulder. The gown is made from a glossy, light-reflecting fabric, and she appears to shine. It emphasizes the colour of her eyes, which stare steadily at the camera: two pools of iridescent blue. "Oh my God!" Julia shrieks. "That's ... that's Maggie!"

It is Maggie – a much younger Maggie than the woman who cleans my house each Monday morning – but definitely Maggie.

I *really* need to sit down now, but the only chair in the room is the swivel-chair behind George's desk and I don't want to sit there because this is where George sat and gazed at the picture of Lake Windermere knowing it concealed a photograph of the woman he loved. So, I hobble out of the study and go back to the kitchen.

Julia storms after me. "Please tell me you didn't know!" she howls.

"I didn't know," I say and drag myself to a chair.

"All this time … coming to the house every week … pretending to be a *domestic*."

"She wasn't pretending."

"Why, Mummy? Why would she do it?"

"I have no idea, Julia."

"I don't believe it! Right under our noses! I tell you, that takes some gumption."

A feeling of complete exhaustion overwhelms me. The world I thought I knew is made of smoke and mirrors; the people I thought I knew are strangers. If this is the final battle with George, then perhaps I am defeated after all.

Julia

My mother is shrinking before my eyes. The painkillers I made her take to relieve the ache in her hip are working, but they can't reach the part of her which my father and Magdalena Bartok have destroyed. She's sitting at the breakfast-table with her head bowed over a cup of now tepid tea. I've urged her over and over again to drink it, but she lifts the cup to her lips then places it back in the saucer as though the effort of drinking is simply beyond her.

"Talk to me," I say. "Why aren't you angry?"

"I don't know."

"Treachery doesn't even begin to describe it."

She looks up. "Are you talking about George or Maggie?"

"I'm talking about *her*!"

A smile hovers on her lips, but this amusement at my response doesn't relieve the sadness in her eyes. She says, "You're always so quick to defend him."

"Because *she's* the one who's been coming to this house for... How many years?"

She thinks about it. "Maybe eleven or twelve, I can't remember exactly."

"Twelve years!"

"I know you're going to find this hard to understand Julia, but there's method in her madness," she tells me. "I'm upset by what she's done: hurt and disappointed mostly because I thought we were ... it sounds silly ... I thought we were friends. But ... when I think about it ... I can see why someone in her position might do this."

She's right, I don't understand. "I'm going to call Richard and tell him," I say.

She reaches across the table and grasps my hand. "When will the scales fall from your eyes? Your father was responsible for all of this. We are where we are today because of *him,* not because of *her.*"

I don't want to hear this. "My father loved me," I say. "I know he did. He would never have left this house to that woman's child if she hadn't influenced him in some way."

A huge sigh escapes her lips. "Well, he *didn't* love me. He made me a *tenant* of this house – my own home, Julia. My own home! Not only that, he kept a portrait of the woman he *did* love behind a picture in plain sight, knowing that I would see it, but it would be his little secret. What kind of man does something like that?"

"I can't explain it."

"That's because it's unnatural, perverse," she says. She clumsily pushes herself into a standing position, staggers slightly as she moves away from the table. "Maybe you should think on that when you're berating Maggie for stealing your inheritance." She stops in the doorway. Her face is a picture of unrelieved misery. "Have you ever considered for a single moment that maybe he just didn't want you to have it?"

I watch her walk up the stairs and go back to her bedroom.

Have I ever seriously considered that he didn't want me to have it? I think if ever that thought has slipped unbidden into my mind then I've quickly pushed it away again, and yet now I'm forced to ask myself if my mother is right. Of course, I know in my heart the answer to that conundrum: I simply don't care.

I waste no time and immediately call Richard to tell him what we've discovered.

"Hang on a second," he says. "I'm at the solicitor's – at Silver, Reid and Bateman."

I wait for him to finish his conversation. From the strident tone of his voice, it sounds like this is going to be more bad news, but before I can tell him *my* news he blurts out, "Julia, I've just come out of a meeting with Miriam. Before you complain, Henry Silver arranged it – he managed to find a telephone number for her."

Well, this is unexpected. Something tells me that it hasn't been a resounding success. "Did you speak to her about Hillcrest?"

"I didn't ask her if she was prepared to share it with us, if that's what you mean," he says. "She was extremely hostile towards me, even went as far as recording the conversation..."

"Richard..." I try to interrupt him.

"Just let me finish!" he snaps. "Apparently, her mother was forced to leave her with her grandparents back in Urk. It sounds like they've both had a pretty tough time since Dad died. I'm telling you, Julia, if you're still thinking of contesting the will then you're going to have a fight on your hands. She wants Mum out of the house *now*! Said it belongs to her and she shouldn't be forced to wait."

I try again, "Richard..."

But the rant continues. "Just to make things even more complicated, Henry Silver has just informed me that Dad made Lena Bartok one of the trustees on this Life Interest Trust. And wait till you hear *this*: the woman's been living here in Shenfield. Can you believe it?"

This time I yell into the receiver, "Shut up and listen to me for a second."

"What is it?" he says sharply as though nothing I have to say can compare with *his* revelation.

"Lena Bartok's real name is *Magdalena*. She's Maggie. Mum's Maggie from Hutton Home Help."

This earth-shattering piece of news is met with stunned silence but eventually he replies, "I honestly don't know what to say. Maggie is Lena Bartok?"

"Yes, Maggie is Lena Bartok. It's hit Mummy really hard. She thought this woman was her friend. A 'friend' of all things! She's been lying about who she is for twelve years, ingratiating herself into our family. You know I really don't understand how you people operate over here," I continue angrily. "When does someone, who you employ to clean your house, become someone you confide your problems to? It's ridiculous! I tell you Richard, I'm absolutely fuming, yet Mummy tells me she's hurt and disappointed."

"That doesn't surprise me," he says.

"Why aren't *you* angry?" I shout into the phone.

His response is to tell me to calm down. "I agree it's a bit of a shock, but perhaps this friendship has come about because of us."

"What's that supposed to mean?"

"I'm just saying, if we'd been there for her when she needed us then she wouldn't have had to look to someone else for support. Maggie – I mean Lena Bartok – wouldn't have had the opportunity to worm herself into Mum's affections in the way that she has."

271

"She had Aggie! Aggie was her friend."

"Yes, and look how that's turned out," he replies glumly.

"We have to confront the woman," I tell him. "Find out exactly what she's been up to."

"You're right," he says. "There's definitely been something fishy going on. I'm busy this afternoon and tomorrow morning, but I can pick you up in the car around four o'clock tomorrow afternoon and we'll have it out with her."

I'm thinking about marching straight over to the offices of Hutton Home Help and having it out with her right now so when I don't immediately concur with this arrangement, he's quick to insist, "You're not to do anything until I can come with you. Are you listening to me, Julia? We don't want to upset Mum more than she is already. This must have shaken her to the core."

Reluctantly, I give my agreement.

Before he hangs up, Richard says, "You didn't tell me how you found out about Maggie?" So, I explain how Mummy and I were searching the study; that someone had left the window open and a sudden gust of wind caused the picture of Lake Windermere to fall and break, revealing the portrait of Maggie hidden behind it. "Don't you think that's a bit strange?" he asks in rather a strained voice. "I mean … that's quite a coincidence isn't it? You searching the room, and then the picture falling down?"

"I told you, it was a gust of wind."

"Are you sure?" he says. "The windows are all locked, Julia. I know because I locked them."

Richard

I've found it hard to concentrate this morning after yesterday's revelation about Maggie. Our new client kept throwing me worried looks. I think he must have sensed that I wasn't really *present* at the meeting arranged to discuss the refurbishment of an old office block he bought last year.

His plan to take out most of the internal walls and rebuild as luxury apartments has been rejected by the local authority for a second time; it wants affordable housing for local residents. He tells me over and over again it's not financially viable, but it is. This is the problem with speculative investors: they hope to make a killing and are disappointed when it doesn't work out.

I tried my best to reason with him, but he was adamant: make some minor changes to the plans and resubmit.

Well, it's his money, I thought to myself.

The meeting didn't end till lunchtime, at which point I had another meeting with a happily satisfied client: the owner of our old friend *Hotel Albatross*. She was organizing a relaunch of the hotel and wanted to hand-deliver my invitation. It's to be renamed 'The Bed of Roses', which goes a long way to explain the floral theme that finally found favour with her – though no doubt she'll change her mind at some point, but that won't be *my* problem.

It's nearly three o'clock before I leave the office and I'm hoping and praying that Julia hasn't taken matters into her own hands, but I missed lunch and I don't like running on empty so I grab a sandwich and a coffee 'to go' from the café at the corner of the street.

Eating and drinking while driving isn't the most sensible way to navigate a busy road and I know I'm going to be late, but it helps to prevent me from thinking too deeply about Maggie's or rather Lena Bartok's photograph hidden behind the picture of Lake Windermere (because it has to be Lena Bartok).

It isn't the fact that my father chose to have the photograph in the house, which preoccupies me – it's just another example of his monstrous conceit. No, the thoughts, which crowd my head, relate to the *finding* of the photograph. I told Julia I thought that something 'fishy' was going on, but I didn't want to tell her that our mother isn't the only person who's experienced strange phenomena. I realise now that it started more than two weeks ago when I was sitting in the kitchen and heard noises overhead – that's when I first discovered my mother had closed up Julia's bedroom. Was I *led* to the room in the same way that I was *led* to the garage? And what happened on Sunday evening? Well, I know what I saw and what I saw was a woman in a red dress, but could it really have been a ghostly manifestation of Aggie leading me to Julia's bedroom once again?

My mind is still reeling with the possibilities when I finally pull onto the drive at Hillcrest.

Julia must have been looking out for me because she's already walking out of the house before I have a chance to even open the door. She climbs into the front seat of the car and says a little breathlessly, "I persuaded Mummy to take an early rest. I just popped upstairs to check on her and she's sleeping. She was still very upset this morning – she wanted me to phone Maggie and ask her to come over."

"I hope you didn't do that," I say.

"Of course, I didn't…" She stops suddenly, and I can almost hear the cogs and wheels grinding while she works out if it's worth bearing the consequences of admitting that she *has* done something I won't approve. From the corner of my eye I see her glance at my face. I know what she's thinking: Is it worth it? I hear her take a readying breath before she says in a low voice, "I did phone her just now. There's no point driving over there if she's not in," she quickly adds. "I told her we want to speak to her about Mummy. I didn't say when, I just asked if we could make an appointment to see her. She said she's free Friday morning."

"I really wish you hadn't," I tell her.

"Well, at least now she won't be expecting us, and she doesn't know we've discovered her real identity."

"Okay, okay," I say. "Let's hope she's still there."

Thanks to the traffic, it's nearly five o'clock when we reach the offices of Hutton Home Help. The sun has disappeared behind a bank of dark clouds and it feels like night is already drawing in. Someone is still working because bright light illuminates the interior. Maggie isn't visible through the glass panel in the door, but when I open the door and walk in, I can see her speaking to someone on the phone.

When she sees us, she doesn't hang up immediately, but she turns her head away, mutters something in a low, insistent voice. She ends the conversation abruptly with, *"Tot later. Dag."* She turns back to us, unsmiling, almost angry. "I wasn't expecting to see you today."

I look around for a second chair and invite Julia to sit down. I know she's primed and ready to launch a verbal attack, but I want to keep the conversation calm. We won't achieve anything by anyone losing their temper.

Maggie looks at us enquiringly. "Does your mother know you're here?"

Addressing us like two naughty children is an interesting gambit under the circumstances and it immediately provokes Julia to say, "You've got some cheek."

I lay a restraining hand on her shoulder. "Let me handle this." I can't think of any easy way to start this conversation, so I cut straight to the chase. "Maggie, we know who you really are."

For a brief moment her face registers unhappy surprise, but she quickly recovers. "I wondered how long it would take you to find out. Your mother told me you wanted her to move so I guessed it wouldn't be long before you spoke to her solicitor. How did you make the connection? Between Maggie and Magdalena?"

"We found a photograph. A professional portrait of you in a white evening dress. It was on the wall of dad's study."

She shakes her head. "I know that's not true."

"It is true!" Julia jumps in. "It was hidden behind the picture of Lake Windermere."

Maggie's eyes widen. "It was there? All this time?"

"As you can imagine, this has been quite a shock for all of us, but especially for our mother," I continue in a calm voice, but Julia has other ideas.

"How could you do that?" she shrieks at Maggie. "Pretend to be her friend. All this while she's trusted you, confided in you, and you're ... you're ... you're a liar and a cheat!"

Maggie's response is to immediately place her hand over her heart. "I never lied to her. I swear it."

"But you didn't tell her that you're Lena Bartok," I point out.

"How could I tell her that?" she flings back at me. "You don't understand. You don't know what it was like for me when George died."

"I know it wasn't easy. I know you lost your home," I say.

She nods. "Miriam told me she spoke to you. Did she tell you I had to leave her with her grandparents?"

"Yes, and I know she wasn't happy there."

A look of pain and sadness sweeps across her face. "She became hysterical when I left her that first time. She was ten years old. She knew what 'death' meant. She knew she'd never see her father again, and then I went away. Can you imagine how that was for her?"

It's a rhetorical question and one I couldn't answer even if I wanted to, but the tension in the room is rising minute by minute and her polished English accent is slowly dissolving.

"Why didn't you bring Miriam back with you?"

She doesn't hesitate to answer. "Because it was impossible. I knew I couldn't live in the house any longer. I only had a part-time job, so I had to find a second job, find somewhere to live. Later ... when I take over this business ... she doesn't want to come back. She's not happy in Urk with my parents but she has friends, she has a new life. Only now, now she wants to live with me again."

"What about my mother?" Julia says sullenly. "It's a great sob story that you've just told us, but it doesn't explain what you did to *her*."

A pleading note enters Maggie's voice. "You have to understand, George told me many things about Lenora, he said..."

I interrupt her. "He told you that she wouldn't agree to a divorce, didn't he?"

Maggie nods.

"But that wasn't true."

She closes her eyes for a brief moment and when she opens them tears threaten to spill down her cheeks.

Julia has been watching her intently all this time and she seems unmoved by this overt display of emotion. "You still haven't explained why you insinuated your way into our mother's life."

Maggie pulls a tissue from her desk drawer and slowly, carefully dries her eyes. It's enough time to restore her composure and answer Julia's question in a quiet, measured tone. She says, "I know it looks bad, but I was thinking of my daughter and her future. I only found out that George had left the house to Miriam and not to you, after he died."

"I don't believe you!" Julia exclaims angrily.

"I didn't know before that," Maggie insists. "When I found out …" She looks up at me and once again her eyes shine with emotion. "I hadn't met your mother then. I didn't realise how unhappy…" She leaves the sentence unfinished and straightens her shoulders. "I knew she had someone from Hutton Home Help cleaning for her – George used to complain about the cost. I got work with them and after a few months they let me work at Hillcrest. I thought I could…" She hesitates.

"Keep an eye on Miriam's inheritance. Make sure that it wasn't sold off or passed on to someone else without you finding out?"

She inclines her head just a fraction but it's enough to confirm that my accusation is correct. "I realise that George wasn't the man I thought he was," she goes on. "And I know that Lenora is a kind, caring person. I should have told her the truth."

"You should have told her," I say. "Especially now that Miriam seems to think she can turn her out of the house."

"Miriam didn't mean to…" she begins, but then she realises that this is an admission of some unnamed guilt.

Of course, she doesn't want to incriminate her own daughter, but I don't want to play good cop bad cop in order to find out if Miriam has already acted to have my mother removed from Hillcrest, so I try to appeal to her good nature. "I know you care about my mother – she thinks of you as a friend – but you need to tell us what Miriam has done. What did she do, Maggie?"

When Maggie answers her voice trembles and she looks away. "She wanted to see the house for herself so one day, when I knew Lenora was going to be away, I brought her with me. It was just a

277

natural curiosity, and nobody needed to find out. It did no harm and it made Miriam happy."

I've spent the last ten minutes watching Maggie fall apart and gather herself together again, but she can't conceal her emotions which is how I know that she's still keeping something from us. I can't think what it might be and then I remember how she reacted when I told her about the garage, and it hits me. "She's been inside the house more recently, hasn't she?"

Maggie's face crumples. "She stole the key from the safe and made a copy of it."

Julia can barely contain her fury. She moves to the edge of the chair and speaks directly into Maggie's face. "Are you saying she could get into the house whenever she wanted?"

Maggie recoils in fear. "She didn't *really* want to hurt Lenora. She just wants to have the house. I had no idea when I told her all about Aggie, about the red dress ... I couldn't know that she'd use it to do what she did."

"What was she doing?" Julia shouts.

I grasp my sister's shoulder and pull her back into her seat. "Just calm down, Julia." I turn to Maggie. "When did you find out?"

"Your mother showed me a perfume bottle – Aggie's perfume. And then the family photographs... I guessed what Miriam had been doing and how she'd been doing it. I told her it had to stop. I took the key from her and I thought that would be the end of it."

"Then I told you about the garage," I say. "And the broken glass. That was her?"

"That was Miriam?" Julia demands. "Every weird thing that's been happening in the house was Miriam?"

Maggie doesn't answer. She doesn't need to because the expression in her eyes betrays her.

"I have to ask you this, Maggie," I say. "Did Miriam push Mum down the stairs?"

"No!"

"How can you be sure?"

"I know because she was here with me," she insists. "That was the day I told her I was going to your mother's house to tell her what Miriam had done: the perfume bottle, the writing on the mirror, the photographs, the red dress ... everything, everything ... so Lenora

278

wouldn't be frightened any more. I told Miriam the house would be hers, but she must be patient."

"She was here when you left?" I ask her.

"No, she left before me, but I went straight to Hillcrest."

"She could have got there before you. Got in through the garage. Where is she now? Do you know?"

"She didn't tell me..."

Julia has been listening to this exchange with rapt attention. "You told her we were here in the office with you, didn't you?" She turns to me and the look of fear in her eyes is mirrored in my own quaking heart. "That means she knows that Mummy's alone in the house, Richard."

I close my eyes for a moment and a picture of Miriam fills my mind. She is my father at his ruthless, heartless worst. "My mother told me that a woman in a red dress with long dark hair pushed her down the stairs. She saw her, Maggie. Miriam pushed her down the stairs."

Lenora

Today has been a day of quiet contemplation for me, but not for Julia. After yesterday's bombshell she's been crashing about the house, turning out cupboards and searching through sundry drawers because she's convinced herself that she'll find something that will 'convict' Maggie. I asked her what Maggie was guilty of and she told me, "Lies and duplicity."

When I said that lying isn't really a punishable crime, she became quite cross.

The strange thing is, I don't feel that Maggie *has* lied to me because she's always spoken openly about her life – at least the life she's lived since George died. Of course, she never referred to her daughter's father as 'your husband', but she did tell me he was killed in a car accident and that for many years afterwards their young daughter had to live with her grandparents in a small, fishing town in the Netherlands. I had all the pieces of the puzzle in front of me; I just didn't put them together.

The even stranger thing is that I don't think Maggie really is Lena Bartok anymore. At least, she's not the Lena Bartok whose photograph was hidden behind a picture in George's study. I fear that radiantly beautiful young woman was very much like the young Lenora, who was once captivated by a handsome man's charm and then bitterly disappointed when she discovered the truth about him. I'm sure he promised her a wonderful life and, though it pains me to admit it, he might even have loved her – as far as a man who thinks only of himself can truly love another – but it doesn't change the fact that when he died he left her only debt and despair. At least I still had a roof over my head.

I've spent most of the day in my room here thinking about the past and contemplating the future. I can't feel what Julia feels. I can't feel angry indignation. She can only think about the legacy that isn't hers and that's why she's been thumping up and down the stairs all day long in the uncertain hope that she'll uncover another piece of evidence. But what has Maggie's Miriam really got? It's only the *promise* of Hillcrest. The actual bricks and mortar might never be hers to possess, because life is unpredictable and uncertain.

At around four-thirty, I heard a car pull up onto the drive and then the front door slammed shut. I know Richard and Julia intend to drive over to Hutton Home Help offices and confront Maggie, but what good it will do them, I'm really not sure.

I've continued to doze since then, but the sound of glass breaking suddenly wakes me. The noise appeared to come from somewhere downstairs. I think it must be a window. At first, I'm apprehensive but then I remember the great pile of metal poles and wooden planks erected beneath Julia's balcony doors. Clearly something has broken loose.

I'm thinking about going down and investigating when it strikes me that the temperature in the room has dropped dramatically. My immediate thought is that the timer on the central heating system needs to be adjusted and I sit up, reminding myself that I have to lead with my operated leg first when I get out of bed.

I'm shuffling my bottom to the edge of the bed as per Frankie the physiotherapist's instructions when a movement on the far side of the room catches my eye. Most of the room is in semi-darkness; only the bed has light. It spills from the table lamp onto the place where I was lying and it doesn't reach into the corners of the room, but I already know what's hiding in the shadows.

I haven't thought about Aggie for several days, not since I woke up the morning after I was discharged from hospital and knew that she was in the room with me. I know that she's in the room with me now. I also know that I'm alone in the house.

I realise, that somehow, I have to get myself to the front door without toppling headfirst down the stairs. In my haste to get away, I knock my walking stick to the ground, but I'm not going to waste time searching for it. On Saturday I screamed my fear out loud, but now it's like a huge weight pressing on my chest: I can barely breathe.

Holding onto to anything that meets my outstretched hand, I feel my way to the door. My hands are shaking so hard that I struggle to hold onto the handle, but I manage to turn it and let myself out onto the landing.

Julia has left a light on downstairs. It shines like a beacon of hope in the darkness. I tell myself I just have to hold onto the bannisters with both hands and keep my wits about me. Don't look down but most of all don't look back, I tell myself.

I've almost reached the head of the stairs when I realise that someone is walking into the hallway from George's study. It's a light feminine tread so I know it isn't Richard. Relief floods through me. "Julia?" I call out. "Julia, is that you?" The voice that calls back to me isn't my daughter, but as soon as I set eyes on the person now standing in the stairwell, I know who she is. It's like looking at a carbon copy of George: the eyes, the nose, the angles of her face, but most of all the cruel twist of her mouth as she smiles mockingly up at me. And now I understand what she's done, how foolish I've been, and I feel the blood rush to my head. She's even wearing the red dress.

"So, that's where you are," Miriam says.

"What do you want?" I call down to her.

"I want what's rightfully mine. I've tried for months and months to *persuade* you to give it up to me, but you're a tough old bird. You even survived that fall down the stairs, so now I'm just going to take it from you."

I hold tightly onto the handrail in front of me, because I know that, once again, I'm in danger of falling. I have no idea what Miriam has planned but I'm not going to hand myself over like some sacrificial lamb. "This house is legally mine until the day I die and I'm not leaving it before that, so how exactly do you propose to take it from me?"

She replies in a voice that would freeze the brandy in a Champagne cocktail, "I think you've just answered your own question."

It takes several seconds for my brain to process what she's said. When I see her place her foot on the first step, my heart beats wildly, but suddenly I feel something pulling me back into the bedroom. I feel hands on my shoulders dragging me away from the stairs; I feel icy breath on my neck and for a moment I panic and struggle against it, but the more I struggle the more insistent it becomes.

282

I'm being forcibly manoeuvred back to where I've come from, and when my legs buckle under me, I'm lifted up by unseen arms and hauled across the length of the bedroom into the en suite shower room with the heels of my feet drumming on the floor. As soon as I've crossed the threshold and the door has slammed shut behind me, I'm left to fall heavily onto the cold tiles.

A small part of my brain is telling me that my new hip joint is a searing ball of agony as the newly healed tissue is torn away, but I don't feel the pain because my whole attention is now focused on the space between the door and the window.

It's dark inside the shower room, but a pillar of rippling white light has manifested. Slowly it begins to take colour and form. It's Aggie. She's wearing her red dress. It's a shimmering swirl of scarlet. Her blue eyes shine out of her pale face like the brightest, shiniest sapphires. She looks into my eyes, and then she's gone, and the room is dark once more, but in that brief moment I saw only love and devotion.

How could I have doubted her?

Somehow, I manage to get to my feet and draw the bolt across on the door, locking myself inside the room. It seems like only moments later that Miriam is banging her fist on the other side of it.

"That won't save you," she shouts at me. "You're going to die, Lenora Oakley!"

I sit back down on the hard floor with my back pressed against the door. "Julia and Richard will be home soon," I shout back at her. "You should go now, before they find you."

"By the time they get back here it will be too late to save you, you stupid, old woman."

Once again, I'm seized by dread and fear. "What have you done?"

She laughs wildly. "I've disconnected the fire alarm and built a bonfire under you. It seemed an appropriate way to end the life of a witch."

The only words I can take on board are 'built a bonfire under you', but this is complete madness. "You're burning down the house?" I cry.

"Not the whole house. Obviously. My father taught me all about fire safety: how to contain them, how to manage the spread, but most of all the importance of keeping doors closed. The paint on the ceiling of the room below you is already blistering by the way. Can you smell the smoke yet?"

I can, but I know Aggie brought me here for a reason, and now I understand why: it's my only hope of survival.

Miriam pounds on the door. "Are you still breathing in there? It won't take long to die, and if you're lucky the smoke will kill you first. But just in case I'm going to open the window in the bedroom here. That should speed things up nicely."

I hear voices outside – someone must have seen the flames through the window – then I hear Miriam running from the room. When I'm as certain as I can be that she's gone, I crawl over to the handbasin and heave myself into a standing position, ignoring the pain in my hip and leg. I push in the sink plug and turn on both taps then I turn on the shower.

I'm frightened to switch on the light, so I feel my way to the cupboard where I keep the towels. I grab an armful of them and throw them into the shower and as soon as they're drenched with water, I pile them up around the door. The basin is already overflowing onto the floor, so I carefully climb into the shower cubicle. My legs are trembling, and my courage is failing me, but I stand under the shower, let the water soak my clothes till I'm wet through to the skin. Only then do I allow myself to sink to my knees.

I don't want to die like this, alone and frightened with the smell of my home burning around me, but if this is the end, at least I know that Aggie, my forever friend, will be waiting for me on the other side. It fills me with an uncertain relief.

Julia

Maggie wants to come with us when we leave.

"Come with us?" I shout at her. "You must be mad! For all we know, you put her up to this."

Richard tells me to shut up. "Come on, Julia," he urges. "Let's get back to the car. It's just a five-minute drive and we've been gone less than an hour."

"She could be in the house already," I tell him as we hurry out of the office.

"She doesn't have a key anymore," he says. "And I've locked the garage so she can't get in that way."

I know this is meant to reassure me, but I don't feel reassured. I haven't met Miriam, but she strikes me as someone who will go to any length to get what she wants.

We reach the car and scramble into our seats. Richard starts the engine, but he doesn't pull away.

"Why aren't we moving already?" I yell at him.

He slowly turns his head to look at me. The colour has drained from his face and his eyes are dark pools of fear. When he speaks, it's barely a whisper. "Miriam doesn't need a key. All she has to do is ring the front doorbell. Mum probably got up when she heard us leave. She'll recognise her, I know she will, and then she'll invite her into the house because *she* thinks it was Aggie, who pushed her down the stairs."

"Why are you wasting time telling me this now?" I say.

He doesn't reply. He puts his foot on the accelerator and the car shoots forward.

Five minutes is an awfully long time when you're counting down the seconds, and when we finally arrive back at Hillcrest, there are people standing in the front garden and in the road in front of the house.

A man motions to us not to pull onto the drive. He points back at the house and that's when we see it: Daddy's study engulfed in flames.

Richard leaps out of the car before me. I hear him shout, "My mother! Has anyone seen my mother?"

"I haven't seen anyone come out," the man says.

I can hear sirens in the distance, but I know it takes just minutes for a whole house to go up in flames. I run over to Richard, who's pacing up and down in front of the house.

"I have to get inside," he says. "She could still be in one of the rooms upstairs."

"You can't go in there. Please don't do it Richard," I plead with him, and I try to pull him back to where the neighbours are standing in a frightened group on the pavement.

He pushes me away. "I'm not going to just leave her to die!" he screams. Before I can do anything to stop him, he's running around the side of the house.

"Richard!"

"The scaffolding," he shouts back at me. "I can climb up!"

When I try to run after him, the man who greeted us grabs hold of my arm. "You stay here," he says. "They'll need to know the layout of the house. You can explain."

The sirens are louder now. I know it's probably just seconds before the fire engine is going to arrive, but the fire has moved into the hallway and thick smoke is billowing up the stairs.

Richard

They say when you drown your life flashes before your eyes. But only when you drown? What happens when you're trapped inside a burning building and smoke is filling your lungs? Is that like drowning?

I can't help it. I can't stop thinking: Is my mother lying on the floor somewhere inside this house and in her mind's eye a procession of pictures whizzing past at lightning speed? What does she remember as the years race by? A happy childhood on the family farm? A chance meeting with a handsome stranger? Her own children as babies and then, in the blink of an eye, a grown man and a grown woman? Does Lena Bartok feature in this rapid cinematic review of her life? And what about Aggie, the girl in the red dress?

I can't bear for it to end like this.

At the rear of the house, I can still hear the low-throated roar of the fire at the front, but the flames haven't reached the rooms overlooking the garden. Back here darkness fills the space, which heightens all my senses and I immediately become aware of the damp smell of wet leaves and light, peppery scent of autumn flowers.

I need a torch, but I don't have a torch, and I don't have time to get one.

I stand back from the scaffolding to get a better view – I know there are ladders fixed to the metal poles.

A movement behind the doors, which lead into Julia's bedroom, catches my eye. They're criss-crossed with chequered tape so I can see them fairly clearly. Without warning, they're opened from inside and Miriam steps out onto the wooden planking. She's wearing a red dress and her long hair is loose and falls about her face. Frantically I call her name, but she doesn't hear me because she's completely caught up with something happening in the room behind her.

Hope soars in my heart. My mother is safe. Miriam's going to help her escape from the house.

But it isn't my mother who demands Miriam's wide-eyed attention.

From out of the darkened room, a hazy female figure in a red dress floats into view. It's like looking at a very old photographic transparency. I recognise who it is straight away, for who else could it be.

Miriam backs away from what's now a large opening in the bedroom wall and her abject terror is visible in the rapid, jerking movements of her outstretched arms.

I try to call out to her, but fear has robbed me of my voice. I run to the bottom of the ladder but in the very moment I place my foot on the first rung, Miriam screams. The sound slices through the air like a butcher's knife. Seconds later, her body hits the flagstones on the patio.

The complete absence of sound and movement proclaims her death.

I have to make a split-second decision. Do I still have time to save my mother from the fire? Before I have a chance to move, uniformed figures are clustering around the bottom of the ladder beside me.

"Just stand back, Mr Oakley," someone orders me. "We'll take it from here."

My eyes search the ground for Miriam but all I can really see of her is the red dress, blood-red in the pale light of the moon. Her broken body is soon surrounded by more uniforms and I'm asked if I know who she is.

I hesitate before answering. Do I want to claim her as my sister? Julia wouldn't hesitate for a second to deny her, and perhaps this time she's right, so I tell them, "Her name's Miriam. Miriam Bartok."

Six Months Later...

Lenora

A fine plume of smoke announces the success of Richard's debut attempt to build a bonfire. We've been outside in the garden for more than an hour, but he isn't inclined to listen to advice even though I've told him that burning green wood isn't like putting kiln-dried kindling in the stove at his pretty, Victorian cottage. But I mustn't complain, because Richard and Silvio worked like proverbial Trojans to get the bungalow ready for me and they've only just moved to a new house themselves. Silvio wanted me to stay with them for a while longer, but I think they need their privacy, and I'm used to living by myself.

Fortunately, my hip replacement has been a triumph of modern medical technology in spite of the setback it faced last autumn. It's taking a little longer for my lungs to mend but as they say, time is a great healer, though Richard has forbidden me from sitting in the outside 'smoking permitted' area whenever we go to a restaurant.

That's also why I've been ordered to stay at the top end of the garden while Silvio strims and weeds and he cuts back overgrown shrubs and tries his best to burn the woody branches. Every now and then my new neighbour pokes his head above the fence. He used to look after the garden for me but a conversation with my son in his smart suit changed his mind.

"Shall we take a break?" I call out to them.

Silvio shakes his head but tells me he would love a cup of coffee.

Richard immediately stops piling wood onto the fire and throws his gloves onto the ground beside it. He trails up the garden after me. "Make a whole pot of coffee," he advises.

"I'll have to find it first," I tell him.

The kitchen in Tyne Lodge is half the size of my old kitchen, and I've had to downsize everything since I moved in here. It was strange at first, but neither Richard nor Julia will countenance me ever moving back into Hillcrest, even though the fire only damaged part of the house. They think it's full of unhappy memories – the memory of being *put to the stake* by poor Miriam is certainly not one I shall treasure – but it was also full of happy memories as well. [Not least being rescued from the en suite shower room by two handsome firefighters.]

After opening up several boxes, because I still haven't unpacked everything, we manage to find the cafetière which Richard and Silvio bought me. It's one of the many *moving home* presents they've given me since most of my own things were either destroyed in the fire or suffered smoke damage.

"Make the coffee nice and strong," Richard tells me. "Silvio requires regular injections of caffeine otherwise he'll be lounging on your new sofa for the rest of the afternoon."

"I don't mind," I say. "I'm just glad you're here."

He reaches across the table, pulls my hand to his lips and places a kiss on my knuckles. "Not half as glad as we are."

Tears spring to my eyes. It's become a bit of a habit since the fire – me welling up with emotion. "You know you really didn't have to move closer. I'm going to be fine."

"We wanted to," he says.

"But…"

He wags a cautionary finger at me. "No buts. This way we get to see you more often and you get to be a part of the extended Mazzi clan."

"It is lovely," I say, remembering how Silvio's sister and brothers and his ferocious Mamma have taken me into their hearts. "I feel like a proper grannie."

"Well, Julia isn't going to surprise you," he observes with a wry grin.

"Oh, that train left the station many moons ago," I say. "Still she seems happy enough on her own."

Richard's face is suddenly serious. "I think Colin has been very fair. I don't think I would have offered her a second chance – not after what happened."

"He's still moving back here though, isn't he? What he's offered her is an olive branch."

Richard nods his agreement. "She stays in Singapore and gets to keep their apartment rent-free for the next two years while she decides what she wants to do."

"I think she'll be okay," I say. "After the fire … when I was in hospital again…" I offer him a rueful smile and he responds with another kiss to the back of my hand. "When I was in hospital," I say again, "Julia told me how and why she started 'Glück Glass'. Apparently, the word 'glück' has two meanings: happiness *and* luck. She said the gallery has actually brought her both of those things, which is why she won't give it up."

"Is she still involved with…? You know, I don't think she ever told me his name," Richard says.

I shake my head. "We talked about lots of things while I was in hospital. I don't think we've ever been this close before." Emotion gets the better of me once again, but this time Richard hands me a towel to dry my tears.

"Did she tell you about the baby?" he asks.

"Yes. She told me that's when she knew there was no future for them."

Richard pours coffee into three newly unpackaged mugs. "I'll take this out to Silvio." He walks to the door holding a mug in each hand then pauses in the doorway. "When you're feeling completely well, I'd like to talk to you about what happened last year."

"If you're going to tell me Maggie wasn't really my friend, please don't," I say.

"Maggie … Lena …whatever it is that she's calling herself these days … I'm not interested, Mum. What I want to talk about is Aggie." His gentle, hazel eyes search mine, seeking my understanding. "I know I should have told you this before," he says, "but you were frightened, and I didn't want to make things worse. It's just that … I'm certain I saw her in the house the night of the fire. And that wasn't the first time; I'd seen her before. I don't think she meant you harm. I think … I think perhaps she was trying to warn you about Miriam."

I want to throw my arms around him, tell him how much I love him. I want to reassure him that everything he did, I know, was done to make me feel safe and cared for, but I don't want to start a conversation about Aggie when there's so much that must remain unsaid, so I smile and tell him, "You could be right. I've been wrong before."

His face lights up and his eyes twinkle their delight. "Wow, Mum! That's quite an admission."

I throw the towel at him, but it misses its target and falls at his feet. "I'm right about most things though. Don't you forget it."

"I'll tell you one thing you're not right about," he replies. "That damned garage at the bottom of the garden. Why won't you let us clear it out?"

"Oh, there's plenty of time for that," I say, hoping against hope that he won't press me to make a decision. "Off you go now or the coffee will get cold."

The freshly ground coffee is really good – it's Italian, a present from Mamma Mazzi. I think it's the kind of drinking habit I could happily acquire although I quite enjoyed the green tea, which Julia persuaded me to try, even if I'm not quite as convinced by the health benefits.

I cast my eyes around the small, square kitchen and I can't help thinking: how on earth did Mrs Bagshot manage to produce the complicated meals she served her family?

My mother had a huge kitchen with an old-fashioned range to cook on, but I'm sure it was mostly used to dry out my father's clothes when he came in from the fields. Dinner was plain meat and veg, and if my mother could put everything into a single casserole dish then that's what we had.

It was a happy childhood though and one where we were encouraged to be independent and free to explore the world around us. I'm not sure I can say the same about Aggie's childhood and sadly she never really escaped it.

Now that I can move more easily, I quickly check that Richard is no longer within earshot.

"Are you there, Aggie?" I say out loud.

Julia explained to me how Miriam died. She didn't give me the graphic details, but she did tell me about the ghostly figure in the red dress at the top of the scaffolding, although her take on the situation was to ridicule Richard for his 'outrageous imagination'.

"Did you push her, Aggie?" I whisper.

I wouldn't put it past you, but I've had a lot of time to think about it, and I've *chosen* to draw the conclusion that everything you did was motivated by care and concern for the people you loved.

I look out of the kitchen window past Richard and Silvio working in the garden; past the ivy-cloaked garage hiding Mr Bagshot's Volvo covered by a huge tarpaulin. My eyes come to rest on the soft sweep of blue sky, which stretches overhead and fades into the far horizon. I'm reminded of that day, a day quite like no other day, when you told me you were responsible for George's death. You couldn't know that what you did would be a life-changing event for many people and not just for me, which is what, I'm certain, you had planned.

"I know you're out there somewhere, Aggie," I say. "I just wanted to let you know, for as long as I live, your secret will be my secret. *Au revoir* my dear friend."

****  ****

Acknowledgements

I would like to thank –

Hilary Barber, Chloe Chong and Kevin Tracey for reading the first draft of this novel. Your comments and observations were as always invaluable.

The late Graham Barber for his work designing the front cover.

Paul Churchouse for proofreading.

And last, but not least, my family: Anthony, Chloe, Liam and Ciara. Your support and encouragement are appreciated more than you can ever know.

About the author

Elaine Chong was born in Essex. She read German with Philosophy at UEA, Norwich. She has lived in Germany, Austria, Singapore and Malaysia, but she returned to Essex, and continues to live there with her family. In 2002, Elaine was a winner in the Essex Book Festival Fresh Talent competition. She is also the author of *Sturstone Hall*. She can be contacted via her Facebook page: elainechongauthor.

Also by this author

Sturstone Hall
A Paranormal Mystery

Sturstone Hall. It sits on the brow of a low hill in a gently undulating Essex landscape, blackened and broken, stubbornly refusing to give way to nature, nursing its secrets, and waiting for the one…

But change is coming.

Colchester hotelier Helen Whelan is restoring the gatehouse to the Hall, persuaded by her husband, Carl, that it will be a new home for them: a place to start a family and perhaps a different life.

When she begins to experience strange, psychic visions, Helen decides to consult university parapsychologist, Doctor David Barton. The meeting sets in motion a sequence of events which will change her life forever.